Rainy Day
Sisters

Center Point
Large Print

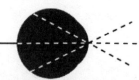

**This Large Print Book carries the
Seal of Approval of N.A.V.H.**

Rainy Day Sisters

A HARTLEY-BY-THE-SEA NOVEL

KATE HEWITT

CENTER POINT LARGE PRINT
THORNDIKE, MAINE

This Center Point Large Print edition
is published in the year 2016 by arrangement with
New American Library, an imprint of Penguin Publishing
Group, a division of Penguin Random House LLC.

The text of this Large Print edition is unabridged.
In other aspects, this book may vary
from the original edition.
Printed in the United States of America
on permanent paper.
Set in 16-point Times New Roman type.

ISBN: 978-1-62899-902-0

Library of Congress Cataloging-in-Publication Data

Names: Hewitt, Kate, author.
Title: Rainy day sisters : a Hartley-by-the-sea novel / Kate Hewitt.
Description: Center Point Large Print edition. | Thorndike, Maine :
Center Point Large Print, 2016. | ©2015
Identifiers: LCCN 2015046460 | ISBN 9781628999020
      (hardcover : alk. paper)
Subjects: LCSH: Large type books.
Classification: LCC PS3619.W368 R35 2016 | DDC 813/.6—dc23
LC record available at http://lccn.loc.gov/2015046460

To my father, George Berry,
for always being there.

Rainy Day
Sisters

1

LUCY BAGSHAW'S HALF SISTER, Juliet, had warned her about the weather. "When the sun is shining, it's lovely, but otherwise it's wet, windy, and cold," she'd stated in her stern, matter-of-fact way. "Be warned."

Lucy had shrugged off the warning because she'd rather live anywhere, even the Antarctic, than stay in Boston for another second. In any case she'd thought she was used to all three. She'd lived in England for the first six years of her life, and it wasn't as if Boston were the south of France. Except in comparison with the Lake District, it seemed it was.

Rain was atmospheric, she told herself as she hunched over the steering wheel, her eyes narrowed against the driving downpour. How many people listed walks in the rain as one of the most romantic things to do?

Although perhaps not when it was as torrential as this.

Letting out a gusty sigh, Lucy rolled her shoulders in an attempt to ease the tension that had lodged there since she'd turned off the M6.

Or really since three weeks ago, when her life had fallen apart in the space of a single day—give or take a few years, perhaps.

This was her new start, or, rather, her temporary reprieve. She was staying in England's Lake District, in the county of Cumbria, for only four months, long enough to get her act together and figure what she wanted to do next. She hoped. And, of course, Nancy Crawford was going to want her job as school receptionist back in January, when her maternity leave ended.

But four months was a long time. Long enough, surely, to heal, to become strong, even to forget.

Well, maybe not long enough for that. She didn't think she'd ever forget the blazing headline in the *Boston Globe*'s editorial section: *Why I Will Not Give My Daughter a Free Ride.*

She closed her eyes—briefly, because the road was twisty—and forced the memory away. She wasn't going to think about the editorial piece that had gone viral, or her boss's apologetic dismissal, or Thomas's shrugging acceptance of the end of a nearly three-year relationship. She certainly wasn't going to think about her mother. She was going to think about good things, about her new, if temporary, life here in the beautiful, if wet, Lake District. Four months to both hide and heal, to recover and be restored before returning to her real life—whatever was left, anyway—stronger than ever before.

Lucy drove in silence for half an hour, all her concentration taken up with navigating the A-road that led from Penrith to her destination, Hartley-by-the-Sea, population fifteen hundred. Hedgerows lined either side of the road and the dramatic fells in the distance were barely visible through the fog.

She peered through the window trying to get a better look at the supposedly spectacular scenery, only to brake hard as she came up behind a tractor trundling down the road at the breakneck speed of five miles per hour. Pulling behind her from a side lane was a truck with a trailer holding about a dozen morose and very wet-looking sheep.

She stared in the rearview mirror at the wet sheep, who gazed miserably back, and had a sudden memory of her mother's piercing voice.

Are you a sheep, Lucinda, or a person who can think and act for herself?

Looking at those miserable creatures now, she decided she was definitely not one of them. She would not be one of them, not here, in this new place, where no one knew her, maybe not even her half sister.

It took another hour of driving through steady rain, behind the trundling tractor the entire way, before she finally arrived at Hartley-by-the-Sea. The turning off the A-road was alarmingly narrow and steep, and the ache between Lucy's shoulders had become a pulsing pain. But at last she was here. There always was a bright side, or at least a glimmer of one. She had to believe that, had clung to it for her whole life and especially for the last few weeks, when the things she'd thought were solid had fallen away beneath like her so much sinking sand.

The narrow road twisted sharply several times, and then as she came around the final turn, the sun peeked out from behind shreds of cloud and illuminated the village in the valley below.

A huddle of quaint stone houses and terraced cottages clustered along the shore, the sea a streak of gray-blue that met up with the horizon. A stream snaked through the village before meandering into the fields on the far side; dotted with cows and looking, in the moment's sunshine, perfectly pastoral, the landscape was like a painting by Constable come to life.

For a few seconds Lucy considered how she'd paint such a scene; she'd use diluted watercolors, so the colors blurred into one another as they seemed to do in the valley below, all washed with the golden gray light that filtered from behind the clouds.

She envisioned herself walking in those fields, with a dog, a black Lab perhaps, frisking at her heels. Never mind that she didn't have a dog and didn't actually like them all that much. It was all part of the picture, along with buying a news-paper at the local shop—there had to be a lovely little shop down there, with a cozy, grandmotherly type at the counter who would slip her chocolate buttons along with her paper.

A splatter of rain against her windshield startled her from the moment's reverie. Yet another tractor was coming up behind her, at quite a clip. With a wave of apology for the stony-faced farmer who was driving the thing, she resumed the steep, sharply twisting descent into the village.

She slowed the car to a crawl as she came to the high street, houses lining the narrow road on either side, charming terraced cottages with brightly painted doors and pots of flowers, and, all right, yes, a few more weathered-looking buildings with peeling paint and the odd broken window. Lucy was determined to fall in love with it, to find everything perfect.

Juliet ran a guesthouse in one of the village's old farmhouses: Tarn House, she'd said, no other address. Lucy hadn't been to Juliet's house before, hadn't actually seen her sister in more than five years. And didn't really know her all that well.

Juliet was thirty-seven to her twenty-six, and when Lucy was six years old, their mother, Fiona, had gotten a job as an art lecturer at a university in Boston. She'd taken Lucy with her, but Juliet had chosen to stay in England and finish her A levels while boarding with a school friend. She'd gone on to university in England. She'd visited

Boston only once and over the years Lucy had always felt a little intimidated by her half sister, so cool and capable and remote.

Yet it had been Juliet she'd called when everything had exploded around her, and Juliet who had said briskly, when Lucy had burst into tears on the phone, that she should come and stay with her for a while.

"You could get a job, make yourself useful," she'd continued in that same no-nonsense tone that made Lucy feel like a scolded six-year-old. "The local primary needs maternity cover for a receptionist position, and I know the head teacher. I'll arrange it."

And Lucy, overwhelmed and grateful that someone could see a way out of the mess, had let her. She'd had a telephone interview with the head teacher, who was, she realized, the principal, the next day, a man who had sounded as stern as Juliet and had finished the conversation with a sigh, saying, "It's only four months, after all," so Lucy felt as if he was hiring her only as a favor to her sister.

And now she couldn't find Tarn House.

She drove the mile and a half down the main street and back again, doing what felt like a seventeen-point turn in the narrow street, sweat prickling between her shoulder blades while three cars, a truck, and two tractors, all driven by grim-faced men with their arms folded, waited

14

for her to manage to turn the car around. She'd never actually driven in England before, and she hit the curb twice before she managed to get going the right way.

She passed a post office shop looking almost as quaint as she'd imagined (peeling paint and lottery advertisements aside), a pub, a church, a sign for the primary school where she'd be working (but no actual school as far as she could see), and no Tarn House.

Finally she parked the car by the train station, admiring the old-fashioned sign above the Victorian station building, which was, on second look, now a restaurant. The driving rain had downgraded into one of those misting drizzlesthat didn't seem all that bad when you were looking out at it from the cozy warmth of your kitchen but soaked you utterly after about five seconds.

Hunching her shoulders against the bitter wind—this was *August*—she searched for someone to ask directions.

The only person in sight was a farmer with a flat cap jammed down on his head, wearing extremely mud-splattered plus fours. Lucy approached him with her most engaging smile.

"Pardon me—are you from around here?"

He squinted at her suspiciously. "Eh?"

She had just asked, she realized, an absolutely idiotic question. "I only wanted to ask," she tried again, "do you know where Tarn House is?"

"Tarn House?" he repeated, his tone implying that he'd never heard of the place.

"Yes, it's a bed-and-breakfast here in the village—"

"*Eh?*" He scratched his head, his bushy eyebrows drawn together rather fiercely. Then he dropped his hand and jerked a thumb towards the road that led steeply up towards the shop and one pub. "Tarn House's up there, isn't it, now, across from the Hangman's Noose."

"The Hangman's—" Ah. The pub. Lucy nodded. "Thank you."

"The white house with black shutters."

"Thanks so much, I really appreciate it." And why, Lucy wondered as she turned up the street, had he acted so incredulous when she'd asked him where it was? Was that a Cumbrian thing, or was her American accent stronger than she'd thought?

Tarn House was a neat two-story cottage of whitewashed stone with the promised black shutters, and pots of chrysanthemums on either side of the shiny black door. A discreet hand-painted sign that Lucy hadn't glimpsed from the road informed her that this was indeed her destination.

She hesitated on the slate step, her hand hovering above the brass knocker, as the rain continued steadily down. She felt keenly then how little she actually *knew* her sister. Half sister, if she wanted to be accurate; neither of them had

16

known their different fathers. Not that Lucy could really call a sperm donor a dad. And their mother had never spoken about Juliet's father, whoever he was, at least not to Lucy.

Her hand was still hovering over the brass knocker when the door suddenly opened and Juliet stood there, her sandy hair pulled back into a neat ponytail, her gray eyes narrowed, her hands planted on her hips, as she looked Lucy up and down, her mouth tightening the same way her mother's did when she looked at her.

Two sleek greyhounds flanked Juliet, cowering slightly as Lucy stepped forward and ducked her head in both greeting and silent, uncertain apology. She could have used a hug, but Juliet didn't move and Lucy was too hesitant to hug the half sister she barely knew.

"Well," Juliet said with a brisk nod. "You made it."

"Yes. Yes, I did." Lucy smiled tentatively, and Juliet moved aside.

"You look like a drowned rat. You'd better come in."

Lucy stepped into the little entryway of Juliet's house, a surprisingly friendly jumble of umbrellas and Wellington boots cluttering the slate floor along with the dogs. She would have expected her sister to have every boot and brolly in regimental order, but maybe she didn't know Juliet well enough to know how she kept her house.

17

Or maybe her sister was just having an off day.

"They're rescue dogs—they'll jump at a mouse," Juliet explained, for the two greyhounds were trembling. "They'll come round eventually. They just have to get used to you." She snapped her fingers, and the dogs obediently retreated to their baskets.

"Cup of tea," she said, not a question, and led Lucy into the kitchen. The kitchen was even cozier than the hall, with a large dark green Aga cooking range taking up most of one wall and emitting a lovely warmth, a circular pine table in the center, and a green glass jar of wildflowers on the windowsill. It was all so homely, so comforting, and so not what Lucy had expected from someone as stern and officious as Juliet, although again she was acting on ignorance. How many conversations had she even had with Juliet, before that wretched phone call? Five? Six?

Still the sight of it all, the Aga and the flowers and even the view of muddy sheep fields outside, made her spirits lift. This was a place she could feel at home in. She hoped.

She sank into a chair at the table as Juliet plonked a brass kettle on one of the Aga's round hot plates.

"So you start next week."

"Yes—"

"You ought to go up to the school tomorrow, and check in with Alex."

"Alex?"

Juliet turned around, her straight eyebrows drawn together, her expression not precisely a frown, but definitely not a smile. "Alex Kincaid, the head teacher. You spoke with him on the phone, remember?" There was a faint note of impatience or even irritation in Juliet's voice, which made Lucy stammer in apology.

"Oh, yes, yes, of course. Mr. Kincaid. Yes. Sorry." She was not actually all that keen to make Alex Kincaid's acquaintance. Given how unimpressed by her he'd seemed for the ten excruciating minutes of their phone interview, she thought he was unlikely to revise his opinion upon meeting her.

And she was unlikely to revise hers; she already had a picture of him in her head: He would be tall and angular with short-cut steel gray hair and square spectacles. He'd have one of those mouths that looked thin and unfriendly, and he would narrow his eyes at you as you spoke, as if incredulous of every word that came out of your mouth.

Oh, wait, maybe she was picturing her last boss, Simon Hansen, when he'd told her he was canceling her art exhibition. *Sorry, Lucy, but after the bad press we can hardly go ahead with the exhibit. And in any case, your mother's not coming anyway.*

As for Alex Kincaid, now that she remembered

that irritated voice on the phone, she decided he'd be balding and have bushy eyebrows. He'd blink too much as he spoke and have a nasal drip.

All right, perhaps that was a little unfair. But he'd definitely sounded as if he'd had his sense of humor surgically removed.

"I'm sure you're completely knackered now," Juliet continued, "but tomorrow I'll give you a proper tour of the village, introduce you." She nodded, that clearly decided, and Lucy, not knowing what else to do, nodded back.

It was so *strange* being here with her sister, sitting across from her in this cozy little kitchen, knowing she was actually going to live here and maybe get to know this sibling of hers who had semi-terrified her for most of her life. Intimidated, anyway, but perhaps that was her fault and not Juliet's.

In any case, when Lucy had needed someone to talk to, someone who understood the maelstrom that was their mother but wasn't caught up in her currents, she'd turned to Juliet. And Juliet hadn't let her down. She had to remember that, keep hold of it in moments like these, when Juliet seemed like another disapproving person in her life, mentally rolling her eyes at how Lucy could never seem to get it together.

And she *was* going to get it together. Here, in rainy, picturesque Hartley-by-the-Sea. She was going to reconnect with her sister, and make loads of friends, and go on picnics and pub crawls and find happiness.

"He's a good sort," Juliet said as she whisked the kettle off the Aga before it had shrilled for so much as a millisecond. It took Lucy a moment to remember whom Juliet was talking about. Alex Kincaid, her new boss. "Tough," Juliet added, "but good."

Lucy didn't like the sound of tough, especially Juliet's version of tough. She wanted her boss to be cuddly and comforting, or maybe a pull-you-up-by-your-bootstraps type, but in a jolly, let's-get-on-with-it kind of way. She had a feeling Alex Kincaid was going to be neither.

"Here you are." Juliet put a mug of steaming tea in front of Lucy, and pushed the sugar bowl and the milk jug towards her before taking her own mug. "So," she said, taking a sip of tea, her face settling into neutral lines. "What did Fiona think of you coming here to stay with me?"

Lucy gave a noncommittal shrug. She supposed she'd eventually have to give Juliet the details of everything that had happened with their mother, but she'd part with them reluctantly and in any case Juliet could find them plastered all over the Internet if she did a search. Maybe she already had. "I don't know. I just sent her an e-mail, telling her I was coming here. We haven't actually spoken since . . ."

"That's understandable," Juliet answered blandly. "I haven't spoken with her in five years."

Lucy didn't know the source of her sister's estrangement with their mother, although she supposed she could guess at it. Fiona Bagshaw was, to put it mildly, a personality. A "force" would be how she described herself. She'd made a name for herself in the world of modern art before Lucy was born, creating sculptures of round-hipped and large-breasted women that reminded Lucy of something you might discover in a prehistoric cave. *Fertility Goddess, circa 2000 BC.* But the figures were immensely popular and now sold for thousands of dollars, along with her latest artistic undertaking, angry-looking phalluses made from handblown glass.

In the last decade Fiona Bagshaw had become as much of a social commentator as an artist. If a newspaper or a television program needed a quote about women's rights or modern culture or just about anything, they went to Fiona. Lucy had become used to her mother's constant theorizing, the endless commentary on what anyone wore, ate, said, did. She couldn't so much as eat a Twinkie without her mother making some remark about it being a phallic representation and a symbol of modern patriarchy.

But Juliet had missed her mother's fame and its effects on Fiona's purpose-built family. She'd left before Fiona had become something of a cultural icon, at least in America. She certainly hadn't lived with it day in and day out the way Lucy had. So why *had* her sister chosen to alienate herself from their mother? Lucy wasn't about to ask. One, she didn't know Juliet well enough to ask such a personal question. Two, she didn't want to think about her mother for the next four months. And three, she was exhausted.

"I'll show you your room," Juliet said, draining her mug of tea. She rose and went to the sink, rinsing the mug out with her usual brisk movements. "You probably want a lie-down, although it's best not to sleep for more than an hour or two. Otherwise you'll be completely off schedule."

And Juliet was someone who seemed to thrive on schedules. Left to her own devices, Lucy would sleep all day. But now she obediently rose from the table and followed Juliet back into the hall. "I'll just get my bags from the car. What time is dinner?" Juliet gave her a rather narrow look. "I only meant, with your other—umm, your paying guests? Are they . . . ?"

"I haven't any guests at the moment," Juliet answered. "They left this morning, and the next lot arrive tomorrow at noon. They're all walkers, and they're usually only here for a night before they move on to the next stop on their route. I don't do dinner for guests, though, so it'll just be the two of us."

"Okay." Lucy jangled her car keys, the sound seeming too loud in the little hall. "I'm happy to pitch in, of course. With cooking and cleaning and all that."

"I'll make a rota," Juliet answered.

"A rota?" Lucy said blankly, and her half sister pursed her lips.

"A schedule," she explained, and Lucy suspected she'd already made one.

"Great." In the short silence after this awkward exchange, she jangled her keys again, and then went for her bags, ducking her head in the persistent drizzle, giving Hartley-by-the-Sea's high street one dubious glance. In the rain it all looked gray and bleak, without a single person to liven up the muted, monochrome landscape of terraced houses. If she were to paint it, she'd use a palette of grays and title it *Loneliness*. Or maybe *Isolation*. Not that she was planning on painting anything here, or ever again. Standing there, she couldn't hear a single sound besides the soft pattering of rain on the hood of her car.

Ten minutes later Juliet had left her alone in a sunshine yellow room at the back of the house, the white duvet cover stitched with daisies and a single window overlooking the sheep fields.

Lucy sank onto the bed, feeling more exhausted than ever and quite suddenly homesick— although for whom or what, she didn't know. She didn't miss Boston, particularly, or her job as a barista at a gallery/café in Cambridge. She didn't miss her mother or even Thomas, to whom she'd given three years of her life. She would have missed his children, if they'd shown her even a modicum of kindness or affection, but as it was, she was relieved to be free of them.

Maybe that was the trouble. She was missing the very fact that she didn't miss anything, that no one was special to her, that she'd left nothing behind that she still wanted. And nobody would miss her.

All right, perhaps that was being a bit maudlin. Her best friend, Chloe, hadn't wanted her to go. She had a small circle of friends and acquaintances who would at least read her Facebook updates, if she could be bothered to post them.

Arrived in Hartley-by-the-Sea! Raining steadily and had a cup of tea.

She had friends; she had a sister who she believed loved her even if she wasn't particularly demonstrative; she had a job. She had her health. Anything else?

Sighing, Lucy kicked off her shoes and turned back the daisy cover. Sleep, she decided. She had the luxury of sleeping for at least four hours, never mind what Juliet had said about one or two. She'd wake up in time to help with dinner, or with whatever job Juliet had written her down for on her precious rota.

2
Juliet

JULIET HAD FINISHED WASHING up the tea mugs, her gaze on the sheep fields that stretched to the horizon, blanketed in a gray drizzle. Upstairs she'd heard the creak of the floorboards as Lucy had moved around, the squeak of the bedsprings. She wondered now what Lucy thought of the room, imagined her taking in the curtains with the daisy chains Juliet had stitched herself, the Edwardian washing pitcher and basin she'd found at the antiques fair in Cockermouth. And then she wondered why she cared.

A mug slipped from her hand and broke in the bottom of the farmhouse sink she'd bought from a reclamation center. She swore softly under her breath and picked up the shattered pieces, swearing again when a jagged shard of pottery cut into her thumb, and a bright red drop of blood welled up. She wrapped the broken pieces in a paper towel and threw them in the bin before putting her thumb in her mouth and sucking at the cut.

Then she reached for a sponge and wiped the table, swiping at the droplets of tea and the sprinkling of sugar granules that Lucy had left. Having her sister stay was going to make a mess in all sorts of ways, and stir up unwanted feelings in herself. And that was something she hadn't expected.

It had seemed to be both simple and generous, to invite Lucy here when her life had fallen apart in spectacular Lucy style. Lucy, Juliet had long noted from afar, never seemed to do anything by halves, or with any modicum of caution. She jumped into situations, relationships, and even college degrees with far more enthusiasm than sense. Juliet had, with a kind of smug pleasure at her own neatly ordered life, periodically checked Lucy's enthusiastic Facebook updates: *Changed my course from history to art! So excited* and *Moved to a converted warehouse in South Boston. Love it!!!!* Never mind that she'd already done two years of her history degree, and changing to art necessitated a further two semesters of college, or that the converted warehouse hadn't actually yet been converted into a livable dwelling. Lucy leaped. Juliet looked.

Except, in this instance, Juliet had been the one to leap, by inviting her half sister to stay. And while it had seemed so easy when she'd suggested it on the phone—here she was, the organized, older sister, swooping in to take care of poor Lucy—now it felt . . . unsettling.

She propped her elbows on the sink and gazed

27

out again at the muddy fields. Peter Lanford was coming down the dirt road from Bega Farm in his battered old Land Rover, probably to check on the sheep he kept in the pasture in back of Juliet's garden. She and Peter had gotten to know each other a little, both through their properties adjoining and being on the village's parish council together. She might almost call him a friend, and she didn't really do friendship. Or even relationships in general, outside of ones that were clearly and comfortingly defined. Employer/employee. Patient/doctor. Innkeeper/guest. What category did half sister fall into?

It had been shockingly disconcerting to open the door and see Lucy standing there in the flesh, with the same sandy hair, gray eyes, and freckles that Juliet possessed, and yet looking so different. Her ballet flats, purple tights, and miniskirt decorated with lemons of all things had been ridiculous and inappropriate for the weather; Juliet was, as ever, wearing jeans and a fleece. Lucy's hair had frizzed about her face, while Juliet kept hers subdued in a sensible ponytail. And yet there could be no denying they were sisters. Half sisters. They even had the same slightly crooked nose. Whoever their respective fathers were, neither of them seemed to have passed on many of his genes.

And as Lucy had stepped into the foyer, seeming suddenly to fill up the space that had always been hers alone, Juliet had had a sudden and overwhelming urge to push her half sister right back out the door and then slam it in her face.

Not exactly the most sisterly of impulses, and not one she'd expected to have. She was being kind and generous to poor, hopeless Lucy. That was what was going on here. That was what she'd signed up for.

A knock sounded on the door, and blowing out a breath, Juliet turned from the sink. A few seconds later Rachel Campbell appeared in the kitchen with her arms full of freshly ironed sheets.

"I thought I'd pop by with the ironing while I had a moment," she said, and with a murmur of thanks Juliet took them from her. Rachel cleaned the house twice a week and did all the ironing, tasks that Juliet was fully capable of doing herself, but Rachel's housecleaning business supported a family of five—a mother, two sisters, and a nephew—and Juliet wanted to help her without seeming pitying. Besides, she hated ironing. "Has the half sister arrived?" Rachel asked, her eyebrows raised, and guilt needled Juliet uncomfortably.

When she'd told Rachel last week that Lucy would be coming, Rachel had said in a voice of such disbelief that Juliet hadn't been able to tell if she was joking, "You have a *sister?*"

"Half sister," she'd said, and Rachel had rolled her eyes.

"Oh, *well,* then," she'd said, and Juliet hadn't answered, because she couldn't, in truth, explain her relationship, or lack of it, with Lucy. Since then she and Rachel had both, in a semijoking way—or maybe not—referred to Lucy as "the half sister."

"Yes, she's here," Juliet said. "Lucy's here," she added, as if there were any question as to who had arrived. She didn't want to call her the half sister anymore, even if Lucy still felt like the half sister. Or maybe even just a quarter sister. Barely related, basically.

"And is she as scatterbrained as you expected?" Rachel asked, making guilt needle Juliet once more. All right, she might have called Lucy scatterbrained. But she hadn't meant it meanly. It had been more a statement of fact.

Juliet leaned against the Aga rail and folded her arms. "She's just Lucy," she said flatly. "And she's only been here about five minutes. She's just gone upstairs to have a nap. Jet lag."

Rachel nodded, her clear-eyed gaze resting a little too thoughtfully on her. "You think she'll get on at the school?" she asked. "Alex Kincaid is a bit of a slave driver, from what I've heard."

Juliet shrugged. She respected Alex and she liked his toughness. She understood tough, because that's what she'd been faced with for most of her life. Lucy, however, didn't know the meaning of tough, their mother's ridiculous grandstanding aside. She'd been cosseted and spoiled since the moment she'd been born and as far as Juliet could tell, she still expected other people to step in and pick up the pieces she'd carelessly dropped.

"She'll have to manage, won't she?" Juliet said, deciding to cut short any more speculation or gossip. "I should get on. I've got three walkers coming in tomorrow, Australian lads. They'll eat me out of house and home, most likely."

"All right." Reluctantly Rachel rose from the table. "I suppose I should get on, as well. Lily's gone to the cinema with a friend. She'll need a lift home."

Lily was Rachel's seventeen-year-old sister, and Juliet knew Rachel had been caring for her more or less since she'd been a baby. She didn't like to think about it too much, though, because Rachel was eleven years older than Lily, the same age difference between her and Lucy. And her relationship with Lucy was so incredibly different. So much *less*.

"You coming to the quiz night tomorrow?" Rachel asked, and Juliet shook her head. Every week Rachel asked her to the quiz night at the Hangman's Noose, and every week Juliet refused. She wouldn't know what to do at a thing like that. She didn't do banter and refused to try.

"See you Friday, then," Rachel said, and headed towards the front door. "I'll do the bathrooms. You'll need it, after these Australian blokes go."

Juliet waved and then hefted the pile of ironed sheets to take upstairs. She couldn't hear anything from Lucy's room; she was probably asleep.

As she made the three guest bedrooms up with the freshly starched and ironed sheets, tucking in the hospital corners and snapping them tight, she told herself that maybe being with Lucy now would close a little bit of the distance they'd had in their relationship. Maybe during these four months they'd actually get to know each other.

The trouble was, Juliet acknowledged as she headed back downstairs, she wasn't sure she wanted to.

3
Lucy

ALEX KINCAID, LUCY THOUGHT, looked *nothing* like she'd expected him to. Forget balding or bushy eyebrows or a nasal drip. The man was amazingly and irritatingly sexy.

It seemed an entirely inappropriate word to attribute to a head teacher, of a primary school no less, but it popped into her head just the same. Dark brown hair cut very short. Navy eyes with thick lashes. And a body that even in a conservative suit looked toned and muscular and, well, *hot*.

Alex Kincaid's good looks were an unexpected perk. She could use a little distraction, not just from everything she'd left in Boston, but from this new life in Hartley-by-the-Sea she was trying hard to like. It wasn't easy. In the eighteen hours since she'd shown up at Tarn House, Juliet hadn't warmed to her in the slightest.

Lucy hadn't expected some kind of *homecoming,* of course, but she'd thought Juliet would be at least a little happy to see her. She'd assumed her sister's invitation meant that Juliet actually wanted her here. And all right, yes, perhaps she'd imagined her sister running her deep bubble baths and pampering her a bit. Was that so wrong? Her life had just been destroyed. She could do with a tiny bit of coddling, the odd glass of wine pressed into her hands, assurances that she was here to relax, to be restored.

If anything, Juliet seemed to resent her presence. After sleeping for three hours yesterday afternoon, Lucy had stumbled downstairs to find her dinner of beef stew left in the warming oven of the Aga, with a note on the table asking her to put her plate in the dishwasher when she was done. Juliet had gone to walk the dogs.

Lucy had eaten alone in the kitchen, feeling once more like a scolded child, the house quiet and creaky all around her. The wind rattled the windowpanes and sent drops of water spattering on the glass, a sound that felt unfriendly. The sun was just starting to set at eight o'clock, but Lucy could barely see its weak rays from behind the heavy gray clouds. She couldn't remember the last time she'd felt quite so alone.

She'd told herself to stop being so melodramatic, and turned on a lamp by the deep window seat that overlooked the gloomy pasture. She felt a little better then, and she made sure to rinse her plate and put it in the dishwasher as Juliet had instructed.

Then she'd heard Juliet come in, her quick, purposeful step, and she'd appeared in the kitchen doorway, hands on her hips.

"Did you get enough to eat?"

"Yes, thank you—"

Juliet had nodded and turned away before Lucy could stumble through any more thank-yous. She'd turned off the lamp Lucy had just switched on and then fished a *tiny* piece of beef from the kitchen drain and pointedly deposited it in the bin. Lucy had bitten her lip to keep from apologizing.

An hour later Juliet had knocked on Lucy's bedroom door and handed her a sheet of paper, the rota she'd mentioned earlier. Lucy scanned it and saw she was down to make dinner on Tuesdays and Thursdays, and clean the upstairs bathroom once a week.

"I'll take you over to the school tomorrow morning," she said with one of those brisk nods Lucy was starting to dislike. "Introduce you to Alex Kincaid." She'd glanced at Lucy's purple tights, her mouth tightening. "You might want to think about what you wear. First impressions are crucial, you know."

And she'd walked away before Lucy could say anything. "Thank you" had not come to mind.

She'd lain in bed, exhausted but unable to sleep, wondering if she'd made a huge mistake in coming here. The last thing she needed in her life was yet another sniffily disapproving person making her feel small and stupid. And yet she couldn't just take off, either. She didn't want to run away again. She wanted something to *work*.

35

So, yes, Alex Kincaid being good-looking was a very nice distraction. Except right now he appeared as stern and disapproving as Juliet.

"Umm . . . sorry?"

"Have you been listening to anything I've said?"

The answer to that would be no. She had been admiring the cleft in his chin, though. Very Cary Grant. "I . . ." She scrambled to think of *something* he'd said, but her mind came up empty. This was definitely not the first impression she'd wanted to make. And first impressions were so *crucial,* as Juliet had said. She had gone for her most sensible outfit too, a brown corduroy skirt and a fuzzy blue sweater and plain black tights because even though it was the last week of August, it was still freezing. She was wearing the clothes she'd brought for the beginning of winter.

"I see," Alex said, the two words bitten out. Lucy supposed she should have expected this kind of attitude from Mr. Kincaid; from the moment she'd met him out in the school yard, he'd seemed hassled and impatient, one sweeping glance taking her in and seeming to dismiss her all at once. He'd turned away to unlock the front door of the school, and then ushered her into the tiny front office with its sliding glass window and enormous photocopying machine. Lucy had breathed in the scent of chalk and new paint and, underneath, the tang of old PE clothes and sweaty boy. That smell had catapulted her back to elementary school,

36

and that had not been a happy time. Junior high had been worse.

Maybe working in a school hadn't been such a great idea.

"I was asking, Miss Bagshaw," Alex elaborated now in the overemphasizing way used by people who clearly thought you were stupid, "if you had any administrative experience."

She'd already told him she hadn't during her phone interview. "No, I'm afraid not."

"Any experience answering telephones?"

Besides her own? "No."

He pressed his lips together, eyes narrowing. He still looked attractive, but it had become much less of a distraction. She was now depressingly aware of how little Alex Kincaid clearly thought of her. "I can make a mean cup of coffee," she offered, and he actually scowled.

"Let me explain your responsibilities," Alex said, his voice turning even in the way of someone who was only just holding on to his temper. "You'll answer any telephone calls, in addition to dealing with any visitors. Maggie Bains, who covered reception in the summer term, will guide you through it for a few days. You'll also do some work for me, as you'll be the closest thing I have to a personal assistant."

"That's no problem at all," she told him brightly. The truth was, she had no idea what a personal assistant actually did. File? Type? She was a *great* barista. But Alex Kincaid hadn't seemed too impressed by that information.

"I'm glad to hear it," Alex answered tightly. He stared at her for a moment, and Lucy held on to the alert, friendly expression she'd been trying to maintain with effort. Then he sighed and glanced at his watch. "Look, I've got a million things to do before school starts, and Maggie can show you around on the first day. Would that be all right?"

"Totally fine." She took a deep breath and stood up, unfortunately at the same time as Alex, making them nearly bump noses in the tiny office. Lucy took a step and felt the photocopier jab into her back. She suppressed a wince. So did Alex.

Resolutely she stuck her hand out. "Thank you for taking me on, Mr. Kincaid. I really appreciate the opportunity." There. That sounded professional, didn't it?

With seeming reluctance Alex took her hand and gave it a shake. "You're welcome," he said grudgingly.

Two minutes later Lucy was back outside in the little school yard, a chilly wind buffeting her. A steep lane ran down to the high street, and above the slate roofs she could see the rolling pasture and the determined twinkle of the sea. The rain had eased off this morning, although the relentless rattling of wind through the trees had kept her up half the night. Now the sky was a pale gray-blue, as if it couldn't make up its mind whether to revert back to rain. The sun wasn't exactly shining, but at least it wasn't a downpour.

Digging her hands into the pockets of her coat, Lucy headed down the lane and back to Tarn House.

The house was full of noise and commotion as she let herself in, squeezing past the three enormous backpacks that crowded the little entry hall. She made her way back to the kitchen, where three young men, of a size to match their luggage, were standing around the kitchen table, chatting in loud Australian accents while Juliet poured tea from a big blue pot.

Her sister looked almost . . . animated. She was smiling, at least, which made Lucy realize Juliet had not actually smiled once since she'd arrived.

And the smile disappeared completely when she caught sight of Lucy.

"You're back," she said, and Lucy just kept herself from inanely agreeing. "So, how did you get on?"

"Fine, I think." Actually, she didn't think she'd gotten on fine at all. Alex Kincaid seemed to take her on sufferance, just as Juliet did. But she wasn't about to say that, especially not with these three linebackers eyeing her with such blatant curiosity.

"Well, it's not rocket science, is it?" Juliet said as she put the teapot back on the Aga. "Answering phones."

Lucy tried to figure out if that comment had

been as snippy and sarcastic as it had felt. She caught the gaze of one of the Australians, who winked at her. "No," she agreed as she backed out of the room. "It's not rocket science."

She went upstairs to her bedroom, the Australians' raucous laughter ringing in her ears. Quietly she shut the door and leaned against it, wanting to duck the tidal wave of homesickness she felt crashing over her and knowing she couldn't.

She thought about calling Chloe, who was practical and matter-of-fact but in a kindly, cheerful way. Unfortunately it was only seven in the morning in Boston, and Lucy didn't think her best friend would appreciate being woken up at that hour just so Lucy could moan. She couldn't even send her an e-mail, because she hadn't worked up the courage to ask Juliet for the Wi-Fi password.

She curled up on the bed, tucking her knees to her chest as she gazed out at the fragile blue sky, which was threatening to be overwhelmed once more by dark gray clouds.

She could explore Hartley-by-the Sea, but at the moment the dark sky and the narrow high street didn't beckon to her with their dubious charms. She'd rather stay curled up on her bed and feel miserable. Sort of.

The Australians thundered up the stairs, and then it seemed as if the whole house rattled as they dumped their heavy backpacks in various rooms before heading downstairs again and then out the door with a loud slam.

The ensuing silence felt like the calm after a storm, interrupted by a light tapping on Lucy's door.

"Yes—"

Juliet poked her head around the door, her gaze taking in the pajamas Lucy had left on the floor and yesterday's clothes kicked in the corner. The contents of her toiletry bag were strewn over the top of the dresser, and she'd dumped all her American change and a crumpled pack of gum in the antique washbasin. Predictably, Juliet's mouth tightened at the sight of all this mess and then her gaze snapped to Lucy.

"I'm going to take the dogs for a walk to the beach. Fancy coming?"

Lucy swallowed past the lump in her throat and nodded. "Sure," she said, and hopped off the bed.

4
Juliet

JULIET ALWAYS FELT A bit flat without guests in the house. She liked guests like the Australian boys: boisterous, cheerful, needing her to bustle around them. The retired couples who came on walking holidays were soothing in their own way, and certainly slotted into the order of things with calm neatness, but they didn't need her the way these lads did, frying them a half dozen eggs each for breakfast and letting them wash out their dirty kit in the kitchen sink.

Now she stood in the doorway of Lucy's room and watched while she grabbed her sweater and reached for an elastic for her hair amidst the detritus strewn across the dresser. How had Lucy managed to make such a mess in less than twenty-four hours? And why did her sister's mess irritate her when she knew she would put up with the Australian boys' muddy boots and dirty socks?

Well, the Australians were leaving tomorrow. Lucy wasn't.

"I'll get the dogs' leads," Juliet said, and turned away.

Back downstairs she jammed on her hiking

boots and reached for her waterproof jacket before looping the dogs' leads around their sleek heads. They always knew when she was taking them out, from the moment she even seemed to think about it. Now they pranced around her with nervous excitement, butting her thigh with their noses.

She heard Lucy coming down the stairs; she'd changed into jeans, but she was wearing those ridiculous ballet flats and her jacket was actually velveteen.

"It's going to rain," Juliet told her. "Don't you have proper gear?"

Lucy glanced at her jacket. "Umm . . . I have a winter parka, but it's kind of heavy, considering it's supposed to be summer."

"You'll need a proper waterproof here unless you want to catch pneumonia." Juliet reached for one of the spare waterproofs she kept for guests and tossed it to Lucy. "Here. You can use that until you can get something suitable. Those flats will be soaked in seconds. The beach is tidal, you know. The sand is always wet." Belatedly Juliet realized how stern she sounded.

"Sorry," Lucy said. Her sister looked like a kicked puppy. She'd looked the same when she'd made that comment in the kitchen about answering phones not being rocket science. And maybe it had sounded a little mean, but honestly. How hard a job could it be?

"You can borrow a pair of boots too," she said

gruffly, leaning down to lace up her hiking boots. "There's probably a pair your size in the hall."

A few minutes later they were heading down the high street, bundled up in coats and boots, their heads lowered against the chill wind.

"I can't believe it's August," Lucy said as she dug her hands into the pockets of her coat. "*August.* It's ninety degrees Fahrenheit in Boston."

"Sounds awful," Juliet answered shortly, and patted her thigh. "Milly. Molly. Heel."

"I suppose it was pretty muggy," Lucy allowed. "But it's bloody freezing here. It can't be above fifty degrees."

"I don't know Fahrenheit," Juliet answered, "but it's not that cold. You just have to dress appropriately."

She sneaked a glance at Lucy and saw she was doing the kicked-puppy thing again. Her shoulders were hunched against the wind, her head lowered, her eyes streaming. But then Juliet's eyes were also streaming; they were walking straight into the wind.

"So how long have you been living here?" Lucy asked.

Juliet narrowed her eyes against the onslaught of the wind. No matter what she'd said to Lucy, it really was freezing out, even for Cumbria. "Ten years."

"What made you choose this place? I would have expected you to live in London or something, doing something important. Stockbroker or solicitor or something."

Juliet let out a bark of a laugh at that. "Solicitor? I didn't even finish university."

"Didn't you?" Lucy's gaze widened and Juliet gritted her teeth. She didn't know what annoyed her more: that she'd told Lucy or that Lucy hadn't known. "Why not?"

"I dropped out. Wasn't for me." Juliet dug her hands into her pockets and started to walk faster. "I did a catering course instead."

"I never knew that," Lucy said, and Juliet shrugged.

"Why would you? We haven't exactly kept in touch."

"I know, but . . ." Lucy trailed off and Juliet didn't fill the silence. What was there, really, to say? Their mother and Lucy had chosen to make their lives in Boston, separate from Juliet. They'd been perfectly happy in their little bubble of fame and fortune, a far cry from the council flat Juliet had grown up in, when Fiona had been struggling through night classes and jobs working in pubs. Lucy had no idea of what life had been like before Fiona Bagshaw had become *the* Fiona Bagshaw.

"So a catering course," Lucy said after a moment. "Have you always worked in the hospitality industry?"

"I got a job at a big hotel in Manchester right

45

after graduation. I worked there for a few years." Until her life had fallen apart, though not in the spectacular way Lucy's had; more of a desperate, quiet crumbling.

"So how did you end up in Hartley-by-the-Sea?"

Juliet dug her hands deeper into the pockets of her waterproof. "I was on a walking holiday up here and I stopped and decided to stay for good."

"Really? You just . . . stayed?"

Juliet shot her a narrow look. "Why all the questions now, Lucy?"

"Because I'm living with you, and I realize I don't even know you, not really. We're sisters—"

"Half sisters." It popped out before Juliet could keep herself from it, and Lucy blinked, clearly stung.

"Half sisters," she agreed, "but we're the only siblings we've got—"

"True enough, I suppose."

Lucy continued stiltedly. "I don't think I've thanked you properly for putting me up. Inviting me here, I mean. I really do appreciate it. I had nowhere to go—"

"You could have stayed in Boston."

Lucy shook her head. "No. I'd rather have gone anywhere than stay there."

Juliet raised her eyebrows. "Even a poky village with the worst weather in all of England? Although to be fair, it *has* been a miserable August. It's not normally quite this cold."

Lucy raised her eyebrows right back at her. "And you told me it wasn't that bad."

"Well." Juliet could feel a sudden smile tugging at her mouth, surprising her. Were they actually joking with each other?

"It's beautiful here," Lucy said, and fluttered her fingers. It took Juliet a second to realize she was trying to touch her hand. "*Look* at that," she exclaimed, and flung the other hand out to encompass the view.

They'd turned off the high street at the train station, and had been walking along a lane aptly named Beach Road, with sheep pastures on either side, the steep, gray-green fells cutting a jagged line out of the horizon. As they rounded a gentle hill, they could see the sea in the distance, glittering under a sun that had emerged from dark storm clouds, offering that syrupy golden light particular to England, even though most of the sky was still a deep, dank gray.

The wind blew their hair into tangles around their faces and tears still streamed from their eyes, but in that moment, facing the stark beauty of sea and sky, Juliet felt her spirits lift.

Lucy must have felt it too, for she grabbed Juliet's hand and squeezed. Juliet went rigid in shock, but Lucy was clearly oblivious. "It really is beautiful," she exclaimed. She turned to Juliet, her smile ridiculously radiant. "I can see why you stayed."

Juliet pulled her hand away from Lucy's and called the dogs forward. "Let's go. Milly looks like she needs a poo."

They let the dogs run about on the beach for a good half hour, racing along the water's edge, wet sand spraying up behind their long, elegant legs.

"So where did the Australians go off to?" Lucy asked as they stood huddled by the concrete promenade that ran along the beach, all the way to the flimsy-looking bungalow with a sign in peeling black paint that was Hartley-by-the-Sea's beach café.

"The pub," Juliet answered. "They'll stagger back when Rob throws them out tonight and then conquer Scafell Pike tomorrow."

"Rob?"

"Rob Telford. He's the landlord of the Hangman's Noose."

"Nice name."

"It adds character."

Lucy gave a small smile, and Juliet gave one back. So apparently she and her sister could chat like normal people, for a few minutes at least.

"So, are all your guests like these Australians?"

"They're almost all walkers or hikers. I get the odd guest who's here for something else, visiting relatives or doing research for a dissertation on Wordsworth or Beatrix Potter. But we're a bit far off the beaten track for that sort of thing, so walking it is."

"I saw a sign for Wordsworth's house, I think, on the road here."

Juliet nodded. "Up in Cockermouth. And Hill Top, Beatrix Potter's house, is in Ambleside. There's not much going out this way, though, besides walking."

"But that's enough to keep you in business, I suppose."

"I manage." Juliet nodded towards the café. "It's not much, but they serve coffee and tea and some toasted sandwiches. You fancy it?"

Lucy beamed at her, making Juliet feel guilty again. She should be kinder to Lucy; it was just that she wasn't always sure *how*. Or if she really wanted to. "Sounds great," Lucy said, and Juliet called for the dogs, who came loping to her, butting their narrow heads against her leg.

"Get off, you're soaking," she exclaimed, but she stroked them all the same before looping their leads around their necks and heading for the promenade that led to the café.

Juliet could tell Lucy was a bit nonplussed by the shabby, muggy warmth of the café, the windows that overlooked the frothing sea fogged up. The small room was scattered with tables with peeling tops and rickety chairs, and only a handful of patrons. It wasn't some upscale Boston bistro, that was for certain.

Mary, the café's owner and a buxom woman with flyaway white hair and a booming laugh, handed them a grease-splattered laminated menu upon their arrival; Juliet had tied the dogs up outside.

"What can I do you, Juliet?"

"A cup of coffee and a toasted ham and cheese, please, Mary." She glanced at Lucy. "What would you like?"

"I'll have the same."

Mary rang up their orders on a till and Juliet took out a ten-pound note while Lucy fumbled with her pockets. "My treat," she said shortly, and Lucy stammered her thanks, which Juliet ignored. "How's the heart, Mary?" she asked, and the older woman made a wry face.

"Still ticking, more or less."

"Hopefully more." Mary gave her the change, which she tipped into the plastic box for the Royal National Lifeboat Institute. "Mary had a heart attack last winter," she told Lucy as they walked to a table by the window. The sun had retreated again and rain spattered the glass.

"Is she okay?" Lucy asked, turning around to gaze at Mary before Juliet tapped her on the shoulder.

"She's not going to fall down dead, so you can stop rubbernecking," she said, meaning it as a joke, but it didn't come out like one. She clearly had trouble with delivery.

"Do you know everyone in the village?"

"No." She didn't actually know that many

people, considering she'd been here ten years. She certainly didn't know many people *well*.

"So, how unusual is this for August, really?" Lucy asked. Juliet had seen that the thermometer outside the café had registered eleven degrees Celsius. "Tell me the truth."

Juliet shrugged. "Not that unusual, I suppose, but we keep hoping for better." Mary came over with the coffees and after thanking her, Juliet stirred hers slowly, her gaze on the gray clouds, a wisp of blue just barely visible underneath. The definition of hope. "When the weather's good here, it's really, really good."

"And when it's bad, it's horrid?" Lucy finished with a smile, and Juliet let out a sudden, rusty laugh that seemed to take them both by surprise.

" 'There was a little girl, who had a little curl,' " she quoted. "Yes, like that." Then, impulsively, she added, "The day I arrived here, I came from Whitehaven on the Coast-to-Coast walk and the sun was just setting over the sea. It was amazing, really. It had been the most wonderful day, pure blue skies and bright sunshine the whole time. And warm, even though it was September. I stood on the top of the head by the beach right there"—she nodded towards the window—"and watched the sun turn the water to gold and I felt as if—well, as if I didn't need to go anywhere else. Finally."

Lucy was looking almost weepy, and Juliet felt a flush rise on her face. She didn't normally sound so bloody sentimental. She didn't think she'd told anyone that story before, or even articulated it to herself. And yet somehow the words had spilled out to Lucy of all people.

"Why—why did you . . . ," Lucy began, stammering a bit, and Juliet braced herself for whatever prying question her sister was going to ask. Then Mary plonked their plates on the table and the moment broke, much to Juliet's relief, although she couldn't quite suppress a flicker of disappointment that Lucy hadn't finished asking her question—not that she'd intended to answer it.

5
Lucy

ON THE FIRST DAY of school Lucy woke up with a stomachache. She used to get them quite a lot when she was younger; seventh grade in particular had been the Year of Stomachaches. Her mother had been commissioned to do a sculpture in Boston Common, and the day before school had started, it had been installed: a huge, lumpy breast with a grotesque nipple pointing heavenwards. Just remembering that awful thing still made Lucy cringe fifteen years later.

It had been controversial, of course, and her mother had always thrived on controversy. She'd been in all the papers, on all the news networks, defending her creation against the "uninformed bigots" who protested against shepherding their children past a huge, ugly boob. Lucy had sympathized with those so-called bigots, although she'd never told her mother so.

And then that first day of school . . . walking into a strange new middle school with everyone knowing who her mother was and the sculpture she'd made. Lucy's stomach clenched at the memory. There had been an outline of a breast, complete with pointy nipple, scrawled on her locker in permanent pen before first period.

In second period a popular boy in eighth grade called her Boob Girl; by lunchtime everyone in the school was calling her that.

By November she was throwing up every morning from stress, and begging her mother to let her switch schools. Her mother had sighed, looking sympathetic for about a millisecond, and then refused.

"If you can't stand up to petty bigots now, Lucy, you never will. Trust me, I'm doing you a favor."

Her mother had done her a lot of favors over the years. She'd endured three more months of teasing, sitting alone at lunch and walking through corridors with a determined smile on her face, as if she could appreciate the joke they were all making endlessly at her expense, until people had finally, thankfully, grown tired of it, and even better, the sculpture had been taken down.

Eighth grade had been better. Her mother had had no major commissions.

But things were different now. She was starting school, yes, but she was twenty-six, not twelve, and her mother was on a different continent. Her boss might have his doubts about her, but she could prove him wrong. Prove herself capable. And best of all, no one in Hartley-by-the-Sea, except Juliet, knew about what had happened in Boston. None of them would have read Boston's newspapers; they probably hadn't seen the blogs and editorials online. They might not have even heard of Fiona Bagshaw.

Smiling a little at the thought, Lucy rose from bed to get ready for the day.

Washed and dressed, she entered the kitchen to find Juliet busy making fry-ups for another group of walkers who had come in last night, two high-flying couples in their thirties with expensive equipment and a van service that would ferry it for them so they could walk with just their day rucksacks.

"Luxury walking," Juliet had told her last night with a wry twist of her lips, almost a smile, and when Lucy had smiled back, she'd almost felt as if they were complicit in something.

She wanted to get along with Juliet so badly, but it wasn't coming easily. She'd been here for four days and besides that surprising admission at the beach café, they'd barely had a conversation. Lucy had tidied her room, worked up the courage to ask for the Wi-Fi password, and spent several gluttonous hours on Facebook, gorging on the details of everyone else's far more interesting lives. She'd returned her car to Workington, a dismal-named town if she'd ever heard of one, and taken the train back that ran along the coast, gazing out at the endless, choppy gray sea and feeling as if she were teetering on the very edge of the world. It wouldn't take much to fall right off, she'd thought, just one good push.

The next day she'd walked up to the post office shop, half-hoping to find a potential friend in its cozy interior, but the man behind the counter was surly and six feet four with tattoos up both arms, and when Lucy had attempted a cheery conversation opener, telling him she'd just moved into Tarn House, he'd simply given her a flat stare before silently putting her change on the counter. Although he looked to be roughly the same age as Juliet, he clearly wasn't one of her friends.

Lucy wasn't actually sure Juliet *had* any friends. She seemed to be consumed by the bed-and-breakfast business, churning out full English breakfasts every morning and making up beds and tidying endlessly in between walking the dogs. Lucy had, tentatively, offered to walk Milly and Molly, to which Juliet had pursed her lips and said, "Wait till they get used to you."

And now she was starting her job and despite her stomachache, she was clinging to her optimism. She could meet people at the school, teachers who would be far friendlier than grumpy Alex Kincaid. Kindred spirits, even. She was still hoping for picnics and pub crawls.

In the kitchen Lucy murmured good morning before grabbing a bowl for her own breakfast of microwaved oatmeal. At moments like this she felt like an interloper and even a freeloader in her sister's house, and she wasn't sure if that feeling would pass with time. Maybe she should offer to pay rent.

"You'd better be getting on," Juliet said after the two couples had left and she'd dumped all the pans into the sink to soak. "You're meant to be there right at eight, aren't you?"

"Yes . . ." Lucy glanced at the clock. It was ten minutes to eight and the oatmeal she'd eaten felt like a stone inside her stomach.

"Get on with you, then," Juliet said briskly, and made a shooing motion. Lucy couldn't tell if she was being encouraging or just wanted her out of the house. "It'll be fine, I'm sure."

Lucy nodded and reached for the proper waterproof she'd bought in Whitehaven, at Juliet's instruction. It wasn't actually raining this morning, although it had been last night.

Now as she stepped outside, she saw the sky was a fragile blue, the sun streaming weakly from behind shreds of cloud. A few people were walking briskly towards the train station, but otherwise the street was quiet and empty.

Lucy took a deep breath and headed up towards the school. As she battled with the school's front door, a sudden gust of wind making it nearly impossible to open, she saw that a woman was already installed in the little reception office. She hurried out to help, closing the door behind her as Lucy blew herself in.

"Sorry," she said, gasping, and tried to force her

now-frizzy hair into some kind of submission. Wind was not kind to hair like hers.

"You must be the Yank," the woman said, and Lucy blinked. *The Yank?* Seriously? The woman gave a booming laugh. "Oh, never mind me, I'm just having you on. Juliet said you were born here, weren't you?"

"In Hampshire," Lucy answered. She slipped off her coat and hung it on the stand in the corner of the office. "I moved to Boston when I was six."

"You *do* sound American." The woman put her hands on her hips and surveyed her, making Lucy aware of how bright and fuzzy her sweater was. She'd paired it with what she considered to be a very sensible black velveteen skirt, but the outfit was a far cry from her companion's lavender twin set and tweed skirt. She was definitely zero for two in the first-impressions department. "Well, then," the woman said. "I'm Maggie Bains."

"Oh, yes. Mr. Kincaid mentioned you—"

"I covered last term. And I'm here for a day or two to show you the ropes, but you'll get the hang of it in no time, I'm sure, and then I'm off to Newcastle to visit the grandkids." She smiled and bustled over to the photocopier. "Now, first things first. Mr. Kincaid is hard, but he's fair."

Just like Juliet's tough but good. Lucy was now officially terrified. Perhaps Maggie read her expression, for she let out another booming laugh and said, "Now, now, don't let him scare you. I'd say his bark is worse than his bite, but he's never bitten anyone, as far as I know. He's a lovely man, really."

"Mmm."

"And he hasn't had an easy time of it, by any means. But *I'm* not one to gossip," Maggie stated, making Lucy think she probably was. "So here's the agenda for the staff meeting this morning," she continued, taking a sheaf of papers from on top of the photocopier. "You'll be responsible for that in future, but don't worry. Mr. Kincaid always e-mails you the points beforehand."

"Okay," Lucy said, trying to sound as if this were no problem at all. Already she felt over-whelmed. What on earth made her think she could do any of this?

"And here's Diana," Maggie announced cheer-fully. "She teaches Year Five." A woman with curly auburn hair and a gap-toothed smile came in the front door, lugging a box of craft supplies. "Hallo, Diana. Have a good summer, did you?"

"Oh, fine," Diana replied. "The usual. Down to Manchester as often as we can to see Andrew."

Maggie clucked sympathetically. "How's the new job, then?"

"It's in Manchester," Diana answered, her voice turning a little flat. "And always will be."

"Diana's husband has been working in Manchester for the last few months," Maggie explained to Lucy. "It's a long commute."

"He comes home for weekends," Diana answered. "Mostly. Although I don't blame him for wanting a break from the kids after a long week's work." She let out a laugh that didn't sound quite convincing. "Can't believe I'm back already. Now, who's this?"

"This is Lucy Bagshaw, the new receptionist," Maggie said, and put one arm around Lucy.

"Ah, you're covering for Nancy? Well, the best of luck to you. It can be a bit of a madhouse here sometimes, but Mr. Kincaid does try to run a tight ship."

"Mmm," Lucy said again. It seemed the safest answer at this point.

The next hour blurred by; Maggie pointed out various office machines and policies, mentioned various children's allergies ("We're a nut-free school") and photocopier codes and the government's new policy on first aid. "No plasters, I'm afraid, just ice packs."

Lucy felt as if her head might explode from all the information she knew she wouldn't remember. It had taken her a few seconds just to remember that plasters were Band-Aids. She really had become American.

There was a staff meeting in a cramped room with a few worn sofas and chairs, a fridge and a sink, and a big notice board with lots of official-looking announcements on it as well as things scribbled on a whiteboard: "Chicken soup is mine,"

"WHERE are the music sheets?!?!" and more. The jumble of it both comforted and surprised Lucy; she would have expected Alex Kincaid to run his staff room with military precision.

He came into the room when all the teachers and staff were already seated, balancing cups of tea on their knees as they chatted about their summers. Lucy stood in the corner, smiling awkwardly. A few people had smiled back, and some had said hello, but she wasn't exactly feeling a part of things. Yet.

"Right." Alex closed the door behind him with a firm-sounding click and gazed around at all the teachers with only the barest hint of a smile. "Welcome to a new year at Hartley Primary School."

A few people clapped; a few others murmured a rather sarcastic "hooray," followed by a few titters. Lucy pressed back against the wall. She hadn't been bold enough to plonk herself down next to someone in the staff room, and she was now positioned, unfortunately, at the front of the room, next to Alex Kincaid, as if she were somehow in charge.

He spared one second's irritated glance for her, and then turned back to his staff and began to drone on about new government policies and repairs that had been done to the school, until Lucy tuned out and wished yet again that she hadn't eaten oatmeal for breakfast.

"Miss Bagshaw?"

From Alex Kincaid's annoyed tone, Lucy was pretty sure that was not the first time he'd said her name. She pinned a wide smile on her face. "Yes!"

"I was just," Alex informed her with chilly politeness, "introducing you to the rest of the staff?" He raised his eyebrows in expectation, and with a bubble of panicked laughter swelling inside her, Lucy wondered how she was supposed to respond.

She widened her smile. "Hello."

"Nancy," Alex informed everyone, "will be back in January." His tone suggested that such a time couldn't come a moment too soon. Lucy kept smiling, trying not to let his comment sting. Good-looking or not, Alex Kincaid was, she decided, pretty much an ass.

Fortunately Maggie Bains made up for him, at least a little. "Mr. Kincaid is always like that," she told Lucy when they were back in the reception office. "Stern, I mean. He's brought the school right up in the league tables, though, so I reckon he knows what he's about. Just do your job and don't pay him too much mind," she whispered conspiratorially, before handing Lucy a much-needed cup of sugary tea.

A few pupils had started coming up the lane, all of them dressed in bright blue polo shirts and gray trousers or pinafores, swinging blue schoolbags with the school name emblazoned on them in red. Lucy thought they looked rather sweet, at least from a distance. Close-up, she tended to find children far more intimidating; at least Thomas's two sons, Will and Garrett, had been. She couldn't remember their glaring faces without suppressing a shudder.

She'd learned her lesson there, at least. No more trying too hard, not with men, not with their children. No more jumping into relationships, convincing herself she was in love just because someone liked her tidying up after him and watching his disagreeable kids.

"Here we go," Maggie said cheerfully, and Lucy watched with some trepidation as parents began to line up by the glass partition. She listened in semi-awe as Maggie efficiently dealt with lunch money, new uniforms, permission forms for everything from music lessons to using the climbing wall, and a variety of other school matters that had her head spinning yet again.

"I'll never remember all this," she told Maggie when the flood of mothers—and two dads—had finally stopped. Maggie patted her arm reassuringly.

"Of course you will."

Lucy had a feeling Maggie was just saying that because she wanted to skip off to Newcastle and her grandchildren. *She* wanted to skip off to Newcastle.

Still, the morning settled down and Lucy found she did get the hang of it, or at least of photocopying staff schedules, which proved to be easy but rather dull. However, even that had its pitfalls, for Alex Kincaid made an appearance just as all the children were spilling out into the school yard for morning playtime, a scowl making him seem, annoyingly, even more attractive. He really had that brooding thing going on, and Lucy wondered how old he was. He had that sort of fit middle-aged quality that made it impossible to tell whether he had just turned thirty or was nearing fifty.

"Miss Bagshaw?"

"Yes?" She lurched out of her seat as if standing to attention, and Alex's frown deepened.

"Did you photocopy these schedules?"

"Er, yes." Lucy tried one of her bright smiles. "Is there something wrong with them?" Stupid question, clearly.

"The paper," Alex explained evenly. "Did you notice anything about it?"

She glanced down at the schedule he held in his hand. "Er . . . it seemed quite thick, actually."

"Yes, it is, Miss Bagshaw. It's card stock, *actually,* and quite expensive. We don't normally use fifty pieces of card stock for staff schedules. We use normal-weight paper. Despite your lack of administrative experience, I think you might have realized that."

Lucy tried to will herself not to flush. She could hear Maggie busying herself in the office behind her, a few teachers slowing their pace as they ushered their pupils past her. She felt everyone's stares.

"I'm sorry," she said, stumbling over the two simple words she was saying far too often lately. "I didn't realize."

"That, Miss Bagshaw, is quite obvious." He glared at her, and Lucy glared back. It was better than the other option, which was to burst into tears. As a barista she'd had her fair share of angry customers whose Americano didn't come fast enough, or whose cappuccino didn't foam quite the way they wanted it to. And when a customer took somebody's else cup? Always her fault.

She'd always laughed it off, and the other staff had laughed it off too, but somehow it hadn't felt as awful as this. She was too raw to be yelled at right now. She needed to grow back a layer of skin before Alex Kincaid tore another strip off.

"Sorry," she said again, and Alex glared at her for another five seconds before turning abruptly on his heel and stalking off.

Lucy sank into her seat; she was actually trembling. Behind her Maggie made a sound that was very nearly a snort.

"I know it's the beginning of term and all that, but it is only fifty pieces of bloody card stock." She sighed and then clapped a hand on Lucy's shoulder. "He is usually fair," she told her. "He must be having a bad day."

Lucy bit the inside of her cheek as she felt emotion bottle up her throat; she wasn't sure whether a laugh or a sob was welling up inside her. She'd been flitting from one over-the-top emotion to the next ever since everything had blown up in Boston. On one hand, it was all so *ridiculous,* whether it was her mother's grandstanding about not showing favoritism or Alex Kincaid's dressing-down about card stock or her sister's seeming resentment of her. And yet, however ridiculous, it could still hurt.

She stared at the closed office door, wondering why Alex Kincaid was so tightly wound. He was head teacher of a lovely little primary school in a lovely little village in a lovely little corner of the Lake District. And the sun was actually shining today. What on earth did the man have to be stressed about?

She sank back into her seat and stared blankly at the computer screen. Why had all the text turned green?

Fifteen minutes later Lucy had managed to turn the text back to black, but had lost a paragraph about PE uniforms in the letter to parents and was frantically trying to find where it had gone. She did not relish the idea of asking Alex Kincaid to resend the letter to her e-mail, and Maggie Bains had "popped off" to feed her cats. Lucy suspected she would be gone for some time.

A sudden cry from the school yard where the

younger children (called, rather adorably, Infants) played had Lucy lifting her head. With nothing short of alarm she watched one of the playground supervisors bring a tiny-looking girl into the office. She knew she was working in a school, but she hadn't actually thought she'd have to interact too much with the children. She had absolutely no qualifications and yet the playground supervisor didn't seem to realize this, for she plonked the girl down on a chair right next to Lucy.

"Can you do something with this little one, then?" the supervisor asked cheerfully. "I've got to get back out there."

"Sure, of course," Lucy murmured, because she could hardly say otherwise. She told herself it couldn't be very hard, comforting such a very small girl, and yet it was her smallness that terrified Lucy.

The girl had huge blue eyes and masses of light brown hair, like a cloud around her pointed, elfin face. She sniffed loudly and then mumbled something so garbled by tears and a Cumbrian accent that Lucy couldn't make out a single word.

"Well, then," she said in the too-hearty voice she knew was so often used by people who werenot comfortable with children. "Let's get you a Band— a plaster, shall we?" Except she remembered as she rose from her chair, Maggie had said the school policy was no plasters, only ice packs. But did you really put an ice pack on a cut knee?

"We can clean it off, at least," she told the girl, although she had no idea if that was government policy or not. Still, a little water surely couldn't hurt. She went to the staff room and ran some warm water onto a paper towel, and then brought it back to the girl, who had thankfully stopped crying but was still sniffling.

"Here we are." Cautiously Lucy dabbed at the cut knee. Once the blood was cleared away, it didn't look so bad. "I just need to fill out an accident report," she said as Maggie's instructions came back to her. She dug through a drawer and filled out the form before handing it to the little girl, who took it with a doleful sniff. "Now you give that to your mum or dad when you get home, all right?"

"I don't have a dad." The girl spoke matter-of-factly, just as Lucy once had. The telltale wobbly tilt of the chin and the defiant glint in the eye were familiar too.

"Well, your mum, then," she said, keeping her voice cheerful. The girl nodded, biting her lip, and the gesture caught at Lucy's heart.

Seeing her sitting there, hunched over, her face tear-streaked and her lip still wobbling . . . Lucy knew *exactly* how she felt. "There, there," she said softly, and impulsively she gave the girl a clumsy hug. *That* had to be against government policy, but this little girl needed a hug. *Lucy* needed a hug. And it seemed like a six-year-old with a scraped knee was the only person who was going to give it to her.

And the little girl must have been grateful, because she threw her arms around Lucy and pressed her face into her shoulder. Lucy was gently easing back when she felt someone's gaze on her. She looked up and froze when she saw Alex Kincaid staring at her with that terrifyingly inscrutable expression from the doorway of his office.

Lucy braced herself for the sharp criticism that was surely coming her way. Only this time she wasn't going to trip all over herself to apologize. She stared back for a moment, her chin lifted in bravado more than actual courage, and then after about two seconds she glanced quickly away. So much for courage. The man had an absolutely basilisk stare.

When she risked glancing at him again, however, he was smiling, rather awkwardly.

"All right, Eva?" he asked, and the girl nodded, wide-eyed. It looked as if most people were intimidated by Alex Kincaid. Although to be fair, he had a rather nice smile. No more than a quirking of his mouth, really, but it softened him a bit.

She straightened and gave Eva a smile of her own. "I think you can go back outside now."

Eva scrambled off the chair and headed out, and Lucy braced herself for Alex's criticism.

"I'm sorry I yelled at you about the card stock," he said stiltedly. Someone was actually saying sorry to her. It was a rather nice feeling.

"That's all right," she answered. "It was only paper, after all."

Which was, she realized, probably not the right response.

By four thirty she was exhausted. She'd regularly worked eight-hour days at the café in Boston, but that now felt like a jaunt at the beach compared with this. Her mind spun with all the information Maggie had thrown at her, despite the older woman's assurances that she'd be "right as rain" by tomorrow afternoon, when Maggie was leaving. Lucy felt panicked at the thought. Or she would feel panicked if she had the energy to summon the emotion.

Yet there were still a few things to look forward to, she thought as she headed out into the glorious September afternoon that Juliet had told her existed, but Lucy hadn't quite believed. The sun was still high in the sky, bathing everything in gold, and the air was warm—or at least warmish.

Standing there, Lucy felt a surge of love for the place, for the potential of it. Some of the teachers were going to the pub tomorrow night, and they'd invited her along. Back at the beach café a few days ago, Juliet had opened up, at least a little, about why she'd moved here. One of the pupils seemed to like her.

Smiling a little, she headed down the hill.

Back at Tarn House, Juliet was out walking the dogs and no guests were due until tomorrow, and so for a little while Lucy had the house to herself.

She kicked off her shoes amidst the jumble of boots in the hall and put the kettle on in the kitchen, stretching luxuriously. Juliet, she saw as she dropped her arms, had left her a note propped against the salt and pepper shakers, reminding her that it was Thursday, and her turn to make dinner tonight. Halfheartedly Lucy wondered if scrambled eggs would suffice.

She wasn't much of a cook. She didn't bother when it was just for herself, and the meals she'd occasionally made Thomas and his boys had never seemed to satisfy them, if the melodramatic gagging and choking noises Will and Garrett had made during dinner had been any clue. Thomas, caught between apology and accusation, had always ordered them takeout.

Just as with those unruly boys, Lucy had a slightly shaming desire to please or even impress Juliet, and yet she recognized that impressing her half sister was going to be about as hard as impressing her mother, something she'd never once managed to do.

She curled up on the window seat with a mug of tea and gazed out at the same view she'd had from the school, only closer up. She could see the deep puddles in the sheep pasture, the wooden five-bar gate that led to yet another field, and from this angle the sea was no more than a twinkle in the distance. The light was syrupy and golden, gilding everything in sight.

The scene was perfectly pastoral and peaceful, and yet there was something a little melancholy about it too. The fields were empty save for a few dirty-looking sheep, and dark clouds threatened to overtake the fragile blue of the sky.

Some of Lucy's hard-won optimism waned. She should check her e-mail, yet she couldn't stomach the thought of the newsy, concerned messages she'd probably received from Chloe—or those she most likely hadn't received. Her mother hadn't spoken to her since Lucy's one tearful phone call after the story had broken, when Fiona had sighed and said she was sorry, but Lucy really needed to develop a bit of backbone.

"So this is you helping me?" Lucy had asked, her voice choked, and Fiona had had enough grace to admit, "I know it doesn't feel like it, Lucy, but yes."

Lucy had hung up the phone, and they hadn't spoken since.

She could call Chloe now, and yet Lucy was reluctant to talk to anyone before her life here seemed just a little more promising. Chloe was someone important in marketing, and even though they'd been best friends since freshman year of college, their lives had taken divergent paths:

Chloe's towards career success, Lucy's less so. And she didn't feel like having Chloe hear just how much less on a phone call.

She was going to the pub, she reminded herself. She had a job. Juliet could, on occasion, thaw a little bit. Given time, things would surely improve.

In any case, she wasn't about to run away again.

She drained her mug of tea, and went to see what Juliet had in her cupboards for dinner.

Half an hour later Juliet walked in with two very muddy dogs, both of which she banished to the utility room before turning to Lucy.

"Something smells good."

"Pasta with egg and bacon. I'm afraid I'm not a gourmet cook."

"Simple works for me," Juliet replied briskly as she washed her hands at the sink. Lucy laid plates on the table and Juliet fetched forks and knives. She took a bottle of red wine from a rack in the pantry and brandished it, eyebrows raised. "No guests tonight, although you've got work tomorrow. Fancy a glass?"

"Oh, go on, then," Lucy answered with a smile, and her heart lightened rather ridiculously as Juliet opened the bottle and poured two glasses. *This* was what she'd been hoping for when she'd come to England. Cozy suppers and confiding chats over large glasses of red.

"How was your first day, anyway?" Juliet asked when they were both seated.

"Overwhelming," Lucy confessed, adding hurriedly, "I know it probably shouldn't be. I'm just answering phones and photocopying—"

"Any first day is bound to be a bit over-whelming," Juliet answered. "It will get better."

"I hope so."

"Alex didn't give you a hard time?"

She thought of his tongue-lashing about the card stock, and then his terse apology. "No, not really." She raised her eyebrows as she took a sip of wine. "Why do you ask?"

"He's known to be a bit tough, as I said. But the school went from Very Good to Excellent in the last Ofsted inspection."

"I'm not even sure I know what any of that means, but it sounds impressive."

Juliet cracked a small smile and Lucy asked impulsively, "Have you heard from—from Fiona at all?"

Juliet's smile disappeared and she looked away. "No, but then I haven't heard from her in about ten years. I called her on her birthday five years ago, but she's never rung or written me."

"Really?" Lucy sat back in her chair, surprised by this admission yet recognizing that she had no real reason to be. She'd e-mailed Juliet on occasion, and they'd communicated a little through Facebook, but that was about it. Around five years ago Lucy had come to London for a spur-of-the-moment weekend and Juliet had taken the train down. They'd had a rather awkward lunch at the café at Selfridges, where they had not talked about their mother at all, yet she had been as present as if she'd been sitting at the table.

Now Lucy recalled Juliet's one visit to America, back when she was nine or ten, and Juliet must have been around twenty. There had been no big argument that Lucy remembered, but Juliet had left after only a few days, and Fiona had acted as if her oldest daughter hadn't visited, didn't exist. It hadn't bothered Lucy at the time; Juliet had just been one more person flitting in and out of their lives.

"Did you two have a falling-out?" she asked now, recognizing even as she said it that it was a rather stupid question. Of course something must have happened to make them so estranged from each other. Although considering they were talking about their mother, self-absorbed, non-maternal Fiona, maybe not.

"We were never *in* anything to fall *out* of," Juliet replied flatly.

Lucy frowned. "What do you mean—"

"Look, she might have wanted you," Juliet cut her off, her voice hardening as she turned to give Lucy a sudden, savage glare, "and paid for a sperm donor so she could be a mother and all the rest of it. But she never wanted me, and she let me know it every single day of my childhood."

6
Juliet

JULIET DRAINED HER GLASS of wine as Lucy stared at her slackly and then abruptly she rose from the table. "I need to walk the dogs," she said, even though she'd just given them a walk, and she left the kitchen without waiting for a response.

In the hall she called for the dogs and they came nervously, wagging their stubby tails, unsure of this sudden change in routine.

She grabbed her coat and the dogs' leads and headed out into the night. She needed to get out of the house, away from her own awful admission and Lucy's stunned stare, even if just for a few minutes.

It was past seven, the sky the color of a bruise, a hint of rain in the air. The wind was starting to stir up as it did most autumn nights, and fallen leaves swirled about Juliet's boots as she walked around the house to the muddy lane in the back that cut through the sheep fields. No one would be out on this rutted track at twilight, and she wanted to be alone.

She had a sudden, shaming desire to burst into tears, which infuriated her. She *never* cried. Anger was far better than tears, and she clung to it as she strode into the darkness, the dogs at her heels. She'd rather be angry at Lucy than miserable about her own loneliness.

She should have expected Lucy to get to her a little. She hadn't seen her sister properly in so long, she'd forgotten how the simple fact of Lucy's existence could hurt, reminding her of why Fiona had needed a second daughter in the first place.

The sky was darkening, and Juliet could barely see the rutted lane in front of her. She heard a gate in the distance banging against a post, a disconsolate sound. The dogs pressed close to her sides; they didn't like being out in the dark, and they quivered nervously, sensing the disquiet of her mood. Overcome by sudden remorse, Juliet dropped to her knees and stroked their heads, murmuring soothing nonsense as they pressed even closer to her. She shut her eyes, taking comfort from the warmth of their bodies, their obvious need of her.

It surprised her, this feeling of loneliness coming back to ride her so hard now. Ironic, really, that it had taken someone coming to live with her to make her realize how alone she really was. She'd been on her own for so long she'd thought she'd become used to it.

The sound of footsteps had her tensing, and she looked up from her dogs to see a man coming down the lane, a dog trotting by his heels. Peter Lanford with his border collie, Jake. She recognized him even though it was dark; there was something unique about his slow, steady gait, the untidy shock of brown hair under a well-worn flat cap, and the dog trotting faithfully beside him. He came closer, squinting in the darkness.

"Juliet? That you?"

Juliet straightened slowly, hating that her emotions were still so close to the surface, making her feel as if she'd lost a layer of skin. "Hello, Peter."

Even in the darkness she could see Peter's smile, a shy thing, but no less genuine. He whistled to Milly and Molly and patted their heads; when they came rushing towards him, Jake sniffed them with disinterest before sitting obediently.

"Has your sister arrived?" he asked, and Juliet just kept herself from reminding yet another person that Lucy was only her half sister.

"Yes, last week." She didn't think she'd actually told Peter that Lucy was coming, but news traveled quickly around Hartley-by-the-Sea. Tell one person something and you might as well have told the whole village.

"How's she settling in, then?"

"Fine." In her mind's eye Juliet saw Lucy's stunned expression as she'd stalked out of the kitchen; she'd looked as if Juliet had slapped her. "She's good."

"And how about you? Not always easy, sharing a house."

Peter gave her a lopsided smile that hinted at too much understanding. He was a man of few words, but Juliet had always appreciated his plain speaking, his steady, stolid approach to village issues at the parish council meetings. They'd worked together on drafting a proposal for a new playground at the beach, and Peter had confronted the Copeland Council on giving the village more litter bins. Small but important things, and they'd shown him to be both trustworthy and dedicated.

That did not, however, make her want to confide even an iota of what she was feeling now.

"I'm used to sharing a house," she said, and was glad to hear how unconcerned she sounded. "I run a bed-and-breakfast, after all."

"Different, that," Peter remarked, and Juliet suppressed a stab of irritation at how he cut to the heart of things with so few words. Sheep farmers weren't supposed to be so emotionally attuned, were they?

"I'm not sure it is," she replied. "Lucy's just like my other guests, except she's staying longer and she doesn't pay."

Too late Juliet heard the bitterness in those words, the way they fell into the silence like stones. She turned away to needlessly untangle the dogs' leads.

To her shock she felt Peter's hand on her

shoulder, a heavy weight that had her whole body tensing even as she registered its warmth and solidity.

"Bound to be hard at first. You're like me, used to being alone."

God, she was far too used to being alone. She was tired of it, desperately so, yet she didn't want puppyish Lucy being the person that ended her isolation.

Juliet stared down at the leads looped through her fingers; the wind blew her hair into her eyes and Peter still had his hand on her shoulder. She had the opposing desires to both shrug it off and keep it there.

"You're not really alone, Peter," she said when she trusted her voice to sound normal. "You live with your father." William Lanford had run the farm before Peter, and although he was elderly now, his health clearly starting to fail, Juliet still saw him out sometimes, with Jake trotting by his side.

After an endless moment Peter removed his hand. "That's different too," he said, and Juliet chose not to ask what he meant.

"I should get back. It's late, and Lucy . . ." Somehow she wasn't able to finish that sentence. *Lucy thinks I hate her? Feels sorry for me? Will still be there, even though I half wish she wasn't?*

Peter tipped his flat cap at her, a gesture that seemed rather ridiculously gentlemanly, almost from a different age. Juliet nodded back and then wordlessly she turned around and headed back to Tarn House.

The house was quiet and dark when she let herself in, and she saw their meal had been cleared away, the dishwasher turned on, the wine bottle corked, the glasses drying upside down in the drainer. When she opened the fridge, she saw that Lucy had left her half-finished plate of pasta on a shelf, neatly covered in plastic wrap, and somehow this small gesture caused a lump to form in her throat, so it hurt to swallow.

She settled the dogs in their beds even though it wasn't much past eight o'clock, locked up, and went upstairs, pausing for a moment in the hallway. She could see light spilling out from under Lucy's door, but she couldn't hear anything except the relentless wind.

Juliet hesitated, staring at that door, and then pressing her lips together in a firm line, she turned and went to her bedroom.

7
Lucy

AFTER JULIET HAD LEFT the kitchen, Lucy had sat at the table for a good fifteen minutes, staring into space, her mind spinning without snagging on any coherent thought. Then she'd gotten up, tidied the remains of their meal, and tiptoed upstairs to her room, even though she'd known there was no one else in the house. She'd heard Juliet calling to the dogs and then the slam of the door.

Alone in her bedroom, she decided to tidy up there too. It wasn't until she'd folded all her clothes away, had thrown out the crumpled receipts and gum from her trip, and was sitting on the edge of her bed that she realized what she'd done. She'd just tried to erase all signs of her presence in Juliet's house. Because Juliet didn't want her here.

It hadn't been her imagination; her half sister actually did resent her. *She may have wanted you, but she never wanted me.*

Was that true? It shamed her that she'd never really thought about her mother's relationship, or lack of it, with Juliet. And it made her feel like laughing or tearing her hair out or both, because Juliet might think Fiona had wanted her, but Lucy had never felt all that wanted. Her whole childhood had felt like an apology for messing up her mother's life.

And Juliet probably felt the same. Perhaps they had something in common, even if her *half* sister didn't think they did.

But she could hardly go explaining that to Juliet now. She didn't even want to face her, and the anger and contempt she'd seen so plainly on her face when Lucy had thought they'd been enjoying a pleasant dinner together.

With a sigh she reached for her laptop. She didn't care anymore that her life here in Hartley-by-the-Sea wasn't as promising as she'd hoped it would be. She needed to talk to a friend.

It took three attempts on Skype to reach Chloe, who was, Lucy realized belatedly, at work at two o'clock on a Thursday afternoon.

"Luce." The Internet connection was so slow that while Lucy could hear Chloe's voice, her friend's face was frozen in a smiling rictus, her eyebrows drawn together in concern. "What's up? You know I'm at work, right?"

"Sorry, I forgot the time difference."

"It's okay. I'm taking a late lunch. I've been thinking about you. How's village life? As charming as you hoped?"

Briefly Lucy remembered talking with

determined airiness about the appeal of English villages. She'd been picturing something vaguely Shakespearean in the Cotswolds, all thatched roofs and clotted cream.

" 'Charming' isn't exactly the word I'd use," she said. Even though Chloe's image was still frozen on the computer screen, Lucy heard a tiny sigh, and then Chloe shifting her chair.

"You need to give yourself some time to settle in, Luce. How's the job?"

Lucy thought of Alex yelling at her about the stupid card stock. "Not great. But that's not really it. . . ." She trailed off, realizing that she didn't actually want to tell Chloe about Juliet, or what she'd said. It felt disloyal, as if it wasn't her secret to share. "It's just a bit more awkward than I expected."

"Well, it's bound to be, isn't it? You and Juliet barely know each other." Chloe spoke bracingly, the way she always did, but it irritated Lucy now. She didn't want a pep talk. She wanted sympathy. She wanted to do the one thing she'd tried to keep herself from, which was to luxuriate in self-pity. To stop looking for the bright side and wallow in the darkness instead.

"I'm not sure she wants to get to know me," she said finally. She pictured Juliet's face right before she'd stalked out of the kitchen. Lucy had never seen such an expression of resentment and *loathing* before. Her mother might have used her as publicity fodder, and her boyfriend of three years might have broken up with her with no more than a shrug of apology, but neither of them had looked at her as Juliet had.

"She invited you," Chloe protested reasonably. "So she must want you there."

"That's what I thought." Lucy tried for a laugh and didn't quite succeed. "But honestly? I have no idea why she invited me. She certainly isn't acting like she wants me here. At all."

"Then maybe you should ask her. Get to the bottom of this."

Which would, of course, be Chloe's advice. Chloe was confrontational, even aggressive. She'd faced down their smarmy landlord when the loft conversion they'd rented in South Boston during college hadn't actually been all that converted. Lucy had hidden behind a stack of old copper piping and watched a huge rat waddle across the floor of their stripped apartment.

"I can't," she said.

"Why not? What have you got to lose?"

"A place to live? Seriously, Chloe. I think Juliet is more than half-inclined to boot me out."

"Why? What happened?"

"It's . . . just a feeling," Lucy said, knowing she was being lame. On the screen Chloe's image had unfrozen and then frozen again, so she was stuck in mid–eye roll. She should have known better than to expect unquestioning sympathy from

Chloe. "It'll get better, I suppose," she said with absolutely no conviction.

"It will if you try," Chloe said. "Maybe this is a chance for you to get to know your sister properly."

"I thought that when I came, but honestly, Chloe, she's not—"

"Get to the bottom of what happened between you two—"

"Nothing *happened*. Before I came here, we had maybe five conversations total."

"And why was that?" Chloe pressed, and Lucy slumped back against the bed, a pillow clutched to her chest.

"Because I don't think Juliet was ever interested in knowing me."

"But she invited you, so something must have changed. Maybe there's some tension, but there's also opportunity."

Chloe always saw opportunity. They'd been friends since they were eighteen and as the years had gone on, Lucy had fallen further and further behind in the opportunity stakes. Chloe had graduated from Boston University summa cum laude; Lucy had barely scraped a 3.0. Chloe had gone to grad school; Lucy had started as a barista. And now Chloe had some high-flying job in marketing and her own office, and Lucy had . . .

A temporary job and a sister who hated her.

"All I'm saying," Chloe persevered, "is try to see the bright side—"

"I've been seeing the bright side my whole life," Lucy cut across her. "You *know* that. But maybe there isn't one here. Maybe I'm stuck in the middle of nowhere, England, with a sister and a boss who both hate me. And it's freezing here, by the way. And it rains. Constantly."

Chloe cocked her head. "Finished?"

"No, I haven't mentioned the wind. It is so windy I am doomed to have a bad hair day for the next four months."

"Now, *that* sucks."

Lucy let out a little laugh. She couldn't hold on to her self-pity for long. "Yes, it does suck. Majorly."

Chloe was silent for a moment, and Lucy wasn't sure it was due to the lag in the Internet connection. "You don't think things could get better with Juliet?" she finally asked.

"I don't know if I want to try." Chloe's image had unfrozen again and she saw her glance at her watch. Lucy straightened and tossed the pillow she'd been clutching back on the bed. "I know you have to go. Thanks for listening."

"Okay. Hang in there. Skype me on Saturday. I'll only be at the office until lunchtime."

"Right." When the call had ended and Chloe's image faded to black, Lucy felt the silent emptiness of the house around her once more. She

87

hugged her knees to her chest as she considered, reluctantly, what Chloe had suggested.

Could she talk to Juliet about what had happened with their mother? Should she apologize?

For what? Being born?

She felt a surge of anger, a sudden white-hot flare of feeling, because it wasn't her fault that Fiona had decided to go the sperm donor route and have another baby. Juliet shouldn't blame her for their mother's choices, but she had no idea how to make her feel otherwise. How did you reconcile with someone who resented your very existence?

Lucy fell asleep sometime towards ten; she'd heard Juliet come in and the sound of her bedroom door closing, but she didn't move from her bed. She just wriggled out of her bra, peeled back the duvet, and snuggled down, content to let the world slip away.

She woke up to the shocking reality of bright sunshine pouring through the window, her cheek stuck to her pillow by drool, and the clock on the bedside table glaring at her accusingly. It was four minutes past eight.

She bolted upright as if she'd been electrocuted, then scrabbled for some clothes. There was a terrible taste in her mouth and she could feel her hair sticking up in about eight different directions. Talk about a bad hair day.

A bad everything day, she decided when she clattered downstairs and grabbed a banana from the bowl on the kitchen table. Both Juliet and the dogs were gone. Lucy grimaced at her reflection in the hall mirror; she'd pulled her hair into a messy bun and grabbed the first clothes she'd found, which had been her lemon skirt, an aqua top, and the purple tights that had seemed to offend Juliet. Not the most coordinated of outfits, and Alex Kincaid would probably have something to say about it, but for once in her life she was past caring.

She was late enough that pupils and their parents were already heading up to the school in a steady stream, so Lucy joined the harried mothers pushing strollers or checking their phones or both. A few gave her distracted smiles, and as she turned up the little lane, someone waist-high reached for her hand.

"Morning, Miss Bagshaw."

Lucy blinked down at Eva, the little girl who had scraped her knee the day before.

"Hello, Eva," she said, and squeezed her hand lightly. "How's the knee?"

"Mummy gave me a plaster." She pointed to a garishly colored Band-Aid with a picture of a cartoon character.

"That looks like an awesome Band-Aid," Lucy said, and Eva giggled.

"She said you had a funny accent," Eva's mother said with a little laugh. She looked like Eva, with an elfin face and wispy blond hair. "You're American."

"Actually, I was born in England, but I know I don't sound like I was. And I thought you guys were the ones with the funny accents."

Eva's mother laughed, and Lucy smiled, her heart lifting. It didn't take much to get her to start hoping again.

"We don't get many Americans around here," Eva's mother said, and stuck out her hand. "I'm Andrea."

"Hi," Lucy said, and shook her hand. "Lucy Bagshaw." She remembered what Eva had said about not having a dad, and wondered if she'd ever get to know Andrea well enough to hear her story.

They chatted all the way into school, and her bad mood had cleared away with the clouds by the time she arrived in the office. Maggie pressed a mug of tea in her hand and gave her a wink. "I told Mr. Kincaid you were in the loo when he asked where you were."

Lucy grinned back. "You're a saint, Maggie Bains."

"I just don't want you to get fired on your second day," Maggie replied with an answering smile. "I'm going to Newcastle, remember."

Lucy took a much-needed sip of tea and sat down in front of the computer. The children were coming into the office with the morning registers; Maggie had explained yesterday that two children from every classroom brought the morning registers to be logged into the computer.

Now Lucy took them with a smile for each of the children, from the too-cool-for-school Year Sixes to the brand-new kindergarten—or Reception, as they called it in England—pupils, only four years old, who held out the registers with wide eyes and trembling hands.

Around her the school was humming to life; Maggie had set the photocopier whirring away, and teachers were dashing in and out of the staff room with piles of papers and mugs of tea. A hassled-looking mum brought in a late Year Four and then gossiped with Maggie across the opened glass partition for the better part of half an hour.

Lucy hunted and pecked her way through the registers, logging each present, absent, or tardy with painstaking slowness. She knew her way around a computer when it came to design and graphic art, but spreadsheets were her nemesis and she always seemed to be leaping to the next box before she'd filled one in completely.

Alex, thankfully, had not left his office, although Lucy had discovered that if she leaned forward in her seat and craned her neck, she could see him at his desk through the window of his office that overlooked the front hall. Not that she would do that.

The still-hassled but more cheerful-looking mum had left and Maggie had bustled back to the photocopier, taking out a stack of parent letters before glancing over at Lucy.

"Are you still on the morning register?"

"Sorry, I'm a bit slow with these spreadsheets."

"I don't suppose it really matters. There's not too much to do, is there?" As if to prove her wrong, the phone rang and Maggie snatched it up with a cheery, "Good morning, Hartley-by-the-Sea Village Primary." She paused for a moment, her forehead wrinkling in a frown, and then launched into a lengthy description of the current issues with the school's boiler. Lucy turned back to her computer screen.

She'd just gotten to Year Three when she stilled, her gaze trained on the middle of the year's register. *Kincaid, Poppy.*

Surely not. Kincaid had to be a fairly common last name. Or maybe Alex had nieces and nephews at the school. Juliet had told her, on that beach walk, that everyone here was related one way or another, and if you weren't, then you were an offcomer, no matter how long you'd lived here.

"Are you an offcomer?" Lucy had asked, and Juliet had smiled grimly.

"I'll always be an offcomer," she'd said.

Maggie hung up the phone with an exasperated sigh and turned back to the photocopier. "Maggie," Lucy said, and she looked over her shoulder.

"Yes, love?"

That was something that would take some

getting used to: near strangers calling her love. Although, actually, Lucy kind of liked it. "Does Mr. Kincaid have relatives at the school?"

"Relatives?" Maggie let out one of her booming laughs. "You could say that. His daughter Poppy is in Year Three. Sweet little thing, poor soul."

Lucy swiveled in her chair. "Poor soul?"

Maggie's expression tightened briefly and she flashed Alex's closed door a wary glance. "No mum. Alex's wife died nearly two years ago now, only a few months after they'd come up from Manchester."

He was a *widower?* Lucy stared at Maggie, unable to form a response. She'd assumed Alex Kincaid was one of those aggressively single men who was your common commitment-phobic workaholic. He hadn't seemed married, and as for being a father . . .

She supposed it shouldn't change how she viewed him, but it did. She couldn't keep sympathy from swelling inside her at the thought of him coping alone with a daughter. Although maybe he had a girlfriend, one of those glossy, coolly competent women who also managed to be kind and lovable with a little girl.

She turned back to the register, her fingers hovering above the keyboard as she squinted at the screen and tried to figure out how to get to the next box on the table. The return button? Tab? She pushed both and watched as a box disappeared and another enlarged, just as Alex Kincaid came into the office.

He frowned at her computer screen and she gave him her sunniest smile. "So, as you might have guessed, my word processing skills are a little underdeveloped."

"That's a spreadsheet application, not a word processing program," he answered, and she wondered if his wife had minded his anal-retentive behavior. *Widower,* a little voice whispered inside her. *Widower and single dad.*

"I think I just proved my point. Now if you wanted me to design a brochure for the school, I could do that, no problem."

Alex's frown deepened. "We're a state school. We don't need brochures." He pronounced it *bro-shurs,* putting equal emphasis on both syllables.

"Just a thought," Lucy murmured, and he brandished a piece of paper at her.

"I have a draft of an e-mail here. It's to the board of governors. There's a meeting next week, and I need them all to receive the agenda. Could you forward this to the board? The addresses should be in the contacts folder on the e-mail server."

"I probably can manage that," Lucy answered. E-mail she could do.

"Thank you," he said, his voice terse, and he turned to head back to his office.

"A bunch of us are going to the pub tonight," Lucy called after him. The words popped out of her mouth before she could think better of them, or consider her motive. "Just for a drink after work. Why don't you join us?"

Slowly he turned around. He looked, Lucy thought, rather dumbfounded by her invitation. "Thank you, but I don't think that's a good idea."

"Why not?"

"People like to relax at those kinds of social occasions," he answered stiffly. "If I was there, they wouldn't be able to."

"Because you're the boss or because—" She stopped suddenly, biting her lip. Behind her Maggie had stopped shuffling papers and was clearly listening to this exchange with avid interest.

"Because?" Alex prompted, his frown fast becoming a scowl.

"You're a bit . . . stern," Lucy allowed, and Maggie suppressed something that sounded like a cross between a cough and a laugh. Alex stared at her for a long moment and Lucy wondered if she was about to get fired.

"Only a bit?" he finally said, and to her amazement his mouth quirked upwards in the tiniest of smiles. Lucy stared at him in shock, and then grinned back. Alex Kincaid had actually made a joke.

"Enjoy your night out," he said quietly, his expression back to its usual stony stare, and he returned to his office, closing the door behind him.

Shaking her head again, Lucy turned back to the computer and from behind her she heard Maggie rustle papers.

"Now, that was interesting," Maggie said, and Lucy decided not to ask what she meant.

An exhausting but fairly productive day's work later, Lucy was closing down the office, the children having all spilled out of the school an hour ago, and was ready to head to the pub with a few of the teachers. Maggie had taken off after lunch, claiming Lucy could handle everything that came her way, although Lucy wasn't convinced of that. She'd managed to disconnect three calls—two of them meant to go through to Alex—and logging the afternoon register—something she didn't see the point of—had taken the better part of an hour.

At half past two Alex had come out of his office to inform her he would take his own calls. Meekly, Lucy had agreed. Transferring calls was not turning out to be one of her skills.

Now Diana, the red-haired Year Five teacher, waited for her by the door. "So, how are you finding Cumbria?" she asked as they left the school together.

Lucy thought of the endless rain and wind, her sister's glare and ensuing silence. "I like it so far. I think."

"So what made you come all this way, then?" Diana asked as she buttoned up her coat. The wind blowing off the sea felt like it was straight from Iceland, which, considering their location, it probably was. "I know you have a sister here, Juliet, but it's an awful long way from America."

"I was at a loose end, and I thought I'd like a change." Diana nodded, and thankfully didn't press. Lucy imagined telling her, or anyone, the full, unvarnished truth. "What about you?" she asked. "You don't sound like a local, either."

"Not precisely. I'm from Carlisle."

"And your husband works in Manchester?"

Diana grimaced. "Yes."

"He couldn't get a job up here?"

"He didn't really try. I came up here last year to be closer to my mum, who's still in Carlisle. My dad died a year ago, and it's been hard on her. Andrew came up planning to get a job locally. He's in real estate—there are plenty of job opportunities."

"But?" Lucy prompted when Diana lapsed into silence.

"He didn't like it here. I don't blame him, not really. He's a city boy, and West Cumbria is about as remote as you can get, unless you move to the Outer Hebrides."

"I don't even know where those are," Lucy answered. She felt sorry for Diana; it had to be hard to be separated from your husband for five days out of seven.

"Well, anyway," Diana dismissed with a smile

and a shrug. "At least we're both working. And this too shall pass, eh?"

Lucy thought of her mother's scathing editorial, the endless blogs and articles that had covered the whole debacle. "Eventually."

"And now I could really use a drink."

A bunch of the other teachers were waiting at the bottom of the school yard, and they all headed down to the Hangman's Noose. Despite the rather dour name, the pub was cheerful and cozy, with a couple of worn sofas and squashy armchairs set around a blazing log fire.

Lucy sat on the end of one of the sofas with a glass of wine and let the teachers' chatter wash over her. They all knew each other well, and were catching up on their summers and school gossip, so while Lucy didn't feel unwelcome, neither did she feel precisely a part of things.

Her mind drifted to Alex Kincaid. He ought to smile more, she thought, especially at the children. She'd watched him give out the Head Teacher Awards at assembly that afternoon, and he had looked so stern. But he'd been kind too, saying something specific about each child—although perhaps he'd been prepped by their teachers.

She wondered how his wife had died, and whether he missed her very much. What was his daughter Poppy like? Lucy had seen the Year Threes file into the hall at lunchtime, but she hadn't been able to identify Alex's daughter among them.

"So what do you think of our head teacher?" Diana asked, and it took Lucy a second to realize she was addressing her. Diana was looking a lot more relaxed; she'd kicked off her shoes and was leaning back against the sofa, sipping a large glass of wine.

"Umm . . . he seems fine," Lucy said cautiously. She didn't mind a good gossip, but she was pretty sure that saying anything indiscreet in Hartley-by-the-Sea was akin to taking out an ad in a national newspaper. And she'd had enough press coverage to last her a lifetime.

"Fine? *Fine?*" Tara, a just-out-of-college teaching assistant with the Year Twos, giggled into her near-empty glass. "I'll say he's fine."

Liz Benson, the long-married Year Six teacher, slapped her on the thigh. "Be good, Tara."

"Well, he is quite good-looking," Lucy admitted, her tone still cautious. Surely stating the obvious couldn't get her into trouble.

"Ooh," Tara cooed, in the manner of one of her pupils, and Lucy flushed. Okay, maybe it could.

"Maggie told me he's a widower," Lucy continued.

Liz nodded seriously. "His wife, Anna, died two years ago now. Horse-riding accident. She fell and broke her neck, died instantly."

"They'd only just moved here a few months before," Diana contributed. "She was friends with

Juliet, Anna was. Kept her horse behind Tarn House."

"Did she?" Was that why Alex had hired her, because Juliet had been friends with his wife? It was strange, thinking of Juliet with a friend, a friend she'd lost. It made her realize all over again how little she knew about any of them.

"I don't know if you'd call them *friends,*" Tara protested. She giggled into her glass again, a girlish gesture Lucy decided was annoying. "Does Juliet even have any friends?"

Liz made a shushing sound and Diana reached over to pluck Tara's wineglass from her hands.

"Right, that's you finished," she said briskly, and Lucy forced a smile. It didn't really surprise her that Juliet didn't have any friends. She'd guessed as much already, but now she felt a twinge of sorrow anyway. Juliet had been living here for ten years.

The conversation moved on to summer holidays, and after a decent interval Lucy put her unfinished wine on the table and made to leave.

"Thanks, everyone," she said, and half a dozen heads turned towards her, eyebrows raised, a few of the smiles a little guilty. "It's been fun."

She reached for her coat just as Liz reached for her hand, causing them to have an awkward little tussle. "Don't take what Tara says to heart," Liz said in a low voice. "She's a bit of a radgee."

Lucy stared at her blankly. "A . . . what?"

Liz smiled. "A radgee. Cumbrian for . . . I don't know, a silly person." She glanced at Tara, who was leaning forward, eyes bright as she gossiped with the Year One teacher. "Although maybe that's a bit hard on the lass. She hasn't had an easy time of it."

"Tara hasn't?"

"She got in with a wild crowd in secondary," Liz explained, her voice low. "Ended up pregnant and alone at seventeen. Her mother wouldn't have naught to do with her, or the baby, which was a terrible shame. So she got into council housing on her own, and saw herself through an NVQ Level One."

"That's impressive," Lucy said, although she had no idea what an NVQ was. "What happened to the baby?"

Liz grinned unexpectedly. "She's in Reception. Emma Handley." She glanced back at Tara. "She doesn't get out much, poor lass. She's just trying to enjoy herself."

Everyone had a story, it seemed, and not necessarily a happy one. "I don't mind what she said," Lucy told Liz. "Trust me, I know Juliet can be a little . . . prickly." She immediately felt guilty for admitting that much, but Liz nodded in understanding.

"Juliet's areet," she said firmly, and it took Lucy a second to realize Liz meant *all right,* and that this seemed to be a compliment indeed. With a smile of thanks for Liz and another wave to the group at large, she headed out into the wet and windy night.

When she got back to Tarn House, she was feeling tired and also very slightly buzzed; Juliet had made a chicken pie and left it in the Aga's warming oven. Several walkers were in the sitting room in their thermal socks with glasses of sherry; not wanting to get drawn into a lengthy conversation about walking gear, Lucy stayed in the kitchen.

Juliet appeared a few minutes later, pausing for a moment in the doorway. Lucy didn't think she was imagining the tension that twanged between them, and she took a bite of pie to avoid it. There was a reason she'd run all the way to England after her life had blown up. Confrontation was so not her thing.

But considering what she'd learned in the pub, and what Juliet had told her about Fiona . . . Lucy swallowed and smiled.

"Hey, Jul—"

"Apparently one of the guests is allergic to cotton sheets," Juliet cut her off, not quite seeming to be addressing her. "Could have told me, don't you think?" She shook her head and went to fill the kettle. "Americans. Sometimes they can be so picky." She put the kettle on the Aga and stood there, one hand on the railing, her expression shuttered but also weary. From this angle Lucy could see a few gray streaks in Juliet's sandy hair.

"Would you mind walking the dogs tomorrow?" Juliet asked abruptly. "I've got an appointment up in Carlisle." She didn't look at her as she said it, and Lucy wondered if this was her sister's idea of a peace offering.

"Sure," she said, although Milly and Molly still made her nervous. Their trembling terror of just about anything put her on edge. She almost asked Juliet about her appointment, but her sister's expression was so closed she decided not to. She thought about saying something else, something about the way their dinner had ended last night, but she couldn't quite make herself, and she didn't know what she'd say anyway.

Why don't you like me? seemed pathetic. And *Why did you invite me, anyway?* could possibly make her homeless. No, silence was better.

8
Juliet

THE IDEA HAD COME to her suddenly, although Juliet knew it had been flirting at the fringes of her mind for a while now, maybe even years. But her confrontation with Lucy, her awkward conversation with Peter, the loneliness she now felt like a palpable thing, always pressing down on her . . . they had, together, made her determined, or perhaps just desperate, to act.

And so she was driving to Carlisle, her hands gripping the wheel so tightly her fingers ached, to have a preliminary appointment with the Cumbrian Fertility Clinic.

She let out a bark of disbelieving laughter, the sound like the crack of a gunshot in the confines of her car. She, Juliet Bagshaw, was thinking about going down the sperm donor route, just as her mother had.

Because if Fiona could do it, why couldn't she? A ready-made family. A person who was new and unspoiled, with no preconceptions about life or parenthood or what a family was supposed to look like. A person who would need her, love her.

A person you could mess up.

Because she had such a great track record with relationships. Because her own mother hadn't loved her, so why would a child be any different?

She was going for a preliminary consultation, Juliet reminded herself. Nothing was definite. She just wanted to *see*.

She drove the forty miles to Carlisle past rolling sheep pastures, the fells a gray-green smudge in the distance, the sea falling away on her left and signs for the nearby lakes of Crummock Water and Buttermere on her right. It was always a bit of a jolt to come into Cumbria's only city and see the rows of terraced houses, the massive Carlisle Castle with its ruins of Hadrian's Wall. With seventy thousand people, Carlisle felt like a teeming metropolis in comparison with Hartley-by-the-Sea.

The private fertility clinic she'd furtively looked up online last night was in a concrete building on the far side of the city, with tinted glass doors and a discreet sign with the letters CFC. Juliet parked in the near-empty lot and headed inside.

The lobby could have been the waiting room for any office; there were the standard uncomfortable sofas and chairs, a coffee table of fake wood, and the usual collection of year-old issues of *Good Housekeeping* and *Woman's Weekly*, plus the odd, ancient copy of the more upmarket *Cumbria Life*. A couple sat on one of the sofas, holding hands and looking down at their laps. Juliet looked away from them.

She gave her name to the bored girl at the desk and was handed a clipboard with a ream of forms to fill out. Her knee started to jiggle as she began to write.

"Miss Bagshaw?" A round-faced man in a creased shirt and gray trousers came to the door just as Juliet was filling out the last page; it was almost as if he'd timed it. "Would you like to come through?"

Stony-faced, clutching the clipboard to her chest, Juliet nodded and followed him to a small office that was decorated with the same utilitarian furniture as the waiting room.

The man rounded the desk, gesturing to one of two chairs in front of it. Juliet sat down, glancing at the empty chair next to her, and felt more alone than she wanted to in this moment.

"So. I'm Dr. Allen." He folded his hands on the desk and gave her a smile that felt cringingly compassionate. She wished he were wearing one of those white lab coats, something to give him a little distance. "You're here today for a preliminary consultation about fertility options?"

"Yes." Her voice emerged as a croak, but clearing her throat felt too revealing. Her gaze moved to the window and she looked out at the square patch of pewter sky, unable to bear looking at Dr. Allen's face again. Coming here had been a mistake, a moment's idiocy.

"Let me just look through your medical history,"

Dr. Allen murmured, and she heard the rustle of the pages she'd painstakingly filled out and handed to him. She kept staring out the window. "I see you're interested in an IUI with donor sperm," he said after a moment, and Juliet nodded, forcing her gaze back to Dr. Allen. "I also see that you've indicated on your medical history that you have only one functioning Fallopian tube."

"Yes." Her throat had gone tight and her hands were clenched in her lap; she was sitting so rigidly she knew he must see and feel her tension. "I had an ectopic pregnancy eleven years ago."

"And it burst, causing damage to the tube?" Wordlessly she nodded and Dr. Allen glanced back down at her notes. "And you've also suffered from endometriosis?"

"Yes."

He took off his glasses and gave her a smile of such genuine sympathy that Juliet wanted to slap him. "I have to tell you, Miss Bagshaw, that IUI might be difficult for you." She didn't say anything, didn't think she could, and he continued in that same kindly tone. "With your medical history, implantation of an embryo would be challenging. Of course, we'd do a full physical and fertility assessment first, and I should let you know that counseling is required when using donor sperm. Would you be using the sperm of an acquaintance, or would you prefer to go through a sperm bank?"

Juliet stared at him blankly. *Of an acquaintance?* Who on earth could she ask to give her some sperm? "A bank," she said, and Dr. Allen nodded.

"Then you should know that you would, in all likelihood, have to go through another country. The United Kingdom has very few sperm donors on register. Most people use a bank in the United States or Denmark, which have the largest number of donors. But it can be expensive."

Juliet's jaw bunched even more tightly. "I see."

He cocked his head, his gaze sweeping over her. Juliet didn't like to think about what he saw. "Perhaps," he said, his voice so very gentle, "this is something you need to think about for a little while."

Five minutes later she was back out in the parking lot, the rain spitting down, her car keys clenched in one hand, cutting into her palm. She'd envisioned the appointment taking most of the morning, not just ten minutes, although granted, that had been long enough. But some naive part of her had vaguely imagined coming out of the clinic with a plan, a promise. Maybe even a pregnancy.

She was utterly hopeless. What on earth had she been thinking, making that appointment? What would everyone in Hartley-by-the-Sea have said when she was suddenly pregnant? Not that it was even likely she could get pregnant. She'd known going in that it was a remote possibility, and yet still she'd hoped. She'd clung to the possibility because at least it had been *something*.

The rain was coming down harder now, stinging her face, and Juliet got back into her car. She didn't want to go home yet, not when she'd intimated to Lucy that she'd be gone for most of the day. And frankly she wasn't ready to face Lucy at all. The sympathy she'd seen on her sister'sface last night . . . even now it made her wince. The last thing she wanted or needed was Lucy's pity.

She ended up parking the car in the center of town and walking around the shopping area known as The Lanes, gazing unseeingly into shop-windows and feeling aimless. She had no guests due at Tarn House until tomorrow, and the house was already clean, the beds made up, the towels laid out. She had absolutely nothing that needed doing and she wanted to be busy, too busy to think, to feel.

She ate lunch at the café on top of Debenhams department store, amidst other chatting shoppers, bags piled by their feet. She watched as two women around her age gossiped over a piece of chocolate fudge cake they were sharing. One of them let out a crack of laughter, and the sound seemed to slice right through her. She turned to gaze out at the rain-washed streets as she picked at a lukewarm slice of steak and mushroom pie and tried to act as if she liked being alone, as if this were her choice.

9
Lucy

SATURDAY DAWNED, RATHER predictably, wet and windy. By the time Lucy came downstairs, Juliet had already left for Carlisle, and after a quick breakfast of cereal and tea she decided to walk the dogs early, while the tide was out; the tide clock above the Aga informed her she had at least two hours before the sea started its relentless surge back towards shore.

She wrapped herself up in a fleece and waterproof, yanked on her already mud-splattered Wellies. "All right, you two," she told the dogs, who trembled in their beds, tails thumping on the ground as they eyed her with trepidation. When Juliet fetched their leads, the dogs raced for the door, quivering with joy. When Lucy did it, they dropped their heads onto their paws.

"Walkies," Lucy said halfheartedly, and stuffed a few dog biscuits into her pocket, which got the dogs up and out of their beds, at least. They still trembled, and suddenly it made her sad. "What happened to you," she asked them, "to make you so nervous? I promise you, I'm not going to hurt you."

Milly and Molly didn't look convinced.

Still, with the help of a few dog biscuits she got their leads on and them out the door, then heading down Beach Road. The wind was brisk but surprisingly refreshing, and although the sky was still gray, at least it wasn't raining anymore. Quite afew people were out, Lucy noticed. Children rode bikes and scooters, and several couples were walking with a rather determined briskness that suggested pedometers and heart monitors were involved.

There were also plenty of dogs, of different shapes and sizes, all of them heading with their owners towards the beach.

The tide was completely out when Lucy reached the beach, an endless stretch of wet sand that was churned up joyfully underneath a thousand dogs' paws. Milly and Molly were straining at their leads to get out there, although Lucy wasn't sure she should risk it. What if they ran off and she couldn't get them back? She imagined telling Juliet she'd lost her dogs and shuddered.

But it wasn't really much of a walk if they didn't get their playtime at the beach, and so with some trepidation she released them. They were both off like shots, quivering with ecstasy or fear, probably both, as they tore down the beach towards the sea. Lucy had brought one of Juliet's old tennis balls for them, but they didn't seem much interested in it, much happier to simply race about and frisk and play with the other dogs.

Lucy stood for a while watching them, her hands in the pockets of her waterproof, her shoulders hunched against the wind. She exchanged a few friendly smiles with other dog walkers, and felt a surprising satisfaction and pleasure in the simple act of having gotten here, in having the stiff, salty wind sting her cheeks. Then she heard a frenzied, terrified barking, and with a lurch of alarm she knew something had gone wrong.

She searched the beach, the shapes of dogs blurring as her eyes watered from the wind; finally she saw Milly and Molly cowering from a rather fat black Lab who looked, Lucy thought, a bit overeager but unlikely to hurt a fly, much less two greyhounds.

She marched off towards the dogs, calling their names and snapping her fingers to seemingly no purpose, when her step faltered and her heart stilled and then sank as she saw the owner of the black Lab.

Alex Kincaid.

He hadn't seemed like a dog person, was her first irrelevant thought as she approached. Alex had managed to get a lead around the Lab's neck and was pulling the dog to heel. The dog, Lucy saw with some amusement, had dug his paws into the sand and was resisting with all his might. She remembered her little fantasy about walking through the fields with a Lab and nearly started laughing.

"Milly, Molly," she called, and then she did laugh at Alex's expression when he caught sight of her. He looked like she was the last person he wanted to be the owner of the dogs that his own dog was frightening.

"Sorry," he bit out as he pulled on the dog's lead. "He's not very well trained, I'm afraid."

Lucy looped the leads around Milly's and Molly's heads with an easy confidence that was both amazing and faked. "Now, that surprises me."

"What do you mean?"

"I would have expected your dog to come to heel at just a look," Lucy answered. "*I* practically do."

For a second she thought he was going to smile; the corner of his mouth tugged upwards slightly, but then his expression ironed out. "I'm not that terrifying, surely."

"Trust me, you are." She kept her voice light, maybe even the tiniest bit flirtatious. Alex was so good-looking it was hard *not* to flirt. "I have to give myself a pep talk in the mirror every morning before I go into school."

His mouth tugged upwards again, but only briefly. "I think that might be your issue, not mine."

She laughed, enjoying this banter. "Actually, you might have a point there." She nodded towards the fat Lab. "So why isn't he well trained?"

"No time. Getting a dog was a somewhat ill-conceived notion on my part, I'm afraid, but it seemed like a good idea at the time."

"It always does, I suppose."

He glanced down at Milly and Molly, who had been butting Lucy's legs rather insistently with their long, pointed noses. "Those are Juliet's two. Are you much of a dog person, then?"

"Not really. I've never had one of my own, anyway."

Lucy could feel the conversation petering out and she wished it wouldn't. She'd enjoyed the round of gentle teasing, was ridiculously glad that Alex Kincaid did, in fact, possess at least a small sense of humor.

The sky had darkened ominously as they'd chatted, and now the first few raindrops spattered onto the sand, the heavy, large kind that almost always preceded a torrential downpour. Even so, Lucy didn't want to leave.

"Look," she blurted before she could lose her nerve, "it looks like it's about to rain. Again. How about a cup of coffee?" She nodded towards the beach café at the end of the promenade. "My treat."

He stared at her for a moment, looking so nonplussed that Lucy felt as if she'd suggested something utterly inappropriate. And maybe she had. Maybe you didn't offer to buy your boss a cup of coffee. Did he think she was asking him out?

Was she?

No, she just wanted a friend, even if it was

grumpy Alex Kincaid. Someone to talk to over a hot drink. Was that too much to ask?

The torrential downpour had started, rain sleeting into both of their faces, and finally Alex answered. "That would be nice," he said, and unable to keep a big, sloppy grin from spreading over her face, Lucy nodded and then they both began half-sprinting to the café, the rain now coming down in sheets, the dogs barking and frisking at their heels.

They tied the dogs up outside under the awning and headed into the warm café, picking a table near a rain-spattered window. Alex grabbed one of the menus and studied it so intently that Lucy had a feeling he regretted accepting her impulsive invitation. She sat down, hanging her coat on the back of her chair and unwinding what felt like a mile of multicolored scarf before reluctantly taking off her hat. She knew her hair was a mess, and as Alex looked up from the menu, she saw him glance at it and she grimaced.

"I must look like a clown. My hair goes really frizzy when it's wet."

"You look fine." He spoke tersely, inspecting her for a second longer before looking back at the menu. At least it gave her a chance to study him. She let her gaze linger on his straight nose, that cleft chin. She wondered what his wife had looked like. *Anna.* She sounded dark and beautiful, Italian maybe. Someone who would tease him out of his grim moods, pull his ears and ruffle his hair and kiss him senseless.

A petite, dark-haired woman with a toddler perched on her hip approached the table, looking friendly but fairly harassed. Lucy wondered if she was related to Mary, the elderly woman with the flyaway hair and the heart condition. "What can I get you two?" she asked, hitching the little boy higher on her hip. He grabbed a strand of her hair and started winding it around his fist. She winced and drew his hand back. "Easy, Noah."

Alex raised his eyebrows at Lucy. "What would you like?"

She ordered a latte and he had a black coffee, which seemed so predictable. Why couldn't stern, sexy men order mochaccinos? The woman went back to the kitchen, the little boy now trailing after her. Lucy turned back to Alex. "So what brought you to Hartley-by-the-Sea?"

He tensed, looking almost trapped by what Lucy had meant to be an innocuous conversation opener. "The job, first of all," he said finally. "But village life seemed appealing."

"Yes, I think I have this rather ridiculous fantasy of life in an English village. I thought the lady at the post office shop would slip me chocolate buttons."

"Too bad for you a man runs the post office shop."

Lucy grinned. "Yes, I've met him." Lucy was

still nurturing hopes that Dan Trenton was more of a gentle giant, but her three forays into the shop had not yet won her more than a flat stare and her change. "So that really wrecks my fantasy, I guess," she said.

"I don't know. He might slip you a button or two."

Which sounded kind of . . . flirtatious. "So what about village life was appealing to you?" Lucy asked.

He traced a coffee ring on the table, averting his gaze. "The whole package, I suppose. Community. Closeness."

Lucy wondered if he would mention his wife, or if she should be the one to mention that she knew. Or, since this was such a small village, would he assume she knew? Should she say she was sorry to hear about his wife's death? This was a whole new territory of uncertainty and awkwardness.

"So has the village met your expectations?" she finally asked, her tone a little too jolly, and Alex looked up with a surprisingly bleak smile.

"I don't think *I've* met its expectations."

Surprise jolted through her at this honest admission. "Why do you say that?"

He spread his hands flat on the table and stared down at them; there was something about the gesture that seemed both contemplative and lonely. "Work has taken up most of my life."

"But as head teacher you're giving back to the

community," Lucy pointed out. She felt she should really say something about his wife, or maybe he should.

He just shrugged and said, "I suppose." Lucy opened her mouth to say something, although *I know about your wife* made her sound like some bad TV detective. Then Alex spoke first. "What about you?" he asked. "You're only here for four months, but what made you decide to come all the way to Cumbria?"

"Well." She considered fobbing him off with the usual *I wanted a change* and then decided she was tired of prevaricating. Alex had been surprisingly honest, so maybe she could be too. "My life in Boston kind of fell apart. Actually, there's no 'kind of' about it. Completely fell apart is more accurate."

"I'm sorry," Alex said after a moment. "That's always difficult."

He spoke as if he understood what she was talking about and Lucy knew she couldn't let the moment pass. "I'm sorry," she blurted, and Alex arched an eyebrow. "About—about your wife."

"Ah." His mouth twisted in a rather grim smile. "You've heard."

"One of the teachers told me she died a couple years ago." He nodded, not seeming inclined to say anything more. "I'm sorry," Lucy said again.

"So am I."

Fortunately the woman brought their coffees,

and Lucy was spared from making any more awkward condolences. Alex's expression was back to the basilisk stare. She turned to the woman, who had the little boy—Noah—clinging to her legs as she struggled to put their coffee on the table. Lucy reached for her latte to help her. "Is Mary all right?" she asked, and the woman jerked back a little in surprise, sloshing black coffee on the tray. Alex took the cup from her, mopping up the spilled coffee with a napkin.

"You know her?"

"My sister does. We came in here a week or so ago."

"She's all right," the woman said, but she sounded resigned. "She had a bit of a turn last week and she needs to rest."

Lucy nodded, not wanting to ask any more questions and seem nosy. With a tired smile the woman left, taking the little boy with her.

"And when you go back to Boston," Alex said as Lucy loaded her latte with sugar and took a frothy sip, "what will you do?"

"Honestly? I have no idea."

She saw remembrance flicker across his face. "You worked in an art gallery, didn't you?"

"Is that what I told you?" He raised his eyebrows at that. "Well, yes, I did work in a gallery, but in the café part. I was a barista. And before you say anything, I know it seems like a waste of a perfectly good education. I do have a university degree, even if you're surprised to know it." Now where had all *that* come from?

Her mother, obviously. *I spent three hundred thousand dollars on your education so you could pour people coffee?*

Lucy had replied, as cheerfully as always, that it was a little more complicated than that. She could operate fairly complex machinery, after all. But she'd taken her mother's point. How could she not?

"In what subject?" Alex asked, and Lucy dragged her mind back to the conversation.

"Art. I know, I know. Most useless degree ever, but I really did want to have a career as a serious artist."

"You still could," Alex answered. "You're what, twenty-six? Not many people are making it professionally as artists by then."

"My mother was." Actually, her mother had been thirty when she'd gotten her big break, winning an emerging female artist award. Lucy braced herself for the obvious question about who her mother was, but Alex didn't ask.

"Well, like I said, you still have time," he said after a moment, shrugging as he took a sip of coffee. Lucy felt a rush of relief that he wasn't going to press. Maybe he wasn't that interested.

They both lapsed into silence, and Lucy gazed out the rain-smeared window, wondering if she'd ever pick up a paintbrush again. The funny or perhaps the sad thing was, she didn't feel tempted to. She didn't miss painting, so maybe her mother had been right. *The brushwork is amateurish at best, revealing a lack of both focus and passion.*

And the whole world had read that. The whole world knew she sucked at art.

"You're frowning."

Lucy jerked her gaze back to Alex. "So are you," she answered, and his usual scowl morphed into a small smile.

"So I am. I was thinking about Charlie. I really should take him to obedience school."

He glanced away, and Lucy had the distinct feeling that he hadn't been thinking about Charlie at all. "No time, you said," she said lightly.

"Right."

"How long have you had him?"

"Eighteen months. He's seven, though. I got him from a rescue center. His last owner had died."

"Eighteen months," she repeated, and he nodded in answer to her silent question.

"Since Anna died. I got him for my two daughters, because they'd been begging for so long." He glanced away again before turning back to her with a wry smile that wrapped right round her heart. "But a dog doesn't make up for a mother."

"No." Belatedly she registered what he'd said: *two* daughters. Just like Thomas had two sons. But it was stupid to compare Alex to Thomas; yes, they were both single dads, and yes, they both happened to be teachers. And yes, maybe they both had a bit of a pompous thing going on, but really, the similarities ended there. And in any case, she wasn't going to date Alex.

"Looks like it's clearing," he said, nodding towards the window. The sun was emerging from behind wispy white clouds, and though the horizon was still dark, bits of blue were breaking through. Perhaps it was because of the discussion of her degree, but Lucy could suddenly imagine how she'd paint the scene: the contrasting darkness and light, the choppy waves breaking on the shore. She'd do it in oils, maybe, rather than her usual watercolors—an insipid medium, her mother had called it. But oils . . . thick, dark oils soaking into the canvas seemed right for such a scene of wild beauty.

"So it is." She turned back to Alex, sensing the dismissal. Twenty minutes of small talk was all Alex was up for, although actually it had ended up not being all that small.

"I should head back." He stood, awkwardly, and Lucy reached for her purse. "I'll pay for the coffees," he said, and she glanced up, frowning.

"I was the one who—"

"I know, but I should have suggested it first," he said firmly. "And a couple of coffees really isn't all that much." He left enough change on the table to cover the coffees and they went out to collect the dogs, saying stilted good-byes over tangled leads before they finally managed to separate.

They ended up walking in the same direction back up the beach road, smiling self-consciously as they fell into step without speaking. The silence stretched on, even more awkward than their good-byes, and so when Milly and Molly stopped to sniff something in the bushes lining the road, Lucy indulged them, letting Alex walk far ahead of her before she tugged on their leads.

Juliet hadn't returned by the time she got back to Tarn House, dried off the dogs, and left her mud-caked Wellies out by the front step. She made herself a cup of tea and stood in the kitchen, the sun streaming through the window, and wondered what she should do. She didn't feel like kicking around Tarn House by herself, and so after finishing her tea and then giving the dogs treats to keep them occupied, she headed back out into the sunshine to explore a bit more of Hartley-by-the-Sea.

The village, she'd already surmised, was made up of only two main streets: the high street with the school, the pub, and the post office shop, and the beach road that stretched through sheep fields towards the sea. Lucy headed up the high street, past the Hangman's Noose and the school, to the top end she hadn't yet seen.

With the sun shining brightly and the sea glinting in the distance, the air fresh and clean, and the only sound the distant bleating of sheep, Lucy decided Hartley-by-the-Sea was just as charming as she'd hoped it would be.

It seemed hard to believe that just weeks ago she'd been in Boston, surrounded by strangers and high-rise buildings. Now she had sheep and the sea. And, as Juliet had told her, a decent fish-and-chip shop five miles away in Whitehaven.

Yet she wasn't missing the culture or restaurants or even a proper *caffé latte* as she continued up the high street, the road becoming both steeper and narrower, the houses now older, low-lying stone farmhouses with slate roofs and tumbled out-buildings, the sea twinkling like a promise when she glanced between them.

She felt as if she were going somewhere, although in reality she suspected the village's main street would peter out to yet more sheep fields. At least there would be a decent view, and she could certainly do with the exercise. And with each step she felt her mood improve, her natural optimism strengthening into determination. She could make this funny little life of hers in funny little Hartley-by-the-Sea work. She could make friends, even with the stony-faced Alex Kincaid, and she could do her job well and she could reconcile with Juliet.

It was the last thought that had her slowing her step, bending over, and resting her hands on her thighs as she tried to catch her breath. She could do it, she told herself. She could do it all. And she'd start today, when Juliet returned from Carlisle. Lucy had no idea how she'd broach that topic of conversation—*Why do you resent me?* seemed like a bit of a loaded question—but she was determined to try.

She wasn't running away anymore.

She was almost at the top of the street; the only buildings she could see ahead were a stucco-fronted bungalow that looked like an afterthought and an abandoned stone barn with its roof fallen in. She took the last few steps; as she'd suspected, the high street fell away to fields, but the long grass glinted gold in the sunlight, and from this vantage point she could see the sea stretching all the way to the horizon, flat and sparkling, and the hazy, violet shape of the Isle of Man in the distance.

A boy she recognized from school came careening around the bungalow, wearing a Manchester United jersey and kicking a battered soccer ball. He came up short at the sight of her.

"Hey there," Lucy said cheerfully. She felt a sudden, overwhelming benevolence towards all of humanity, even this gap-toothed, tousle-headed kid.

He stared at her, nonplussed, and then he stuck out his tongue.

Lucy blinked in surprise and then she stuck out her tongue right back at him. He grinned, unexpectedly, before he kicked the football across the weedy garden and ran off after it.

She laughed aloud then, so thankful to feel genuine joy. She'd been miserable for so long, trapped by her mother's scorn and expectations, clinging to her optimism by her fingernails, always waiting for things to happen. For her art to take off. For Thomas to make their relationship more serious. For life to begin.

Well, it was beginning now. She'd just pushed the start button. Humming softly under her breath, she started down the street, back to Tarn House. Impulsively she ducked into the post office shop and bought a newspaper. Dan Trenton was at the till, looking as surly as ever.

"So what brought you to Cumbria?" Lucy asked, determined to make the man speak more than a monosyllable. "Or are you from here?"

He stared at her for a moment and then said, "I left the army after half my men were killed in a raid in Afghanistan." His voice was as flat as his stare. "Found out my wife was cheating on me with my brother, and decided I needed to do something different." Lucy stared at him open-mouthed as he pushed twenty pence across the counter. "Here's your change."

10
Juliet

JULIET HEARD THE FRONT door open and then the sound of Lucy humming under her breath. Her half sister was in a good mood, apparently, or at least in a better mood than she was. She'd spent the hour drive from Carlisle alternating between despair and determination.

So the sperm donor thing probably wasn't going to work. The pregnancy thing wasn't going to work, not with her dodgy medical history. She veered away from that line of thinking, though, because to remember those bleak days alone in the hospital, everything in her aching, was a form of self-torture she did not intend to practice.

Anyway, she'd told herself as she drove past Workington, she was fine as she was. She enjoyed her work and her guests; she was a productive member of her community; she had a couple of friends. What was there to complain about?

By Whitehaven she'd had to pull into a lay-by. She'd pressed the heels of her hands to her eyes and drawn one long, shuddering breath. Then she dropped her hands, checked her mirrors, and pulled back onto the A595. She didn't think about anything at all for the five miles back to Hartley-by-the-Sea, and she was still wrapped in that much-needed numbness now as she tidied the kitchen—tea bag left in the sink, sugar sprinkled across the countertop—and heard Lucy come in.

"Juliet!" Her sister sounded happy to see her, which didn't make sense. "How was your appointment?" Lucy asked, and Juliet turned to the sink, taking her time to wring out a dish towel.

"Fine." She kept her back to Lucy as she hung the towel on the rail of the Aga, made sure it was straight. "Would you mind putting the tea bags in the compost bin instead of leaving them in the sink?" It was a reasonable request, yet it was met with silence. She didn't trust herself just yet to turn around, and so she straightened the dish towel some more.

"Juliet . . ." Lucy's voice sounded soft and sad. "Do you . . . do you regret inviting me here?"

Oh, not this. Not now. Not when she was feeling so raw and revealed already. "Don't be stupid, Lucy," she snapped, and then steeled herself to turn around. "I was just asking you to tidy up a bit."

Luck blinked in that kicked-puppy way of hers that Juliet was really starting to dislike. "I know that. I didn't ask because of the tea bags. It's just that ever since I've arrived, you've been acting like you don't like having me here—"

"Oh, so it's my fault?" Juliet cut her off, the

words exploding out of her with far too much anger. "I'm not welcoming enough, am I? Not spoiling you and saying 'Poor Lucy, put your feet up while I get you a cuppa'?" Juliet heard the sneer in her voice and she knew Lucy did too. A distant part of her was shocked at the vitriol spewing out of her, and another part felt the relief of saying it all, like ripping a plaster off a wound. Painful but necessary. "I suppose you came here expecting to be coddled and fussed over. You've had *such* a hard time, with your mother slagging off your paintings. Poor, *poor* Lucy." She shook her head, felt the ugly way her features had contorted, and couldn't seem to get her face back into its normal, sane shape. She turned away from Lucy, whose face had drained completely of color. Damned if she'd apologize. It was no more than the truth.

"Is that what you really think?" Lucy finally asked in a low voice.

"And if it is?" Juliet answered. She had her hands on the Aga's railing, her fingers curling around the metal bar so tightly her knuckles stood out like bony little hills.

"Then . . . then why *did* you invite me, Juliet? Why on earth did you invite me, when you seem to hate me so much? I barely know you. You've hardly ever spoken to me, and yet you act like you've had all this *experience*—" She broke off, and Juliet stared down at her hands.

"I've seen your updates on Facebook," she said, which was about the lamest response she'd ever heard. Lucy must have thought so too, for she let out a snort of disbelief.

"Oh, *okay,* then," she said. "And we all know how Facebook updates are an accurate picture of someone's life, someone's soul."

"Don't be so melodramatic."

"I'm not the one who started this," Lucy shot back. "I'm actually *trying*—"

"You don't think I tried?" Juliet demanded. "I invited you here—"

"And it seems you'd rather I left!" Lucy took a deep breath. "*Would* you like me to go?"

"Where to? You have a job, remember—"

"I don't mean leave Hartley-by-the-Sea," Lucy said, and shock jolted through Juliet. "I mean leave here. You."

The flatly spoken statement, the rejection of it, made Juliet recoil. "No," she said, and knew as she spoke that she meant it. "I don't want you to leave."

"But I don't think you want me to stay, either."

Juliet let out a long, weary sigh. "Look, Lucy, I admit I haven't been all that friendly. I didn't . . . I didn't expect to feel so . . ." She broke off, unable to put into words just what she'd felt at having Lucy catapult into her life. Opening the door and seeing her half sister there, the daughter Fiona had chosen, had actually *wanted* . . . "This isn't about you," she finally said. "I know it's unfair of me to take it out on you."

"You mean it's about Mum," Lucy said, and Juliet didn't answer. She'd never, not once, called Fiona *Mum,* not even as a child. Fiona had never wanted her to. "What happened between the two of you?" Lucy asked, and Juliet pushed away from the Aga, reached for a sponge.

"I told you before, nothing happened. She never wanted me, that's all." She swiped at the already-clean counter.

"And you think she wanted me."

"Considering she went the sperm donor route to get you, yes, I'd say so."

Lucy didn't say anything and Juliet kept wiping the counter. "I didn't feel all that wanted," she said after a long moment, and Juliet stilled for a nanosecond before she continued cleaning. "Trust me—"

"No, *you* trust *me,*" Juliet cut her off. She was, quite suddenly, nearly shaking with rage. She could not, *would not* listen to poor little Lucy's sob story about how she'd felt ignored. How Mummy hadn't hugged her enough at bedtime. "You have no idea what it feels like not to be wanted. No bloody idea, Lucy." Juliet could feel Lucy's shocked silence, and she turned around. "When you were six, Fiona threw you a pony party. Do you remember?"

Lucy blinked. "I think so," she finally said hesitantly.

"You think so? Well, I remember it perfectly. She hired a pony to come give rides to all your friends, your entire class, in our back garden. And there was a cake, this huge pink sparkly thing with a little porcelain pony on top. And you had a new dress, as well as the most ridiculous little outfit for riding that damned pony. She bought a six-year-old *jodhpurs*."

Lucy blinked again. "None of that stuff—"

"Mattered? Well, it mattered to me." Lucy looked confused and Juliet clarified impatiently, "I didn't want a stupid pony party. I was seventeen. But it mattered because Fiona had never even acknowledged my birthday, not once, much less thrown me a party or given me a present." She threw the damp sponge into the sink, where it landed with a wet thwack. "So yes, it mattered," she said, quietly now, her rage depleted. "Stupid as that may sound."

"It doesn't sound stupid," Lucy answered after a moment. She sounded shaken. "I just never knew . . ."

"Well," Juliet said tiredly, "now you do."

11
Lucy

SHE'D FORGOTTEN ABOUT THAT stupid pony party. As Juliet left the room to go make up some beds, Lucy sank into a chair at the kitchen table. And to think she'd been so full of optimism, so *determined* to reconcile with Juliet. What a joke. Juliet didn't want to reconcile. Not remotely. Her sister's anger had shocked her, because despite Juliet's obvious reluctance to have her here, she hadn't realized the emotion ran that deep.

She stared out the window, oblivious to the uncharacteristically bright sunshine, as she remembered that long-ago afternoon. The pony. The party. And, yes, the jodhpurs. What a miserable day it had been. Not, she knew, that Juliet would understand that. And maybe her sister had a point. She'd still had the party, something Juliet had never had. But it hadn't been for her. She'd never even liked ponies and had been too scared to ride one on that awful, endless day.

The pony party, like so many other things in her childhood, had been Fiona's way of showing the world she was both an incredible artist *and* a loving mother. She didn't consult Lucy about what kind of party she wanted; she didn't even talk to her for most of the day. She simply arranged the party and then became annoyed when Lucy had refused to have a ride. Afterwards, in her misery, Lucy had eaten too much cake and been sick. But at least she'd had a cake. And, to be fair to her mother, Fiona had tried to give her something nice, even if it wasn't what Lucy had wanted. Her mother had tried in a way that she obviously hadn't with Juliet.

It was hard for Lucy to separate Juliet's anger from her own hurt, but she knew she needed to. Needed to get to the bottom of what was—or, really, wasn't—between her and Juliet. Like Chloe had said, this could be an opportunity.

She just wasn't sure it was one she wanted.

She took a deep breath and then, for lack of anything more useful to do, wrung out the sponge and replaced it on its little dish by the sink. The kitchen was otherwise spotless, and so she went upstairs in search of her sister.

She found her in one of the four guest rooms, smoothing an already perfectly smooth duvet. Lucy stood in the doorway and watched as sunlight touched Juliet's hair, showing up the streaks of gray by her temples.

"Juliet."

"Don't." Juliet didn't even look up. "I'm sorry, all right? I shouldn't have said all that. I know it wasn't your fault you had a pony party, or the rest of it. I just don't want to talk about it now."

Lucy hesitated, with no idea how to breach her sister's defenses. The easiest thing, the thing she actually *wanted* to do, was to quietly agree and tiptoe away. They could call a truce, tense as it would be, and learn to work around each other. She could have a perfectly satisfactory life here in Hartley-by-the-Sea without Juliet actually in it.

But that was the same as running away, and she'd told herself she wasn't going to do that anymore.

"I won't talk about the pony party," she finally said. "Trust me, that's not something I care to remember."

"Oh, why not? The pony wasn't pretty enough?"

"Juliet—"

"Look, I know I'm bitter, all right?" Juliet looked up, and Lucy saw the ravages of emotion on her sister's face. "I get it. It's a stupid pony party you had when you were six. I understand that to mention it twenty years later and act like I'm still angry about it is—pathetic." Her face tightened briefly with that word, and she went back to making the bed.

Lucy watched her for a moment, at a loss. Finally, because she didn't have any better idea, she ventured, "I don't actually think you can get that duvet any smoother."

Juliet let out a snort of laughter and shook her head. "Now that's just stating the obvious."

"I'm sorry," Lucy said, and realized she meant it, maybe even more than she'd meant any "sorry" she'd ever said. "I'm sorry I had a pony party."

"I said not to talk about that," Juliet answered, and Lucy couldn't tell whether she was joking.

"I know. But I'm sorry I never even realized . . ."

"Why would you? You went to America when you were six, right after that party, as I recall. I wouldn't expect you to be emotionally attuned to what had been going on in my life, Lucy."

"But afterwards," Lucy admitted, searching for words that would bridge this awful chasm between them. "I never even really thought . . ."

"Why would you?" Juliet repeated wearily. She sat on the bed, creasing the duvet. "I was never a part of your life."

The words seemed to echo through the room, fall into the stillness. What could she say to that? All she could do was agree, or attempt some cringingly corny expression of how she wanted Juliet to be in her life now. And truthfully, considering how difficult every interaction with her sister was, she wasn't even sure she did.

"Anyway." Juliet rose from the bed and started smoothing it all over again. Her hair had fallen out of its usual neat ponytail, obscuring her face. "I should get on. I've got two Scottish blokes coming to do the Coast-to-Coast walk tomorrow morning."

It sounded like a dismissal, and Lucy decided to take it as one. She'd had enough angst-ridden interactions with her sister for one day.

No, she decided as she went back to her own room, she'd hold on to the successes of the day: her coffee with Alex and her walk through Hartley-by-the-Sea. The little boy sticking his tongue out and Dan Trenton's surly confidence in the post office shop. It was all progress.

She and Juliet seemed to have reached that tense truce Lucy had envisioned by the next morning, when Juliet busied herself in the kitchen, in preparation for the arrival of the next batch of walkers. Lucy thought about trying to make herself useful, but then she decided she could best help Juliet by staying out of her hair.

She ended up catching the train down to Ravenglass and wandering around a different, and slightly quainter, village; Ravenglass had, in addition to replicas of Hartley-by-the-Sea's pub and post office shop, an impressive set of Roman ruins and a miniature railway that traveled several miles through the fells to Eskdale, passing one of the county's lakes that Lucy had yet to see. It was sunny but chilly out, and Lucy spent a good part of the afternoon cradling a paper cup of coffee as she sat on a park bench by the miniature railway and watched all the families cram into the tiny seats, smiling and laughing, although, to be fair, some of the mothers looked a bit hassled, trying to keep their toddlers from climbing out of the train.

Still, it looked like fun.

She headed back to Hartley-by-the-Sea late in the afternoon on the Northern Rail train with all the families she'd seen in Ravenglass, their children now cranky and tired, as well as the parents. The train trundled along the coast and half a dozen families unloaded themselves along with Lucy at Hartley-by-the-Sea.

Home, she thought with a funny little pang. *Sort of.*

Eva and her mother, Andrea, were among the passengers who got off the train, and they caught up with Lucy as she stared towards Tarn House.

"Had a day away?" Andrea asked.

"Yes, down to Ravenglass. Trying to catch some of the sights." Lucy smiled at Eva, who was dancing on her tiptoes as she clung to her mother's hand. "Where have you been?"

Andrea made a slight face. "Down to Barrow for a doctor's appointment."

Eva did a little twirl. "I get to draw pictures and talk about my *feelings.*"

"An art therapist," Andrea said. "We go on the weekends." She drew a quick breath and added, her voice so low Lucy had to strain to hear her, "Her dad and I split up last year and it wasn't . . . friendly. It's been tough on her." She gave Eva a quick, concerned glance, but the girl was oblivious.

"I'm sorry. Divorce is tough." It had been hard on Thomas's two boys and Lucy's attempts at helping certainly hadn't worked.

"It's also a blessed relief," Andrea said, and then let out a guilty laugh. "Sorry, I know how that sounds. But I'm glad Eva and I are shot of him. He wasn't a nice man."

"I'm sorry," Lucy said again, helplessly. Despite Andrea's laughter and easy smile, a darkness lingered in the woman's eyes and in the tightness of her mouth. She reached once more for Eva's hand.

"I should get on. Have a good night," Andrea called, and hurried up the main street.

Tarn House was quiet when Lucy entered, and guiltily she wondered if she should have come back sooner. She could have helped Juliet with dinner, although that thought hardly inspired happy images of them chatting while chopping vegetables.

Lucy shed her coat and walked into the kitchen, struck again by the coziness of the room—and how many discouraging conversations she'd had in it.

Juliet was out with the dogs, and Lucy didn't dare start making dinner on her own. Juliet was the kind of person, she was quite sure, who knew exactly what was in her fridge at all times, and would be seriously annoyed if Lucy used up something she wasn't supposed to.

But she was hungry and tired after spending all

day wandering around, and she felt like eating her favorite comfort food, scrambled eggs and toast. Resolutely, a little defiantly, she got out the eggs a local farmer delivered every Monday morning and cracked two into a bowl. She was *living* here. She should be able to make herself a meal. And she'd talk to Juliet about contributing to the grocery bill and paying rent. Feeling both better and worse at the thought, she made herself eggs and toast and ate them at the kitchen table, gazing out at the sheep fields, thinking about Andrea and Eva, about Dan Trenton and Mary from the beach café, and, yes, about Alex Kincaid. All of them with sorrows and stories to tell.

She'd cleaned up everything, wiped the counter and stove top until they gleamed, and even inspected the sink drain for bits of egg, when Juliet came in. Her narrowed gaze took in the kitchen, the plate Lucy was about to load in the dishwasher, and absurdly, she felt guilty.

"I was just thinking," Lucy said, her voice sounding a little too loud, "that I should contribute to household expenses. And I'll pay rent."

Something flashed across Juliet's face but was gone before Lucy could figure out what it was. "That sounds like a good idea," she answered tonelessly, and Lucy swallowed.

"So if you think of an appropriate amount . . ."

"I think one hundred pounds a month should cover both bed and board."

"Okay." Lucy had seen a sign in the post office shop advertising a room for rent for a hundred pounds a week. Juliet was being generous, even if it didn't feel like it. "Great. I'll . . . get a bank account, I guess." She hadn't even organized how she was to be paid at school. "When would you like me to . . . pay?"

"It doesn't matter," Juliet replied, her tone both flat and brisk. "Whenever you get around to it."

"Okay." And then, because it was painfully obvious they had nothing more to say to each other, Lucy started upstairs. The last thing she heard was the sound of Juliet closing the dish-washer she'd left open.

Juliet was out with the dogs when Lucy left for school the following morning; it was another crisp and sunny day, and her spirits lifted at leaving Tarn House—and, she had to admit, at seeing Alex again. Would he be different towards her, now that they'd had a coffee together and could, perhaps, consider themselves friends?

That question was answered when Alex stalked by reception without so much as a glance at her, or even his usual muttered hello. Lucy felt the expectant smile fade from her face as Alex disappeared into his office, shutting the door behind him with a very firm click.

Okay, so maybe they weren't friends. Maybe he'd just had a difficult morning. Still, a hello would have been nice.

Moodily Lucy started up the computer and watched the first trickle of pupils come up the hill. She could hear their excited chatter and laughter, and something inside her twisted and ached.

She'd wanted that once. A husband. Children. An actual family, something she'd never experienced. She'd tried to find it with Thomas and his sons. She'd met the boys first, two towheaded imps who had come into the gallery café and careened wildly around, arms out as they pretended to be airplanes. Thomas had come in after, looking handsome and harassed, and something in Lucy's heart had squeezed.

She'd made the boys chocolate milk shakes with extra whipped cream and sprinkles, and chatted to them—they'd been to the Boston Aquarium and their father was a professor at boring *Harvard*—while Thomas had sipped an Americano and had looked, in retrospect, quite self-consciously wryly self-deprecating.

Still, Lucy had fallen for it. She'd fallen for the whole package: the adorable, if a bit wild, boys, the winsomely nerdy academic father, the image of the four of them spending lazy Sunday after-noons on Boston Common.

She'd served Thomas another Americano on the house (actually it had come out of her wages) and listened to him drone on for half an hour about eighteenth-century politics (most boring subject ever), and then his cell had rung and he'd spoken tersely to someone named Monica, who Thomas had explained after the call was his nasty ex-wife. Actually, Lucy remembered, he didn't call her nasty. He just implied it while insisting that he couldn't speak badly of her because of the boys.

The boys, Lucy had suspected then, had easily understood the subtext. She'd been the only one off in la-la land, feeling sorry for Thomas and his virtually motherless children, and thinking how she could come in and heal everyone and everything.

"Lucy?"

She jerked out of her reverie to see Alex standing in the doorway of the reception area.

"Yes?"

"The photocopier in the staff room needs paper. Would you see to it?"

"Yes, of course." She stared at him, willing him to say something about Saturday, but he looked as purposeful and indifferent as ever.

She watched him disappear back into his office and wondered just what she'd been expecting. For Alex to perch on the edge of her desk and ruffle her hair as they shared some nonexistent in-joke?

Well, not quite.

Actually, sort of.

With a groan Lucy buried her head in her hands. She was so ridiculous. Her insistent sense of optimism verged on fantasy—about Thomas, thinking that their relationship was actually going somewhere; about Juliet, thinking they could reconcile; and even now about Alex. But she wasn't going to make the same stupid mistake again.

She wasn't going to fool herself into thinking they were flirting or even friends simply because he'd bought her a cup of coffee.

And anyway, she was here for only four months and as she was coming out of a long-term relationship, she had no intention of dating or even flirting with anyone for a long time.

She heaved herself out of the chair and went to find the paper for the photocopier. She'd get that right this time, at least.

The rest of the morning passed uneventfully save for two scrapes at playtime—a tearful Year One followed an hour later by a stoic Year Five who had bloodied both elbows pretty badly but was determined not to cry. It wasn't until Lucy had applied the ice pack and filled out the accident report that she realized it was the boy she'd seen at the top of the village, kicking his soccer ball.

"Hey, you," she said, and wagged her finger at him. He looked as nonplussed as when she'd said hello.

She stuck her tongue out as a reminder, and after a second's stunned pause he gave her that cocky grin back.

"I can tell you're trouble," Lucy teased. "What's your name?"

"Oliver."

"Oliver from Year Five. I'm going to keep my eye on you." She was only teasing, but she watched as Oliver's grin slid off his face and he gave an indifferent shrug. Then he slipped from the stool, jamming his hands in the pockets of his gray flannel trousers.

"Can I go out again, miss?"

"Yes, just keep those elbows protected." Lucy watched him go, frowning. Then she swiveled around to her computer and checked the attendance records she'd been logging in every day. Oliver Jones in Year Five had been late every day since school had started.

She stared at the record for a moment, wondering what was going on, and then glanced up as Diana came into the office with her afternoon attendance log.

"Two children out for dentist appointments." She noticed Lucy's frown with one of her own. "What's wrong?"

"I was just noticing that Oliver Jones has been late every day this term."

"Ah, Oliver." With a weary sigh Diana braced her shoulder against the doorway. "Poor little lad."

"He seems like a cheeky little so-and-so to me," Lucy answered, and Diana nodded.

"He is, but it's hard on him. His father works on the oil rigs in the North Sea for eight months of the year, and his mother . . ." She hesitated, and

145

Lucy waited. "His mother gets depressed," Diana finally said. "Sometimes she can barely make it out of bed of a morning."

"And no one can help?"

"Neighbors help out when they can, but in a place like Hartley-by-the-Sea . . ." She paused, her gaze faraway. "Most people know when to step in and when to butt out."

But he's nine, Lucy wanted to say. Instead she just nodded. Her mother hadn't suffered from depression, but Lucy had gotten herself to school most mornings. She knew what it was like not to be able to depend on your mother.

Lucy was still thinking about Oliver an hour later when she took a rather terse phone call from someone at Cumberland Academy for Alex.

She put through the call and leaned forward to see Alex at his desk through the glass, his brows drawn together in a frown, the phone receiver pressed to his ear. He pinched the bridge of his nose and closed his eyes before hanging up.

Lucy threw herself back into her chair and he came into the reception area a few minutes later.

"Lucy."

She looked up, smiling brightly. "Yes, Mr. Kincaid?"

"You can call me Alex, you know. I have to leave school for about half an hour. If anyone rings, please take a message."

"Of course."

"Thank you." She watched him head out into the school yard, saw something tired and defeated about the set of his shoulders as he walked towards the staff car park, and wondered all over again what that phone call had been about.

Half an hour later Alex returned with a very sulky preteen in tow. The girl slouching into the school behind him was beautiful, although you wouldn't necessarily notice that first off. Her dark, silky hair was covering half her face, and her black school blazer was far too big, with the tie worn loose and the skirt quite short.

She gave Lucy a deliberately bored look, and Lucy saw that the girl's eyes were a lovely, clear hazel. Her Cupid's bow mouth was painted an unfortunate fire-engine red.

"In here, Bella," Alex said tersely, and pointed to a chair in the reception area. Lucy scooted closer to her computer, as if doing so gave Alex and this girl any kind of privacy. At least it gave them some space.

With a loud, sneering sigh, the girl flung herself into the swivel chair and sat there sprawled, her tights-clad legs flung out in front of her, her bags and coat at her feet. She looked up at Alex with her eyebrows arched, a mocking smile on her face. She reminded Lucy of the mean girls she'd encountered in seventh grade, all acid sweetness and deliberate contempt.

"What, I'm going to sit in here all day?" she

asked, spinning around in the chair, and Alex glared at her.

"Yes," he bit out, "you da—you are."

"Language, Dad," Bella mocked, and Alex's eyes snapped with fury, his mouth tightly compressed.

So this was the other daughter he'd mentioned at the café. Lucy would have expected Alex's daughters to be quiet and cowed, but then since he didn't have his dog under control, why should he have his daughter? And Bella Kincaid definitely looked like a handful.

"Just stay here, Bella," Alex said. "Since you managed to get yourself suspended from school in only the second week of term, you can face the consequences."

"Which is to be bored out my mind?"

"That's the first one," Alex snapped, and then turned to Lucy. "Lucy, I'm sorry to inconvenience you, but I trust my daughter will behave herself and not cause you any trouble this afternoon."

That, Lucy thought as Alex stalked back to his office, was some incredibly wishful thinking on Alex's part.

She slid a sideways glance at the girl, who was still lounging in the chair, studying her chipped black nail polish with such obvious boredom that Lucy almost wanted to advise her not to try *quite* so hard.

She turned back to her computer, the afternoon's register blurring in front of her. She could feel

Bella's curious and contemptuous gaze burning into her back. How on earth was she supposed to concentrate with this girl staring at her all afternoon?

She might be able to give a few five-year-olds cuddles and ice packs, but this type of child—this querulous, unpleasant, on-the-cusp-of-adulthood, malevolent *force*—was something else entirely.

The exaggerated sighs, the narrowed looks, the eye rolls, the lip curls . . . she'd had it all before with Thomas's sons. And she'd been trying with them, not that it had ever done much good. If anything, those two boys had put her off children completely.

She turned back to the register and tried to work for ten endless minutes, with Bella heaving gusty sighs and spinning in her chair, before she couldn't take it anymore. She swung around in her chair and gave Bella a sunny smile the girl very obviously ignored.

"So, what you'd get done for?"

Lucy watched Bella hesitate, torn between keeping up her too-bored-to-live act and actually answering the question. She turned so her back was to Lucy.

"Nothing too bad."

"Oh." Lucy loaded the single syllable with disappointment. "I thought you might have set fire to the chemistry lab or something." Not, she realized, that she should be giving the girl ideas.

Bella certainly looked capable of a major act of arson. But she'd had quite enough of her too-cool-for-school attitude. She was *so* over that.

"I just bunked off PE," Bella said after a moment, spinning round in her chair again to face Lucy. "Teachers overreacted as *usual*."

"Hmm." A suspension for skipping a single class? Lucy doubted she was hearing the whole story. She turned back to her computer and continued to enter the register numbers into the afternoon attendance spreadsheet. She was getting a lot faster at it, thankfully. "Why PE?" she asked after several minutes had passed. "I mean, math or physics or something like that I could understand. But PE? It's fun."

"It's stupid," Bella said with sudden viciousness. She spun again in her chair, faster, so her hair flew out, and Lucy could see her face properly.

Spinning there, legs and hair flying, she looked very small, very young. Her face still held a puppyish roundness. And instead of reminding Lucy of the mean girls she'd encountered in junior high, Bella Kincaid reminded her of someone else.

Herself, at the same age. Vulnerable, lonely, so very unhappy—and hiding it any way she knew how.

"Some of it's stupid," Lucy agreed, turning once more back to the computer. "I hated swimming, for example. Getting wet in the middle of the day is *so* not fun."

Bella didn't answer, and Lucy mentally shook her head at herself. Why was she trying so hard? She didn't care why Bella Kincaid had been suspended from school. She didn't care about Bella Kincaid at all.

Except somehow she couldn't keep from caring, at least a little. Surely Bella's difficulties had something to do with her mother's death. The girl still had to be grieving, and that alone, Lucy knew, was enough to soften her already too-squishy heart towards her.

"It was netball," Bella said in a low voice. Lucy stilled, her hands resting on the computer keyboard; even her heart seemed to have stopped beating for a moment. "Stupid effing netball," Bella said viciously, and then to Lucy's shock she burst into noisy tears.

Lucy spun around and saw Bella with her arms over her face, her bony shoulders shaking.

"Oh, sweetie . . ." She tried to pull the girl into a hug, but Bella was no six-year-old Eva, grateful for a cuddle.

"Geroff," she snapped, her voice muffled against her arm as she cringed away from Lucy.

"Sorry," Lucy muttered. She felt her face flame as she sat there helplessly, not knowing how to make it better but wanting to. "I hate netball," she finally said, and then added, "Is that like basketball?"

Bella let out a snort that Lucy hoped was a

laugh. With her face still buried in her arms she said, "You don't even know what netball is?"

"Well, it *obviously* sucks."

Bella lifted her tear-streaked face from her arm to peek at Lucy. Her mascara had run and she'd bitten off all her bright lipstick. She looked even younger now, and far too vulnerable. "I don't even *care* about netball," she said, and wiped at her cheeks. "And my dad doesn't let us say 'sucks.'"

"Hey, you said 'effing,'" Lucy answered. "Isn't that worse?" Actually, she wasn't sure if it was a really bad swearword, or if she should have repeated it. Leaving the country at six years old had given her a limited Brit vocabulary, especially when it came to curse words.

Bella shrugged defiantly. "He wasn't here."

"I won't tell him."

She gazed at Lucy, the traces of her tears still visible on her face, along with the streaks of mascara. "Why are you sucking up to me?" she asked, her eyes narrowing. "Are you trying to, like, get in with my dad?"

"Get in with your dad?" Lucy repeated with a nonchalance that sounded awful, almost as bad as one of those fake, hearty laughs stuffy adults gave when talking to kids.

Her mother's friends had laughed like that when she'd been trotted out like some tarnished trophy at her mother's showings. *Heh, heh, heh, Lucy, well, aren't you getting bigger?* Then they'd turn away and her mother would give her a little push, indicating that she should make herself scarce. She'd usually ended up hiding under the refreshment table, her knees tucked to her chest, as she watched all the shoes go by.

"I'm afraid I'm kind of hopeless at this whole receptionist thing," she told Bella with a shrug. "And frankly, your dad seemed so ticked off at you that being nice to you isn't going to score me any points, is it?" Not that she wanted to score points with Alex. Or score anything.

Bella's gaze remained narrowed, as she seemed to assess the truth of her words.

"So if it's not netball you don't like," Lucy asked, "what's the big deal with PE?"

Bella shrugged, hunching her shoulders and drawing her knees up to her chest. "Nothing," she muttered, and looked away.

Lucy waited for a few minutes, and then when she'd finally finished logging in the afternoon register, she turned back to Bella, who was still sitting with her knees tucked up. "Why don't you clean up?" she suggested, and Bella regarded her suspiciously.

"What are you talking about?"

Lucy tried for a kindly smile. "Umm . . ." She gestured to her cheek. "Mascara."

"Oh." Bella nibbled her lip and then with an attempt at an insouciant shrug unfolded herself from her chair. "Fine."

"You know where the bathroom is?"

She gave Lucy an utterly scathing look. So much for solidarity over netball. "I used to go to school here?" she said in the "well, duh" tone that seemed to be a universal language for teenagers.

"Right."

Bella stalked out of the room, her arms wrapped around her body but her chin held high, and Lucy sank back into her chair. Children were hard work, she thought, then amended that to other people's children were hard work.

How much emotional energy, not to mention money and time, had she expended on Will and Garrett? Three years of her life poured into those boys. Reading them bedtime stories. Showing up at their soccer matches. Giving them presents, and not just gift cards or the latest electronic toy, but thoughtful items that had taken effort and time.

For Will's twelfth birthday she'd made him a bird feeder in the shape of the Tardis, which might have been a bit on the bizarre side, but birds and *Doctor Who* were Will's two favorite things. A week later she'd seen it stuffed into the recycling bin. She hadn't known whether to burst into tears or clock him over the head with the thing. She'd done neither, just smiled and pretended she hadn't seen it. Of course.

Lucy turned back to the computer. Time to log in the amount of lunch money paid this week.

Time to stop thinking about Bella or Alex or any Kincaid.

Five minutes later Bella slouched back into the room. Her face had been scrubbed clean, which made her look about six. She stood in the center of the reception area for a moment, her expression uncertain, and the pale sunlight streaming through the windows touched her in gold—and shone right through her thin cotton uniform blouse.

The girl wasn't wearing a bra. And preteen or not, she needed one.

Lucy didn't think she'd been staring, but Bella must have sensed her gaze, for she abruptly pulled her blazer closed and threw herself into the chair, angling her body away from Lucy so she was all sharp elbows and knees.

"I left my jumper at school," she muttered, and Lucy sat back in her own chair, her mind spinning. No bra. No mother to buy her one. Skipping PE, most likely because she had to change for it. It came together in her head with an almighty clang.

Bella Kincaid needed someone to buy her a bra.

12
Juliet

THERE WAS A SHEEP in the back garden. Juliet braced her elbows on the sink and leaned closer to the kitchen window; in the settling dusk she could just make out the dirty white shape. The stupid beast was eating her autumn roses.

She turned from the window and reached for her fleece. The Scottish lads had gone out to the pub, and after a tense, silent meal of pasta bake, Lucy had gone upstairs. Juliet still felt a cringing mix of guilt and shame at the argument they'd had. And when Lucy had mentioned paying rent, she'd felt both satisfied and hurt. She was a mess of contradictory emotions, and she was too weary in too many ways to attempt some sort of semi-reconciliation. This tiptoeing around each other, grim and silent as it was, was easier.

She stepped outside into the chill night air; as soon as the sun went down, the temperature had dropped rapidly, promising a frost that night. She walked around to the back garden where the sheep stood, rose petals protruding from its mouth as it chewed contentedly.

"Stupid animal," she said. It had to be one of

Peter Lanford's, and after the awkward conversation they'd had in the lane, she didn't relish seeing him again. She took a step towards the sheep, who eyed her with beady suspicion before shuffling backwards. Juliet kept walking towards it, slapping her thigh, and the sheep, used to being herded by Jake, began to beat a retreat, back down the dirt track towards Peter's house. She walked behind it, slapping her thigh anytime it stopped, and finally reached the field where the rest of its flock were huddled against a drystone wall.

Juliet opened the five-bar gate and the sheep hurried in; as she was closing it, she saw that the fence on one side had fallen down into a tumble of rocks. She'd have to tell Peter.

Sighing, she turned away from the gate and headed up the track to the Lanford farmhouse. Night had fallen by the time she reached the low, rambling house of whitewashed stone, a drystone wall surrounding its garden; Peter's mud-splattered Land Rover was parked in front.

The place looked small against the dramatic backdrop of the stark fells, the rolling sheep pasture stretching onwards all around it. She could see the sea in the distance, no more than a sweep of black in the darkness, and behind her the lights of the village twinkled comfortingly. She hadn't realized how remote the Lanford farm was; even though it was only a mile from the village, it felt cut off from everything, nestled between the fells and the sea.

A light gleamed in what Juliet supposed was the sitting room, but the rest of the house was dark. She knocked once on the door, and then again, but no one answered. There was no door-bell, and thinking that Peter might not have heard her knock, Juliet pushed the door open and stuck her head inside, taking in the gloom of a very dirty kitchen.

Cups and plates littered most surfaces, and stacks of newspapers and unopened post covered the kitchen table. Curious now, as she'd never been inside before, Juliet stepped into the kitchen and saw the huge, ancient Aga, frying pans with congealed grease on the bottoms left on top. A smell of old cooking hung in the air; she could see a pile of muddy clothes left by the washer.

Peter Lanford's house was a mess.

She heard sounds from the sitting room and guiltily Juliet realized she was snooping. "Peter?" she called out, heard the note of uncertainty in her voice. What if he was entertaining? She had no idea if Peter had a girlfriend, although she suspected he didn't. Surely in a village the size of Hartley-by-the-Sea she'd have heard something, and anyway, Peter had told her he was alone. As alone as she was. "Peter?" she called again, and picked her way through the mess to the doorway that led to the sitting room.

She stopped on the threshold, arrested by the scene in front of her. Peter's father, William, was in an armchair, his head tilted back, his face lathered up, while Peter gave him a shave. A bowl of warm water was by his feet, and Juliet watched, strangely transfixed, as Peter gently ran the old-fashioned straight razor along William's cheeks, dabbing his face with a towel to catch the drips.

"There you are, Dad," he said, his voice as gentle as his movements. "Nice and still. We'll have you looking right smart, won't we?"

William looked far older and frailer than Juliet had expected; she'd only glimpsed him from a distance, walking through the sheep fields with Jake at his heels. Now she saw his hair was sparse and white, his chest sunken in under the old flannel shirt he wore, and the hands that gripped the arms of the chair were reddened and knobby with arthritis.

Instinctively Juliet took a step backwards, into the kitchen. Watching seemed like an intrusion. She stood there amidst the mess of the darkened room, wondering if she should slip out the door even as she itched to tidy the place up a bit. More contradictory impulses.

In any case, she didn't have time to do either, because before she could move, she heard the clink of the bowl as Peter picked it up and then, murmuring something to his father, he came into the kitchen. He froze as he saw her standing there in the dark, and Juliet froze too; it suddenly seemed almost offensive that she was standing uninvited in the middle of Peter Lanford's kitchen.

"Juliet . . . ?"

She forced her lips into some semblance of a smile. "Hello, Peter."

"What—"

"Your sheep got into my garden," she hurried to explain, her voice, in her nervousness, coming out more tersely than she meant it to. "I got it back into the field, but I noticed you have a hole in your fence, and I thought I'd tell you." She gestured to the door. "You didn't hear my knock." Peter still just stood there, the bowl of soapy water in his hands, and Juliet muttered a final, "Sorry." She took a step towards the door.

"No, don't go, now that you're here." Peter walked over to the sink and dumped the water down the drain. "Let me just get Dad settled first."

"Okay," Juliet said, but she took another step towards the door. She couldn't fathom why Peter would like her to stay, and she couldn't decide whether she wanted to or not.

He went back into the sitting room, and Juliet tried to simultaneously listen and not listen to him talking to his father. After a few minutes she heard the creak of both the chair and old joints, and then the shuffling step of slippered feet up the stairs. Still she stayed by the door; when Peter returned a few minutes later, she had one hand on the knob.

160

He glanced at her, his steady gaze seeming to take everything in, or at least more than Juliet would like. She dropped her hand from the door and just stood there, smiling awkwardly. At least she hoped she was smiling.

"Whiskey?" Peter asked, and took a bottle of Glenfiddich from the cupboard above the sink.

"Oh . . . all right, then." Juliet couldn't remember the last time she'd had a whiskey; maybe a few Christmases ago, when she'd had a retired couple booked in for the holidays. They'd invited her to sit with them in front of the fire, and Juliet had cradled a glass of whiskey between her hands, feeling strangely like a guest and more at home in her own house than she had in a long while.

Peter poured them both healthy measures and handed her a glass. He glanced ruefully around the kitchen before turning back to her. "Sorry, I'm not much in the housekeeping department."

"You're busy." He nodded and Juliet felt compelled to mention his father, although she wasn't sure why. "Your dad . . ."

"He's not very well." Peter took a long swallow of whiskey. "Dementia," he clarified quietly. "It's got a bit worse in the last few months. He can't do much by himself these days, but he likes a good shave, same as any other man."

"Oh, Peter." Juliet shook her head helplessly. "I'm sorry."

He lifted one shoulder in a shrug. "It happens."

161

"Yes." His stoic acceptance of what life had to offer matched her own, although since Lucy's arrival, Juliet realized, she'd been feeling a lot more bitterness. A lot more everything. She took another sip of whiskey.

"So how are things with your sister?" Peter asked. "Lucy, isn't it?"

"Yes." Juliet's hand tightened on her glass. She shouldn't have come here. She should have known Peter would make small talk, although the man had been virtually monosyllabic before; Juliet had no idea why he was so chatty now. Not that a single question actually constituted chatty. "Things are . . ." She was about to say "good," but her throat closed around the word. Things with Lucy weren't good. They weren't remotely good. "It's kind of hard, actually," she shocked herself by saying. "Having her here." She drained her glass then, and Peter nodded, seeming unsurprised.

"Bound to be. Family's hard."

"Is it? I thought family was meant to be easy because it's, you know, family."

Peter let out a rusty laugh. "I don't know what your family's like, but mine hasn't been like that."

"No?" She nodded towards the sitting room. "You get along with your dad, though."

"Aye." Peter's face closed up a bit at that, and Juliet decided not to press.

162

"Do you have sisters or brothers?" she asked, thinking this was something she should have known.

"A brother, David. He lives up Carlisle way. Runs one of those hobby farms." He spoke without inflection, but Juliet still sensed hurt behind the words.

"Hobby farm?"

"You know, one of those places where you feed the animals and ride toy tractors and that. He does well with it."

"I suppose loads of farmers have to do the same, just to keep the farm going," Juliet said. She tried to picture toy tractors and a petting zoo at Bega Farm and failed. As if Peter sensed her thoughts, he offered a crooked smile.

"Not going to happen here, though."

"No."

He finished his whiskey in one long swallow. "So what is it that's hard?" he asked, and Juliet realized he was talking about Lucy.

"Everything," she said bleakly. "Absolutely everything."

"Were you not close, as barneys?" he asked, and she smiled a bit at the Cumbrian word for children. Peter's genealogy stretched back to the Vikings, she suspected, who had come to the Cumbrian coast a thousand years ago. There were some who said the old Cumbrian dialect was closer to Icelandic than to English.

"No, we weren't. I'm eleven years older than Lucy, and we have different fathers."

He nodded slowly, and for a moment Juliet didn't think he'd say anything more. And maybe that was better. Did she really want to talk about how much she resented Lucy? It would only make her seem petty and childish.

"But you invited her here, all the same," he finally stated.

"Yes, but I didn't expect it to make me feel so . . ." She stopped then, not wanting to put it into words.

"That's what family does, though, don't they? Make a hocker-up of everything."

"A hocker-up . . ."

"A bloody mess," Peter said with an unexpected grin. "You've been here near *dick* years, Juliet, and you don't know the Cumbrian yet?"

She laughed, surprised and strangely gratified to be teased. "*Dick* years. Sounds a bit dirty. Would that be ten years?"

He nodded. "Surely you've learned the counting."

"Only *yan, tan, tethera.*" She knew many sheep farmers, and even some schoolchildren in the playground, used the ancient number system for counting sheep.

"*Methera, pimp, sethera, lethera, hovera, dovera, dick,*" Peter finished.

"Definitely sounds a bit dirty," Juliet said, and wondered if she was actually *bantering* with Peter

Lanford. She felt unbalanced by the conversation, or maybe just the whiskey. "Anyway, I'm still an offcomer, aren't I?"

"Only in your mind, maybe."

And just like that, the teasing tone dropped and she felt exposed, revealed by his words and his perception, and she had nowhere to look, nowhere to hide. She stared at him helplessly, unable to come up with a response. Fortunately—or perhaps unfortunately—Peter Lanford didn't seem to need one.

"Well, it's bound to get easier with time, if you let it." He took her glass. "And I'll see to that wall on the morrow. Can't have my ewes moidering you and eating all your rosebushes."

"They're not moidering me," Juliet protested, the Cumbrian word for "bothering" sounding as awkward coming from her as it did easy coming from Peter. "And I didn't say they were eating my rosebushes."

Peter gazed at her, a smile lurking in his eyes. "You didn't have to." Juliet stared back, discomfited, sensing a depth behind Peter's silent stillness that she'd had no idea was there. It felt akin to jumping in the sea and finding out it was far deeper than you'd imagined, and instead of resting your feet on solid, sandy ground, you kicked uselessly through the water, in over your head.

"Thank you for the whiskey," she finally said.

"Anytime, Juliet," Peter answered. "Anytime."

She left Peter's house and strode down the dirt track, stumbling a bit in the darkness. Back at the house she tidied up the kitchen before going up to bed; she'd told the Scottish lads to lock up after they came back after the pub's last call. She paused for a second on the landing, but all was quiet from Lucy's room.

She'd just changed into her sensible fleece pajamas and was getting into bed to read the gritty crime thriller that was a blessed escape from her own life when she heard a soft, hesitant knock on the door. She slid out of bed and went to open the door, surprised to see Lucy even though it couldn't have been anyone else.

"Do you . . . do you have a moment?" Lucy asked, and Juliet nodded. Lucy came into her bedroom, looking young and vulnerable with hair frizzing all about her face; she was wearing a pair of pajamas covered in dancing Snoopys. Juliet waited, arms folded. "How well do you know Alex Kincaid?"

Juliet blinked. "Not very well."

"Do you know him well enough to know how he might take a . . . a bit of advice?"

"It depends what the advice is regarding."

She must have had some kind of skeptical look on her face, because Lucy let out a little laugh and said, "I know you're probably thinking there's nothing I could advise him on."

"I don't have an opinion on the subject." She sounded so prickly. So prissy. And yet she didn't know how to keep herself from it.

"Well, it's what I would be thinking," Lucy said. "Except in this case . . ." She hesitated, and Juliet raised her eyebrows.

"In this case?" she prompted, a touch of impatience to her voice. Clearly Lucy wanted her to ask.

"I think his daughter Bella would appreciate this advice," Lucy said. "Eventually."

"Bella?" Juliet stared at her. She'd seen Alex's daughters in the village, two solemn-faced girls, the older one slouchy and sullen and the younger dreamy and lost. She'd said hello to them a few times, both before and after Anna had died, but that was all. "How do you even know Bella?"

"She came into school yesterday. She's been suspended."

"For what?"

"Skipping PE."

"They suspend children for bunking off PE now?" Juliet asked, and Lucy shrugged.

"I think there's more to the story."

"So what advice do you want to give Alex?" Juliet was curious now, in spite of her intention to remain removed.

"Well . . . Bella kind of needs a bra," Lucy said, and then added, "Actually, there's no 'kind of' about it."

Juliet stared at her. "A bra," she said, without inflection, because that was just about the last thing she'd been expecting.

"I don't think her father realizes it. Which isn't all that surprising, really."

Lucy gave a wry smile while Juliet just stared, and then all of a sudden, because it was so absurd, or maybe because her emotions were so close to the surface, she burst out laughing. Lucy stared at her in shock as Juliet sank onto the bed, her arms wrapped around her middle, and then Lucy started laughing too, her hands pressed to her mouth, both of them in the throes of the kind of silent-shaking, eyes-streaming, helpless laughter that took them over completely.

It felt good to release all the excess emotion. Finally she pressed the heels of her hands to her eyes and took a steadying breath.

"A bra," she said. "Poor Alex."

"Poor me, because I'm the one who's got to tell him."

"And he's got to buy it." Juliet's laughter subsided completely then, because while the situation was funny, it was also desperately sad.

Lucy must have sensed the shift in her mood because she asked quietly, "Were you friends with his wife?"

"Anna?" Juliet considered. "I wouldn't say friends, exactly." She didn't know whom she'd call her friend, except maybe Rachel.

Then she thought of Peter's steady gaze on her as they drank whiskey in his kitchen, and pushed the memory away. "We were friendly," she told Lucy. "She kept her horse in the stables behind the house and I'd chat with her when she got ready to go riding. She didn't seem very happy here, though."

"She didn't?"

Juliet shrugged. "She spent a lot of time riding, and I got the sense she was more of a city girl."

"Why did Alex move here, then?"

"Why does anyone move here? Anyway," Juliet said, rising from the bed. "If Bella really does need a bra, then you have to tell Alex. I don't think anyone else will."

"Surely someone . . ."

"He's a bit of a loner. Works all the time. I'm sure some single mums in the village have set their sights on him, but not enough to do him that kind of favor."

Lucy grimaced. "Except for me."

"Except for you," Juliet agreed. The laughter they'd shared had loosened something between them, and now she felt it inexorably tightening again. "It's late. I should go to bed." Which was unsubtle code for *Get out of my room.*

Lucy nodded; message received. "Thanks," she said, turning to Juliet, taking a step forward as if she might actually hug her before she stopped. "Thanks for listening."

Juliet swallowed. Lucy's gratitude made her feel guilty for how little she'd offered. She nodded, and Lucy headed back to her room. Quietly Juliet closed the door. Her stomach muscles actually ached from laughing. She couldn't even remember the last time she'd laughed like that; she knew only that it had been a very long time.

13
Lucy

LUCY SPENT A SLEEPLESS night debating how to handle the rather sensitive topic of Bella and her bra—or lack of it. She was pretty sure Alex had no idea what his daughter needed. And Bella had no way to go into town and buy herself one, if she were so inclined, which Lucy doubted she was. She remembered the first time she'd bought a bra with her mother and cringed, even now. It had been utterly mortifying.

But the girl couldn't go to school without a bra, and while Lucy knew it wasn't her problem—she didn't want it to *be* her problem—she also knew that she had to say something.

But how?

She was still mulling over the dilemma the next morning, after she'd fired up the computer and the kettle, as she stared out at the school yard, now bathed in golden light. Alex came in with both Bella and his younger daughter, Poppy, in tow.

"Is it all right if Bella spends the morning in here?" he asked, and Lucy wondered what he would do if she said no. "She's brought her homework."

"Of course, no problem." Lucy gave them both a sunny smile; Bella was wearing a huge black jumper that came down to her skinny-jean-clad knees. At least it covered her properly. Lucy swallowed a nervous laugh. "Umm . . . make yourself comfortable."

That bit of politeness earned her a curled lip from Bella, who threw herself into the chair in the corner, dropping her bag by her feet. It was, Lucy suspected, going to be a very long day.

She turned back to find Poppy inspecting her solemnly. "You talk funny."

That nervous little laugh she'd swallowed escaped in a bubble of sound. "Actually, I think you talk funny. So I guess we're even."

Poppy considered this for a moment before nodding in acceptance. Lucy met Alex's gaze above his daughter's head and her heart lurched at his expression, which was unreadable as always, and yet—

Was it just wishful thinking to believe there was something tender beneath the sternness?

Yes, Lucy told herself resolutely. Yes, it was.

Alex went to his office and Poppy skipped off to her classroom, and Lucy was left with Bella, who filled the tiny space with her silent malevolence.

The hours dragged by as Bella picked her nails and refused to do any work. She asked if she could use the Internet on Lucy's computer, and let out a long-suffering sigh when Lucy refused. She took herself off for lunch with the older school pupils, and Lucy breathed a sigh of relief. A whole half hour to herself. Thank goodness.

"Is everything going all right?"

"Oh." She looked up to see Alex standing in the doorway, his expression caught between a scowl and a smile.

"Yes, fine."

"She goes back to school the day after tomorrow." He shook his head, his expression closing, his arms folded. "She never used to do this. Bunking off class."

"Maybe there's a reason," Lucy ventured, and Alex shook his head again.

"I asked, and she wouldn't give me one. Send her to me if she gives you any trouble." He turned to go back to his office, and Lucy felt her heart start to beat hard. Her hands went clammy.

Taking a deep breath, she rose from her desk. "Umm . . . Alex?"

He glanced back at her. "What is it?"

"Could I talk to you for a sec? In your office?"

Alex frowned, and then nodded. Lucy followed him into his office and closed the door, resisting the urge to wipe her damp palms along the sides of her skirt. She shouldn't be nervous about this.

"What's going on?" he asked, his voice touched with impatience.

"It's about Bella."

"She *did* cause trouble—"

"No, it's not that. It's just . . . I think I know what's causing her problems at school."

Alex's forehead furrowed. "You do?"

"Yes . . . I spoke to her while she was in the office yesterday. . . ."

"And she said something to you?"

Lucy couldn't quite make out Alex's tone, whether he was surprised or disbelieving or even a little miffed. "It's more what she didn't say."

"What do you mean?"

"Look, Alex . . . I know your wife died a year and a half ago. . . ."

He folded his arms. "What does that have to do with anything?"

"Don't you think losing her mother might have something to do with Bella's problems?" Lucy asked. How emotionally clueless was this guy?

"Look, I know Bella and Poppy are grieving," he answered, his voice tight. "But as I can't bring their mother back, there's not much I can do about it besides what I already do. And while I appreciate this illuminating psychological insight, I'm not sure what you're trying to get at." He glared at her, his arms still folded.

"Look, I'm not trying to offer some *illuminating psychological insight,*" Lucy told him, her voice taking on a slight edge. "I'm just pointing out that Bella hasn't had a woman around to help her out with—some things."

"She has me," Alex said staunchly, and Lucy just about kept herself from rolling her eyes. "All right, look, Alex, here's the deal. Bella needs a bra." Alex's expression didn't change. He blinked several times, opened his mouth, and said nothing. "I think that's why she got suspended. She'd been avoiding PE because she doesn't want to change her clothes in front of everyone." The words came in a rush as she remembered her own miserable middle school years. Being bullied *sucked,* and that, at least, was something she had no qualms telling Alex about. "I think kids are teasing her about it. I think maybe they're taking her sweaters, too."

"Her jumpers?" Alex sat up straighter. "She's lost two since school started. I shouted at her about it, told her she needed to keep track of her things."

"I'm guessing kids are hiding them—"

He turned to her, his expression now fierce. "You think some bully is nicking my daughter's clothes?"

"I think," Lucy answered, "that someone is making your daughter's life miserable. She's being bullied because she doesn't have a bra. It might seem like a small thing to you, but girls can be vicious. Taking her sweaters and teasing her during PE could be just the tip of the iceberg. Why did she get suspended exactly, anyway? It wasn't for missing just one class, was it?"

Alex didn't answer for a moment. "She skipped PE," he finally said flatly. "As you know. She hid in the bathroom and when the teacher found her, she refused point-blank to go. Said some nasty things about the teacher and the class and—*damn*. I should have . . ." He shook his head, then closed his eyes and pinched the bridge of his nose. "She told you all this?"

"Not exactly."

"What do you mean?" Alex opened his eyes and subjected her to a rather narrowed gaze. "You're just guessing?"

"I'm a pretty good guesser when it comes to crap that happens in middle school," Lucy answered shortly. "I was bullied myself when I was Bella's age. I recognize the signs." Although she hadn't lashed out the way Bella was. She'd just kept smiling.

Alex was silent for a long moment. Finally he glanced up at Lucy, and the vulnerability in his eyes made something in her ache. She clamped down on the feeling, hard. She wasn't going to go start *feeling* things for Alex Kincaid and dreaming of the way she could help him and his poor, motherless family. No, she really wasn't.

"What should I do?" he asked, and there was that ache again.

"Buy her a bra, for starters."

Alex winced. "I don't . . ."

"*Alex.* Come on. You've got two daughters.

You're a single dad. They need you to do this kind of stuff for them."

"Talking to Bella about undergarments would mortify her. As you've seen, our relationship isn't that great to begin with."

Undergarments? Seriously? She saw that the back of his neck and the tips of his ears had gone red. He was embarrassed, although to be fair she had started out that way. Now she was possessed with a resolute determination to see Bella properly clothed. "Well, how is she supposed to get one, then?" she asked, exasperation creeping into her tone.

"I could buy it off the Internet—"

"She needs to try it on."

His ears went even redder. "I can't . . ." He glanced up at her. "What about you?"

"Me?"

"You could take her shopping," Alex said, clearly having a lightbulb moment, and Lucy's jaw dropped.

"Alex, I met her yesterday. I'm a complete stranger—"

"She told you more than she's told me or any other adult," Alex cut her off, his voice taking on that steely, determined quality she was coming to recognize. "Why not you?"

"Surely there's someone else who is closer to her," Lucy protested, but Alex shook his head.

"We—we don't have people like that in our life."

She eyed him with both curiosity and an insuppressible compassion. "No one?"

"Her grandmother would do it, but she lives down near London and we're not going down there until half term. This sounds urgent."

"It is urgent," Lucy said firmly.

"Well, then?"

It was ironic, really, that for three years she'd tried to insinuate herself into Thomas's sons' lives, only to be continually pushed away. And here she was, not long in Hartley-by-the-Sea, determined not to make the same mistake again . . . going bra shopping with a preteen she wasn't sure she even liked. "Fine. I'll do it. When is she going back to school?"

"Thursday."

"I'd go tomorrow, but I think the shops close at four." She'd learned last week, to her amazement, that Whitehaven emptied out by late afternoon.

"Country hours," Juliet had informed her. "All part of the West Cumbrian charm."

"You can have the afternoon off, fully paid," Alex said quickly. "I'll ask Maggie—"

"She's in Newcastle."

"We'll manage," he said firmly. "If you're here for the morning rush of calls, we should be fine. I don't mind taking my own calls. I did it at the start, you might recall."

"Hey, I don't drop that many calls anymore," Lucy protested, and Alex gave her a small smile.

178

"There has been some improvement," he allowed.

"Well, thanks for that. But back to Bella." Lucy leveled him with a look, or tried to. "You need to be able to talk to her about these things, or find a woman in your life who can. She'll probably get her period soon—"

Alex winced but met Lucy's gaze. "I have actually thought of that," he told her. "A little."

She gazed at him; his ears and neck were a normal color now, but he still looked pretty uncomfortable. Lucy was half-amazed at all the things she'd said. What on earth had possessed her?

Just a scorching memory of her own middle school years. If she could save any girl that misery, she would. "I'll talk to her now," she said, and Alex eyed her with undisguised relief.

"Thank you, Lucy. I really do appreciate this."

"I bet you do," she retorted, and he smiled again, just a little quirk, but it still made Lucy grin back. She turned away from him and went in search of Bella.

Lunch had finished and so she headed out to the school yard, where Years Five and Six were playing. She scanned the playground, and caught sight of Oliver Jones tussling with a boy a lot smaller than him.

"Hey, Oliver." She waved at him and he

179

loosened the headlock on the other boy. "Easy there, okay?" She softened the scolding with a smile; if she could keep Oliver out of trouble and reassure him at the same time, she'd consider it a job well done. He needed somebody in his life to look out for him. He let the boy go and scuffed his shoes along the ground, and Lucy dared to ruffle his hair for a millisecond before she went in search of Bella.

She found her hunched against the brick wall, her arms wrapped around herself. Lucy had decided on the way there that she'd speak as plainly to Bella as she had to Alex. She knew Bella would see instantly through any kindly meant ploy, and she imagined how scathing the girl's incredulous scorn would be.

No, better to just lay it all out there. Bella already had, whether she'd meant to or not.

"Hi," she began brightly, and Bella gazed at her with the same narrowed look at which her father was so adept. "Look, Bella, I'm just going to say this," she said, keeping her voice upbeat with determination. "I think I know why you got suspended—" Bella raised an eyebrow. "I mean I think I know why you skipped PE," Lucy amended. "Because you didn't want to get changed. Because you're being bullied."

Lucy saw how still and trapped Bella became, like a beautiful, dark butterfly pinned to a board. She felt a hard tug of sympathy for the girl. "I

180

was bullied when I was your age. It *sucks,* and I told your father so."

"You talked to my father about this?" Bella asked in a suffocated whisper, her gaze on the ground.

"A little," Lucy admitted. "He wants to help you—"

"Yeah, *right.*" She looked away, hugging herself all the more tightly.

"We don't need to bring your father into this right now," Lucy said after a moment. "The important thing is to get you suited up as soon as possible."

"Suited up?"

Lucy stepped closer so no one could hear, even though there wasn't anybody nearby. "You need a bra," she said quietly. "I can take you shopping tomorrow."

Bella closed her eyes, her face going bright red. A tear squeezed out of her eye and she dashed it away furiously.

"Look, I know this is embarrassing," Lucy said calmly. "I get it. I had to ask my mother to buy me a bra and that was the trip from hell, let me tell you. She spoke in this super-loud voice the whole time, about womanhood and my—I'm not kidding you—buds of femininity, and I just wanted to disappear." Bella let out a choked laugh, her eyes still closed. "I promise I won't do that. This will be a very discreet trip."

"I can't believe we're talking about this," she muttered.

"I'm talking," Lucy pointed out. "I'm monologuing here. But no worries. You can meet me here at the school at one, okay? And we'll take a trip into Whitehaven."

Bella didn't say anything for a long moment and Lucy waited, knowing the girl needed to process this very unexpected conversation. *She* had to process it. Finally Bella gave a tiny nod, her gaze averted.

"That's sorted, then," Lucy said cheerfully. She stepped back, relieved that at least one hurdle had been cleared. "I'll see you tomorrow."

Bella didn't answer, and with one last reassuring smile Lucy turned and walked back into school.

14
Juliet

JULIET COULDN'T SEEM TO settle to anything. She tidied up after the Scottish lads, who had left that morning with their rucksacks and walking sticks, and then did a load of laundry and weeded the front flower beds. She walked the dogs, updated the Tarn House Web site, and renewed her advertisement in the back of *Cumbria Life*. And all the while her mind flitted restlessly from this to that, from her conversation with Peter to her laugh with Lucy to poor, motherless Bella Kincaid.

She felt an unexpected kinship with Bella; she'd been virtually motherless too, although Juliet didn't know which was worse: having your mother die or having her hate you.

She was glad when Rachel came by after lunch to clean the bathrooms; Juliet needed to be diverted from her own circling thoughts. Rachel was always like a breath of clean, cool air breezing through the house, as brisk and practical as Juliet yet without being prissy or remote.

"*Someone* doesn't lift the lid when he goes for a wee," she announced as she came downstairs.

"Who was staying in the blue room? I practically needed a hazmat suit for the en suite."

Juliet gave a half grimace, half smile. "You're a saint."

"Saint of the toilet plunger," Rachel agreed, blowing a strand of hair out of her eyes.

She was just collecting her mop and pail of cleaning supplies when Juliet asked, "Fancy a cuppa?"

"I wouldn't say no," Rachel answered, and left her things in the front hall before following Juliet back to the kitchen. "So, how's the half sister these days? You rubbing along together?"

"Her name is Lucy," Juliet reminded Rachel as she filled the kettle. "And rubbing along together is about right. We're not going to be best mates, by any stretch."

"I don't know any sisters who are," Rachel answered.

"Don't you? I feel like plenty of sisters shop and do each other's nails and hair—" Juliet broke off with a self-conscious laugh as she caught sight of Rachel's eloquently disbelieving look. "What, you're not painting Lily's nails?"

"Hardly. I'm usually reading her the riot act about working towards her A levels. She wants to drop biology after this year and I've told her she can't."

"Why not?"

"Because," Rachel answered with surprising

force, "I want her to get somewhere in life, and I'm sorry, but a BTEC in media studies is not going to do it."

Juliet was silent, surprised by this bit of academic snobbery from Rachel. Plenty of people did fine with BTECs, herself included. "Is she even interested in biology?" she asked, and Rachel rolled her eyes.

"Don't you start, as well. The point is, she needs decent A levels to get into a decent university—" She broke off, her expression hardening. "So many people take it for granted. University's an *assumption*—"

"Loads of people don't go to university and are fine," Juliet answered mildly. It felt good to be talking about someone else's issues instead of dwelling on her own. "Myself included."

"You?" Rachel looked surprised, and then discomfited. "I thought . . ."

"I dropped out after the first year. Wasn't for me. And maybe it's not for Lily."

Rachel shook her head, fierce again. "Lily *will* go to university. She'll be the first person in our family to get a degree." She held up a hand. "And I'm not going to argue with you or anyone about it, Juliet."

Juliet was saved from replying by the sound of the door opening, and then Lucy coming into the kitchen. Rachel eyed her with undisguised interest; they hadn't met yet, and Juliet could see her examining Lucy's colorful outfit—a dress in sky-blue corduroy that resembled a bright potato sack, matched with green tights and chunky ankle boots. At least the shoes were sensible, more or less.

"Rachel, this is my sister, Lucy. Lucy, Rachel," Juliet said briskly. "Rachel helps out with the laundry and cleaning." She was determined to keep this normal, and to keep Rachel from asking Lucy any awkward questions about their relationship.

"So you're Lucy," Rachel said, and Juliet suppressed a groan.

"And you're Rachel," Lucy answered lightly. "Although I can't say Juliet said anything about you to me." She glanced at Juliet, her expression both curious and guarded. "But you obviously know who I am."

"Juliet mentioned you were coming to stay," Rachel told her. "And not much escapes notice in this village. How are you finding Hartley-by-the-Sea?"

"Friendly," Lucy answered, her tone cautious. "For the most part."

Friendly, save for the half sister who didn't want her here? Juliet remembered laughing with Lucy last night and she decided to make more of an effort, although whether it was to prove to Lucy, Rachel, or simply herself that they could get along, she wasn't sure. "How did you get on today with the big discussion?"

"What big discussion?" Rachel asked, and Lucy shot Juliet another one of those looks she couldn't quite decipher. Was her sister angry or annoyed or hurt? Something fairly negative, at any rate.

"You don't mind if Rachel knows," she told Lucy. "She can keep a secret."

"Ooh, this all sounds quite interesting," Rachel said, propping her feet on another chair and taking a sip of tea. "Tell all."

"Alex Kincaid's daughter Bella needs a bra," Juliet stated. "And Lucy was the one to inform him of the fact." She glanced back at Lucy. "You did talk to him, didn't you?"

"Yes." Lucy poured herself a cup of tea from the big blue pot and joined them at the table. She seemed to have relaxed a bit. "Most awkward conversation *ever*."

"Talking to Alex Kincaid about bras?" Rachel snickered. "But he is a hottie."

"Which made it even more awkward," Lucy answered. She leaned her head back against the chair. "But the kicker is, he asked me to go with Bella to buy her the bra."

Rachel's mouth dropped and Juliet shook her head. "He did not!"

"He did."

"That's hardly in your job description," Rachel said, and Lucy sighed.

"I'm doing it as a favor."

"What a chicken he is," Rachel said, seeming to

luxuriate in this statement. "I bought my sister Lily her first bra. It's not that bad." There was a moment's silence, and Juliet wondered what Lucy was thinking, if she wished her big sister had been around to buy her bras and tell her about getting your period. By the time Lucy had hit puberty, Juliet had been out of her life for six years.

"My mother bought me my bra and it was awful," Lucy said after a moment. "She kept speechifying about how I was entering the realm of womanhood, a flower with buds of femininity."

Rachel let out a crack of laughter and even Juliet managed a smile. When she'd needed a bra or anything at that age, Fiona had given her some money and dropped her off at the Meadowhall Centre in Sheffield. She'd shopped for herself, and Fiona hadn't even asked about her purchases. But at least there had been money then; before Fiona had made it as an artist, when they'd been living in a council flat and eating beans on toast nearly every night, Juliet hadn't had new clothes at all. A kindly neighbor had passed on her daughter's well-worn hand-me-downs, which Juliet had accepted gratefully. Fiona had neither noticed nor cared.

But now Juliet decided she was glad she'd bought a bra for herself at age twelve rather than Fiona posturing so ridiculously, using everything in her life to make some kind of cultural or political point.

Although would she have preferred it when she was twelve, or would she have rather Fiona shown an interest in her, any interest, even if it was just to throw yet more attention onto herself?

That was a question Juliet couldn't answer.

"So when will you take her?" Rachel asked Lucy.

"Tomorrow. She's suspended from school at the moment, so we'll go during the day. Alex is even giving me time off work, fully paid."

"He really is desperate," Rachel remarked.

"I think he is," Lucy answered quietly. "It's got to be very tough, raising two daughters on your own."

Had their mother had it tough? Juliet had never spared a single moment of sympathy for Fiona, and she wouldn't now. She'd ignored her first daughter and chosen to have the second on her own. She'd deserved whatever difficulties she'd encountered.

"Good thing he's got you, then," Rachel told Lucy cheerfully. "Although God only knows what he's going to ask you to do next."

Lucy blushed at that, and Juliet wondered just what her half sister felt for her boss.

A knock sounded at the back door, and all three women turned to gaze at the blurred figure standing behind the pane of glass. Juliet felt her insides lurch as she recognized that still, solid form, the untidy shock of brown hair. Peter.

189

"What on earth . . . ?" she murmured, and felt herself blushing just as Lucy had as she went to answer the door.

"Afternoon, Juliet." Peter stood there, a potted miniature rosebush in his hands. He held it out to Juliet, who stared at it. "For you. To make up for the one that got et."

"It was just a few petals," Juliet muttered. Her face felt fiery. She couldn't remember the last time she'd actually blushed.

"Peter," Rachel called, and Juliet heard a gleeful interest in her friend's voice. "Why don't you come in and put your feet up for a bit? We're all having a cuppa."

Peter glanced at Lucy and Rachel sitting at the table, both of them staring at him rather avidly, and gave a slow smile. "Don't mind if I do," he said, and stepped around Juliet. He put the rosebush on the counter. Rachel poured him a cup of tea, while Juliet simply stood there, like a lemon.

"You must be Lucy," he said with a nod for her sister, and Lucy looked slightly startled that he knew her name.

"Yes . . ."

"Peter's a neighbor," Juliet explained stiffly. "And everyone knows everything in this village, anyway." She sounded almost spiteful, and there was a moment's awkward silence before Rachel broke it.

"Sheep getting out, then?" she asked as she loaded Peter's tea with milk and sugar. "Wandering into Juliet's garden?"

"Just the one," Juliet said. She whisked the rosebush off the counter and put it on the windowsill, simply to have something to do. "Really, Peter, you didn't have to go to such trouble."

"It wasn't any trouble," Peter answered. Even though her back was to them, Juliet could feel Lucy's and Rachel's speculative looks. This was awful, and yet she realized she didn't feel angry or annoyed. Discomfited, yes, definitely. But also . . . elated.

"So who's going to the pub for quiz night?" Rachel asked, gazing at each of them in turn. "Lucy? You fancy giving it a whirl? You'd trump everyone on any American questions."

"I don't know about that," Lucy said. "American reality TV shows, maybe. What's a pub quiz?"

"Exactly what it says on the tin," Rachel answered, which earned her another blank look from Lucy. "You go to the pub, have a pint or a glass of wine, and answer twenty questions. You work in teams of four, and the winner gets a free bottle of plonk."

"Plonk . . ."

"Wine!" Rachel shook her head, laughing. "I thought you were British."

"I left this country when I was six. Plonk and pub quizzes were not part of my childhood vocabulary."

"Well, you need to get up to speed, then. It's Thursday night. Juliet?" Rachel turned to her, and Juliet could tell she was on a mission. "You'll come with Lucy." It was not a question.

Everything in Juliet both yearned and resisted. She'd lived in Hartley-by-the-Sea for ten years and she'd never gone to a pub quiz. She'd barely gone to the pub, except after a parish council meeting, when everyone had gone out for a pint, and she had shyly, tentatively joined them, staying silent.

"We've got a team right here," Peter said. "The four of us, unless you're already on a team, Rachel?"

"They can do without me," Rachel answered airily. She glanced around at everyone, smiling with beady determination. "So it's settled."

Peter smiled back, slow and easy. "I guess it is."

Juliet gave a little shake of her head, incredulous at how quickly it had all been managed. She sneaked a glance at Peter, discomfited all over again at how natural he looked, sitting there in her kitchen, one of her pottery mugs cradled between his big hands. He wore dirty, faded jeans and an Aran jumper with a frayed hem and holes in both elbows. His fingernails were rimed with black dirt, as any farmer's were, and there were deep creases by his eyes from spending a life in wind and rain, as well as the occasional bout of sunshine.

He met her gaze, and Juliet realized she'd been staring at him. Worse, she could tell he'd noticed. He gave her a very slight smile, and she could see knowledge and understanding and a touch of humor in his eyes, and quickly she turned away, moving the rosebush from the windowsill to the counter again, just because.

15
Lucy

LUCY CAME DOWNSTAIRS THE next morning buoyed by a determined optimism to enjoy her afternoon outing with Bella. She'd had a good time last night, chatting with Peter and Rachel and Juliet. Rachel had intimidated her at first, with that knowing smile. Plus she was about eight feet tall and had masses of red hair. Lucy had felt like Minnie Mouse standing next to Boudicca.

But Rachel had invited her to the pub quiz, and Juliet had even agreed, and they were actually going to be a team. Plus there was the very interesting Peter, who'd brought Juliet flowers.

"He's just a neighbor," Juliet had told her dismissively when Lucy had asked who he was, after Peter and Rachel had gone. "A sheep farmer. We're on the parish council together."

"Parish council?"

"The local governing body for the village," Juliet explained. "We liaise with the county council, and organize village events, and start campaigns for everyone to clean up their dogs' poo. Stimulating stuff."

"Important stuff," Lucy had answered. "I nearly

stepped in dog poo this morning, so you'd better do your job." Juliet hadn't even cracked a smile; since Peter and Rachel had left, she'd seemed rather brittle, and she kept moving the rosebush around the kitchen.

The exchange had been enough for Lucy's optimism to return in full force, and now she headed off to school, determined to rock this afternoon with Bella.

"Bella's here," Alex announced just after lunchtime.

Lucy glanced up, blinking the world back into focus. He stood in the doorway of the reception area, lines of tension bracketing his mouth as Bella came up the school lane. Somehow one o'clock had crept up on her and now, despite all her cheery optimism, butterflies swarmed in her stomach.

"Super."

He cleared his throat. "Let me give you some money. . . ."

"No, I'd like to do this for Bella, and a couple of bras don't cost much."

Color touched Alex's cheekbones, although whether because she'd said she'd pay or used the b-word, Lucy didn't know. "I insist," he began, but Bella was coming inside the school and so with a nod he left it, at least for now.

Bella studiously ignored her father as Lucy gathered her coat and purse. She'd checked the trains to Whitehaven and seen there was one just a little bit after one o'clock; they could come back on the four o'clock train, which would give them long enough for what they needed to do, she hoped. She'd thought about asking to borrow Juliet's car, but she was terrible at driving stick shift and the afternoon had enough potential obstacles already.

"Ready?" she asked Bella in that same over-bright voice she'd used before, and the girl didn't answer. Still, this was going to go well. Lucy would make sure of it.

She kept up a cheerful monologue, saying whatever came into her head, which included a lot of inane facts about reality TV shows and her favorite Disney movies and why Hartley-by-the-Sea's pub was called the Hangman's Noose, all the way to the train station. Bella didn't speak at all. By the time they'd boarded the train, Lucy had lapsed into a weary silence, realizing that three hours with Bella was going to feel long indeed.

Lucy had been to Whitehaven only once before to buy the waterproof and Wellies she'd forgotten to bring, so her only acquaintance with the town was the one pedestrianized street with a variety of shops, including the hiking store where she'd bought her gear. She'd done a search online last night, however, and found a department store on Lowther Street with a lingerie department.

Bella slouched after her, deliberately staying

several paces behind as Lucy walked past a florist's and a gourmet coffee shop, a café and a museum about rum smuggling, looking for the shop in question.

"Ah, here we are," she said brightly, and held open the door for Bella.

"I can't believe we're doing this," Bella muttered, and Lucy followed her into the shop.

"To be honest, I can't believe we are, either," she answered as she wove her way through the shoe and accessory departments. The store had a lovably slightly shabby quality to it; clearly it had been around a long time, although the escalator that dominated the center of the space looked shiny and new. She could see the lingerie section in the distance, a lacy sea of white and pale pink with the occasional splotch of crimson or black, and turned to give Bella a reassuring smile. "Shouldn't take long."

Bella just folded her arms across her chest and stared straight ahead. Poor girl. No matter how nice Lucy tried to be, the whole experience still had to be mortifying.

Lucy inched her way across an aisle of what looked like G-cup satin Wonderbras, looking for the teen section. She really, really, for Bella's sake—and, okay, a little bit of her own—didn't want to have to ask.

"Oh, no," Bella muttered under her breath, and Lucy turned to see a buxom sales assistant heading towards them like a ship in full sail, a wide smile on her face.

"Hello, my lovelies. Can I help with anything?"

Next to her Lucy felt Bella stiffen. She shook her head firmly. "Just looking," she said, and the sales assistant retreated a few feet away, watching them expectantly. Lucy moved to the next aisle.

"Thank you," Bella whispered after a pause, her head lowered, her hair hanging down to hide her face.

"Believe it or not, I remember being your age," Lucy answered in a low voice. They'd reached the end of the lingerie department and had no luck finding the appropriate bras. "However, I think we might be stuck. I can't find what we're looking for and I might have to ask Miss Double D over there."

Bella let out a huff of laughter, quickly smothered. "Keep looking," she muttered, turning away from the sales assistant. *"Please."*

Fortunately they found a "Young Miss" section at the end of a rack of sports bras, kept in boxes and left there almost as an afterthought. Lucy scooped up a couple in different sizes, and then impulsively grabbed a bra in her size to cover the incriminating boxes. "Okay, we're good," she told Bella. "But you do have to try these on, I'm afraid."

Bella eyed her with disbelief. "Are you kidding me?"

Lucy glanced down and saw she'd managed to pick up a purple satin push-up bra. She let out a little laugh. "That one's for me, just for cover," she explained. She gestured to the boxes. "These are yours."

Bella's face was bright red and she looked away. "Fine."

Lucy marched to the changing rooms, brandishing the purple bra. "I'd like to try this on," she told the assistant, who gestured to a row of empty, curtained stalls.

"Just give us a shout if you need a different size," she said cheerily, and Lucy nodded.

"Will do."

Alone in the corridor of changing rooms, she turned to a still-mortified Bella. "Okay, I'm going to try on this purple monster, and you try on yours. They should fit well, not too snug, not too loose, okay? The panel in the middle should touch your breastbone, not pull away from it. If it pulls away, you need a larger cup size."

Clearly that was TMI for Bella, for she wordlessly grabbed the boxes and disappeared into one of the stalls. Lucy glanced down at the purple bra and decided that she might as well try it on.

And actually, she decided a moment later, having never owned a push-up bra before, she could definitely see the appeal. She'd never looked so perky.

"How are you doing in there?" she called to

Bella, and received a suffocated "Fine" in response.

A couple of minutes later they met back out in the corridor; Bella's bras had been stuffed back into the boxes.

"Did you find one that fits?" Lucy asked, and she nodded and held out one of the boxes. "Great. I'll go get a few in that size and you can take yourself off to another department if you want. Just in case the sales assistant feels like having a conversation about our purchases."

With obvious relief Bella hightailed it out of the lingerie department. Lucy found a couple of bras in the same size, in various colors, and brought them to the register. The sales assistant engaged her in a detailed conversation about the escalator, which had been bought from the London Olympics for the impressive sum of four hundred thousand pounds. It was, the woman told her proudly, Whitehaven's only escalator.

"We had a little party when we opened it. Champers, even, and a Tom Cruise look-alike."

"Wow, that sounds amazing," Lucy told her, quite sincerely, and then, bag in hand, went to find Bella.

Bella was loitering by the cosmetics counters, reminding Lucy that she'd been wearing quite a lot of war paint yesterday. Somehow she doubted the girl had paid for all of it herself, and Alex didn't seem like the kind of dad who shelled out for eyeliner and crimson lipstick.

"Hey." Lucy joined her by a display of sparkly eye shadow in every color of the rainbow, the bras safely hidden in an opaque plastic shopping bag. She nodded towards the eye shadow. "What do you think? I'm fond of the purple, myself." She lowered her voice to a whisper. "It would match my new bra."

Bella's mouth quirked in a tiny smile—sort of like the way her dad's did—before she turned away. "Who are you trying to impress?" she asked in a deliberately bored drawl. "My dad?"

Lucy hesitated, then decided for lightness. "Somehow I don't think the eye shadow or the bra would impress your dad, Bella. But if you're worried I'm trying to make a move on him, I promise you, I'm not."

Bella turned back to her, eyes narrowed. "Why not?"

"What do you mean, why not?"

Bella shrugged. "He's single. He's not that old. You're single, right?"

"Yes, but—"

"He's okay looking, for a dad. So why aren't you interested?" She subjected Lucy to a challenging stare, making her realize she wasn't fooling anyone with her paltry promises.

"Well, I'm only here for four months, first of all," she said after a moment. "And yes, I'm single now, but I just got out of a long-term relationship and I'm not looking for another one quite so soon.

And your dad is okay looking, true, but you might have noticed he can be a little scary? A little intimidating?" She tried to elicit a smile, but Bella just looked away.

"Whatever," she said in a dismissive tone, making Lucy feel as if she rather than Bella had brought Alex into the conversation. She decided to drop it. She really didn't want to talk about Alex with Bella, and she definitely didn't intend to trip all over herself trying to explain why she wasn't interested. Because she was afraid that wasn't even true.

Sighing, she nodded towards the door. "How about we hit Boots for a mini shopping spree and then have a hot chocolate before we go home?"

Interest lit Bella's eyes even though she still looked wary. "A mini shopping spree?"

"I think you could use a new lipstick," Lucy said easily. And preferably not one she suspected Bella had shoplifted. "Maybe in a slightly more subtle shade, something your father wouldn't mind you wearing out of the house?"

"He hates everything I wear," Bella answered with a shrug. "Everything I do."

Lucy chose to let that one go and they headed back out to Lowther Street.

She bought Bella a lip gloss in a neutral shade and some purple eye shadow, and then they headed over to a café that promised bowl-sized cups of hot chocolate with lashings of whipped cream.

Seated across from Bella as she slurped a spoonful of whipped cream, Lucy wondered what on earth they would talk about now.

Bella surprised her by asking her suddenly, "Why were you bullied in school?"

Lucy licked her spoon clean before stirring her hot chocolate with it. "Well, surprisingly, it also had to do with boobs. Well, boob singular, actually."

Bella let out a snort of incredulous laughter. "What do you mean?"

"My mother is an artist. Modern stuff, very cutting-edge, or so everyone says. She made a giant sculpture of a boob and it was displayed in a public park in Boston. It was a huge deal, in the newspapers, everything. And on the first day of seventh grade I was nicknamed Boob Girl."

Bella didn't laugh, much to Lucy's surprise. She'd been speaking lightly, inviting her to share the joke, even though the memory still stung, perhaps because her mother *still* had the power to make her life miserable.

"That sucks," Bella said after a moment. She slurped a spoonful of whipped cream from her hot chocolate. "Didn't she know how it would affect you?"

"I don't really think she thought about it."

"Did you tell her?"

"I tried. I asked to change schools actually, because, you know, the damage had already been done. Even if the sculpture had been removed, which it was eventually, I'd still be called Boob Girl."

Bella nodded wisely. "Yeah, you would have been."

"So I thought changing schools might help, although in retrospect I don't think it would have. Kids would have still known about the sculpture."

"So what happened?"

"Well, my mother refused to let me change schools, because she said I shouldn't care what small-minded people thought." Bella rolled her eyes, and Lucy smiled. "I pretty much had the same reaction. And it did go away eventually. The sculpture as well as the teasing."

"You mean people stopped calling you that?"

"Yes, after a while."

Bella slowly stirred her drink. "Do you think people will stop teasing me?" she asked in a low voice, her head lowered. Lucy had the sudden motherly urge to tuck her hair behind her ear. Thank goodness she resisted. She didn't want to care about this girl, didn't want to care about whether Bella cared about her, but already she felt her resolve to stay disinterested and uninvolved slipping.

"Yes, definitely," she said, "although I can't promise it will happen tomorrow, or even next week. But bullies get tired of making the same lame joke over and over, trust me. And sadly, they usually just move on to someone else."

"As long as it's not me."

"Well, you could stand up to them," Lucy suggested. "I know it's not easy, but I realize now that bullies are actually secret cowards. They can dish it out, but they can't take it. So if you act like you don't care, like you think they're the pathetic ones for making their lame jokes, you might be surprised at how they scurry back to their holes." She'd tried to act as if she hadn't cared, had kept smiling even when everything inside her had heaved with misery. And while they hadn't precisely *scurried,* the bullies had left her alone eventually.

Bella didn't seem to agree. She shook her head, licking whipped cream off her spoon. "I don't think they would."

"You don't know unless you try. And if you're already being bullied, it's not like you have a lot to lose."

Bella stared down at her hot chocolate again. "I wish I hadn't been bullied in the first place," she said in a low voice. "I wish my stupid mum had bought me a stupid bra."

Unthinkingly, wanting only to comfort Bella when she was so obviously hurting, Lucy reached over and covered the girl's hand with her own. After barely a second, Bella yanked her hand away. "I'm sorry," Lucy said quietly. "You must miss your mum a lot."

"What do you know about it?" Bella huffed, and

Lucy didn't answer. She didn't know much about it at all. She didn't miss her mother; she missed the mother she wished she'd had. But she couldn't explain that to Bella.

They wandered around Whitehaven after they'd had their hot chocolates, looking at the shops and killing another hour. Lucy tried to engage Bella in conversation, but each time Bella's answers became more monosyllabic and unfriendly and finally she stopped speaking altogether, so Lucy stopped trying.

By the time they boarded the train back to Hartley-by-the-Sea, Lucy was feeling unaccountably tired. She was so weary of trying with people and feeling as if she were getting nowhere at all.

Just once she wanted someone to try with her. Too bad no one was lining up for that role, in any capacity.

The clouds had cleared and the sky was a lovely, deep blue as they headed down the high street to Alex's house. Lucy was a little curious as to where Alex lived; she certainly wasn't expecting the tumbledown terraced Victorian with the crooked and cracked front steps, a wild, unmanageable garden, and a sharply peaked roof of weathered slate. It was in need of a lot of love and DIY, but it was charming too, the kind of house that should have elves living at the bottom of the garden.

"It's a mess, I know," Bella muttered, opening

the gate, which squeaked in loud protest. She walked up the front steps and fiddled with a key before she managed to unlock the front door. "Dad's not home yet," she tossed over her shoulder. "You don't have to wait or anything."

Lucy hesitated, then followed Bella up the steps and into the dark front hallway, which was a mess of cluttered papers, books, boots, and coats. Charlie, the Lab she'd met at the beach, came lumbering out of the kitchen, his tongue hanging out expectantly. Bella dropped down to her knees and petted him while he slobbered over her before turning to Lucy.

"Umm . . . good doggy." Lucy patted him on his head. Apparently this was enough to win the Lab's devotion, because he threw himself onto the floor, his chunky body draped over her feet as he offered his tummy to be scratched.

Bella rose and kicked off her clunky boots, adding them to the jumble on the floor. "You don't have to stay," she said again, and Lucy couldn't tell from her tone whether she wanted her to.

She should just take herself off, she supposed. Check in at school before heading back to Tarn House. Juliet's warm and cozy kitchen was a sight more enticing than the cold darkness of Alex's house.

Alex's house felt unlived in, unloved. The kind of house that felt empty even when there were people in it. Bella had slouched into the kitchen, and Charlie scrambled to his feet and trotted after her. After a moment Lucy followed.

The kitchen was even more of a disaster than the hall; breakfast dishes littered the circular table by the window, the bowls half-filled with milk and soggy cereal. A cereal box lay on its side, trailing bits of granola. A single cup of coffee, only half-drunk, had been left by the sink, along with a pint of milk, which was now probably sour.

Lucy wasn't particularly tidy, but she had a mad urge to clean everything up and make some nourishing meal for Alex and Poppy to come home to. To turn this cold, dark, depressing house into a place that was cozy and comfortable, warm and welcoming.

Not your problem, she reminded herself. Even so, she put the milk back in the fridge.

Bella let Charlie out into the back garden and then turned to face Lucy belligerently. "Why are you still here?" she asked, not bothering to disguise her hostility, and Lucy blinked before shaking her head slowly, her hand still on the door of the fridge.

"I don't know," she said honestly, and took a step towards the door. "I'll leave you to it, then. Your dad will be home soon, I'm sure."

Bella shrugged, but Lucy thought she saw disappointment or even hurt in the girl's eyes.

No, she was being fanciful. Wishing Bella needed her, wanted her, when really the girl didn't.

"Okay, then," she said, and with Bella giving her the death stare of indifference, she turned around and headed for the hall.

Stupid to care, she told herself. *Stupid to feel hurt. You barely know these people.* She wrenched open the front door and stepped out, only to collide with what felt like a brick wall but was, she realized almost instantly, Alex Kincaid's chest.

He grabbed her by the shoulders, holding her still for a second, before he thrust her away from him so hard and fast she nearly fell over.

"Lucy." He stared at her, his expression unreadable and yet also strangely fierce. "You're back," he said, and Lucy nodded.

"Yes, I dropped Bella off. I was just leaving. Mission accomplished, so . . ."

"Thank you," he said, and she could tell he really meant it. "But you can't just run off. . . ."

"She could stay for dinner," Poppy offered, ducking out from behind him to offer Lucy a wide smile. "Are we having sausages again?"

"No—," Alex began, and Lucy blinked at the blatant rejection.

"No, of course not, I don't want to intrude," she said quickly, practically tripping over her words. She sidled past Alex, trying not to touch him again, and stepped out onto the front stoop. "I was just seeing Bella home, and I'll see you tomorrow at school. You too, Poppy." She waved, a bit frantically, and then stilled in shock when Alex put his hand on her shoulder.

"I didn't mean no to you staying for supper," he said. "I meant no to sausages. We've had them two nights in a row and I'm sick of them. And in any case, we don't have any more. I can't promise a stellar meal, but it—it would be nice if you stayed for supper."

Lucy just kept her jaw from dropping. She blinked at him instead. Was this just a thank-you for buying the bra, or . . .

No, best not to think about motives. "Well . . . ," she began, her gaze sliding to Bella, who was standing in the hallway, her arms folded, definitely not looking thrilled by the prospect.

"Oh, please!" Poppy cried, dancing forward on her tiptoes. "We never have anyone over, ever, and you're so nice at school. *Please.*"

Lucy's heart softened at that—how could it not? Then she looked back up at Alex, who was staring at her rather grimly. "I don't know," she began, because she really didn't. She had a feeling only one of the Kincaids wanted her to stay, and she was seven years old.

"I do mean it," Alex said. "We would like you to stay."

Bella let out a dramatic, excuse-me-but-I'm-here-too-you-know kind of sigh, and Alex gave Lucy a wry smile that just about melted her heart. She nodded. "Okay, I'll stay. Thank you."

With a scowl Bella turned on her heel and flounced upstairs. Alex watched her go before turning to Lucy. "Shopping trip went all right?"

"Yes, actually." Lucy glanced up the stairs. "I'm not sure . . ."

"Trust me, that's par for the course. Don't take it personally."

"Sometimes it's hard not to," Lucy answered, "but I know what you mean."

Poppy pirouetted down the hall into the kitchen, dropping her arms as she came to a stop in the doorway.

"Daddy, the kitchen is a mess."

"Oh . . ." He glanced around the kitchen, his face reddening. "Sorry," he muttered as he whisked a few cereal bowls, Cheerios encrusted to their sides, off the table and dumped them in the sink. "We had a rushed morning."

"I'm not exactly a neatnik myself," Lucy replied, and righted the cereal box, folding the cardboard flaps back in before sweeping a mess of granola off the table and into her hand. She looked around for the trash can and Alex pointed to the corner.

Meanwhile Poppy had opened the fridge and was peering into it dispiritedly. "Daddy," she said, turning to look at him over her shoulder with a grave expression, "there's nothing to eat."

Lucy watched as he came to stand behind her, resting one hand on her shoulder in a way that made her insides ache. Did he hug his children? He was obviously trying with both of them, even if he was having a hard time.

"You're right, Poppy," he said. "I suppose I need to do a shop." Lucy could see that the only things left in the yawning, brightly lit expanse were some sad-looking lettuce, the pint of milk she'd put back, a piece of moldy cheddar, and a few pots of yogurt that she suspected were past their sell-by date.

"Hmm," she said, and when she risked a glance at him, she saw he was smiling at her. She looked away; that one shared smile seemed to energize every nerve ending.

"How about fish and chips?" he suggested, and Poppy clapped her hands.

"Ooh! Yes! I love chips!"

"There's a takeaway in Egremont that does a good one," he told Lucy. "I can nip out and get us some, if you don't mind waiting here with the girls."

"Sounds good," Lucy said. "I haven't had fish and chips in ages."

"I don't have to eat the fish, do I, Daddy?" Poppy asked, and he ruffled her hair.

"No, Poppy, you don't. You never do."

"What about Bella? Is she a fan of fish and chips?" Lucy asked.

"I'm not sure Bella is a fan of anything at the moment," he said, and then winced as they both saw his oldest daughter scowling at them from the kitchen doorway.

"I'm not hungry," she snapped, and turned to go back upstairs.

"Don't, Bella," Alex barked. "You can stay here with Lucy."

Wonderful, more time with Bella. "Great," Lucy said, trying to inject her voice with enthusiasm she most certainly didn't feel.

Alex shot her one quick, grateful smile and grabbed his car keys before heading towards the door.

"So." Lucy smiled at both girls. "How about we tidy up and set the table?" Bella didn't answer, but at least she started chucking things into the sink. Hopefully she wouldn't break a bowl. Poppy put the cereal away and Lucy loaded the dishwasher. This all felt surreal, being in Alex's house, doing his dishes, looking after his daughters.

She should have said no to dinner. For her own sake, as well as for Poppy's and Bella's. The girls were obviously fragile; the last thing they needed was to become attached to someone who was going to leave. And the last thing she needed was to start caring about people who weren't going to let her into their lives, not really. Not enough.

She turned to Poppy. "Where do you keep the plates?"

By the time Alex came home with cartons of chips and paper-wrapped fish, the kitchen was tidy and the table was set. Poppy had chatted to Lucy the whole while, and Bella had suffered her in silence, but overall Lucy decided their time together had been a success.

Alex came into the kitchen and blinked in surprise, then did a self-conscious double take that had Lucy smiling. There was something about the way Alex joked that was endearing; it was as if he had to think about it first.

"I thought I'd walked into the wrong house," he said as he put the bags on the counter. "Poppy, will you get the milk?"

"That smells really good," Lucy said. The scent of fish and chips was wafting from the bags as Alex unpacked them.

"Good and greasy."

They all sat down at the table and Charlie wiggled underneath it, clearly hoping for the crumbs. Alex dished out the fish and chips while Lucy poured milk, after surreptitiously sniffing it first. It hadn't gone sour. Bella was still doing her surly, silent thing, but Lucy decided to let it roll off her. She'd gotten along with Bella, more or less, this afternoon.

Poppy's happy chatter dominated dinnertime, and afterwards Bella disappeared upstairs again and Poppy went to watch TV in Alex's bedroom; he told Lucy it was the only TV in the house because he didn't want it overtaking their lives. Lucy, who had a secret passion for reality TV, the more obscure the better, had simply nodded.

Now she stacked the dirty plates in the dishwasher, conscious that she should head home and yet not willing to end the evening.

"You don't have to clean up," Alex said as he came into the kitchen, tossing the empty chip cartons into the bin. "You've done so much already."

"It's not a big deal."

He watched her for a moment, his hip braced against the counter. "Coffee?" he finally asked, and Lucy looked up, fully intending to tell him no, she needed to go home, it had been a lovely evening, and so on.

"Yes, please."

Mentally she shook her head at herself. She finished loading the dishwasher while Alex made them both coffees, and then took them into the sitting room, which was a surprising oasis of quiet and calm. Distantly from upstairs Lucy could hear Bella's music and Poppy's television program.

"This room isn't too much of a mess," Alex said with a rueful glance at the overstuffed sofa, which had only a few of Poppy's stuffed animals scattered across it. "Mainly because we hardly ever use it."

"It's a lovely room." A coal fireplace with a painted tile surround took up one wall, and French doors overlooked the untidy garden in the back.

"Yes, I always liked this room," Alex agreed.

He'd joined her on the sofa, and although there was an entire seat cushion between them, Lucy still felt conscious of him: his body, his heat, his whole presence. Charlie had lumbered in after them and now he threw himself down at their feet with a theatrical groan of contentment.

Lucy curled up on the cushions, cradling the coffee mug in her hands, striving to make the scene seem normal. And it did seem normal, in a hyperaware sort of way. "It must be hard, to keep things going all the time on your own," she said. "I don't know how single parents do it, really."

Alex gave a little grimace. "Neither do I."

"You mentioned grandparents? Are those your parents?"

"No." He spoke rather flatly. "Anna's parents. They live down near London, but they like to see the girls as often as they can."

Lucy nodded, noting the way he'd spoken about them wanting to see the girls, not him, and wondering if that was significant. "And what about your parents?"

"They're both dead."

"I'm sorry."

He shrugged, his gaze sliding away from her. "What about you?" he asked after a moment. "This famous artist mother of yours?"

Lucy shrugged. She'd rather talk about anything than her mother. "That's all there is to say, really."

He turned back to look at her with a faint smile. "Surely not. Is she very famous?"

"In certain circles." She hesitated, then said, "Her name is Fiona Bagshaw. Have you heard of her?"

He gave her a quizzical look and shook his head. "Can't say that I have. Should I have done? I'm a bit of a Philistine when it comes to modern art."

"Thank goodness for that," Lucy answered, and then felt stupidly disloyal to her mother. It wasn't as if her mother had been loyal to her. "She does sculptures and installations for museums and public parks, stuff like that. She also tends to be quoted in articles and on TV, at least in America. If a newspaper wants a controversial opinion, they generally ask her."

Alex nodded slowly. "I see." He paused, his gaze sweeping over her. "And let me guess. Your artistic endeavors are a little different from hers?"

"You could say that." She gave him a crooked smile, even though her mother's scathing contempt for her work still burned. Still *hurt*. "Twee water-colors, she called them. Distinctly uninspired and amateurish."

"Ouch."

Lucy shrugged. "She was probably right."

"You can't say that."

"Neither can you, since you haven't seen them."

He stretched his legs out, resting one arm along

217

the back of the sofa, his fingers only inches from her shoulder. "Still, I think I like the sound of them, at least compared to whatever it is your mother does." He arched an eyebrow, waiting, and Lucy managed a smile.

"She started out sculpting breasts. Huge, lumpy ones."

Alex winced and a little giggle escaped her. She was glad *someone* wasn't taking her mother's art seriously. "What has she moved on to, then?" he asked.

"Oh, well. Um . . . the male anatomy."

"I think I definitely prefer the watercolors."

"Even if you haven't seen them?"

"Even so. What are they of, exactly?"

"I do nature scenes. Wildflowers, mostly." The antithesis of what her mother did, essentially, although whether she'd set out to be her mother's opposite, artistically anyway, Lucy didn't know.

"They definitely sound like more my kind of thing." He held her gaze then, or perhaps she held his; and suddenly she was intensely aware that the arm he'd stretched out along the back of the sofa was quite close to her. If she leaned back and tilted her head to one side, his fingers would brush her hair, maybe even her cheek.

She had no intention of doing that, of course.

Just thinking about it. Quite a lot.

"So what happened to make you leave Boston?" Alex asked. He broke their locked gazes, shifting in his seat, the second's worth of intensity now sliding into awkwardness. "If you don't mind me asking."

Amazingly, she didn't mind. She'd wanted to keep it secret, or at least separate from her life in Hartley-by-the-Sea, but she felt Alex might understand, maybe even sympathize, which was an incredible thought, considering a week ago she'd thought he was an ass.

"You don't have to tell me," Alex continued when Lucy hadn't said anything. "It's not really my business. . . ."

"It's going to sound kind of lame," Lucy said. "Or maybe ridiculous. I don't know."

"Now I really am curious."

"I was working as a barista in this gallery café, like I told you before. It was just a way to pay the bills and get a toe into the art world."

"Didn't your mother give you a toe in?" Alex asked, and Lucy made a face.

"That was part of the problem." She felt a familiar tightness in her chest. It had been over a month since this had happened and yet it still hurt to remember. "I didn't want to succeed because of who my mother was," she explained. "Is. I wanted to do it on my own. So I worked at the café and spent every spare waking minute working on getting a portfolio together, something I could show galleries." She took another breath, let it out slowly. In the distance she heard a burst of staccato laughter from the television. It sounded like gunfire.

"And did you get a portfolio together?" Alex asked after a moment.

"Yes, and the gallery where I worked agreed to show it. My boss said he thought I had promise. But it turned out he'd only agreed so my mother would come to his gallery. She had—has—that kind of pull. I told him she would come because, well, she's my mom. I thought she would come for me."

"She didn't come," Alex stated flatly.

Lucy let out a laugh. "That would have been bad enough, I suppose, although I think I could have handled it. I hope I could have. But she did more—or less, depending on how you look at it. She wrote an editorial about it—about me—in the Boston newspaper."

"What?" Alex lurched upright, and even in her remembered misery Lucy smiled to see him look so indignant on her behalf. "What about, exactly?"

"It was titled 'Why I Will Not Give My Daughter a Free Ride' and it was all about how genuinely terrible my work was and how she couldn't support it simply because I was related to her by blood. How endorsing such"—she made her hands into clawlike quotation marks—"*tedious mediocrity* would compromise her artistic integrity, and encourage other, similar would-be hacks to pick up a paintbrush." She practically had the whole, awful editorial memorized, which was pretty sad in itself.

Alex swore under his breath and Lucy forced a smile. "Of course, when my mother makes a statement in the press, everyone takes it up and runs with it. She thrives on being controversial. So for a while every blog and gossip site seemed to have it. Someone found a photo of one of my paintings and that went up too." Along with the thousands of comments Lucy couldn't keep from reading; so many of them had been in a similar vein as her mother's editorial, and although her friends had told her not to pay attention to Internet trolls, it had still hurt. A lot.

"That must have been pretty terrible," Alex said quietly.

"My boss withdrew the offer of the showing. The bad press was simply too much, he said." She thought about telling Alex about Thomas, about how he'd said all the media attention was "bad for the boys," and how Lucy had tried the cheapest, oldest trick in the world and threatened to break up with him, just so he'd beg her to stay.

He hadn't.

But she'd told Alex enough of her sob story. So instead she just shrugged and leaned her head back against the sofa. "Yeah, it all pretty much sucked." She made a face. "Sorry."

Alex frowned. "For what?"

"Bella said you don't let her say that word."

He smiled then, that lovely little quirk. "You're not Bella. And in any case, you just heard me swear. I'm a bit of a hypocrite."

"You're allowed."

"Am I?" His smile disappeared then and for a second he looked so sad that Lucy wanted to put her arms around him, just for a hug. Okay, and yes, maybe to feel that wonderfully hard chest against her one more time. She was only human, after all.

"Solo parenting has got to be really challenging," she said, willing her gaze to move upwards from his hard chest to his face. Although looking at his face made her think of other ways she wanted to touch him. Her thumb against his lips. Her palm cradling his cheek.

"It is. And I'm doing a crap job of it, to be honest." He smiled wryly, but his eyes were still dark and bleak.

"You're doing the best you can, Alex. That's all anyone can do."

"And my best is crap."

"Keep saying that and you might need to put some money in the naughty jar."

He raised his eyebrows. "The naughty jar?"

"A jar you put money in every time you say a bad word."

"Did you have one of those growing up?"

"Yes, but funnily enough it was my idea. My mother had no limits on language, or on anything really. She was all about pushing boundaries, indulging whims." Her own, at least.

"So making a naughty jar was your way of creating limits," Alex filled in thoughtfully, and Lucy made a face.

"That's a neat bit of psychoanalysis."

"True, though?"

She nodded slowly. "Maybe." She'd certainly wanted the typical, normal childhood, the dog and the picket fence and definitely the dad. Fiona had scorned all those things, and believed Lucy should too. *I'm raising you to be a freethinker, Lucy, to be free of the shackles of a patriarchal society that insists you believe the lie that is domestic slavery.*

"So did your mother ever put money in the naughty jar?" Alex asked, and Lucy shook her head, her cheeks heating, because a naughty jar suddenly sounded . . . well, *naughty*. And she was starting to think some definitely naughty thoughts.

The silence lengthened between them, stretching tautly as they stared at each other again.

Another burst of laughter sounded from the television upstairs, and they both jumped, and then laughed nervously. If there had been a moment, and Lucy wasn't entirely sure there had been, at least outside of her fantasies, it was well and truly broken now.

Alex glanced at his watch and she rose from the

sofa, nearly tripping over Charlie, who let out a contented groan.

"It's getting late, isn't it?" she said, practically babbling in an effort to sound normal. "Really late. You'll want to put Poppy to bed. I should leave you to it."

He rose too, and as he moved, she breathed in the clean scent of soap that lingered on his skin. "Thank you, Lucy," he said, "for all you did today."

"It wasn't really that much."

"It was. I was clueless about what was going on with Bella, and I needed you to point it out. I'm very grateful."

"Will you talk to her?"

"About her purchases? I don't know. I don't think she'd want me to."

Lucy thought of how defensive and lonely Bella had seemed this afternoon, when they'd had hot chocolate. "She might not admit it, but I think she would."

He grimaced. "Maybe, but I'm not much good at that kind of thing."

"Talking?" Lucy teased, but he took her seriously.

"Pretty much. If it's not work related, if I can't put on my head teacher hat, I'm kind of hopeless." He smiled, but Lucy knew he believed what he'd said.

"A head teacher hat. What does that look like? I wonder."

"Bulletproof helmet. And invisible, of course, since head teachers are superheroes."

"You have to be, to manage a whole school. I can barely manage the reception area."

"You're doing well out there."

She arched an eyebrow. "Card stock and disconnected calls aside?"

"I never said there wasn't room for improvement."

"Oh!" Teasingly, thoughtlessly, Lucy punched his shoulder, and in an equally unthinking reflex Alex caught her hand.

Lucy stilled, her breath coming out in a rush as she felt his large, dry hand encase her much smaller one. This time she didn't think she was imagining the pulse of attraction between them.

Then he let go of her hand, even pushed it back a bit as if he were returning something she'd dropped. How much of that scenario had been in her own head? Lucy gave him a weak smile and turned to go.

Outside it was growing dark, the sky a deep indigo, the village mired in night save for a few streetlights.

"Do you need a torch?" Alex asked. "You're not in Boston anymore."

"Am I in Oz?" Lucy teased, or tried to. She was still feeling shivery from that moment in the sitting room, and she hoped Alex couldn't notice

225

in the dim light of his entry hall. She fumbled for her coat, pushed her arms through the sleeves, and struggled with the zip. "I'll be fine. Tarn House is just up there, anyway." She pointed up the high street; she could see the train station and the pub in the distance.

"All right, then," Alex said, and stepped back, well out of touching range, which Lucy took as a signal.

She walked down the garden path and opened the gate, which squeaked loudly in the stillness of the night; for once, there was no wind. She could feel Alex watching her, and she wondered when he would go back inside.

16
Juliet

JULIET GAZED AT HER wardrobe full of jeans and fleeces and wondered what she should wear to the pub quiz tonight. She had all of four dresses: one for weddings, one for funerals, and two for any festive occasions, one summer, one winter. None of them were appropriate for a pub quiz.

Not, Juliet acknowledged, that she even knew what you were meant to wear. Presumably Lucy would wear something arty and outrageous, and Rachel would smarten up a bit, as she liked to do of an evening. Peter, Juliet could not imagine would wear anything but his usual jeans and holey Aran jumper. And as for her?

"Oh, why bother," she muttered crossly, and grabbed one of her many fleeces. She didn't want to make an effort, or rather, be *seen* to make an effort, and yet she also felt a flicker of dissatisfaction at putting on her same old clothes. Maybe this whole thing was a mistake.

"It's just a bloody pub quiz," she told herself as she yanked a brush through her hair. "Get over it already."

She could hear Lucy humming in the bathroom;

she'd been in a good mood ever since last night, when she'd come home quite late from the bra shopping expedition. Juliet had been up in bed, reading, when she'd heard Lucy come in, humming just as she was now, practically floating up the stairs. She hadn't left her bedroom to ask Lucy how it had gone, and Lucy hadn't come to talk to her, which didn't surprise Juliet and yet still left her just a little bit disappointed.

The next morning she'd taken the plate of sausages and mash she'd left for Lucy out of the warming oven and scraped it into the bin.

Now, with one last glance at her reflection, she left her bedroom and headed downstairs to wait for Lucy. The latest set of walkers had arrived that afternoon, a retired couple who were already tucked up in bed, exhausted from their day of walking from Ennerdale. Juliet settled the dogs and tidied the already-spotless kitchen, her stomach seething with butterflies. *It's just a pub quiz,* she told herself yet again, annoyed with how nervous she was. She was thirty-seven, for heaven's sake, and she was acting as if she were thirteen.

But she didn't do socializing, never had. Her childhood had been spent in isolation, being ignored by Fiona and with no other family that she knew of. After Fiona had become famous when Juliet was nine, life had improved somewhat, even if their relationship hadn't. Juliet had made a few friends in secondary school, boarding her final year with a friend's family. She'd attempted a normal life at university, derailed by her own folly in confronting her mother. In demanding answers.

And in the seventeen years since then, she'd chosen to live a quiet, solitary life. She'd told herself she preferred it. She *had* preferred it until Lucy had come barreling in, stirring up all these feelings, reminding her of how lonely she was.

"You look nice!"

Juliet turned to see Lucy coming down the stairs, grinning at her. "What do you mean?" she asked sharply. "I look like I normally do."

"Which is nice," Lucy answered. "Anyway, you look a little different. Your fleece is pink instead of gray or blue and you've left your hair down. I don't think I've ever seen it that way."

Instinctively Juliet reached up to touch her hair, and then dropped her hand. "And you look like a yeti," she said, glancing at Lucy's fuzzy blue sweater.

"A blue yeti," she agreed. "I love this sweater."

Juliet watched as Lucy slipped her feet into totally unsuitable ballet flats—it had rained most of the day—and her velveteen blazer. She looked pretty and young and so natural, all things Juliet didn't think she'd ever felt. She'd been bitter about Lucy, resented the hell out of her, and right now she realized she felt a little jealous. She wanted to be as relaxed as Lucy was, able to make friends with ease and collect relationships like trinkets. What had happened with Alex Kincaid last night that had Lucy coming home at nine o'clock at night, humming under her breath?

"Ready?" she asked, opening the door, and Lucy nodded.

"Ready to rock this pub quiz. How hard do you think the questions are?"

"I have no idea," Juliet said, and walked outside.

The Hangman's Noose was bustling with people, a fire burning cheerily in the inglenook fireplace, when Juliet entered with Lucy at her side, the warmth of the place seeming to both wrap around her and slap her in the face. Already she felt uncomfortable.

"Oy! Juliet! Lucy! Over here!" Rachel was waving at them from a table in the corner; she already had sheets of paper and stubby pencils laid out, along with a bottle of red wine. "I thought I'd get us a bottle," she said as they made their way over. Juliet nodded to a few people she recognized; the smile on her face felt too tight, almost as if it hurt her skin. Lucy, she saw, had stopped to chat with Diana Rigby. A gale of laughter rose up from both of them and Juliet looked away.

"This is cozy," she told Rachel as she sat on a stool, her knees brushing Rachel's under the table. "Where's Peter?"

"At the bar." Rachel cocked her head towards the bar of polished mahogany that ran the length of one wall, Rob Telford, the owner, filling orders behind it. "He wanted a pint of bitter instead of a glass of red. Imagine that."

Juliet picked up a pencil and twisted it between her fingers. "So how does this work, exactly?"

"Pretty simple. Rob asks the questions and we write down the answers. Then we exchange papers with another table and everyone marks the quizzes. Winner takes home a bottle. And hopefully we all enjoy ourselves." Rachel's eyes glinted teasingly. "Think you can do that, Juliet?"

"I'll try," Juliet replied without humor. She could see Peter making his way across the crowded pub, a pint in hand. Lucy was still talking to Diana.

"Hello, Peter," Rachel called as he approached, then turned to yell at Lucy. "Get your skates on, lass, we're about to start!"

Clearly, Juliet thought, Rachel saw herself as the social organizer of the evening. She'd already registered the speculative, steely glint in her friend's eye and wondered uneasily what it meant.

"Hello, Juliet." Peter's smile was as affable and easy as always as he crammed his big body onto one of the little three-legged stools; his knees barely fit under the table. And, Juliet realized, one was pressed against hers. She tried to shift a little bit, but as Lucy plopped herself down on the stool next to her, she realized there was no room to move. She could feel Peter's knee, and even some of his thigh, pressed against her own leg.

"How about a glass?" she asked a little too loudly, and Rachel poured her a large glass of wine as Rob came out from behind the bar to start the quiz.

"Areet, areet, you lot know the rules," he called out, and received much good-natured ribbing and catcalling in response. It was nine o'clock and Juliet could tell that everyone had been having a merry time for a while already. She took a sip of her own wine, and then another, needing to feel just a little less conspicuous. A little less uncomfortable.

"I read the questions," Rob continued. "You write down the answers. And if you hear someone's guess at a nearby table . . . well, talk quieter, you lot!" He glanced at a table of boisterous women whose laughter rose like a flock of crows every few minutes. "Think you can manage that?"

"Oh, aye, we'll manage areet," one of them answered with a saucy wink, and Rob grinned.

Juliet felt as if she'd landed on an alien planet. She'd come to the pub before, but it had always been generally tame, with a few farmers leaning against the bar with their pints, a few tables with people conversing quietly. Nothing like this.

And yet Rachel and Lucy and even Peter seemed to be getting into the spirit of things, judging by the way the women laughed and Peter gave a small smile, his pint raised to his lips. He had on a button-down shirt that actually looked ironed, and a pair of chinos. She couldn't remember the last time she'd seen Peter in anything so fancy, except maybe at the Christmas Eve service at church.

"Right, first question," Rob called, and the room, to Juliet's amazement, went silent. "How many years did the Hundred Years' War last?" This was met with a moment of taut silence, followed by sudden guffaws of laughter.

"A hundred years, mate," someone called, "or can't you count?"

Rachel leaned forward, and Lucy and Peter followed, so Juliet, somewhat reluctantly, did as well, and all four of them sat at the table, their heads touching. "So it's obviously not a hundred years," Rachel stated in a low voice. "Anyone do history A level?"

This was met with more silence. "A hundred and one?" Lucy ventured. "It's got to be close to a hundred, for it to be called that."

"Good point," Rachel answered, and then pressed a finger to her lips. "Nicholas Fairley runs the Hartley Historical Society," she whispered. "And he's sitting right behind us."

Instinctively Juliet glanced round, only to have Rachel hiss at her not to be so obvious. "But that's cheating," she objected, and Rachel rolled her eyes.

"That's all part of a pub quiz, Juliet." She shook her head. "Damn, he's already written something down. All right, we'll go with a hundred and one."

"Next question," Rob bellowed, and a respectful hush followed. "What is the capital city of Australia?"

"Oh, that's easy," Juliet exclaimed. "Canberra."

"Pipe *down!*" Rachel hissed as the people at several tables near them began writing frantically. "You want the whole room to know?" She started to write. "You're sure, though?"

"Yes. I was thinking of emigrating there, a while back." Everyone looked at her and Juliet took another sip of wine.

"When was that?" Rachel asked.

Juliet shrugged. "A long time ago, before I moved up here."

"Sometimes I think we might as well be in Australia," Lucy said, and Rachel guffawed at that.

"At least there aren't any poisonous snakes here."

"There's adders up Ennerdale way," Peter ventured, and Rachel gave him a look.

"Did I really need to know that, Peter?" she demanded. "Adders. God help us."

"Next question!" Rob bellowed, and they moved on.

As the questions rolled on—*What is the motto of the British Special Forces? Who composed the opera* Peer Gynt?—Juliet felt herself relax. Maybe it was the better part of Rachel's bottle of red she'd drunk, or maybe it was the good-natured joking that flew around her, making her smile even if she couldn't quite take part in it.

By the time they were exchanging quizzes to mark, followed by lots of teasing about cheating and giving half marks for good guesses, Juliet was feeling loose-limbed and a little bit sleepy.

"You areet, Juliet?" Peter asked, his eyebrows raised. She smiled at him. She felt almost dreamy.

"Oh, I'm fine."

"You're drunk," Rachel stated, holding up the empty bottle of wine. "I've only had one glass! You owe me, Juliet Bagshaw."

"Fine," Juliet answered with a shrug, and Rachel let out a laugh.

"Now I know how to get you to relax. I should have twigged it ages ago."

Juliet drew herself up, annoyed now that she could sense everyone was laughing at her. "I'm not drunk," she told Rachel shortly. "I've only had a couple of glasses of wine."

"More like four," Rachel answered, but she dropped it since they were announcing the winners of the quiz. Their table missed winning by two. "Still, it was a good showing," she said as she rose from the table. "I've got to get home and make sure Lily's done her homework. Same time next week? We'll have to come up with a name for our team."

"The Cumbrian Quizzers?" Lucy suggested, and

Rachel rolled her eyes. "The Seaside Smarties?" she tried again, and Juliet interjected, her voice slurring only slightly:

"How about the Village Idiots?"

"You ought to get her home," Rachel told Lucy. "If you can."

"I'll walk you both," Peter offered. "It's on my way."

Juliet simply sat and watched; she felt so very tired, but also as if the evening were slipping away from her. She didn't want to go home.

"Come on, then," Lucy said, and reached for her hand. Juliet shook her off.

"You all seem to think I'm falling-down drunk," she snapped. "I'm fine." And she showed them just how fine she was by walking very slowly, very carefully out of the pub.

The evening's rain had dropped to a misting drizzle and the cool, damp air brought some clarity—not sobriety, since she wasn't actually drunk. Lucy and Peter walked on either side of her, and Juliet wondered if they were afraid she was going to fall down. *Honestly.* This was what happened when she tried to relax and enjoy herself.

"You areet, then?" Peter asked as they came up to Tarn House, and Juliet whirled around to face him.

"I'm very much *areet,* Peter," she snapped. "I'm fine. I had a paltry couple of glasses of wine and everyone's acting as if I'm three sheets to the wind!"

Her voice, Juliet realized distantly, was ringing out so loudly it was echoing through the empty street.

Peter gave her a small smile. "I was just saying good-bye," he said mildly, and belatedly Juliet recalled how Cumbrians greeted one another—"you areet" was "hello," "good-bye," and "how are you?" all rolled into one. She knew that. Of course she knew that. She'd been living here for *dick* years, after all.

"Well, good-bye, then," she said, rather ungraciously, and turned to go into Tarn House. Lucy followed her, closing the door behind her, and Juliet sank onto the bottom stair, her stomach lurching.

"Juliet?" Lucy dropped the keys on the hall table. "I'll ask it for real, this time. Are you all right?"

"No," Juliet half moaned, her face buried in her hands. "I think, to use the Cumbrian word, I might bowk."

"I think I can guess what that means," Lucy said. "Do you want me to get a bowl, or can you make it to the toilet?"

Juliet took a deep, shuddering breath. She could feel cold sweat prickling on the nape of her neck and between her shoulder blades, and her stomach lurched again, and then thankfully settled. A little. "No," she said. "I'm all right."

Lucy sat down next to her on the stairs. "I think you mean areet."

"Oh, hell." Juliet shuddered again. "I was terribly rude to him, wasn't I?"

"Honestly? No more than you usually are."

She let out a laugh then that subsided into a groan. "I'm sorry," she said after a moment, knowing she would never say this if she weren't drunk. "I'm sorry I'm such a bitch."

"Oh, Juliet." Lucy's voice was soft with sadness and Juliet felt her sister put her arm, rather awkwardly, around her shoulders. "You're not a bitch."

"I'm not a very nice person."

"Not a *very* nice person, no," Lucy agreed after a moment, and Juliet couldn't tell if she was teasing. "But reasonably nice, yes."

Juliet dropped her hands from her face and pressed her forehead to her knees. "I've been living in Hartley-by-the-Sea for ten years," she said, "and I've never gone to a pub quiz."

Lucy was silent for a moment. "Why do you think that is?" she asked eventually.

"Isn't it obvious? Because I don't have friends. I can't make friends."

"You have friends, Juliet. Rachel and Peter—"

"I'd barely call them friends—"

"Well, what would you call them, then?" Lucy asked in exasperation. "They certainly seem like friends to me. And maybe Peter could be even more than a friend—"

"Don't," Juliet said sharply. "*Don't.* There's nothing between us, and there never will be."

"And why is that?"

"Just because you're having some little thing with Alex doesn't mean—"

Lucy's jaw dropped. "I'm not having some little *thing* with Alex!"

Juliet narrowed her eyes, although that made her vision even blurrier. "Just where were you last night, then, not coming home until nine o'clock?"

"Oh, nine o'clock," Lucy retorted, throwing up her hands. "Such a shocking hour."

"In Hartley-by-the-Sea it is."

"We had dinner," Lucy said, dropping her hands. "With Bella and Poppy. That's all."

"That's all? It's more than I've ever had." And once again she was sounding jealous and bitter. What a *shrew* she was. Wearily she rose from the stairs. "I'm going to bed. I have to get up early for breakfast. The Seatons want to be out of here by seven o'clock."

"I'll make breakfast," Lucy offered, and Juliet swung around to stare at her. "Seriously. I have to be up early anyway, and you can sleep in. Sleep it off."

"I'm *not* drunk."

"Whatever you say, Juliet," Lucy said with a smile, and headed upstairs. Juliet didn't bother answering.

17
Lucy

TRUE TO HER WORD, Lucy got up early to make breakfast for the retired couple while Juliet slept in. The bacon was a bit blackened in parts and the eggs were runny, but at least the coffee was good. Lucy drank a mug of it while the couple gathered their things to conquer Scafell Pike; she'd gotten used to the ebb and flow of B&B life, with walkers coming and going most days. Juliet kept a calendar on the kitchen wall of arrivals and departures, and Lucy saw that a large crowd was expected on the weekend, four couples. They would be fully booked both Friday and Saturday nights.

They, not just Juliet. Was she naive or fanciful in thinking that there was a *they,* that she and Juliet were on their way to becoming real sisters, and not just strangers linked by the genes of a woman neither of them actually liked?

She put her mug in the dishwasher, left the pans to soak, and made sure the kitchen was as tidy as she could leave it. Then she headed out into a rather bleak, gray morning, a chill wind funneling down the high street and making Lucy go back inside for her winter coat. To think it was only mid-September.

As she headed up the street, she felt that expectant fizz in her stomach at the prospect of seeing Alex again. He'd been away from school all day yesterday at a head teachers' conference in Barrow, but Lucy hoped that things might have changed a bit between them since their dinner.

Not that anything had actually *happened* during their dinner, even if her hormones had started doing a happy dance when they'd sat on a sofa together. And not as if Alex would ever act anything but professional in the workplace, but . . .

Was it too much to expect some banter, a bit of loitering by her desk, a casual invitation to the pub, just the two of them?

Apparently it was.

By midmorning she could say Alex's attitude had thawed a little, but he was as stern looking as ever, and hadn't even made the most offhand of references to their dinner together.

Weren't they friends now?

She wasn't the only one who thought so, for a few days after Lucy had had dinner with Alex and his family, Diana stopped by the reception desk before school, leaning towards Lucy confidingly.

"So, give me the crack."

"The crack?" Lucy repeated blankly, and Diana grinned.

"West Cumbrian for gossip."

"And here I was thinking you meant drugs," Lucy joked, but Diana shook her head, impatient now to get down to whatever the *crack* really was.

"Someone told me you were leaving Mr. Kincaid's house at *nine o'clock at night*." She spoke in a mock-scandalized tone, but Lucy could tell she was curious.

"Oh—that. It was nothing, really." And right on cue, she started blushing as if she were hiding something, which, unfortunately, she wasn't.

"Nothing? I don't think Mr. Kincaid has had anyone into his house, ever. And you've been here all of two minutes?"

"Three weeks since the start of term, actually. I just did a favor for him, that's all." In case Diana decided to read some sexual innuendo into that, Lucy clarified hastily, "A bit of—ah, business for Bella, his daughter. No big deal, honestly."

"What kind of business?" Diana asked, and Lucy just about kept herself from retorting, *Not yours.* This, she supposed, was the downside of village life.

"Who told you, anyway?" she asked.

"Mrs. Henshaw lives across from Mr. Kincaid. She plays bridge with my neighbor on a Tuesday."

"Ah."

With a theatrical sigh Diana pushed herself off the counter. "I can see you're not going to tell me anything juicy."

"I would if there was anything juicy to tell,"

Lucy answered lightly, and Diana pursed her lips, her eyes glinting.

"You have to admit that our head teacher is just a little bit gorgeous," she said in a stage whisper, and Lucy gave a noncommittal shrug. "*And* single."

"He's been recently widowed," Lucy pointed out, and Diana shook her head.

"Nearly two years ago. And he has two motherless daughters. He's ready to jump back in the dating pool, I should think."

Lucy just shrugged again. She could see the top of Alex's head as he worked at his desk and she cringed inwardly at the thought of him hearing any part of this conversation.

"He *is* hard to get to know," Diana allowed. "And he's kind of distant from most of his staff. But you're not really staff, are you? Being temporary, I mean." She leaned forward again, eyes dancing. "You could have a Cumbrian *fling*."

"It sounds like some kind of dance," Lucy joked.

"All I can say is I wish I were young and single with a handsome head teacher to obsess about." She spoke lightly, but Lucy sensed something else going on.

"How are things in Manchester?" she asked.

Diana made a face. "Oh, things are *grand* in Manchester," she said, a note of bitterness creeping into her voice. "So grand my husband is thinking of buying his own one-bedroom flat."

"Where was he before?"

"He's been staying in a short-term let. I know buying a place makes sense financially. He's in real estate, after all. But . . ." She trailed off, and Lucy waited. "He said he'd look for a job back here after six months," Diana finally said quietly. "He said he'd *try*."

"I'm sorry," Lucy said, wishing she could say something more helpful, and Diana gave a little shrug.

"You can't make someone want something, can you?"

"Unfortunately not." She'd certainly tried that tactic, unsuccessfully, with Thomas. With a sigh Diana moved on and Lucy turned back to her computer.

She wondered how Diana and Andrew would resolve their separate lives, and then how quickly the *crack* got around in a village as small as Hartley-by-the-Sea. Was anyone asking Alex what he'd been doing, having his temporary receptionist over at his house in the evening? Juliet had clearly wondered the same, although she hadn't mentioned Alex or anything in the last few days. They'd gone back to truce status, minus some of the tension, or so Lucy hoped. Juliet had been busy with guests and Lucy had been busy with school, and neither of them had been inclined, it seemed, to have a heart-to-heart conversation.

As for Alex . . . she might be having a few harmless daydreams about him liking her, flirting with her, but she didn't want anyone else thinking that way. She was leaving in four months, first of all. Just a little over three now, actually. More importantly, she didn't want to embroil herself in a family where she wasn't sure she was wanted. Bella had been hostile enough, certainly. Poppy could change her mind in a moment. And Alex . . . who knew what Alex really thought or felt?

The next man she dated would be child free, with no emotional baggage whatsoever.

Several days later Alex appeared in the door-way of the reception area during recess. It was a lovely, warm day in late September, with sunny skies gilding the fells in gold and a gentle breeze ruffling the sea, which twinkled in the distance. From her open window Lucy could hear the shouts and laughter of the children in the school yard.

"Do you have a minute?"

She looked up, her heart seeming to slam against her ribs at just the sight of Alex. His dark hair was a little mussed, as if he'd unthinkingly run his hand through it. His eyes looked even bluer in the sunshine.

"If the boss says I do, then I suppose I do." She pushed away from her desk. "What's up?"

"I just wanted to float an idea by you."

"Sounds intriguing."

He gestured to the stairs that led to the school

hall and the rest of the classrooms. "Do you mind?"

"Not at all." Lucy followed him through the hall, now with all the chairs pushed back as the dinner ladies cleaned up after lunch, and then down a narrow hallway into the newer part of the building.

The school was still a bit of a maze to Lucy; the original building was Victorian, but there had been various additions built over the years that meant you had to go through one classroom to get to another, and a hallway might dead-end against a newer wall.

Alex walked with quick assurance, weaving through empty hallways and classrooms before he stopped in front of a door. "This is our old resource room," he explained. "We acquired a new computer room in the latest renovation, so this room is a bit redundant." He opened the door and ushered her in. It was a long, narrow room in the older part of the building, with a table in the middle and an old stone sink in the corner. A couple of flimsy cupboards of prefabricated wood lined one wall. "Who knows what it was a hundred years ago?" Alex said with a small smile. "Maybe part of the kitchens."

"Mmm." Lucy glanced around, trying to summon an expression of interest in the empty room when she had no idea why Alex had brought her here.

"The thing is," he began, and to her amazement he actually sounded a little nervous, "we don't have any specialist teachers. No budget for them, I'm afraid."

"Specialist?"

"You know, things like PE, French, music." He paused, his gaze resting meaningfully on her. "Art."

"Art—"

"The teachers have to do it all themselves, and frankly some of them have trouble with it. It's all right for something like PE, when all you have to do is grab a ball and head outside. But music and art require a little knowledge, a little skill."

"I suppose . . ."

"You have both, Lucy. And you're good with children."

"No, I'm not—"

"You are," he insisted. "I've seen you when one of them gets a bumped head or a scraped knee. They like you. People like you."

Yes, but they don't love me. Thankfully those words didn't pop out. She had an easy time making friends; it was the more important people that she failed to win over.

"So what are you suggesting?" she asked warily.

"If you wanted, and only if you wanted, you could teach an art lesson once a week, just to the older pupils to start. We could add some lessons for younger children if it seemed to be working."

"And who will be on reception when I'm teaching?" Lucy asked. It seemed easier to focus on the practical; she had no idea how she felt about what Alex was suggesting. Terror was the word that came to mind first.

"We'll manage. It would only be forty minutes, after all. I'm afraid we don't have much in the way of supplies, but we could most likely rustle up some paint and pots, or felt-tips, or whatever you think you need. And I couldn't pay you any more than you're already being paid—the budget is tight."

"I don't want more money," Lucy protested. She wasn't even sure she wanted to teach.

"I know you don't. And if you don't want to teach, that's fine. I just thought it might be a way for you to get back into art a little, without your mother breathing down your neck."

"That's . . ." She blinked, so touched by his thoughtfulness that for a moment it was difficult to speak. In the month since she'd been in Hartley-by-the-Sea, she'd *thought* about painting, when she'd seen the light looking syrupy and golden, or when the blackberry bushes along the beach road had begun to drip jewellike berries. But she'd never been tempted to put pencil to paper, or even to go into the little art and crafts store she'd seen in Whitehaven and browse there. "That's very kind. But I'm really not sure, Alex. I've never taught before, and children, frankly, scare me a little."

He raised his eyebrows. "Bella didn't scare you."

"No, she terrified me. Seriously. I'm not sure I'd be good at it. And you don't even know if I'm any good at art. Have you even seen one of my paintings?" She'd meant it rhetorically, but Alex took it at face value.

"Yes, I looked one up online."

"Oh." She flushed, because if he'd seen it online, he'd also seen some of the awful blogs and gossip sites, the thousands of comments trashing her and her art. "Well."

"I liked it," Alex said. "It might not get everyone worked up, talking about how cutting-edge it is, but it was pretty."

Pretty. She smiled, a shaky thing. "Well. Thank you."

"So you'll think about it?"

"I . . . I don't know." The thought of trying something new, something that could actually matter to her, and failing was terrifying. As terrifying as the children she'd be forced to face. "Maybe."

"That's enough for me," Alex answered.

Apparently, though, it wasn't enough for Liz Benson, the Year Six teacher, who marched up to Lucy as she was getting ready to go home. "So, I hear you're dragging your feet over this art business," she announced with a beady stare, hands planted on her ample hips. "And I'm here to tell you that's nonsense."

Lucy stared at her, taken aback even as she

fought the urge to laugh. Liz, a kindly, grandmotherly type who had always had a smile for her, looked amazingly fierce.

"It's not nonsense," she protested as she wrapped her rainbow-colored scarf around her neck. "I'm not a trained teacher."

"It's one lesson in a specialist subject," Liz replied. "It's not rocket science."

Which was what Juliet had said about answering phones. Lucy had been so stung then, but now she felt only bemused. "No, thank goodness. But I've leapt into enough situations in my life, Liz, trust me. I'm trying to learn my lesson and be more cautious."

Not that it was really working. For as nervous as she was, there was a part of her—a big part—that wanted to leap in headfirst, as she did with everything. A bigger part, however, did not want to make a fool of herself, or feel like a failure. Again.

"What do you really have to lose?" Liz persisted. "So it doesn't go well. You stop." She shrugged. "And we look for another specialist art teacher who's willing to work for free."

"Ah, now I see why you're keen for me to start teaching."

"Seriously, Lucy." Liz gave her a stern teacher's glare. "Hartley-by-the-Sea is the type of place where everyone pitches in and gets the job done. You're part of that, aren't you?"

Was she? She knew she wanted to be. She'd come here wanting people to love and accept her, but maybe she needed to fulfill her half of that bargain. "Okay," she said, and held up a hand to keep Liz from offering any more arguments—or making her feel any guiltier. "I'll think about it."

"Good," Liz said. "Because I'm the one teaching art to the Year Sixes right now and I can barely manage stick figures."

Lucy's heart was both light and full as she headed back to Tarn House. She stopped in at the post office shop, as she'd occasionally taken to doing; after Dan Trenton's terse explanation of how he'd ended up in Hartley-by-the-Sea, he had graduated to gruff hellos whenever Lucy came in. Lucy counted each one as a triumph.

"Hey, Dan," she greeted him cheerfully as she stepped into the single room, its shelves crowded with tins of baked beans and loaves of bread.

"Hello." He was counting bills at the register, the muscles in his tattooed forearms rippling, and Lucy saw the tiniest smile quirk the corner of his mouth. *Progress!*

She grabbed a copy of the *Whitehaven News*, which she'd started reading; the local-interest stories fascinated her. Where else could a primary school's bake sale make the front page?

"So, how are things?" she asked as she put the paper on the counter. This was new territory; she hadn't attempted more than a hello before.

"Hey!" Dan's shout made Lucy jump a little, and then he marched from behind the counter and grabbed the arm of a boy who Lucy hadn't noticed was loitering by the candy rack. "You little bugger. I saw you nick that."

With her heart seeming to both sink and rise to her mouth, Lucy saw the boy was Oliver Jones.

"Get off," Oliver yelped, trying to twist away from the huge man. "I didn't steal anything."

"What's this, then?" Dan demanded, and yanked a bag of chocolate buttons from the pocket of Oliver's school trousers. Oliver glared at him in stony silence, and now Lucy's heart really did sink.

"I'll buy them," she said quickly. "I don't mind—"

"Maybe I mind," Dan growled, and gave Oliver's arm a little shake. "How often have you been nicking things?"

Oliver didn't answer, and Lucy took a step towards them. "Look, he won't do it again," she told Dan, and then gave Oliver as stern a look as she could. "Will you? Because it would be really, really stupid if you did." Neither of them spoke and Lucy continued, a bit desperately now. "Look, Dan. He's only nine. And . . . well." She could hardly mention Oliver's home situation. "Give him a break. It's only seventy-five pence. Please, for my sake."

"Why do you care?" Dan demanded.

"I was nine once too. We all did stupid things when we were young, didn't we?"

After a long, tense moment, Dan let Oliver's arm go. "Fine. But I'm warning you. . . ." He shook a finger at the boy. "If I catch you doing something like that again, it's straight to the police. You ever heard of Lancaster Farms?" Warily Oliver shook his head. "It's a prison for kids who get into trouble. Not a nice place." Dan glowered at him meaningfully. "You don't want to end up there."

Lucy put a comforting hand on Oliver's shoulder. "Okay, so seventy-five pence for the chocolate buttons, and a pound for the paper." She slid a two-pound coin across the counter. "And we're all good?"

Slowly Dan nodded, and then handed her twenty-five pence change. Lucy turned to the door, her hand still on Oliver's shoulder.

"Right," she said once they were outside. "What did you do that for?"

Oliver jerked away from her. "Thanks for the chocolate," he said, sounding decidedly ungrateful. He started walking up the main street.

"You don't get off that easily," Lucy said, and fell into step alongside him.

Oliver looked at her suspiciously. "What are you doing?"

"Walking you home."

"You going to tell my mum?"

"Should I?" Lucy asked, and he snorted.

"She wouldn't even care."

"What about your dad?"

He shrugged. "I haven't seen him since April."

"Still," Lucy said, "I don't think he'd like to know you'd been nicking things from the shop."

"You can't tell him, though," Oliver pointed out as he opened the bag of chocolate buttons. "He won't be home till after Christmas."

"Oliver . . . ," Lucy began, watching as he took a button from the bag. "I know it might seem like grown-ups don't care about you or what you do—"

He jerked around to face her, swallowing the chocolate with an audible gulp. "What do you know about it?" he demanded.

"I know what it feels like to be alone—"

"You don't know naught," he said, and tossed the bag of buttons into the bin on the sidewalk. "I can see myself home."

Lucy slowed as Oliver took off up the street, and then disappeared around the corner.

She was still mulling over how she could have better handled the situation when she came into the darkened kitchen of Tarn House and saw Juliet curled up on the window seat, her bleak face resting against her knees.

"Juliet—what's happened? What's wrong?"

"Nothing's happened," Juliet said with a sniff. She averted her face from Lucy. "I'm just having a bit of an off day," she said, her voice muffled against her knees. "I'm allowed, aren't I?"

Lucy dropped her bag by the table and hung up her coat. Outside the sun was still high in the sky despite its being past five o'clock, gilding the fields with gold.

After a moment's deliberation Lucy filled the kettle and plonked it on top of the Aga. Then she turned on one of the lamps on the Welsh dresser and, pulling a chair from the table, sat down near Juliet. Maybe she needed to fulfill her half of the bargain in other ways too.

"So why is this an off day?" she asked. Seeing Juliet look so dispirited made Lucy wonder if her stern sister was as emotional and fallible as she was.

It didn't seem likely, but it was time they both started talking more honestly.

"No real reason," Juliet said after a moment, her face still averted, and Lucy let out a sigh.

"Juliet, I know we don't actually know each other very well, and that you resent my very existence. Maybe you hate me. I don't know." Juliet had not rushed to refute any of these assertions, and taking a deep breath, Lucy plowed on. "But you still had the kindness and generosity to offer me a place to escape when my entire life fell apart. I hope your life isn't falling apart the way mine did, but I'd like to be here for you, whatever is going on." She paused, considering her next question, not sure if she wanted to lob that particular grenade into the conversation. But it was there already, so she asked, "Is this about Fiona?"

Juliet let out a trembling laugh. "No, actually, it's not. Not directly, anyway. Not everything is about our mother, despite what she thinks."

Lucy smiled at that. "I don't think anyone has dared tell her that. So what is it about?"

"Can't I just have an off day, no explanation needed?" Juliet asked, a familiar edge of irritation entering her voice. "Maybe it's just PMT."

"I assume that's the same as PMS?" Juliet shrugged and nodded. "If it was, why didn't you just say so in the first place?"

The kettle startled whistling shrilly and Juliet rose from the window seat, her face now set into its usual stern lines. She grabbed the kettle from the Aga and made them both mugs of tea. Lucy waited.

"I was thinking about having a baby," Juliet said abruptly, and Lucy blinked.

"Okay," she finally said, her tone cautious. Juliet raised her chin a notch.

"Our mother did it, didn't she? She was a single mum both times round, and I think I could be a much better mother than she ever was, at least to me." She fetched the milk from the fridge and poured some into both mugs before thrusting one towards Lucy. "You don't think so," she stated flatly, and Lucy blinked again.

"Think what? That you won't be a better mother than Fiona? No, I definitely don't think that. But," she added, "you're not setting the bar very high."

"You have no idea," Juliet answered grimly, and Lucy set her mug of tea on the table.

"Then tell me, Juliet. Tell me about you and Mum. Not just about the stupid pony party, but what was really going on. Why do you think she didn't want you?"

Juliet stared down at her mug of tea. "Because she told me," she said, and she didn't sound angry, only tired.

"Told you?" Lucy repeated. "Like, actually *said*—"

"Yes, Lucy. She said, and I quote, 'I never wanted you.' Satisfied?"

Lucy didn't know why she was surprised. Their mother had shown just how insensitive and cruel she could be on many occasions, and yet . . . she'd still been their mother. Amidst all the awfulness and disappointment, there were a few happy memories from her childhood. She could picture her mother dancing around the kitchen after she'd sold a sculpture, and once they'd emptied a gallon of strawberry ice cream straight onto the table and sculpted it into funny shapes before digging into the mess with two spoons. A few times Fiona had sat by her bedside while Lucy had gone to sleep, usually talking about the art world, which had mystified her as a child, yet she'd just been so pleased to have her mother *there*.

Yet now it seemed as if Juliet had no happy memories at all. "When did she say that?" she finally asked.

"When I pushed and pushed her to name my father. I came over to see you both in the States. I was twenty."

"That visit," Lucy remembered. "You left so suddenly—"

"I didn't feel much like staying, after that." She bent her head towards her mug, closing her eyes as the steam from the tea hit her face. "I don't know why it shocked me, to have her say it. She'd certainly shown me every day of my life." She opened up her eyes, looking up to give Lucy a bleak smile. "Honestly, I don't even know how I survived my childhood. She must have fed and bathed me as a baby, kept me in nappies. But I can't imagine she did it happily."

"Why do you think . . . ?" Lucy began, and then stopped. The question she'd been about to ask wasn't exactly sensitive. Juliet, however, guessed it anyway.

"She had me? Kept me, even? I have no idea. I wish she hadn't. I'd probably be less screwed up if I'd been adopted." She pressed her lips together and looked away. Her sister was clearly angling to end their cozy little chat, but Lucy wasn't going to give up just yet.

"You're not screwed up, Juliet."

"No?" She braced her hands on the sink and stared out the window at the sheep fields, the dirt track twisting between them. "Maybe no more than the average person, I'll grant you," she said after a moment. "But it's enough to be going on with."

"And this idea for a baby?" Lucy ventured. "What's that about?"

"What do you think it's about? My biological clock is ticking. I'm thirty-seven with limited fertility—"

"Limited fertility—," Lucy began to ask, and Juliet pressed her lips together in a line.

"I've only got one Fallopian tube, and endometriosis besides," Juliet said, and turned around. "No matter how I go about trying to get up the duff, it's not going to be easy."

"You could adopt," Lucy suggested, and Juliet just shrugged. "How come you only have one Fallopian tube, anyway?"

Lucy didn't think her sister was going to answer, and now that she thought about it, the question had been rather personal.

Then Juliet said tersely, "I had an ectopic pregnancy eleven years ago. The tube burst then. It was lucky I got to keep both my ovaries."

Lucy stared at her in shock. "I'm sorry," she said after a moment.

"Surprised, eh?" Juliet cracked a small, bleak

smile. "What about? That I could have been pregnant, or that I had someone in my life to make me pregnant?"

"Well, both actually," Lucy admitted, not quite joking. "Were you . . . was it serious?"

"It bloody well was. I almost died."

"I meant . . . the relationship?" Although after this conversation she was going to Google ectopic pregnancies, because she really didn't know anything about them, except that they were dangerous. Obviously.

"Oh." Juliet shrugged. "Not really. Sort of. I don't know." She let out a sudden, harsh laugh. "He was married. Not to me." She raised her eyebrows at Lucy. "Now you're really surprised."

"Well . . ." Okay, yes, she was. For a lot of different reasons. "Tell me about it," she said, and Juliet laughed again.

"What is there to tell? He was married. I knew he'd never leave his wife."

"Was this here—"

"No, in Manchester, while I was working for a big hotel. He was in management there."

"Did you love him?"

Juliet thought about this for a moment. "No," she finally said. "I don't think I did."

Lucy pondered too, about how different she and Juliet really were. Juliet kept herself from loving people, while she swan-dived into the emotion with abandon and glee.

"What about the baby?" she asked Juliet. "Did you . . . did you want the baby?"

Juliet's face contorted for a second and then her expression ironed out. "Yes," she said tonelessly. "I wanted the baby."

"Oh, Juliet . . ."

Juliet shrugged off any sympathy Lucy had been about to give. "It was a long time ago."

"But it must have been awful," Lucy said quietly. "Going through that alone . . ."

"Yes," Juliet agreed after a slight pause. "Yes, that part wasn't much fun." She took a deep breath and then continued, her voice low. "The man in question wasn't keen on me having a baby, of course. He wanted me to have an abortion, and when I refused, he stopped speaking to me altogether. I didn't mind so much then, but when I was in hospital with the burst tube and I was unconscious . . ." She paused, her gaze shuttered and distant. "The hospital called him, as my emergency contact. And he refused to come."

Lucy's heart ached to imagine Juliet alone in the hospital, her very life in danger, and the father of her would-have-been child refusing even to see her. No wonder her half sister had a few issues.

"I'm so sorry," Lucy whispered. And then, because she wanted to show her sister that *she* wouldn't reject her, she stood up and opened her arms up for a hug. Juliet simply stared. Lucy started walking towards her.

"What are you doing?" Juliet asked, her voice cracking.

"I'm giving you a hug, silly."

Juliet stood woodenly while Lucy put her arms around her, and didn't soften into the hug in the least. After a moment Lucy took her arms away and stepped back. So maybe they'd try that again someday.

"So, you still want a baby." Juliet eyed her warily and said nothing. "What are you going to do about it?" Lucy asked.

Juliet hesitated, and then answered, "My appointment in Carlisle a few weeks ago was at a fertility clinic. I was looking into going the sperm donor route."

"Oh, don't," Lucy cried, and Juliet raised her eyebrows.

"Why not? It seems a sensible option."

"Because I hated not having a dad. I still do. Even kids with divorced parents have someone, you know. A deadbeat dad is better than nothing, a man who doesn't even know you exist."

"You can contact a sperm donor when you turn eighteen. Did you think about doing that?"

"Thought about it," Lucy admitted. "But I never did. It just seemed too . . ." *Risky.* She didn't really need another parent in her life who wasn't interested in her. "Didn't you wish you had a dad?"

Juliet frowned. "I wished I knew who my dad was."

"And don't you think your child would be the same?"

She shrugged impatiently. "It hardly matters. Like I said, I have limited fertility. I got a reminder from the clinic today to go in for my fertility consultation. *Assessment.*" She pressed her lips together, and Lucy guessed this was what had put Juliet into a dark mood.

"So what are you going to do?" she asked.

"I don't know. Forget it, probably. It was a stupid idea."

"Having a baby isn't necessarily a stupid idea. If your biological clock is ticking—"

"What does that even mean, anyway?" Juliet said, and Lucy smiled.

"I don't really know. But what was motivating you, then, to even think about sperm donors?"

Juliet took a sip of tea, her expression turning both thoughtful and guarded. "I suppose," she said slowly, "I just want someone to belong to. And someone who belongs to me."

A lump rose in Lucy's throat. Wasn't that what she wanted, had always been looking for?

"What about going about it the old-fashioned way?" she asked after a moment.

Juliet shook her head. "I don't have time for relationships. Do you know how long it would take to meet someone, decide if he's right for me, work our way towards settling down, marriage, the whole thing?"

"How long?" Lucy asked with a little smile, and Juliet shook her head again, more firmly this time.

"I'm not cut out for romantic relationships. I'm going to do this my way. Alone."

"So you're going to go ahead with the assessment? The sperm donor?"

Uncertainty flashed across Juliet's features, making her look vulnerable and surprisingly young. "I don't know. I still hate not knowing my father. I'd rather be able to tell my child who his or her father is, even if he's not involved, but . . ." She trailed off, shrugging.

It sounded to Lucy like a potential minefield of hurt and disappointment, the kind they'd both experienced in different ways. "Single parenting seems tough to me, Juliet," she said. "I was talking to Alex and—"

"Oh, were you? Getting cozy with Alex?"

"Not cozy," she said. "Friendly. Maybe."

Juliet's gaze narrowed. "What do you mean, maybe?"

"We've had one dinner, and he asked me to teach an art class to the older pupils. Satisfied?"

"Not really." Juliet emptied her mug into the sink. "Be careful, Lucy."

"What do you mean?"

"There are a lot of people involved who could get hurt if you and Alex start something. And I'm not just talking about you."

"Of course not," Lucy answered dryly, but Juliet steamrollered over her.

"You're leaving in a little less than three months. Alex has two girls who are in a vulnerable place."

"I know that, Juliet." She was in a vulnerable place too. She didn't need Juliet telling her what a bad idea being interested in Alex Kincaid was, never mind actually starting something.

"If they became attached to you—"

"Trust me, you're not saying anything I haven't already thought myself," Lucy said. "We're just friends," she said. *Maybe.*

"That's for the best, I think," Juliet answered, and even though she knew her half sister was probably right, Lucy wasn't sure she could agree.

18
Juliet

"AND NOW IF ANYONE has any more points of business . . ."

Louise Walker, the chair of Hartley-by-the-Sea's parish council, looked up from the minutes of their meeting, eyebrows raised expectantly.

"None for me," Rob Telford stated, his legs stretched out in front of him. The eight other people round the table echoed him one by one, starting with Peter Lanford, who sat next to him, hands resting on his jeans-clad thighs, his voice a low rumble.

"Juliet?"

Juliet blinked and saw Louise was gazing at her with an expectation that bordered on annoyance. Like Juliet, Louise liked these meetings to be short and sweet. She had four children and three Patterdale terriers at home, and she was on half a dozen committees. The woman was practically a machine of efficiency.

"Nothing from me," Juliet said hurriedly, and glanced away again, trying not to fidget.

Ever since she'd told Lucy about wanting a baby, she'd been determined to do something about it. Telling her sister had made the desire both more real and more dangerous; if she didn't do anything, she would look and feel pathetic. Even worse, nothing would change. And if there was one good thing Lucy had done for her, it was make her realize she needed to change.

And to change, she needed to act. Tonight.

Louise had concluded the meeting and everyone started rising from their chairs, heading out into the chilly evening. It was the first week of October, but it felt more like December. Juliet watched Peter out of the corner of her eye; he rose from his chair slowly, smiling and nodding towards several of the other parish council members who filed outside.

Taking a deep breath, she headed across the room. "Hello, Peter."

"You areet, Juliet," Peter answered with one of his slow nods and smiles.

She'd seen a fair bit of Peter over the last two weeks; thanks to Rachel's determination, they'd become something of a fixture at the Thursday night pub quiz. Juliet had even started to relax a little, answering questions and enjoying herself, although it still felt strange to be sitting there among friends. She always stuck to a single glass of wine.

Peter had also stopped by Tarn House several times for a cup of tea; the first time he'd come by, Juliet had been alone, cleaning the oven, her hair piled on top of her head and yellow rubber gloves up to each elbow. She'd been flustered to see him there, standing at the back door as if it were a usual occurrence, then taking off his mud-caked boots when she, stammering, had invited him in.

She'd gotten stuck, removing the rubber gloves, and Peter had reached over and tugged one off in a gesture that felt—well, *suggestive.* Of course it wasn't, Juliet had told herself crossly, but she still could feel herself reacting as she turned away to put the kettle on.

Their conversation had gone in fits and starts, with Juliet needing to fill the silence; Peter had seemed content to simply sit, a mug cradled between his hands.

After a few of these impromptu chats it had become easier simply to talk, and then it had started to feel shockingly natural to have him in her kitchen, chatting about nothing in particular, his sock-clad feet stretched out towards the Aga. Once, at her invitation, he'd removed his wet socks; Juliet had been unsettlingly transfixed by the sight of his knobbly toes.

Part of her relished these changes to her life; another part of her felt how pathetic she was, to be pleased by such small things. And it was that ever-present sense of her own inadequacy that made her even more determined to act.

She'd gone back to the clinic, and suffered through a fertility assessment and its expected results: "Limited fertility, but with the proper course of treatment, a pregnancy might be viable." Now she just needed a dad. A donor.

She'd looked into the banks in the US and Denmark, and realized that going that route was going to cost her thousands of pounds, and make her baby's father a stranger. Then she remembered what Dr. Allen had asked—*Are you going to use an acquaintance's sperm?*—and so now she was here.

"I was wondering," she said to Peter, her voice just a little too strident, "if you fancied having a drink at the pub. With me."

He didn't answer for a moment, which made Juliet feel both nervous and tetchy. Then he nodded. "That'd be areet."

Juliet nodded back, no more than a jerk of her head, and they headed outside. They didn't speak as they walked from the village hall to the pub; Juliet could feel everything inside her coiling tighter and tighter.

In the pub Peter said hello to a few people and then asked Juliet what she wanted to drink.

"I'll buy—," she began, to which Peter responded with a decisive shake of his head.

"No, you won't. Now, what will it be? Glass of red?"

"All right," Juliet relented. She had bigger things to worry about than who bought the drinks.

She found a table in the back corner, the most

private one in the place, and sat down with her back to everyone else. She sucked in a breath and told herself she wasn't actually asking Peter for that much: fifteen minutes and a paper cup. Some sperm. No responsibility, no commitment, no *feelings*.

Peter returned with their drinks, a glass of red for her and his usual pint of bitter. He slid onto the chair and raised his glass in a toast. "Cheers."

"Cheers." Juliet heard how nervous she sounded, her voice going up nearly an octave, and she took a sip of wine. Maybe she shouldn't have picked the pub for this conversation. No matter how private their table, it felt like a very public place for what was going to be a very personal conversation.

But asking Peter in the cozy comfort of her own kitchen would feel much too intimate, as if by inviting him into her house, she was inviting him to share her life. The pub put this meeting on terms she could live with.

"How's your dad?" she asked, deciding that a few minutes of small talk might smooth the way.

Peter lifted one shoulder in a shrug. "Same, I suppose. It's not going to get any better."

"You could have some help," Juliet suggested. "Professionals who come in—"

Peter shook his head. "Dad wouldn't like that. And we manage areet as it is. He doesn't wander, and he can look after himself for most of the day. I check on him often enough. Jake helps."

There was something faintly repressive about Peter's tone, making Juliet feel that his father had not been a wise choice for a topic of conversation.

"What about you, Juliet?" Peter asked. "Things rolling along?"

"Well. Yes." She cleared her throat, and then decided there was nothing for it. She'd have to jump right in, after all. "Actually, Peter, I was hoping you could do me a—a favor."

His heavy brows drew together as he frowned at her. "Of course I could," he answered, and the unquestioning simplicity of that statement nearly brought a lump to Juliet's throat.

"Well. Good." She cleared her throat. "I'm glad to hear that."

"What needs doing?"

For a horrified second Juliet pictured exactly what needed doing and suppressed a near-hysterical laugh. "Umm. Well, I'll get to that. The thing is, I actually . . ." She lowered her voice. "I'm actually trying to have a baby. Well, I'd like to try. I haven't tried yet."

Peter went very still, which was saying something for him. He was usually such a still, silent man anyway, yet now he seemed utterly immobile.

"I mean, as a single parent," she hastened to explain. "On my own."

"Oh, aye?" he said, and Juliet couldn't tell anything from his voice. He took a sip from his pint of bitter, waiting.

Juliet swallowed; her throat felt constricted, the words hard to get out. "Yes. You know, I'm thirty-seven, and I suppose my biological clock is ticking, as clichéd as that sounds." Still nothing. "And so I've been looking into options. I've done a fertility assessment, and while a pregnancy isn't going to be easy for me, it's possible." She waited for him to say something, and he finally did.

"Seems as if you've got yourself sorted, then."

"Well, a bit," she agreed, latching on to his words like a drowning woman reaching for a life preserver. "But I'm also aware—you see, I never knew my father. My mother refused to name him. And Lucy doesn't know hers, either. Fiona—our mother—decided to go with a sperm donor with her. We've both disliked that, the not knowing, in different ways."

"Aye," Peter said after a moment, his voice definitely wary.

"So I realized," Juliet continued, relentless now, "that I want my child to know his or her father. And so that brings me to—" She swallowed convulsively, the gulping sound audible, she feared, even over the din of the pub. "—to you." No response, but Juliet knew she could hardly expect one. "I wanted to ask you, Peter, if you—if you would donate your sperm."

What a cringingly awful, awkward question, and yet how else could she have phrased it? Peter had gone rigid, his pint glass raised halfway to his lips, his eyes widening as he stared at her.

"Donate—," he began, and then stopped. "You want me to be the father of your child?"

"Well—yes. I think you'd make a good father, Peter." Too late she realized how that sounded. "Not that you'd actually be involved, of course. I wouldn't expect anything from you but—well, the obvious. I mean, just the sperm." In case there was any question.

"Let me get this areet," Peter said, and his voice was low, thrumming with emotion. Bad emotion. "You want me to wank off into a paper cup so you can have my sperm for your baby, and then raise that baby in front of my nose, but not have me involved?"

Was there any good way to answer that? "I just don't want you to feel beholden," Juliet finally said.

"Beholden? *Beholden?*" Peter's voice had risen so a few people nearby started shooting them openly curious glances. Out of the corner of her eye Juliet saw Maggie Bains, recently back from Newcastle and a terrible gossip, turn towards them. She definitely should not have chosen the pub for this conversation.

"I only meant," Juliet said coldly, retreating into hauteur, "that I wouldn't expect you to actually act as a father. I'm going to do this on my own, but I wanted to be able to tell my child who his or her father was—"

"And you could also say," Peter cut across her, his voice low but intense, "that you can go up the road and see him anytime you like. The man who fathered you but can't have aught to do with you." He shook his head, clearly disgusted.

"Don't overreact," she snapped. "I didn't mean it like that—"

Peter shook his head again, the movement so vehement, so scornful, that any retort she'd been going to make stopped with the breath bottling in her lungs.

"I know how you meant it, Juliet," he said. He placed his pint glass on the table with a final-sounding clink. "And I'll tell you this. If I bring a child into this world, it will be to love and cherish it, not just walk off as if I hadn't a care in the world." Juliet opened her mouth and nothing came out. "And I'll tell you this, as well," he added, thrusting his face close to hers. "If I decide to have a barney, I'll go about getting it the old-fashioned way!"

And with that startling pronouncement, he got up and stalked out of the pub.

19
Lucy

LUCY STRAIGHTENED THE CHAIRS in front of the two rather rickety tables that Alex had brought into the school's old resource room and tried to pretend she hadn't noticed her hands were shaking. It had been a week since Alex had asked her to teach an art class, a week since she'd agreed, and in precisely three minutes twenty-four Year Six children would be coming in for their first art lesson.

She was terrified.

She'd spent endless evenings on her laptop, garnering ideas from the Internet, going over lesson plans. She'd spent an enjoyable afternoon with Diana Rigby, sorting through the school's craft supplies, joking and laughing as they discarded ancient bottles of poster paint with dried-up drips down the sides, and tried every felt-tip marker in a box of five hundred to make sure they worked.

Diana had seemed more cheerful; she'd told Lucy she was taking her two boys down to Manchester for the half-term break at the end of October, to see Andrew and look at properties.

"I thought I should at least have a say in what flat he buys," she'd said. "And you know, 'if the mountain won't come to Mohammed . . .'"

"That seems like a good solution," Lucy had said. She was all for optimism.

After she and Diana had sorted through the old art supplies, Lucy had spent a happy hour in the art shop in Whitehaven, filling in the gaps in the school's cupboard. It had felt surprisingly familiar, almost like coming home, to touch the crisp, thick pages of a sketchbook and run her thumb along the waxy edge of a pastel. She hadn't thought she'd missed art, but standing in the middle of the shop, she knew she had. She just hadn't wanted to admit it to herself.

And now she was here, with a neatly typed lesson plan, sheets of pristine white paper on the table in front of every chair, and plastic tubs of oil pastel crayons placed every few seats.

She picked up a red pastel and tossed it from hand to hand. She felt so unprepared for today, and yet also so desperate to prove herself—not just to her pupils or Alex or even the whole village, but to herself.

And to her mother.

Too bad her mother didn't even know she was teaching an art class, hadn't spoken to her in nearly two months now. And even if she did know? Lucy could imagine Fiona's response. *Well, of course such mediocre talent would find its home in teaching art to primary school pupils. What do they do but scribble?* A small, teasing smile. *You know what they say. Those who can, do. Those who can't . . .*

Never mind that her mother lectured at a university. She'd already proven her artistic talent many times over, from the time she'd won an emerging artist award before Lucy was born, to the phallic sculptures that could be seen in several prominent museums around the world.

It was stupid to be arguing as if her mother were here, or even cared. Pathetic to let her mother influence her decisions and plague her with self-doubt from thousand of miles away. In the five weeks since Lucy had come to England, Fiona hadn't called or e-mailed even once.

And yet Lucy could still hear her mother's voice in her head.

Now she heard the sound of boisterous voices coming down the hall, and she tossed the pastel back in the tub as her stomach plunged with nerves. They were coming. And they sounded like a horde of wild animals.

A few seconds later twenty-four rowdy Year Sixes trooped in, hot and disheveled from recess. Lucy could tell the troublesome ones straight off: a gaggle of girls who hung by the door, giggling behind their hands and shooting her scornfully speculative looks. Two boys, clearly the coolest in the class, sprawled, legs open wide, in the chairs. One of them grabbed a pastel and sent it flying across the room, a bright-colored missile that bounced harmlessly off the wall. The other kids noticed, and they watched Lucy, waiting for her reaction.

"Everyone, sit down, please," she called out, her voice coming out in a croak. She retrieved the pastel from the floor and returned it to its tub with a pointed look for the boy who had thrown it. Not the most effective discipline, but it was all she was capable of at the moment.

The children took their seats more or less obediently, and Lucy stood there, a tense smile on her face, every inspiring word she'd practiced vanishing from her head.

She heard someone whisper; then a titter came from the far side of the room. Children, she decided, were devils.

She looked up, and her panicked gaze rested on the figure standing behind the door to the room. Through the single narrow pane of glass she could see Alex smile at her, and then give her a thumbs-up.

Relief flooded through her, a cold, sweet rush. Someone, at least, thought she could do this. Or maybe Alex just didn't want a riot on his hands.

"All right, everyone pick up a pastel," she said loudly, clapping her hands. "Only one, thank you," she added as the boy who had thrown the crayon earlier reached for a handful. She plucked them from his hands and deposited them back in the tub. "This is not archery class," she told him, and someone giggled. Lucy felt a surge of confidence and even elation.

"Now I want you to draw a line on your paper. It can be any line, in any color: wavy, curvy, straight, diagonal. You choose. But only one."

The children looked at her, nonplussed for a moment, and Lucy raised her eyebrows in expectation. "Well?" she asked. "What are you waiting for?" And she only just kept from sagging in relief as they all started to draw.

Forty minutes later twenty-four children trooped out of the resource room, and Lucy let out a shuddery sigh as she sank into a chair.

"How did it go?" She looked up to see Liz smiling at her from the doorway.

"Okay, I think. I wasn't too much of a disaster, I hope."

"I think you most likely weren't a disaster at all," Liz answered. "Did Simon and Rupert give you any trouble?"

The two too-cool-for-school boys who had lounged in their chairs. She'd kept a beady eye trained on them all lesson, overlooking the minor misdemeanors and, at one point, confiscating a spitball.

"A little," she admitted, and Liz nodded knowingly.

"They're a handful, those two."

"Yes, I think they are." Lucy remembered her moment of paralysis when they'd come into the classroom, all cocky indifference, and suppressed another shudder. "They also had me almost falling apart before the lesson even began. I don't think I could ever be a real teacher."

"But you are a real teacher," Liz reminded her. "You just taught a lesson."

"Yes, but—"

"Don't put yourself down," Liz admonished, wagging a finger. "There are enough people in life who will do that for you."

Yes, Lucy thought, *there certainly are.* And Liz was right; she had been putting herself down. Always jokey, always with a smile on her face, but she'd been self-deprecating about herself for so long, she'd forgotten how to be anything else. Silly, scatterbrained Lucy, who leaped before looking, who was a walking disaster, who had a BA and was only a barista. Talentless Lucy, who painted wildflowers, barely a step above posters of kittens stuck in wineglasses.

"You're right, Liz," she said. "And the truth is, I enjoyed teaching that lesson, once I got over my nerves."

"I think the children enjoyed it too. They were all talking about their lines as they left." She raised her eyebrows expectantly and so Lucy explained, a bit self-consciously just in case it really was a stupid idea.

"I had them all draw one line on their papers. Then they had to exchange papers and use someone else's line as the beginning of a drawing."

"Very clever," Liz said with a nod of approval. "Next we'll have the Year Fives begging for lessons."

"I don't know about that—"

"Children like you," Liz said frankly. "Can't you feel it? Even the stroppy ones. And I've seen the little ones in the school yard. If anyone has a scraped knee, they ask for Miss Bagshaw."

"Well . . ."

"It's a talent, you know," Liz said. "Not everyone has it, an ease with children. Not even every teacher, unfortunately."

"You do," Lucy answered with a smile. "I've seen you with the children, and with some of the younger teachers too." She thought of Tara, whom she'd seen earnestly talking with Liz after school on more than one occasion, her daughter, Emma, on her lap. "You're like a mum to them."

Liz smiled a bit sadly. "I never did have any of my own," she said. "It just never happened for my husband and me. But I ought to go sort my lot out. They're ready for maths."

After Liz had left, Lucy tidied up the classroom, humming under her breath. Maybe Liz was right, and children did like her. She'd bought into everyone's criticism for so long, but for the first time Lucy considered that a man's two sons disliking his new girlfriend was not proof that she was terrible with children. Nor did her mother's opinion of her art mean she was a talentless hack.

She felt a sense of freedom, a burden she hadn't realized she'd been carrying slipping from her shoulders. She didn't have to be defined by a few people's opinions of her.

Even your own mother's?

"So, Liz tells me it went well."

Lucy turned to see Alex standing in the door-way, that endearingly crooked smile curving his mouth.

"Yes, I think so. Actually," she amended, emboldened now, "I know so. It was fun, and I think the kids had fun too. Amazingly."

"Why amazingly?"

She shrugged, not wanting to go into it. "Anyway, it turned out all right today. Thank you for giving me the opportunity."

"Thank you for taking it."

They smiled at each other, awkwardly now because there was nothing left to say and yet Alex was still standing there, hands shoved into the pockets of his trousers, rocking a bit on his heels, and now that Lucy looked, the tips of his ears had gone red.

"So . . . ," she said, the only opener she could think of. Thankfully Alex took it.

"So I was wondering if you were free this

weekend, to go to the Crab Fair with me and Poppy and Bella."

He'd spoken in such a rush it took Lucy a moment to comprehend that he was asking her out. Sort of. "Oh," she said, stupidly, because her mind was spinning.

The tips of his ears went redder and he continued tersely. "Poppy wanted me to ask you. She's taken a shine to you, and frankly I'd do just about anything to make my daughter happy."

Okay, so he wasn't asking her out. Not willingly, anyway. The smile she'd felt dawning across her face slid right off. "Including suffering through a Saturday with me?" she said, lightly enough, but Alex must have heard the edge of hurt in her voice because he answered, "There would be no suffering involved. I didn't mean . . ." He trailed off, and Lucy waited, bemused, wondering if he'd dig himself out of the hole they'd both created. "I'd like you to come with us," he finally said. "If you want to."

Lucy didn't answer for a moment. She wanted to—of course she did—but she still felt wary. She still couldn't tell if Alex wanted her to come for his sake or just his daughters'.

"Of course, if you're busy," Alex said, "I understand. It's no problem. . . ."

"What's a Crab Fair?"

"Oh." He looked relieved that she hadn't refused him, and that made Lucy smile a little.

Made it also a lot more likely that she'd say yes.

"It's an autumn festival, I suppose. Crab refers to apples, not crustaceans. It's one of the oldest fairs in the country—King Henry III granted a charter for it in 1267."

"You're obviously a teacher," Lucy teased, and Alex cracked a smile, eyebrows raised expectantly.

"So . . . ?"

"Yes, thank you, I'd love to come." Alex nodded, and Lucy couldn't tell what he felt. She still didn't know if this counted as a date. "What time do you want me?" she asked, and then winced inwardly at the blatant suggestion of that question.

Judging from the now fire-engine red of Alex's ears, she was pretty sure he'd gotten the unintended innuendo. "Ten?" he suggested. "We can have lunch there, if that's okay."

"Great."

She nodded, and he nodded back. Their social dynamics, Lucy thought, were on par with seventh grade. Then the phone rang and she heard a teacher's heels clicking down the hall, and with another nod Alex turned and went back to his office.

20
Juliet

IN THE WEEK AFTER Peter stormed out of the pub, Juliet retreated into a familiar, comforting blanket of numbness. It was how she'd reacted during the worst hurts inflicted by her mother: the Leavers' Day at the end of Year Six, when Juliet was the only one there without a parent; the teacher in primary school who had, in front of Juliet's entire class, shouted at Fiona for missing every single parent/teacher conference, and Fiona had simply stared at her, stonily indifferent. When she'd been twenty-six and in hospital, her baby bleeding out of her, and she'd had absolutely no one to call or come to visit.

So this wasn't that bad, in comparison. It wasn't as if she'd actually been *friends* with Peter. He'd turned down her offer, fine. She'd find someone else, or she'd cough up the money to get a donor from the US, pick a profile from the database.

Except as the days passed, she didn't call the clinic; she didn't even let herself think about the clinic. She tried not to think about anything.

She kept busy, though; busy was good. She had a steady stream of walkers who came hoping for autumnal color; the wind tended to blow the leaves from the trees in Hartley-by-the-Sea before they'd turned, but Juliet promised her disappointed guests that it was better towards Keswick, and the walks around Crummock Water and Buttermere, two of the nearest lakes, were spectacular.

She dug over the old stone troughs she used as flower beds in front of the house, and filled them with chrysanthemums in a riot of reds and yellows. She redesigned the B&B's Web site, adding a guest book and more links to local restaurants and pubs. She even volunteered to organize the village's Bonfire Night on the fifth of November, a monumental task that involved coordinating with the Women's Institute, which handled the food stall; the local authority, which had to approve the fireworks; and the primary school, which sold the tickets. For the last she simply gave the tickets to Lucy with strict instructions to keep the money separate from the school dinner money.

"I think I can manage that," Lucy had said with a smile, and it had occurred to Juliet how much more confident and relaxed and even *happy* her sister seemed. Hartley-by-the-Sea was good for her; Lucy clearly enjoyed working at the school, and if her secretive little smile was anything to go by, she was becoming friendlier with Alex Kincaid.

It seemed both ironic and fitting that Lucy's life was getting better and bigger while Juliet's was falling apart.

Except she wasn't going to think about that.

Yet she found she couldn't *not* think about it. At night she lay in bed and stared up at the ceiling, listening to the wind rattling the windowpanes as she went over in excruciating detail the last conversation she'd had with Peter. She remembered the look of scornful disgust on his face, the way he'd shaken his head at her and raised his voice so it had practically rung through the pub.

Remembering it all, she vacillated between self-righteous anger—her request hadn't been *that* unreasonable—and shame. A shame she hated to feel, and so she clung to her anger and pretended she didn't feel it.

She also avoided Peter as much as she could, which was aggravatingly difficult in a village the size of Hartley-by-the-Sea. When she walked into the post office shop, he was buying a newspaper, and she kept her head lowered and intently studied the cover of *Cumbria Life* until Dan Trenton had given Peter his change. Peter walked out without a word for her, and she saw Dan raise his eyebrows at her before he sold her some stamps. If even surly, silent Dan Trenton noticed something was going on between her and Peter, things had to be bad.

When she walked the dogs down at the beach, avoiding the lane to Bega Farm, Peter was emptying his recycling into the bins by the promenade. He stared at her for a moment across several yards of concrete before turning back to chuck empty milk cartons into the big metal bin. Juliet pulled the dogs towards the sea.

She cried off the pub quiz the following week; Lucy informed her, with a narrowed look, that Peter hadn't shown up, either.

"We had to join Liz Benson and Tara Dunwell," Lucy said. "I like Tara, and I know she's had a hard time, but she talks constantly. Even Rachel couldn't get a word in edgewise."

"Liz is good value," Juliet answered, not meeting Lucy's eye, but her half sister would not be put off.

"Has something happened between you and Peter?"

"What do you mean?" Juliet asked, and then hurried on without waiting for Lucy to clarify. "We're acquaintances. How could something have happened?"

"I thought you were friends." Juliet said nothing. "Rachel thought something was happening between the two of you. Something a little more than friendship—"

"Rachel should mind her own business."

"Seriously, Juliet. If you want to have friends, you've got to—"

"The last thing I need," Juliet cut across her, "is a lecture from you."

"From me?" Lucy blinked, looking hurt. "Ouch."

"I'm fine," Juliet snapped, and she almost believed it.

Yet standing by the sitting room window, watching Peter drive by in his Land Rover before she ducked behind the net curtains, she knew she wasn't. She was miserable and she missed him; something had opened up inside her and no matter how she tried to close it again, she couldn't. It felt like a gaping wound, a yearning she hadn't let herself feel before.

"He came over maybe three times," she told herself crossly one afternoon as she waxed the hall floor, another attempt to stay busy. "Get over yourself."

"Talking to yourself is a bad sign, you know," Lucy told her cheerfully as she came into the house. "But I've been doing it for ages. Why do you need to get over yourself?"

Juliet sat back on her heels and blew a strand of hair from her eyes. Yes, Lucy was looking very cheerful these days. She even did a little twirl as she hung up her coat.

"You're in a good mood," she remarked sourly. They'd reached a holding pattern in their relationship; they weren't doing each other's nails, but neither were they arguing or ignoring each other.

"Is that a crime?" Lucy countered, and walked

right across Juliet's newly waxed floor into the kitchen. Juliet heaved herself up from the floor and followed her sister.

Lucy was putting the kettle on top of the Aga, whistling as she did so. Her good mood was becoming seriously aggravating. She turned to glance at Juliet. "Cup of tea?" she asked, and Juliet nodded reluctantly. She didn't really want to have a cozy chat with Lucy about her sister's promising love life, but neither did she want to exist in this vacuum of loneliness. She leaned against the radiator and folded her arms.

"So what's got you in such a good mood?"

"Nothing in particular," Lucy said in a tone that made Juliet think it was very much something in particular. "It's not raining for once. Isn't that reason enough?"

"It hasn't rained for a week." Drizzling didn't count.

Lucy shrugged as she got out the mugs and the milk. "Even more of a reason, then." She turned around, a smile tugging her mouth upwards. "I also taught my first art class today, and it wasn't terrible."

"Sorry I forgot," Juliet said gruffly. "So, not terrible, eh?"

"I think that's fair to say."

"I'm sure it was better than that," Juliet answered, "judging by your grin."

"I enjoyed it," Lucy admitted. "And it felt—I

don't know—validating. After Mum . . ." She trailed off, her smile starting to slip.

"Don't tell me you take anything our mother has to say seriously."

Lucy turned to her with a sudden, surprisingly bleak look. "Don't you?"

"No—," Juliet began, only to stop as she realized she did take what Fiona had said seriously. Not the ridiculous posturing for the press, but the flatly stated fact. *I never wanted you, Juliet.*

Yes, she'd taken that rather seriously.

"Juliet?" Lucy's voice held a lilt of uncertainty and Juliet tried to shake off the dark mood that threatened to fall on her like a shroud. She didn't want to think about Fiona now, not on top of everything else.

"Fiona does everything for show these days," Juliet said, keeping her voice brisk. "You know that. I'm sure the only reason she rubbished your artwork in the news is because it would gain her more coverage, and all the while she could say it was because she was protecting her integrity." Juliet rolled her eyes and Lucy managed a small smile, but she didn't exactly look convinced.

The kettle began to whistle shrilly and Lucy turned to move it off the hot plate. Juliet watched her, frowning.

"I've never actually seen one of your paintings," she said. "What are they like, anyway?"

"Nothing spectacular," Lucy answered, her back still to her. "Just insipid little watercolors of wildflowers."

"That's how you describe your own work?"

"Well . . ." Lucy turned around. "That's how Mum described it."

"How about you let me judge for myself?" Juliet suggested, and Lucy's eyes widened.

"Seriously?"

"Seriously."

"I don't actually have a painting here," she hastened to explain. "I mean, I don't lug them around or anything. But I set up a catalog online, in case anyone . . ." She trailed off, biting her lip. "Well, you know, to be professional."

"So show me," Juliet said, even as she wondered why she was asking. Did she really care about Lucy's paintings, insipid or not? Then, to her surprise, she realized she did.

"Okay," Lucy said. "Let me get my laptop."

Juliet finished making their tea as Lucy went upstairs. At least Lucy's paintings would provide a distraction from her own gloomy thoughts.

"Here we go." Lucy set up her laptop on the kitchen table and Juliet handed her a mug of tea before sitting down. "They're not statements," Lucy warned her. "I mean, my art isn't political or anything. . . ."

"Thank God for that. And stop making excuses. Let them speak for themselves."

"All right," Lucy answered, and pushed the laptop towards Juliet so she could see the screen.

Juliet hadn't really considered what to expect when it came to Lucy's paintings. She hadn't thought about them all that much, but if she was honest with herself, she would have expected them to be a little simplistic, a bit amateurish, and yet heartfelt. Kind of like Lucy herself.

What she hadn't anticipated was that they'd actually be quite good. They weren't going to set the art world on fire, by any means, but there was something warm and welcoming about each painting: bluebells in a shadowy wood, daisies blowing in a breeze. She captured a scene and made you want to enter it. And yet there was a surprising sorrow about the paintings too, as if the artist knew that flowers were fleeting, that the scene was nothing more than a moment in time.

"I like them," Juliet said at last.

"You have to say that."

She arched an eyebrow. "Do you really think," she told Lucy, "I wouldn't tell you if I thought they were rubbish?"

"Well . . ." Lucy considered this and then let out a laugh. "Of course you would. So that gives you an admirable amount of credibility."

"They're not mind-blowing or anything," Juliet continued, determined to be both honest and fair. "But not everything has to be. They're comforting; they make you want to walk in that field or that wood. I like them," she said again, stating it firmly, and Lucy smiled.

"Thank you," she said, her voice soft, and Juliet knew it meant something to her, that she did actually like them. And it felt surprisingly good to realize Lucy cared about her opinion.

"So come on, really. What's going on with you and Peter?" Lucy asked, and Juliet lurched upright, nearly spilling her tea in the abrupt change of subject.

"I told you, nothing—"

"Come on, Juliet. I'm not an idiot. Something happened between you two. You're avoiding each other—"

"How would you know? You're at school all day—"

"I live with you, and this is a small village. People notice things, like you not going to the pub quiz, for starters."

"I only went three times."

"And so did Peter. Coincidence? I don't think so. Other people don't, either."

Juliet stilled at that, a horrible thought creeping up on her like a cold Cumbrian mist. "What do you mean?" she asked, hardly wanting to ask the question. "Has someone said something to you?"

"Maggie Bains told Diana Rigby that she saw the two of you in the pub last week," Lucy answered, "and she said Peter walked out in a hurry."

Juliet rose from the table on the pretense of fetching a dish towel, but more as an excuse to hide her face from Lucy, and the appalled expression she could feel contorting her features.

"What a load of nonsense," she managed as she swiped at the nonexistent spills on the table. Lucy had, for once, not scattered sugar everywhere.

"Is it?" she asked. "Were the two of you at the pub?"

"Well, obviously. I don't think Maggie is a pathological liar."

"Then what happened?"

"Nothing. We had a drink and a chat and Peter had to leave. The end. *Honestly,* this is ridiculous." She turned away, the towel clenched in her hand.

"Juliet." Lucy's voice was soft, almost tender. "Don't bullshit me."

"What gives you the right to get into my business?" she demanded, but it came out less stridently than she'd wanted it to.

"Nothing gives me the *right,*" Lucy said after a moment. "But you're my sister and I am actually quite fond of you, even if we had a rocky start and you can be kind of awful sometimes—"

Juliet gave a snort of laughter. "Now don't start getting all mushy on me."

Lucy ignored her, continuing more seriously. "I care about you, Juliet, and I can see that you're hurting—"

"Okay, really, now stop." She shook her head,

dragged a breath into lungs that felt like concrete blocks. "I can't stand this kind of sentimental claptrap. It's nauseating."

Lucy sat back with a little smile and sipped her tea. "So tell me, then."

Juliet hesitated, torn between the contrary desires of wanting to both unburden and protect herself. She decided to try for both. "I just made a practical suggestion and Peter took it entirely the wrong way." She twitched her shoulders as if to dismiss the subject. "He can be such an *oaf* sometimes."

"A practical suggestion," Lucy repeated after a moment. "What kind of practical suggestion?"

"Nothing that onerous, really," Juliet hedged. She didn't want to get into details, because she had a strong feeling that Lucy would side with Peter. "Just . . . helping me out with something."

"This wouldn't be helping you out with the baby thing, would it?" Lucy asked, and Juliet twitched her shoulders again. Her sister was too perceptive by half.

"Maybe."

"Oh, Juliet." Lucy sighed and shook her head. "So what exactly did you suggest?"

"I asked him to donate sperm," Juliet answered, all brittle indignation now. "I wanted my baby to know his or her father. I didn't think it was too much to ask, just an afternoon at the clinic in Carlisle—"

"Juliet." Lucy looked appalled, just as Juliet had thought she would. "You know it would be more than that," she protested. "He'd be your child's father."

"But I told him he wouldn't have any obligation—"

"And I bet *that* went over well."

Juliet pressed her lips together. "Not too well," she admitted. "He was angry," she continued reluctantly, feeling she somehow owed Lucy the details now. And she realized she wanted to confess them. "Offended, really."

"And why do you think that was?"

"Don't play psychiatrist with me, Lucy," Juliet snapped. "We both know why it was. Because he's not the sort of man to father a child and then just go about his business." She blinked rapidly, and then set her jaw. She hadn't admitted that to herself, much less to anyone else, but she knew it was true. They were talking about Peter Lanford, after all. A man who carried on his family's flagging farm, who cared for his ailing father. Who believed in responsibility and duty and even honor.

"If you knew that," Lucy asked, "why did you make the suggestion to him?"

"Because I didn't realize . . ." Juliet felt her throat go tight and she swallowed in an attempt to ease the soreness. "When I was thinking about it, it didn't seem so . . . I don't know. I was just focused on my child knowing his father. And Peter is a good man. . . ."

"He's cute too."

"Oh, honestly, Lucy. If you like holey jumpers and knobbly toes."

Lucy's eyebrows shot up. "How do you know he has knobbly toes?"

"He took his socks off once—oh, *never mind.*" Juliet rose from the table and dumped her half-finished mug of tea in the sink. "This conversation is pointless, because I did ask him, and he got rather cross, and I'm not sure we'll ever be on speaking terms again."

"You could say 'sorry,'" Lucy suggested. "Wait till he cools down a bit, and then talk to him?"

"It's been over a week. I don't think he's going to cool down much more."

"But have you tried—"

"I'm not sure there's much point." And the thought of talking to Peter again, of seeing that awful contempt on his normally gentle face . . . no. She couldn't do it. She wouldn't.

"Can I ask you something?"

Juliet gave her sister a shrewd glance. "I think you're going to anyway."

"Why didn't you just let things happen naturally with Peter? I mean, he obviously liked you—"

"He didn't. Not that way." The response was automatic, although Juliet couldn't even say why.

"Juliet, he did. He brought you that rosebush.

He came to see you. The only reason he agreed to come to the pub quiz was because you were going—"

"You don't know that."

"No, but I think it's a fair assumption. I might not be great with my own love life, but I can see what's going on in other people's."

"I don't even have a love life," Juliet retorted. "Nothing has happened between us in that way."

"But it might have, if you'd given it time," Lucy countered. Juliet shrugged, not able to voice or even acknowledge what she felt. It hurt almost unbearably to think she might have messed up even more than a friendship. "Can I say something?" Lucy asked, and Juliet rolled her eyes.

"What, again?"

Lucy gazed at her steadily. "I think you didn't let something happen with Peter because you're afraid. Afraid of being rejected the way our mother rejected you. The way that married jerk rejected you."

Juliet simply stared, trapped by the knowing compassion in Lucy's eyes. Trapped and horribly, horribly exposed.

"It's hard to try again, Juliet," Lucy continued. "Trust me, I know that."

"Do you?" Juliet managed, the two words squeezed from her throat with painful difficulty.

"Yes, I do. I'm not attempting to equate my

experience of our mother with yours. I know you had it worse. But having her criticize me so terribly in public, having the entire world take notice and do the same?" Lucy let out a huff of sad laughter. "Yes, I know how rejection feels." Juliet didn't say anything, and Lucy took a deep breath, staring at the ceiling. This conversation was almost as hard for her, it seemed, as it was for Juliet.

"I dated this man, Thomas, for three years back in Boston," Lucy said. "He had two sons. I was trying hard with them, but they wouldn't have anything to do with me, the turds." She let out a long, shaky sigh. "Anyway, when the whole thing blew up in the paper, he called it off. Well, technically, I called it off. He said I shouldn't come around for a while because the publicity would be bad for his boys. I told him I needed his support and all I got was silence."

"And what happened then?" Juliet asked.

"I called it off, but I was really just bluffing. I wanted him to realize he needed to be there for me, and guess what?" She finally looked at Juliet, her face bleak. "He didn't."

Juliet thought about asking Lucy if she was thinking about trying again with Alex, but decided not to. She didn't trust herself to manage a coherent sentence just then.

"I'm saying all this because I can see how it would feel easier to keep yourself from caring about anyone, from putting yourself out there, even if it's a little lonely."

"A little lonely?" Juliet said, her voice torn from her, a ragged thing. "Lucy, you have no idea."

"Then tell me." Juliet shook her head, knowing she didn't trust herself to put it into words. "Juliet . . ."

"I haven't been a little lonely," she finally said, her voice hoarse and grating. "A little lonely is a night at home with the TV. I've been . . ." She stopped, gasping for air as if she'd run a mile, or forgotten how to breathe. "I've been *drowning* in loneliness. Or frozen in it, a great big ice block of isolation." She drew in a ragged breath, hating that Lucy was seeing her like this.

"Oh, Juliet," Lucy said softly, and she shook her head, vehement now, her voice choking.

"Don't. *Don't.*" She could feel the tears gathering in her eyes and she blinked them furiously back. "Maybe you're right. Maybe I'm afraid. Maybe I just don't know how. It doesn't matter, anyway, because I *can't.*"

"You could try—"

"You don't get it, do you, Lucy?" Juliet said, her voice sharpening. Anger was better than grief. "I'm not like you. I don't bounce around making friends and sending little rays of sunshine everywhere like some kind of do-gooding fairy. There's no trying with me. I can't, and that's that, and this discussion is *over.*"

21
Lucy

WAS IT A DATE? Lucy asked herself, not for the first time, as she headed to Alex's house the following Saturday. Had Alex Kincaid really asked her out on a date? And did she want it to be a date? She was here for only three more months, and he had two damaged daughters, *and* he was her boss, which might even make dating him illegal. Maybe there was some school policy against fraternizing with staff. She couldn't exactly ask.

After several days of deliberation she decided to play it the way Alex had pitched it: as a favor to Poppy. Stay safe. Not what she'd advised Juliet, but after witnessing her sister's heart-wrenching near breakdown, she could see the merits in emotional cowardice.

In the few days since then, Juliet had gone back to her brittle self. And Lucy had let her, because she understood about needing to claw back some composure after you'd been rubbed so emotionally raw.

She stopped in front of Alex's house, took a deep breath, and ran a hand over her frizzing hair.

Before she could knock, the door flew open, and Poppy stood there, already dressed with a coat and backpack, grinning widely.

"You look like a sausage!" Poppy exclaimed.

"Umm . . . thanks?" It wasn't the look she'd been going for, but Poppy seemed pleased.

"She means," Alex said, coming behind Poppy and resting his hands on her shoulders, "that you're wearing red and yellow." At Lucy's blank look he clarified, "Mustard and ketchup. Poppy puts loads of both on her sausages."

"Ah." Lucy glanced down at her yellow top visible under her unbuttoned coat and her red corduroy skirt. A sausage it was. She glanced up again, taking in Alex's weekend wear of faded jeans, a T-shirt, and a crew-neck sweater. He definitely could rock the casual look, and deliberately she moved her gaze back up to his face.

Bella slouched downstairs, dressed all in baggy black, her arms folded ominously. Lucy braced herself. She was not going to spend the day trying to win Bella over. Been there, done that, and no desire for a repeat trip.

"Hello, Bella." Her voice rang out, manically cheerful. Seemed she couldn't keep from trying.

Bella muttered a hello back, which was better than silence, if only just.

"So I looked up this Crab Fair on the Internet," Lucy said, "and it looks wicked cool."

Poppy frowned. "Wicked?"

"Sorry, that's American slang for completely amazing." She ruffled the girl's hair gently, grateful that at least one of the Kincaid girls liked her. "Did you know about the gurning competition?"

"The what?" Alex asked, and reached for his coat.

"Gurning. I'd never heard of it before, but apparently there's a competition to make the strangest face. How cool is that?"

"Oh, Daddy, you should enter," Poppy cried, and Alex made a face that Lucy thought wouldn't remotely win, but it was still kind of cute.

"Me? I don't think so."

"You should, Dad," Bella said suddenly, and this surprising contribution to the conversation had them all turning to her.

"You think I should?"

"Do you remember how you used to make faces at us when we were little? To get us to take our medicine."

Alex blinked, and Lucy felt her heart give a dangerous little twist at the sight of the bittersweet memory on his face. "I'd forgotten that." He turned to her to explain. "Both Bella and Poppy were prone to ear infections, and they hated the rounds of antibiotics they were put on—"

"Daddy used to pull funny faces to make us open our mouths, and when we did, Mummy would spoon the medicine in." Now Poppy made a face. "It tasted *awful*."

Lucy smiled in sympathy, even as she felt a dozen different conflicting emotions collide inside her in a kaleidoscope of feeling. Sadness, for the mother they'd lost. A little shameful jealousy, because Alex and Anna sounded like such a loving team. And hope, because clearly there was more to Alex than the stern taskmaster he was at school.

"I think we should all enter the competition," Lucy said. "Apparently you have to make the face through a horse collar, which just adds to the craziness. They call it 'gurning through a braffin.'"

"What's a braffin?" Poppy asked, wrinkling her nose.

"A horse collar, I guess," Lucy answered. "Are we all ready?"

Charlie gave them all a morose look before Alex shepherded him into the kitchen and appeased him with a full water bowl and a dog treat. A few minutes later they piled into Alex's car; Lucy noticed the papers littering the front passenger seat, along with a browning banana peel.

"Sorry," he muttered, sweeping it all into a pile and tossing it into the back.

"I've never owned a car," Lucy said, "but if I did, it would be a complete mess, I know. It would be like having another closet."

He laughed, and Lucy saw Bella shoot him a

sharp look before turning to stare determinedly out the window. Okay, so it was becoming clear that his daughter did not approve of her friendship with Alex. She wasn't going to bend over backwards to make Bella change her mind.

They drove along the coast road towards Egremont, the sea sparkling on one side and sheep pasture stretching out on the other. Lucy saw a sign for Buttermere and said, "Do you know I haven't actually been to a lake since I've been here? I saw Bassenthwaite on the drive down, through the fog and rain. But considering this is the Lake District, I feel gypped."

"This is the *Western* Lake District," Alex said. "We're nine miles from the most westerly lake, Ennerdale."

"Sometimes we walk Charlie there," Poppy piped up. "He likes to swim in the water."

"I'll have to check it out."

"You could go with us," Poppy suggested blithely. "Couldn't she, Daddy?"

Alex stared straight ahead, flexing his hands on the steering wheel. "I suppose she could."

Which wasn't the most promising invitation, and so Lucy kept silent.

The fair was in full swing by the time they arrived, after having spent a taxing twenty minutes trying to find a parking space while Poppy clamored to be let out and Bella kept sighing loudly.

"You're going to wish you hadn't come," Alex told Lucy, when they finally made it down the hill to the town's market square, where the fair's main activities were being held.

"It takes a little more than that to put me off," Lucy answered, and then wondered if he would read more into that statement than she'd meant—although she wasn't even sure what she meant.

What was she doing, tangling herself up with this widower and his lonely kids?

Poppy ran back to tug on Alex's sleeve. "Daddy, the parade is starting!" she cried, and they both turned to see a crowd of people coming down the high street, led by the year's crowned Crab Fair Queen, a teenage girl in a ball gown and a tiara.

They watched the procession of classic cars, dancers, a brass band, several floats for various causes and charities, and finally the apple cart, which was the highlight of the parade. Following the ancient tradition, apples were tossed to the children lining the street, and they ran around, laughing and shouting, as they gathered them up. Even Bella got into it, although she tried to be cool, and Alex turned to Lucy.

"Why don't you think you're good with children?" he asked, and she blinked, disconcerted by the sudden, unexpected question.

"What—"

"You said you weren't good with them before. Why?"

She shrugged, her eyes on the children scurrying for apples as she wondered how much she should say. Then she decided, for once, to tell the truth. "I suppose because the two I tried with the hardest were pretty unimpressed."

Alex was silent for a moment, seeming to sift through her words before he asked lightly, "So who were these brats?"

"Their names were Will and Garrett. I don't think they were actually all that terrible, but they certainly didn't like me." She paused, and then continued. "They were the sons of a man I dated for a couple of years. Thomas."

Another silence, and Lucy kept her gaze on the hunt for apples. "And then what happened?" he finally asked.

"I suppose it's really a question of what didn't happen." She tried to keep her voice both light and matter-of-fact, the only way she knew of lowering the intensity of the conversation. "They never accepted me, even though I tried so hard. Maybe *because* I tried so hard." She sighed, her gaze still on the children, and decided to go for broke. "I wanted to be part of their family. Thomas was divorced, and their mother married someone else and had a baby, and so Will and Garrett were kind of left out in the cold. At least I thought they were. But maybe that was wishful thinking. I wanted to fill a space in their lives that wasn't really there."

"Maybe they were confused about their mother's

new relationship," Alex suggested. "And the took it out on you, because that was easiest."

"Maybe," Lucy agreed. This was definitely starting to feel like a very charged conversation, although she couldn't discern its actual currents. "But it certainly made me miserable, and I ended it, accidentally, I suppose, after everything blew up with my mother and the art showing."

"What do you mean?"

"Thomas suggested I not come around for a while, because of all the media attention. He felt it would be bad for the boys."

"Pillock," Alex muttered, and Lucy shook her head although she was smiling.

"You really need a naughty jar."

"So did you stay away?"

"I did the classic stupid female thing and gave him an ultimatum. I told him I was going to break it off if he didn't support me and he said fine, more or less. Actually more. It made me realize how unimportant I was to him as well as to the boys." She sniffed and looked away.

"I thought he'd realize what he was losing," she said after a moment. "I imagined he'd come charging to me, stand up for me to my mother and the press and everyone. I wanted a knight in shining armor, and I'm afraid I didn't get one." She sniffed again. "Sorry. I thought I was over this. And I am over Thomas, because leaving him didn't actually hurt that much. It was just realizing how stupid I'd been, how easy it was for him to let me go, that hurt."

The apple cart had moved on, and Bella and Poppy were returning with the fronts of their hoodies full of apples.

Alex didn't say anything, and Lucy was starting to wish she hadn't just off-loaded a whole Dumpster of emotional garbage. Just what Alex wanted from this day. He was probably freaking out, wondering if she was equating him with Thomas, and his girls with Will and Garrett. What if he came out with some awful line about how they were just friends? And what had happened to her resolution to keep today light and unthreatening for Alex and the girls? She knew Bella was suspicious of her, if her obvious silence and endless sighs were anything to go by. Poppy was easy to love; she'd slipped her hand in Lucy's as soon as they'd left the car.

And knowing herself, Lucy acknowledged, she'd love Bella too. She'd love all of them, if they'd just give her a chance, and that's what scared her. She didn't want to end up as she had before, trying so hard and getting nowhere. Having a man choose his children over his girlfriend, a choice Lucy agreed with in some ways but that she hadn't wanted Thomas to have to make. She certainly didn't want Alex to make it.

So what was she doing here, holding Poppy's hand and confiding in Alex? Why was she upping the ante with every moment she spent with this family?

"What on earth are you going to do with all those apples?" she asked the girls. Time to get back some lost ground, and make this light again. "Make loads of applesauce?"

"Apple crumble!" Poppy crowed, and then made the mistake of dropping her hands from her hoodie, so the apples rolled everywhere. "Oh, no!" Her eyes filled with tears and her lip wobbled and before Lucy could even think about what she was doing—or why—she was down on her knees, chasing after the apples. Bella made some kind of snorting sound and belatedly Lucy realized how ridiculous she must look, cavorting around on all fours after a bunch of apples you could easily buy in the supermarket.

This was what she did, she acknowledged as she reached for another bruised apple. She tried too hard. She acted pathetic and ridiculous and something about it pushed people away.

Slowly she got to her feet, a few of the apples cradled in her arms. The knee of her tights was ripped, she saw, and they were a new pair. Not that she cared about her tights, or even the apples. She cared about Poppy, about Bella, and, yes, about Alex, and she was afraid it was already too late to stop herself from caring even more. From getting hurt.

"Here you go," she told Poppy, thrusting the

apples she'd collected back into the little girl's hoodie. "Sorry I couldn't get them all."

"You didn't have to do that," Alex said, and Lucy forced a smile.

"I know."

Then Poppy hurled herself at Lucy, wrapping her arms around Lucy's waist. "Thank you," she mumbled, her face pressed against Lucy's middle, and Lucy's arms came awkwardly around the girl.

She glanced up from Poppy's head still pressed to her stomach to see both Alex and Bella watching them, their expressions unreadable. Then Bella turned abruptly away and Alex smiled.

"Shall we have a look at all the food stalls?" he asked.

Lucy quickly caught up Poppy's hoodie full of apples before they spilled again. They all walked along the market square, looking at the food stalls and different exhibits for a while, and Lucy was glad to relax a little. Maybe she needed to stop obsessing over every little action and just enjoy the day, accept whatever it brought. Easier said than done, of course, but she'd try.

A man with a megaphone blared right next to them. "Last chance to enter the greasy pole competition! Winner gets a whole leg of lamb!"

"Daddy—," Poppy began, and Alex shook his head firmly.

"You've got to be kidding me, Poppy. There's no way I'm doing that."

Lucy glanced in bemusement at the greased pole that was festooned with ribbons and had, amazingly, a leg of lamb perched on the top for the lucky—and greasy—winner.

"You sure you don't want to try?" she teased, and Alex emphatically shook his head.

"I think you should, Dad," Bella suddenly said, her eyes glinting a challenge. "You're pretty strong, for an old guy. I reckon you could manage it."

"Thanks, Bella," Alex answered dryly, "but this old guy intends to stay with his feet planted firmly on the ground."

"Of course you won't even try," Bella said, her face tightening as she looked away. Watching the exchange, Lucy had the feeling that Bella had been challenging her father for more than just amusement's sake. Did she want Alex to prove himself somehow?

"Maybe you should, Alex," Lucy said, and he stared at her in amazement.

"Are you having me on? It's practically impossible, and frankly I have no desire to be covered in grease—"

"Don't be such a prig."

"A *prig*—"

"I think you should try."

"Last chance," the man with the megaphone reminded them. Lucy nodded towards Bella, who had hunched her shoulders and was looking away.

Alex's gaze narrowed. "You really want me to climb a greasy pole for my daughter's sake?" he said in a low voice that only Lucy could hear. "I'd rather buy her a bra."

"How about you do both?"

"Competition starts in two minutes, mate," the man said, and Alex heaved a resigned sigh.

"All right, fine, I'll do it."

Bella turned around, her face lighting up with amazement. "You will?"

"I didn't say I'd *win,*" Alex told them, and Poppy clapped her hands.

"Oh, but you will, Daddy! You've got to." She turned to Lucy with a confiding air. "I love lamb."

Lucy watched as Alex peeled off his sweater, revealing a brief, tantalizing glimpse of his toned abs before he yanked his T-shirt down. He tossed his sweater to Bella, who caught it with a small smile.

"The things I do for you," he said with an answering smile and a shake of his head. "If I win, we'll be eating lamb for a month."

"I like lamb too," Bella offered, clutching her father's sweater to her chest. Lucy smiled even as she remained slightly apart, sensing that this was between Alex and his daughters. Who knew what was going on in their hearts and minds, but somehow climbing a greased pole had become bigger than any prize that might be perched at the top. It was about showing his daughters that he loved them, that he'd do anything for them.

Even look ridiculous and get really dirty.

The competition began, and half a dozen brawny-looking lads managed to shimmy halfway up and snag one of the ribbons before they slid down, good-natured and covered in grease.

Alex gave Lucy a dark look. "I'm going to get filthy."

"You can shower when you get home."

Finally it was Alex's turn. Bella and Poppy waited, their breath held, their hands clasped in front of them, as Alex started up the pole. It was clearly a lot harder than he'd anticipated, because he started sliding down almost immediately.

Lucy's breath caught in her throat. It was stupid, she knew; it didn't really mean anything, and yet . . . she wanted him to win. The girls wanted him to win.

Wrapping his arms more tightly around the pole, Alex started to shimmy up again. His biceps bulged impressively and Lucy spared a second's thought for how utterly fit Alex Kincaid really was.

"You can do it, Daddy!" Poppy screeched in excitement, and, startled, Alex slid down half a foot before he managed to stop himself. He was past the halfway mark now and people had started to cheer him on, Poppy and then even Bella, loudest of all.

Lucy realized she was cheering too, and as Alex loomed closer to the top of the pole and the leg of lamb, she started screaming as loudly as the girls, all of them jumping up and down, caught up in the moment.

Alex spared them a glance, which cost him another foot, and then he made one last herculean effort and lunged upwards again, one hand outstretched as he grabbed the leg of lamb.

It must have been heavier than he thought, for it wobbled alarmingly and people jumped back in case it fell on their heads. Alex brought it to his body like a football, lost his grip on the pole, and came sliding down in a greasy rush as his daughters broke out into cheers.

"Your prize, my lady," Alex said, and with a mock bow he handed the lamb to Bella. She took it with a surprised, shy smile.

"You were great, Dad," she said quietly, and the sight of Alex's answering smile nearly burst—or broke—Lucy's heart. Either way it overflowed with emotion, and she turned away so they wouldn't see how affected she was, when she had no right to be.

This was their moment, their time, not hers.

She wasn't part of it.

22
Juliet

THE MORNING OF THE Crab Fair Juliet woke early and left with the dogs; she and Lucy had been tiptoeing around each other since her awful almost-breakdown a few days ago, and she had no desire to sit silent and glum while Lucy got ready for her big day out.

Lucy had played down the invitation, of course, claiming she was going only for Poppy's sake, but Juliet knew better. She could see the sparkle in her sister's eye. It would have gotten on her nerves if her misery wasn't weighing her down so much.

She'd pulled herself back from the brink of her breakdown, thankfully; she'd ended the conversation and started making dinner and Lucy had let it go. The next morning she'd kept herself brisk, if a little brittle, and Lucy hadn't said anything.

But her words, for better or worse, rattled around in Juliet's brain. She knew she was afraid of rejection, of course. Who wasn't? But what Lucy had said made Juliet realize other, unwelcome

317

aspects of herself. Like the fact that she was a master of the art of self-sabotage masked as self-protection. Why had she knowingly embarked on an affair with a married man? Because she knew it could never go anywhere. Because she'd thought she could be content with a little, and keep from getting hurt. Or maybe she just thought she didn't deserve more.

It was, she suspected, the same reason she'd opened the bed-and-breakfast. Because running a B&B was the closest thing to a family home and life she could hope to have. Because people came in and out of your life so quickly, and she stayed safe.

Except now she yearned for more, even as she retreated back into her sad little shell. And people noticed.

Rachel did, coming in after Lucy had left for the Crab Fair. She'd scoured the upstairs bathrooms and she plopped herself uninvited at the kitchen table.

"All right, Juliet. What's going on with you?"

Juliet, who had been cleaning the inside of the Aga, looked around, eyebrows raised. "I don't know what you mean."

"Don't sound so priggish. I mean, why are you avoiding everyone and cleaning your house like that murderer in the Bradbury story?"

Juliet stared at her blankly. "Pardon?"

"It's a short story about a man who kills this

bloke and then gets so obsessed about leaving fingerprints he ends up cleaning the whole bloody house, and when the police arrive, he's up in the attic, where he'd never even gone." Rachel cocked her head and swept her with a far too speculative gaze. "He was hiding something. What are you hiding?"

"Not a dead body," Juliet retorted, but Rachel was undeterred.

"But something. You haven't been to the last two pub quizzes—"

"And until last month, I hadn't gone to one in ten years. I'm hardly acting out of character, Rachel."

"No," she agreed slowly, "but I thought you were changing. Thawing, a little."

"I don't need to thaw," Juliet snapped.

"So you're happy, then, bustling around after strangers and keeping your house sparkling?"

"Yes." Juliet glared at her, refusing to say more. She would not justify her existence.

"Okay, then," Rachel said lightly, and rose from the table. "I'll leave you to it."

It wasn't until Rachel had left that Juliet realized how much she'd brushed her off. And while that was exactly what she'd intended to do, success felt more like failure.

She spent the rest of the day feeling restless, trying to occupy herself. She had plenty of work to do for Bonfire Night, and she spent a productive hour making calls, arranging various aspects of the evening.

Liz Benson, who ran the Women's Institute, promised to provide soup, bacon sandwiches, and tea and coffee on the evening, and just as Juliet was about to ring off, she asked casually, "Everything all right, Juliet?"

"Yes, of course," she answered as she tensed. "Why wouldn't it be?"

"Just wondering," Liz said, her voice still casual. "It's a small village. People care about each other."

"Thank you," Juliet answered gruffly. "But I'm fine." She supposed she should be grateful that people did seem to care about her, even if she kept putting them off. The trouble was, she just didn't know how to respond. How to open up. She'd told Lucy she couldn't and she'd meant it.

Even if she now wished she could change.

By late afternoon she'd done all she could do for Bonfire Night, and weeded the already-weeded flower beds, as well. Her last set of walkers had left yesterday, and the next lot was coming that evening. Juliet decided to bake scones for their arrival, something she'd always felt too busy to do, except now she seemed to have endless time to kill. Why was that? Why had her days suddenly become so long and empty?

She'd been happy before Lucy had arrived, she thought with a sudden surge of resentment. Or at least, she'd convinced herself she'd been happy. Wasn't that almost the same thing?

By seven o'clock her guests had arrived and left again, for steak and chips at the Hangman's Noose. Juliet ate leftovers alone at the kitchen table, and then wandered around restlessly, wondering when Lucy would be back. She decided to walk the dogs, even though the sun was starting to set, and she stepped outside into the brisk night air, breathing in the autumnal smell of damp leaves as twilight settled softly over the village. It was nearly the middle of October now, and night was coming on faster and colder.

She'd intended to walk up the village to the pastures at the top and let the dogs run free for a bit, but her feet didn't seem to be connected to her brain, because she turned instead and walked around Tarn House, then started down the dirt track towards Bega Farm.

She told herself she wasn't going to go see Peter; this just happened to be a pleasant and convenient walk. Never mind that her boots sank into mud and puddles she couldn't see in the darkness, or that the wind coming from the sea seemed to slice right through her. She'd walk to the gate that led to Bega Farm, which was a natural stopping point, and then turn around.

By the time she got to the gate, a few stars twinkled high above in a cloudy night sky. A light gleamed in the window of Peter's farmhouse, making it seem even smaller and more insignificant against the looming fells. Juliet stood there for a moment, her hand on the top bar of the gate, the dogs nosing her impatiently, wanting to either move forward or turn around.

An emotional crossroads, and she knew then that she'd come here for a reason. To move forward or to go back.

Slowly she reached for the latch on the gate and lifted it. Then she pushed the gate open and walked towards Bega Farm.

She knocked on the front door, her body and brain both cloaked in numbness in an entirely new way, as if she were a spectator watching herself from afar. The door opened, and Peter stood there, a flicker of surprise creasing his features before his expression ironed out implacably. He didn't speak. Part of her thought in a distant, surreal way, *I wonder what that poor woman will say.*

"I'm sorry," she blurted, the words tumbling out of her. "I'm sorry for asking you to—well, you know."

"Yes," Peter said flatly. "I know." His expression hadn't altered in the least and Juliet felt both cowed and more determined to say . . . something.

"May I come in?"

Silently Peter stepped aside and Juliet left the dogs huddled on the step and came into the kitchen; it was as cluttered and dirty as it had been

322

the last time she'd been there. She wished Peter would say something, anything, but he remained tight-lipped and silent as she wiped her damp palms down the sides of her jeans and gave him what she hoped was a smile.

"How's your dad?"

"You don't really care, do you?"

She blinked, startled by Peter's flatly stated reply. "I—I do care," she stammered, hating how wrong-footed she felt. How wrong-souled. "I wouldn't have asked, otherwise. I know how difficult it must be. . . ." She trailed off, willing Peter to take up the conversational slack, but he said nothing. Again. And she was afraid to try another opener.

"Peter, I came here because I really am sorry that I offended you by asking you to—to donate your sperm. I realize now I shouldn't have . . . that is, I should have realized . . ."

Peter arched an eyebrow, his arms folded. She'd never seen him look so forbidding. "And what should you have realized, Juliet?"

She felt like an unruly pupil called to the front of the class. By *Peter*. "That you wouldn't take kindly to my request," she answered. "That you're not the kind of man . . . that you *are* the kind of man who would take his responsibilities seriously. And that you'd see bringing a child into this world, no matter how, as your responsibility."

Peter just nodded, his jaw tight. "Well, I'm glad

you realized that," he said, and it sounded like a good-bye.

Juliet swallowed. "I really didn't mean to offend you . . . ," she tried again. She wanted him to give her his slow, easy smile and say in his deep Cumbrian burr that they were *areet* again.

"That doesn't make it much better, Juliet. If anything, it makes it worse."

She stared at him in miserable confusion. *"How?"*

Peter glanced up at the ceiling, seeming to struggle for words. "You and me," he finally said, choosing each word carefully, "we're used to being alone. Stuck in our ways a bit, I think."

"Y-y-y-yes," Juliet stuttered. "I know."

"But I was *trying,* Juliet. Trying in my own thick way, I know, but still. I thought . . . I thought you saw that. I thought you were coming around." He finally looked at her, and the misery in his gaze startled her. It also matched her own.

"But I was just being stupid," she whispered. "I was just being so stupid, Peter."

Slowly Peter shook his head. "No, you weren't. You were showing me what you really thought of me. Showing me how stupid *I* was, because I didn't even see it."

"No," she protested. "No. It's because I thought so well of you that I—"

"Wanted to use me? I know I might not be the finest specimen of man around, but I hope I'm

324

still good enough to be more than a stud." He shook his head, taking a step back, away from her. "Good night, Juliet."

Juliet gaped at him, horrified that it was going to end like this, that her apology hadn't been enough. Not remotely enough. And yet she had nothing else to offer. Nothing Peter wanted.

"Good night," she choked out, and then turned and walked back out into the darkness.

She stumbled down the track back to Tarn House, the dogs hurrying at her heels. She felt frozen, yet as if Peter had taken a hammer to her, and she'd shatter into tiny shards of ice at any moment. She just had to hold it together until she got inside.

Tarn House was cloaked in darkness and quiet; Lucy was still out with Alex and his daughters. Juliet settled the dogs in their beds and walked upstairs. She closed the door to her bedroom; she undressed and put on her pajamas and brushed her teeth.

Then she sat on the edge of her bed and clasped her hands together to keep them from shaking.

It didn't work. And it wasn't just her hands shaking; it was her shoulders, her whole body, as the sobs she'd managed to keep inside for so long came hurtling out, overwhelming her. She bowed her head, her hair falling in front of her face, her whole being racked with a pain that felt too intense to endure for more than a moment.

Surely this couldn't go on. Surely she couldn't feel this much and still live. And yet she could; she wrapped her arms around her middle as the tears poured down her face and she cried for her wrecked friendship with Peter, and for all the relationships she'd never dared to have. For the lonely little girl she'd been, longing for her mother to love her, and for the fact that at thirty-seven she still felt like that lonely little girl.

When the sobs finally stopped, she felt both exhausted and empty. She pulled back the duvet and crawled underneath the covers, shivering as if she had a fever. Eventually her body relaxed a bit, even if the ache in her heart didn't ease. She felt leaden and heavy now, and the thought of getting up from bed ever seemed like an impossible task. She closed her eyes, and eventually she slept.

23
Lucy

THE REST OF THE Crab Fair had passed by in a blur of happiness.

After the greasy-pole competition Alex had washed up a bit in the public bathrooms, and they took the apples and lamb back to the car. Then they went in search of lunch. The sun was still miraculously shining as they ate sausages and chips on a park bench with the antics of the fair all around them. Bella had relaxed a little, and was even smiling, if still studiously ignoring Lucy. She tried not to mind, but the girl's rejection of her rubbed her raw in places that had barely healed over.

"Thank you," Alex said quietly, leaning closer to her on the bench so the girls couldn't hear.

"What are you thanking me for, exactly?" Lucy asked lightly, but Alex's gaze was serious.

"For realizing that climbing that blasted pole was something I needed to do. For them." He nodded towards his daughters, who were immersed in the sights of the fair. "For Bella, especially."

"Your clothes won't thank me," Lucy teased,

because she wasn't sure how to handle Alex's sudden, sincere intensity.

Alex glanced down at his grease-spattered jeans. "No, probably not. But I'd sacrifice my entire wardrobe, such as it is, to reach Bella. I don't know where I went wrong, but I know it happened a while ago."

"Before your wife died?" Lucy asked, and Alex considered the question.

"Unfortunately, yes. I've been a workaholic my entire adult life. It only got worse when we moved here."

"Even though you were looking for the community life," Lucy stated, and Alex gave a nod.

"Ironic, I suppose, but the closer I get to something, the farther away it feels."

"Or maybe it just doesn't feel the way you thought it would."

"That too, I suppose."

"You must get the summers off, though," Lucy said. "Most people don't get that kind of holiday."

"Head teachers don't, either. I have to work for at least half of it. And if I'm honest . . ." He stopped, his unfocused gaze resting on Bella and Poppy. "It's not just a work issue."

"What is it, then?" Lucy asked. She leaned forward and Alex smiled bleakly.

"It's a *me* issue."

She wanted to ask what he meant, but she didn't get the chance, because Poppy had finished her sausage, spilling ketchup all over herself, and after the necessary cleanup they headed over to the children's races.

Bella warmed up enough to stagger through a three-legged race with Poppy as Alex and Lucy cheered them on. They watched some of the gurning competition, with various people pulling all sorts of funny and grotesque faces, and listened to some live music in the town hall until Lucy saw that Poppy was flagging and they decided to wrap things up.

A bucket of popcorn and far too much candy floss later, they headed back towards the car. Lucy had wondered how the day would end, if she should just ask Alex to drop her off at Tarn House, and she was still dithering about whether to say something when he turned to her and said, "Why don't you stay for tea?"

"Are we having the lamb?" she teased, and he smiled.

"I'm afraid not. It needs to roast for about six hours, I imagine. But how does pasta and tinned sauce sound?"

"Delicious."

Bella, thankfully, didn't make a fuss about Lucy staying, and Poppy was delighted. When they got back to the house, Alex disappeared upstairs for a shower—despite his ablutions in the public bathrooms, he was still pretty greasy—and Lucy put on a pan of water for the pasta, got out the tinned sauce, and added some chopped onion and pepper to it to make it a little tastier.

It felt so cozy, so wonderfully normal, to be pottering around in Alex's kitchen, chatting absently to Poppy as she searched for forks and knives and tidied up some of the breakfast things that had been left out.

She felt far more at ease, more at home, here than she ever had in Thomas's sleek penthouse apartment. Yet she still had no idea what could happen between her and Alex, or what he—or even she—wanted to happen.

A few minutes later Alex came back downstairs, dressed in faded jeans and a T-shirt. His feet were bare, his hair damp and spiky, and as Lucy looked at him, her mouth dried.

Okay, she knew what she wanted to happen. She wanted him to kiss her. A lot.

"Smells good," he said with a smile, and reached out to ruffle Poppy's hair. Poppy gave him a quick smile before running off and Alex watched her go, his smile fading.

"She's woken up with night terrors since school started."

"Night terrors?"

"She's awake but not awake. Screaming and crying, and there's nothing I can do to make it better." He sighed, shaking his head. "Sometimes it feels like there's nothing I can do to make anything better."

"Losing their mother is a huge thing," Lucy said quietly. "You can't make that go away, or forget about it."

"I know, but it's been almost two years. I feel like we should all be moving on more than we are." He glanced at her then, as if he'd suddenly realized just how much he'd revealed. "Sorry. I shouldn't be unloading this onto you."

"I don't mind."

"I know, but . . ." He stopped, swallowed. "Lucy . . ."

She tensed, afraid he was going to start in with the "I like you, but . . ." spiel, and that was a conversation she didn't want to have just then. Not when his hair was damp and he smelled like soap and their dinner was bubbling away on the stove. No, he could tell her at school, when he looked stern and forbidding and they had a desk and a photocopier between them.

"I think the pasta's ready," she said, her voice too quick and bright, as she went to drain it.

The rest of the evening passed easily enough; they ate, they chatted, and Alex didn't try to let her down gently, for which Lucy was thankful. Maybe she was a coward, but she wanted to enjoy being with him without being told there wasn't going to be anything more. Surely they could save that conversation for another day.

After dinner the girls cleared off upstairs, and in what felt like a routine even though it had happened only once before, Alex made them both coffees, which they took into the sitting room.

Lucy curled up in the same place she had before, Charlie flopping at her feet, everything about the moment so perfect and poignant she didn't want it to end.

"What made you decide to become a teacher?" she asked, simply because she wanted to learn more about this man.

Alex frowned slightly and took a sip of his coffee. "I had a good teacher myself, once."

"Only once?"

"It was enough."

"What year?"

"Year Six. I was on the brink of becoming a juvenile delinquent, and he pretty much saved me. Saved me from myself."

Lucy's jaw nearly dropped. "*You* were a juvenile delinquent?"

"Well, that might be exaggerating a bit. I was in and out of foster homes as a kid, and I got into a bunch of trouble. But my Year Six teacher, Mr. Benson he was, gave me a talking-to and basically scared me sh—senseless." He smiled shamefacedly and Lucy grinned back.

"So why were you in foster homes?" she asked after a moment. "What happened to your parents?"

Alex shifted on the sofa, his gaze sliding away

from her. "My mum cleared out when I was barely more than a baby, and my dad was a drunk. He'd get his act together sometimes, and I'd go back to him. Then something would happen, he'd fail to show up to a meeting or someone would report him, and it was back to the foster home." He gave a little shrug. "She wasn't a bad lady, my foster mother. Allison. She had four different foster kids to look after. She was run off her feet, but she had a good heart."

"Still, it's not the same as your own family," Lucy said.

"No," Alex agreed. "No, it's not."

Her childhood had been lonely, but she couldn't imagine what Alex's had been like. "And here I was," she said, "feeling sorry for myself because I was called Boob Girl in seventh grade."

"That's quite a nickname."

"Yeah, but . . ."

"Don't feel sorry for me, Lucy," he said. "I don't usually tell people about my childhood because I don't want pity. It's so . . . demoralizing."

"I don't pity you," she protested. "If anything, I admire you, Alex. You rose above all that to become an amazing teacher, and then to marry and raise a family. You've had a lot of hard knocks and you're still going strong. That's pretty impressive, in my book."

He glanced away. "I don't know how strong I am," he said in a low voice.

"Hey, you climbed a greasy pole today," she reminded him. "And you did it for your daughters. I think you're pretty darn strong."

He turned to look at her then, and the expression on his face made Lucy feel as if the breath had been vacuumed from her lungs. She wanted him to kiss her so badly it hurt.

But he didn't.

He just smiled and gave a little shake of his head before saying quietly, "Thank you."

"No problem," she croaked.

Alex didn't answer, and the moment spun on. Reluctantly Lucy unfolded herself from the sofa. "I should go," she said, even though she didn't want to. She held out her hand. "Can I take your coffee cup into the kitchen?"

"Thanks." He handed her his cup and then followed her out of the sitting room, his hands jammed into the pockets of his jeans.

She rinsed out both of their coffee cups and put them in the dishwasher, conscious of the silence stretching between them. This was end-of-a-date awkward, and she didn't even know if today qualified as a date.

"Thanks for today," he said, moving to the side of the doorway so she could get past him in the hall.

"You don't need to keep thanking me, Alex," she said as she reached for her coat, which she'd hung on the newel post. "I enjoyed it."

The hall was dim and quiet save for the tinny sound of the TV from upstairs; Poppy was watching in Alex's bedroom and Bella's door was closed. The intimacy of the dark hallway, the two of them nearly brushing shoulders, felt cringingly suggestive.

"I enjoyed it too," Alex said, and cleared his throat. The noise sounded like a gunshot in the quiet of the hall. God save her from moments like these.

"Well . . ." Lucy buttoned up her coat and moved towards the door. "I guess I'll see you on Monday."

She was at the door, one hand on the knob as she turned for a final good-bye. Why she turned at all, she didn't know. Maybe she really had been hoping all along.

"Lucy . . ." Alex began, and she felt her heart stop for a second, and then start beating hard. The very air around them felt electric. It was going to happen. Thank God.

He reached out and placed his palm flat on the door, his arm brushing her hair. Lucy waited, everything in her stilling and yearning all at once.

"Lucy," he said again, and then with a little grimace, as if he were saying *Screw this talking crap,* he lowered his head and kissed her.

The first brush of his lips against hers reminded Lucy what a kiss felt like, what it was meant to be. How sweet and lovely and *important* it was.

And while it had started as a simple, fairly

chaste good-night kiss, it quickly morphed into something else. Alex pressed Lucy against the doorway, his hands sliding down her body as he deepened the kiss, and Lucy angled her head back and wrapped her arms around his taut middle and thought, *Yes*.

Then a few seconds later a tinny blast of laughter came from the TV upstairs, and they both stilled. Lucy could feel her heart racing as Alex pulled away, raking a hand through his hair.

"Sorry," he muttered. "I don't . . . I just . . ."

She touched her buzzing lips. "Please, don't be sorry about that."

"I suppose . . . I suppose I got kind of carried away."

"I didn't know you had it in you, Alex," Lucy couldn't keep from teasing. "But I'm glad you do."

He grinned, and then to her delight he pulled her to him and kissed her again. This one he kept sweet, but she still clutched handfuls of his T-shirt, her mouth opening under his.

"Good night," he whispered against her mouth, and she smiled against his lips.

She was still smiling as she slipped out the door and walked back to Tarn House.

24
Juliet

THE NEXT MORNING JULIET lay in bed and considered the possibility of never getting up again. The bed was soft and warm, and she could happily—well, comfortably, anyway—live the rest of her days there without so much as moving. She wondered, distantly, whether she'd need food or water first. Then she realized she'd probably need the toilet before either. But she had an en suite bathroom, so she could stay in her bedroom rather than just her bed. Lucy could bring her meals.

She lay there for another hour past her usual waking time, staring at the ceiling, keeping her mind deliberately blank, before she heard a tentative knock on the door.

"Juliet? Are you in there?" Lucy called.

She considered not answering, but what was the point? She couldn't live in either her bed or her bedroom, as much as she wanted to. "Yes," she called back, her voice coming out in a morning croak.

"It's just—the dogs are getting anxious for their breakfast, and I don't know how much kibble they are meant to have."

Oh, the dogs. The only creatures on earth who actually needed her. With a sigh Juliet tried to rise from the bed, but her body felt so leaden that she flopped back down again. "They have one scoop each," she called to Lucy, her voice still croaky. "Can you manage it?"

"All right, then," Lucy answered, and Juliet heard her sister's footsteps go back down the stairs. She closed her eyes.

What felt like a few minutes later but was actually an hour, Lucy knocked on the door again. "May I come in?"

"I suppose." Juliet opened her eyes; she didn't think she'd fallen back asleep, but maybe she had.

Lucy came into the room, a mug of tea cradled in her hands. She put it on Juliet's bedside table and perched on the edge of the mattress. "I thought you might like a cuppa."

"Thank you," Juliet answered, her voice flat and lifeless. It was thoughtful, but she didn't want a cup of tea. She didn't want anything.

"Are you ill?"

"No."

"What's wrong, then?"

Juliet took a deep breath and let it out in a long, low rush. "I only took your stupid advice and went and talked to Peter," she said, throwing her arm over her eyes. She didn't think she had any more tears to cry, but she wasn't risking it. "And it didn't go over well, as I predicted, so thanks for bloody nothing."

Lucy was silent and after a moment Juliet drew her arm back and glanced at her sister. Lucy, she thought sourly, looked . . . incandescent. So something had happened with Alex last night. She covered her eyes once more.

"So what happened?" Lucy finally asked.

"He accepted my apology," Juliet answered. "But it didn't change anything. Whatever we had . . ." She paused, struggling to keep her voice even, not to torment herself with what they could have had. *I was trying in my own thick way.* "It's over," she said flatly. "He doesn't want to have anything to do with me."

"Oh, Juliet." Lucy put a hand on her shoulder, and for once Juliet didn't shake it off. She craved the physical comfort of another person's touch, the solid warmth of it.

"Thanks for the tea," she managed.

"I'm sorry," Lucy said, her hand still on Juliet's shoulder. "About Peter. That just . . . sucks."

"Yes, it does." Juliet drew her arm away from her eyes and tried to sit up a little, wincing as she did so. "I don't know if I feel like I have the flu or am hungover. Both, I think."

"An emotional hangover is the worst," Lucy said, and Juliet reached for the mug of tea and took a cautious sip.

"That's a term I haven't heard before."

"Binge crying. I'm an expert."

Juliet closed her eyes as the hot, sugary tea—Lucy had forgotten she didn't take sugar—hit her system. "I'm not."

"What a surprise."

Juliet smiled a little at that. Her tears had dried on her face last night and her skin felt tight as her mouth curved. She must look like an utter disaster.

"So if you're willing to take some advice from an expert," Lucy began, and Juliet rolled her eyes.

"Here we go."

"Don't stay in bed all day. It's tempting, I know, but you only feel worse when you do eventually get up."

"Maybe I won't ever get up," Juliet countered. The prospect still held a definite appeal.

"Seriously, Juliet." Juliet took another sip of tea to hide the discomfort she felt at seeing Lucy's face all soft with compassion. Her sister could afford to feel charitable, she thought with a tired spurt of bitterness. Her life was going swimmingly. "Why don't we do something today?" Lucy suggested. "Get out, go somewhere."

"Where? The only thing to do around here is hike." That wasn't really true, but Juliet didn't feel like listing the charms of the Western Lake District at the moment. She didn't feel like seeing the charms of anything or anywhere.

"We could go on the miniature steam train," Lucy said, and Juliet stared at her in disbelief.

"The La'al Ratty? That's for children."

"It's not. I mean, yes, children enjoy it, but so can adults. I read the brochure several times when I went to Ravenglass."

"When were you in Ravenglass?"

"One weekend when—oh, when I was kicking around." *When she would have rather been anywhere than with me,* Juliet filled in silently. She wasn't even surprised. She'd been awful to Lucy when she'd first arrived; she wasn't that much better now.

Sighing, she placed the mug of tea back on the bedside table. "I don't know."

"Come on, it'll be fun, and it's better than moping around here."

"Don't you have plans with Alex?" Juliet asked, a bit waspishly, and Lucy's expression went from startled to guarded.

"No, why would I?"

"Something happened last night." She didn't make it a question.

Lucy shrugged. "He kissed me," she admitted. "And it was . . ." Her mouth curved in a smile that lit up her whole face.

"Don't tell me," Juliet said with a groan. She sank back against the pillows. "I don't think I can stand to hear about your little romance just now."

"All right, then get up and we'll go on the Ratty. And I promise we won't talk about men, any men, all day long."

It took Juliet a while to get up, and even longer to get ready; her head felt fuzzy, her brain disconnected from her body. She managed finally to shower and dress, and an hour after Lucy had brought her the tea, they were outside heading for the train station.

The day was dark and gray, a chill, damp wind buffeting them as they walked with their hands dug into the pockets of their coats, their heads lowered against the onslaught.

Lucy, thankfully, seemed content just to be, and Juliet's head was aching so much she didn't think she could manage to put two coherent—or civil—words together.

The train pulled away from Hartley-by-the-Sea and she watched the choppy waves froth and foam as they rode down the coast. At Ravenglass they walked up the hill to the La'al Ratty, tiny and forest green, filled with families even on this less-than-glorious day.

Lucy bought them both coffees at the station café and they managed to find seats in the part of the train that was under cover, sitting opposite each other so that Juliet's knees were jammed up against Lucy's.

"Well, this is cozy," she said dryly, and took a sip of coffee.

"Have you been on the La'al Ratty before?" Lucy asked.

"No." The La'al Ratty was for tourists and families, not for sour single women who screwed up everything in their lives. But she wasn't going to wallow in self-pity. Not today, at least.

The whistle blew and with a chugging sound the train started to move off. Juliet gazed out at the rolling fields and gray-green fells cloaked in mist and felt her mood start imperceptibly to lift.

"Thank you," she said abruptly, and Lucy's eyebrows rose. "I know I don't seem appreciative, and I can be quite a difficult person," Juliet continued. "But I am grateful that you got me out of bed and brought me here." She swallowed and added, "You're a good sister to me, Lucy." Lucy blinked rapidly and Juliet rolled her eyes. "Now don't go getting all blubbery on me. *Honestly*," she said.

"I won't." With a smile Lucy dabbed her eyes. "But do you know, that's the first time you haven't called me your half sister?"

"Is it? Well." Juliet looked away. "You are my sister. The only one I've got." She hadn't meant to sound quite so terse, but Lucy didn't seem to mind because she launched herself towards Juliet, and she jerked back in surprise, spilling her coffee as Lucy gave her a bone-crunching hug.

"Thank you, Juliet, for saying that. You're the only sister I've got too."

"No need to state the obvious," Juliet muttered, and wiped ineffectually at the coffee stain on her jeans. Wiped at her eyes too, because it might be obvious now, but she didn't think it always had been.

25
Lucy

LYING IN BED ON Sunday night after what had turned out to be a pretty fabulous day on the La'al Ratty with Juliet, Lucy turned her thoughts inexorably to Alex. She relived that delicious kiss the way you savored a gourmet chocolate, remembering just how deeply Alex had kissed her, with such raw, unbridled passion. She'd teased him that she hadn't known he'd had it in him, and she really hadn't.

Alex had kissed her like a man dying of thirst and she was water. It had felt fantastic to be kissed like that. To be so wanted and needed.

She stretched her toes towards the end of the bed. Moonlight spilled onto the floor; the wind started up, rattling the windowpanes and making the leaves rustle.

What was going to happen now, on Monday? She pictured Alex coming into school, giving her a secret smile, pulling her into his office for a quick—or not-so-quick—kiss. . . .

Although that last bit seemed unlikely. There had to be some policy about head teachers dating their staff. Temporary staff, in her case, but still . . .

what if Alex regretted what in retrospect could very well be seen as a single moment of reckless passion?

Lucy turned on her side and tucked her knees up to her chest. That kiss *had* been reckless and a little bit wild . . . and perhaps totally unplanned. What if Alex came into school Monday morning and gave her the I'm-sorry-but-it-was-a-mistake talk?

And maybe it was a mistake. She'd been telling herself all along that she didn't want a relationship, wasn't ready. Maybe she'd been fooling herself on that score, but surely she'd learned to be a little cautious by now, to think about the consequences.

By Monday morning she'd thought so much about how Alex would or wouldn't react when he saw her that she was annoyed with her endless navel-gazing, and almost with Alex simply for being so much in her thoughts.

She got to work early, flipped on the kettle for a much-needed cup of coffee, and began to open the reception area, switching on the computer and the photocopier, answering the first calls of the day, which were invariably about children who were missing school because of illness.

She kept glancing towards the school yard, waiting for Alex, her heart leaping every time a figure came up the steep little lane. Teachers arrived in a steady trickle, talking about their weekends, their lessons, the hope of half term, which was just two weeks away.

Diana stopped by the desk to tell her about the weekend she'd spent in Manchester. "Andrew asked us to go down there instead of him coming up here, which seemed fair enough. At least he wants to see us."

"And how did it go?" Lucy asked, trying not to look too often for Alex.

"Fine, I suppose. The children loved it. They miss the city, their old life. We've only been here a year, you know."

"Do you think they want to move back?"

Diana grimaced. "That isn't really an option, with my mum."

"No, but you could do a switch," Lucy suggested, her elbows propped on the counter. "Why couldn't Andrew have the kids during the week, and you have the bachelorette pad in the country? You could go to Manchester for the weekends."

Diana gave a surprised guffaw of laughter. "I can't see Andrew agreeing to that."

"But your kids are in high school, right? So it's not as if they're toddlers. They can practically take care of themselves."

"You've never lived with a teenager, have you?" Diana asked wryly.

"Well, no," Lucy admitted, and Diana moved past her, down the hall towards the classrooms.

"Thanks for the laugh, anyway," she called over

her shoulder. "I might suggest it to Andrew, just to see the color drain from his face."

The teachers had all arrived, and the pupils were starting to come up the lane, a bobbing sea of blue and gray. Still no Alex.

Lucy busied herself making coffee, and then putting up the new notices on the board. She told all the relevant teachers about the day's absences, and then as the last pupils came up the hill, she saw Alex among them, holding Poppy by the hand, looking none too happy.

Lucy ducked out of the way, mindlessly feeding more paper into the photocopier. Not a good sign, that look on his face.

She heard the door open behind her and then Poppy's sweet, piping voice.

"Hi, Lucy!"

Lucy turned with a bright smile that felt as if it could slide right off her face. "Hey, Poppy."

Poppy skipped off towards her classroom, and Lucy's gaze moved to Alex. Her breath caught in her throat. He still looked grumpy and tired and harassed, but he also looked . . . wonderful.

"Hi," she whispered, and his mouth tugged up in one of his tiny smiles.

"Hi." He cleared his throat. "I . . . I've been . . ."

The door banged open and Liz Benson blew in with a gust of wind and rain. "What a day! Blue skies when I left ten minutes ago, but look at it now." She shook both her head and her umbrella, spraying Alex with raindrops. He stepped aside, giving Lucy a wry smile that felt like a private message, a promise to continue their conversation—or so she hoped.

Then he disappeared into his office, and Lucy turned back to the photocopier.

All day long she kept waiting for that conversation to happen, even as she told herself not to.

And the truth was, she had a *life* here in Hartley-by-the Sea. She'd actually made one she enjoyed, with friends from the school and a sister who loved her. All right, Juliet might not have *said* she loved her, but yesterday Lucy had felt closer to her sister—no "half" needed—than she ever had before. And she was enjoying her art classes, and life in the village, and frankly she didn't need Alex Kincaid, amazing kisser or not.

Still she jumped when a door opened, when someone came into the reception area, when the phone rang. She gave in to temptation a couple of times and craned her neck so she could see Alex in his office, but he was always immersed in work or on the phone, which wasn't unusual but felt as if he was avoiding her.

An entire day passed without him talking to her at all. He'd e-mailed her about various work-related issues; he'd given her a distracted smile when he'd gone into the hall for lunch. That was it.

He *was* avoiding her. He regretted their kiss,

regretted everything, and he didn't know how to tell her. And she, Lucy knew, was too much of a coward to push the issue. She'd rather live in ignorance and hope than with disillusionment and disappointment.

Still, when another three days had passed without Alex saying anything personal at all, Lucy knew she had to start a conversation. She deserved better than this.

She waited until Alex was alone in his office, the teachers and pupils all safely in their lessons, and then she took a deep breath and marched to his door, rapping on it rather loudly.

"Come in."

He looked startled to see her at first, and then wary. Lucy's heart plummeted like a penny off the Empire State Building. Down, down, down, so hard and fast it would leave a little crater in the pavement.

Carefully she closed the door behind her. Alex waited, watching her with that same wary expression, and belatedly Lucy realized she hadn't actually considered what she intended to say to him.

She'd wanted *him* to say something. Although looking at his face now, she was pretty sure she didn't.

"Look, Alex, I came in here to tell you that you don't have to avoid me." She heard the hurt in her voice, reminding her of the sound of feet crunching on broken glass. Cringeworthy. Pain-inducing.

"Avoid you?"

"Are you going to tell me you aren't?" She raised her eyebrows, hurt giving way to anger. Was he really going to pull that lame male trick of pretending he had no idea what she was talking about?

"No," Alex said after a moment. He placed his hands flat on his desk as he gazed up at her. "I'm not going to tell you that."

Her anger left her in a rush, and the hurt returned to fill in all the empty spaces. "So you are, then."

"Well . . . a bit."

"A bit?"

"To be fair, I've had a rough week. Poppy's been up every night and Bella's getting into trouble at school again."

"Oh, no." For a moment her worries paled in comparison with those of Alex's daughters. "What's happened? Is it PE again?"

"No, she's mouthing off to some teachers. Acting out. She's risking another suspension." Wearily he rubbed a hand over his face. "I tried asking her what's troubling her, but she won't tell me anything. I even suggesting counseling again, and she just rolled her eyes."

"I'm sorry." And now Lucy felt like a heel.

Alex dropped his hand and glanced up at her

with wry honesty. "But you're right, I have been avoiding you, Lucy, and that's because I don't know what to say to you. I had a wonderful time on Saturday and—and Saturday night."

"So did I," she whispered.

"But the truth is I don't know where this is going. Where anything between us can go. You're leaving in a couple of months and I don't even know if I'm ready for a relationship. Or if my daughters are ready for one. And that's without even asking you what you want. I know you recently broke up with a bloke who was saddled with kids, and I can't imagine your wanting to jump into that scenario all over again."

He waited, and Lucy wondered what he wanted to hear. That she did? Or was he hoping she'd give him the easy out?

"I don't know," she said slowly. "All of this is unexpected."

"Yes, definitely," Alex agreed. "I wasn't looking for . . . well, anything. Frankly at this point my life is more about survival mode."

"Right." So this was the letting-her-down talk, and the trouble was he did it so nicely. She felt sorry for him, but it still hurt that he wasn't sweeping her into his arms and kissing her senseless as he apologized for ignoring her for the last three days. Poor Lucy, ever the optimist.

"So . . ." Alex raked a hand through his hair, shrugging up at her, and Lucy decided to help him out. Help herself out, and end this misery.

"So maybe we should just leave it?" she finished with as practical a tone as she could muster. "It was fun, but . . . ?"

Now it was his turn to finish. And for a second she thought she saw disappointment flicker in his eyes. No, that was probably more of her deluded optimism.

"Fun, but," he repeated after a moment. "Yes, I suppose that sums it up."

Nodding slowly, the heart that had free-fallen like a penny now heavy as a stone, Lucy turned and walked back to reception.

A week dragged by, an awful week where Lucy exchanged cordial hellos with Alex and not much more. Once he'd come into the office and attempted some chitchat, but it had been so painfully awk-ward for both of them that they'd left it.

Lucy told herself she didn't mind, insisted she had enough going on in her life to be happy about. And she *did*. She was teaching art to the Year Fives as well as the Year Sixes now, and she, Rachel, and Juliet had started a new team for the pub quiz with Abby, the granddaughter of Mary Buxton from the beach café and a single mum to a three-year-old boy.

Abby had been living in Newcastle but was staying in Hartley-by-the-Sea for a little while. "Until Mary gets on her feet," she'd said, although

Juliet had told Lucy privately that Mary wasn't likely to do that anytime soon.

"So what do you think Abby will do?" Lucy had asked.

"Stay, I suppose. Mary's the only family she's got, as far as I know. Abby grew up here, but she left as soon as she'd finished school."

"Do you think she's glad to be back?" Although they'd done a pub quiz together, she hadn't gotten to know Abby very well. She hadn't spoken except to offer a few tentative answers, and she hadn't even stayed to hear the results, needing to get back to Noah.

"I don't know," Juliet answered slowly. "I never got the sense she hated it here, but more that she wanted to see the world. She's only twenty-four now."

Lucy and Juliet had taken to spending their evenings together, chatting over dinner and sometimes watching brainless TV shows. Lucy was trying to convince Juliet of the merits of reality TV, and so far she thought she'd had some success.

"It's such rubbish," Juliet would exclaim as contestants dumped buckets of mud over each other's heads on one particularly inane program, but she was smiling.

"You just love to criticize," Lucy answered, and threw a pillow at her.

Some evenings they spent chatting with whatever guests were staying: retired couples or gap year kids or the occasional bus tour of pensioners or pupils. Lucy liked hearing all their different stories and accents, learning a little bit about their lives before they moved on. Juliet, she thought, seemed to like it too, although she never said as much.

So really, Lucy told herself as she swept mascara onto her lashes in preparation for another day at Hartley Primary, she had nothing to complain about. So she wasn't going to dive headfirst into a relationship. With her history, it was better this way. Really.

It was the last day before half term, the week-long break at the end of October, and Lucy had nothing planned for the holiday week except helping Juliet out with the steady stream of guests booked into Tarn House. Poppy had already told her, confidingly, that Alex was taking her and Bella to see his in-laws down in London, so Lucy wouldn't even have the paltry hope of accidentally on purpose bumping into him on the beach when he walked Charlie.

It was just as well, Lucy decided as she started packing up that afternoon. The children had left at half past one, shouting and running down the hill, delighted to be off school for an entire week. And maybe some time away from Hartley Primary would help to get Alex out of her system. She'd certainly be busy enough helping Juliet.

"So what's going on with you and our head teacher?"

"What?" Lucy looked up to see Diana standing in the doorway, eyebrows raised expectantly. "Nothing's going on. Why do you even ask?"

Diana glanced furtively at Alex's closed door; he was working, right up to the last minute. "Because I have it on good authority that you've been to his house twice. Late at night."

"This is your bridge-playing neighbor."

"That's the one."

"I'm friendly with Bella and Poppy," Lucy said with what she hoped was a convincing shrug. "It's no big deal."

"No? Because two dates in Hartley-by-the-Sea is the same as getting married."

"They weren't dates."

"In Hartley-by-the—"

Lucy held up one hand. "Enough, I get it. Trust me, Diana, nothing is going on. You'll have to find someone else to gossip about."

Diana must have finally believed her, because she sighed and said, "Pity. I always thought the two of you would make a good couple. You'd bring him out of his shell and he'd keep you tethered to earth."

Lucy smiled at that but then shook her head. "It's not going to happen."

"I suppose you are leaving soon."

That was something she most definitely didn't

want to think about. "I still have almost two months left," she protested, but in her head she was calculating the days and she realized her time in Hartley-by-the-Sea was half-finished. How had that happened?

Two months wasn't a very long time, she realized as she headed back to Tarn House. The first two had gone by in a flash. She had a feeling the next two months would pass even more quickly.

The next week certainly went fast as she helped Juliet; Rachel was away visiting universities with a reluctant Lily, and so Lucy and Juliet did all the housework as well as the fry-up breakfasts and the afternoon teas. Lucy had never done so much physical labor before, but she enjoyed herself too, chatting with Juliet as they developed a system for the morning (Lucy handled toast, and Juliet manned the Aga), and spending the evenings with guests or on Thursday at the pub doing the quiz.

By Sunday night Lucy was exhausted, and contemplated returning to school the next morning with less than her usual enthusiasm. She didn't relish seeing Alex again, although the pain of having him back off had, with time and effort, lessened just a little.

Since they were free of guests, Juliet brought a bottle of wine and two glasses into the sitting room; Lucy lay back on the sofa, propping her feet on the arm, something she suspected would have given Juliet fits a few months ago, but which she now eyed slightly askance, saying nothing. Progress, of a kind.

"So what about this baby thing?" Lucy asked when they were both settled with full glasses of wine. It was progress of another kind that she felt brave enough to ask the question.

Juliet glanced warily at her, and then shrugged. "It was a crazy idea. I must have been mad even to think of it. As for asking Peter . . ." She closed her eyes, cringing. "Definitely mad."

"Biology is a powerful force."

"I don't think it was just that. It was more . . ." She sighed and stared at the ceiling. "A baby is like a blank slate. Someone to love, someone to love you, without any of the emotional baggage."

Lucy considered this for a second before asking carefully, "Don't you think we're both bound to bring our baggage to motherhood, Juliet?"

"Well, yes. I suppose. But a baby is genetically programmed to love its mother. I think that was the idea I was fixated on." She made a face. "Pathetic, really."

"No, not pathetic. Or if it is, then I'm in that boat with you. I stayed with Thomas for so long because I wanted someone to love and need me. And I've been looking at Alex the same way." Now she was the one to make a face. "Here is this widower with two motherless daughters in desperate need of someone like me to make them all better."

"It helps that he's a hottie," Juliet pointed out.

"Well, yes. There's that too. Too bad he didn't feel the same way." She'd told Juliet, a while back, about the whole "fun, but" conversation. Juliet had made a rude noise, which had made Lucy feel a little bit better.

Now they were both silent for a moment, lying on opposite sofas, staring at the ceiling, drinking their wine. "So here we are," Juliet finally said, "with no men and no babies."

"At least we've got each other."

"Girl power," Juliet replied dryly, and Lucy grinned. She felt happier than she had in a long, long time. Happier, perhaps, than even when she'd been with Alex.

"Don't knock it, sister."

"Oh, please." But Juliet was grinning back. "Have you thought about what you're going to do when you go back to Boston?" she asked a few minutes later, and Lucy's smile faded. She'd managed not to think about returning to Boston for the whole half term, and she didn't particularly want to think about it now.

"Not really." She took a slug of wine. "I have no job, no apartment, no boyfriend. There's not much to go back to."

"You must have friends. . . ."

"Yes," Lucy said, and thought of Chloe. She'd

Skyped with her a few times, although not in recent weeks. "Yes, I have friends," she told Juliet. "But I also have friends here."

"You could stay," Juliet said, and Lucy blinked at her, startled.

"What . . ."

"I mean, if you wanted to. Only if you wanted to. You'd be welcome here, of course—"

Of course? A few months or even weeks ago there would have been no *of course* about it. "That's very kind of you . . . ," she began, and Juliet rushed in, stumbling a bit over the words.

"I'd understand if you wanted to get your own digs. But if you're happy in Hartley-by-the-Sea, if you've made a life for yourself . . ."

It was all too tempting. Juliet was right; she was happy here. She had a life. And if she stayed here, maybe Alex would change his mind about starting a relationship. Not like that was her main reason, of course.

"The trouble is," she said to Juliet, "I don't have a job after Christmas."

"You could find one," Juliet answered. "Make one, even. Start a business offering arts and crafts parties for children. Exhibit your paintings locally. The beach café would put them up."

The beach café. A far cry from an upscale Boston art gallery, and yet she didn't really mind.

"If you wanted to stay, you could make it happen. It's just a question of whether you want to."

"Do you want me to?" Lucy asked. "Really? I wouldn't cramp your style, horning in on your territory?"

"Oh, Lucy." Juliet bit her lip, and then shook her head. "No, I'd love if you stayed. But don't stay just for me."

Yet Juliet was perhaps the best and most important reason to stay.

26
Juliet

THERE WAS A MAN in her garden. Juliet braced her elbows against the sink as she leaned forward and peered out the kitchen window. Since the clocks had turned back last week, the sun set at four o'clock and the days felt wintry. And the man in her garden, she could see as she squinted, looked like he was wearing only a pair of trousers.

He stumbled past her rosebushes, and Juliet wondered if he was a drunk who had made his way down from the pub. Then the moonlight caught his white hair and she realized with a lurch who it was. William Lanford. Peter's father was wandering half-dressed in her garden with no shirt or coat after dark.

Juliet grabbed her coat and shoved her feet into her hiking boots before opening the back door and stepping outside. "William?" she called. "Mr. Lanford?"

He swung around to stare suspiciously at her. "Who the devil are you?"

"Juliet Bagshaw. You're in my garden."

"No, I'm not. I'm going to the pub." She saw a heartbreaking mixture of belligerence and fear in his rheumy eyes. "A man deserves a drink at the end of a long day."

"Yes, he does." Juliet could see from the porch light that William Lanford was shaking from the cold; worse, his feet were bare and bloody from walking all the way from Bega Farm. She'd seen Peter leave an hour ago in his Land Rover, and had no idea how to reach him. She didn't have his mobile number. "It's a filthy night to be out, though," she said to William, trying to keep her voice mild. "Even for a drink at the pub." He simply snorted at this. "Why don't you come in here for a drink?" Juliet suggested.

"Do you have any whiskey?" William demanded.

"No," Juliet admitted, "but I've got some nice sherry."

"Sherry!" William quivered with indignation. "That's a lass's drink."

Juliet almost smiled at that. She should have known better than to suggest sherry. A shudder ran through his body and Juliet knew she had to get William Lanford inside quickly, and preferably back to Bega Farm.

"How about I drive you back to your place?" she suggested. "I know Peter has a good whiskey back at Bega Farm. Glenfiddich." William didn't answer, but she could see the dawning confusion in his eyes, an awareness that things were not as he thought they were.

"I don't know. . . ."

"It's so cold out," Juliet continued, hoping she sounded persuasive. "And I think it's starting to rain." A few raindrops had spattered in her face as they'd spoken and William's whole body was now shaking from the cold.

"It's not far," William insisted. "And I've come a long way already."

"Let me at least get you a coat," she said. "You must have forgotten yours in the rush for that drink. It's freezing out, William."

Confusion contorted his features as he looked down at himself, and the lucid part of him realized he'd gone out only half-dressed. "What's hap-pened to my shirt?" he muttered. "Someone's gone and taken it."

Juliet had read that people suffering from dementia could become paranoid and aggres-sive. Understandably so, but she didn't know how to deal with that now. "Come on, William," she said as gently as she could. "Let's go find your shirt." She reached for his arm and he shook it off, glaring at her.

"Who are you?" he demanded, his voice trembling. "Where am I?"

"I'm Juliet Bagshaw, a neighbor of yours," Juliet answered steadily, although she felt strangely emotional. "And you're in my garden."

William shook his head, his face crumpling with the bewilderment of a child. "But I was just trying to go to the pub."

"I know you were. And you deserve a nice big tot of whiskey, after this." Smiling, trying to reassure him, she reached for his arm again. This time he didn't resist, and holding her breath, hoping he'd continue to cooperate, Juliet guided him towards her car. Thankfully her keys were in the pocket of her coat, and she helped William into the passenger seat before climbing into the driver's side and starting the engine.

She reached over and did his seat belt for him, drawing it over his bare, sunken chest, and he stared at her with troubled eyes. "Peter won't like this."

"He might be worried about you," Juliet allowed. "But he'll be glad you're safe."

"I shouldn't have gone out." William plucked at the seat belt. "Peter told me not to go out. I shouldn't have gone out."

'We'll get you back home, William," Juliet soothed, and started driving down the dirt track that led to Bega Farm. It wasn't meant for a car like hers, and they bumped and juddered down the road while Juliet silently prayed the car wouldn't get a flat tire.

Finally Bega Farm appeared, its lights twinkling in the vast darkness. As Juliet parked the car, she saw the front door had been left wide open, and the rain was blowing in.

With a quick smile for William, who had not spoken during the journey, Juliet got out of the car and hurried around to the passenger side. She sucked in a breath when she opened the door and saw that blood from a cut on his foot had soaked into the foot well. The cut was deeper than she'd thought.

William followed her gaze to his feet and then glanced back at her, panic starting in his eyes. Juliet reached out a hand and drew him up to standing.

"Let's get you inside, shall we?"

Painstakingly, her arm around William, she guided him into the house. He was limping badly now and Juliet knew he would need his foot seen to. Inside the house was as much a mess as ever. Juliet led William past the kitchen with its forgotten dishes and dirty clothes to the sitting room, and helped him to the faded easy chair where he'd sat when Peter had given him a shave.

"Now then, let's get you comfortable," she said as cheerfully as she could. "I'll just go find something for your feet."

William didn't answer; he seemed exhausted, his face gray and haggard. Juliet fetched a bowl of warm water and a towel, and after a second's hesitation she ventured upstairs to find a clean shirt for William. The floorboards creaked as she walked down the upstairs hall, feeling guiltily that she was violating Peter's privacy, but knowing she didn't have much choice.

She peeked in several bedrooms that looked

unused and forgotten, and then paused in the doorway of what was obviously Peter's room. A big bed, unmade and rumpled. One of his Aran jumpers tossed on a chair. She saw a book and a pair of reading glasses left on a bedside table, and unable to keep herself from it, she tiptoed closer to have a look. It was an Agatha Christie, Inspector Poirot, which made her smile a little. She liked Poirot.

Quickly she backed out of the room. The next room she looked in was William's, and she found a stack of neatly folded, ironed laundry on his bureau, which was surprising considering the general state of the house. She took a shirt from the top of the pile and hurried downstairs.

When she came back into the sitting room, she saw that William had fallen asleep, his head lolling against the back of the chair. He woke when Juliet started bathing his feet, dabbing at the cuts and scratches, but kept his head back against the chair and didn't say anything.

At least one of the cuts looked quite deep, and with a quick smile for William, Juliet went in search of some antibiotic ointment. She found an old, cracked tube in the cupboard above the sink, and decided it was better than nothing.

Fifteen minutes later she had William's feet bathed and bandaged and had managed to help him into the clean shirt. He was docile through it all, depressingly so, as if the will to engage in any way had leached out of him. Juliet tried to keep up a stream of cheerful chatter, but she was no Lucy and her conversation petered out after just a few minutes. William didn't seem to mind.

"There you are," she said when she'd settled him back into his chair. "Now for that tot of whiskey."

But when she returned to the sitting room with the promised drink, William was asleep. Juliet left the whiskey on the table by his chair and went back into the kitchen. She gazed around at all the mess for a moment, and then, since she didn't have anything better to do, she started to tidy up.

She loaded the dishwasher with the dirty dishes and left the grease-covered pots and pans in the sink to soak. She scrubbed down all the surfaces and dug out an ancient bottle of enamel cleaner from underneath the sink and had just given the Aga a good scouring when the lights from Peter's Rover shone through the window and she heard the sound of a car door slamming, and quick steps down the path.

Peter threw the door open, striding in, still dressed in waterproofs and mud-caked Wellies.

"I thought it was your car. Has something happened?"

She saw the panic etched in every line of his face and said quickly, "It's okay. Nothing serious—"

"My dad," Peter said, not a question, but Juliet nodded as if it had been one.

"He was in my garden. He was a little disoriented."

Peter's mouth opened, but no sound came out. "I told him to stay here while I moved the sheep," he finally said. Juliet could hear both guilt and confusion in his voice. "He's normally very good about staying put when I ask him to."

"He told me he wanted to go to the pub," Juliet explained. "But I got him back here and saw to his feet—"

"His feet?"

"He was barefoot," Juliet explained. "And without a shirt. He must have walked all the way from Bega Farm to Tarn House."

Peter raked a hand through his hair, his fist clenching on the flyaway strands. "I shouldn't have—"

"He's all right, Peter."

"Let me go check on him." He moved past her to the sitting room, tracking mud across the kitchen floor. At least, Juliet thought, she hadn't gotten round to mopping up yet.

A few minutes later Peter returned to the kitchen. He stared at her for a moment, and then his gaze moved to the cleaned kitchen. "Thank you," he finally said. "You've been very kind."

"It's nothing."

Peter didn't answer; his face was still pale, his expression dazed. Juliet had an urge to hug him, but she doubted that would go over well and in any case she wasn't sure she could manage it. She felt as jerky and awkward as a wooden marionette; it had suddenly become difficult to know what to do with her arms.

She decided he could use a shot of whiskey instead, and she could, as well. She fetched the bottle of Glenfiddich and poured them both measures before handing one to Peter, who took it almost absently, his gaze unfocused.

"Thank you. . . ."

"Drink up, Peter."

He took a sip, blinking as the alcohol hit the back of his throat, and then he drained his glass and placed it on the counter. "I won't be able to manage on my own anymore," he said, and Juliet shook her head.

"No, probably not. But having a caregiver in could be a good thing."

"Dad won't like being meddled with."

"He was all right with me."

"But some stranger . . ."

"You could interview someone," Juliet suggested. "Find someone he likes."

Peter gave her a bleak look. "There's not enough money to be choosy."

Juliet nodded. There was no such thing as a rich sheep farmer, not in Cumbria. "I'm sorry," she said, because she didn't know what else to say, and she was.

"I'm sorry too," Peter said. "And I don't mean

my dad. I'm sorry I've . . . I haven't been more forgiving."

Juliet stared at him, dry-mouthed, before she finally managed to stammer back, "I'm—I'm sorry I did something you needed to forgive."

And finally, *finally* Peter gave her one of those slow smiles she'd missed this last month. "We areet, then, Juliet?"

"We're areet," she answered with a return smile. She couldn't keep from feeling a little twist of sorrow, though, for what they might have had, and missed out on. All because she'd been so bloody stupid. So afraid.

"I should go." She took a step towards the door.

"Thank you for everything," Peter said. "I'd drive you back, but—"

"You don't want to leave your dad. And I have my car. I understand, Peter. And if you need help, you know you can ask me." She looked at him seriously, almost sternly, because she knew Peter was as proud as he was gentle, and he wouldn't like asking for help. "If you need someone to come and sit with your dad, or you could bring him up to Tarn House for a change of scenery. I'm around most days."

"He might like that," Peter said, which was as close to a yes as Juliet would get. She nodded, and Peter nodded back, and then, reluctantly because she knew she wanted to stay, she left.

27
Lucy

THE WEDNESDAY AFTER HALF term Lucy watched with a sinking heart as Oliver Jones was marched towards reception. Diana stopped by the counter, her mouth tightening as she watched the boy slouch into Alex's office.

"I try to cut him some slack, honestly I do, but he pinched another boy in the class, hard enough to leave a bruise. I can't have that."

"I know," Lucy said, but her heart ached for Oliver.

Alex's door closed and fifteen minutes later a woman came hurrying up the lane. She stepped inside the foyer, her expression pinched, her eyes dark and shadowed.

"I'm here for Oliver," she said, and with a start Lucy realized this was Mrs. Jones.

"He's just in with Mr. Kincaid," Lucy said. "I'll go check for you." She knocked on Alex's door, and after he answered tersely, she opened it and stuck her head around the doorframe. "Mrs. Jones is here." Oliver, she saw, had his head bowed and was scuffing his shoes along the floor.

"Please send her in," Alex said, and Lucy motioned the woman forward.

She felt twitchy and tense for the next half hour; she could see the tops of all their heads through Alex's window, but she had no idea what was going on. She hoped Alex would consider Oliver's situation and not come down too hard on the boy.

Finally the door opened and Mrs. Jones came out, one hand on Oliver's shoulder. "Thank you," she murmured to Alex, who had walked out behind them, looking unhappily resolute. "Come on, sweetheart," she murmured to Oliver, who was leaning into his mother. "Let's get your things."

Lucy watched them covertly, surprised by the tenderness Oliver's mother showed the boy, and the way he clearly craved her comfort. She'd assumed Oliver's mother was both uncaring and indifferent, but in that moment she realized Mrs. Jones was doing the best she could, just like everyone else.

They left a few minutes later and she turned to Alex. "Why is he leaving school in the middle of the day?"

"He's suspended for two days."

"That seems harsh—"

"It was his third infraction," Alex said flatly. "I can only make so many exceptions, Lucy."

"You know about his mother—"

"I make it my business to know as much as I can about every pupil's home situation. But I can't let Oliver's behavior go unpunished, no matter what's going on at home." He sighed and ran a hand through his hair. "This job is hard sometimes, and there are no easy answers. But Lena Jones said she'd try to get some help, so that's something." With another sigh he disappeared into his office.

The Saturday after half term Lucy bought the *Whitehaven News* and scoured the Help Wanted section. There were plenty of jobs she wasn't remotely qualified for, and a few she was and didn't want. Nighttime office cleaning? No thanks. Working in the cafeteria at the secondary school? A possibility, but she wanted to stretch her wings a little more, maybe even do something with art, as Juliet had suggested.

Well, she had time, she told herself. It was only the first week of November, after all. Plenty of time.

Guy Fawkes Day was that week, and the following Monday was Bonfire Night for the village.

"You do remember Guy Fawkes Day, I hope," Juliet said severely, on the morning of the bonfire. Lucy gave her a sheepish look.

"Umm, sort of . . ."

"Guy Fawkes almost blew up Parliament in the early sixteen hundreds," Juliet explained, sounding very much like a schoolteacher. "So since then, to celebrate the king's escape from assassination, we have fireworks and a bonfire." She paused, wrinkling her nose. "People used to put a straw man on the bonfire, meant to be an effigy of Fawkes. Some still do."

"You burn a straw man on a bonfire?" Lucy exclaimed. "And this is a holiday for children?"

Juliet shrugged. "It's just an excuse to have fireworks, really," she said. "But I'm in charge of Bonfire Night, as you know, and I could use some help running the thing."

The whole village, Lucy saw that evening, came out for Bonfire Night. It was held on a sheep field at the bottom of the village; men in fluorescent vests guided cars into a makeshift parking lot on another field, but most people just walked. Lucy watched them come down the high street in a steady stream; she was meant to be collecting tickets, but judging from the other woman who was collecting, it was more of an excuse to chat with various people. More than once, the woman waved someone towards the bonfire, smiling. "Ah, you're areet, John. Come along, then."

Lucy felt rather shrewish demanding people show her their tickets, and so she ended up just smiling at everyone and waving the tickets she'd already collected rather feebly. Maybe Juliet should have assigned her to the food stall.

The bonfire was impressive, though, the flames leaping twenty feet towards the sky. The smell of woodsmoke drifted on the air, and people laughed and chatted as they sipped from paper cups of soup and nibbled sausage rolls bought from the food stall, run by a formidable Liz Benson, wielding a large ladle and sternly informing everyone not to jump the queue. Since it seemed as if most of the people had already arrived, Lucy abandoned her post as ticket collector and went to join the line for a cup of soup.

"How was the week in Manchester?" she asked Diana after she'd gotten her soup and was standing near the leaping flames of the bonfire.

Diana gave a little grimace. "Okay, I suppose."

"That doesn't sound all that okay." The last time Lucy had talked to Diana about Andrew being in Manchester, her friend had seemed upbeat. "What happened?"

Diana blew out a breath. "We looked at some of the flats and they were . . ." She hesitated, her distant gaze on her two teenagers, waiting in the line for hot chocolate.

"Small?" Lucy suggested, and Diana shook her head.

"No, it wasn't that. They were . . . bachelor pads." She let out a slightly bitter laugh. "Sleek, modern places with tiny kitchens and one bedroom and everything made of chrome and glass. And the *buildings* . . . let's just say there weren't many married couples in those places, and absolutely no families."

"But you wouldn't all be living in a place like that," Lucy said after a moment. "Would you? I thought it was just meant to be a weekday place for him."

"Yes, it was. Is. But the thought of Andrew

having a life down there, in a place like that, while I'm cooking sausages and mash and going to teachers' meetings and all the rest of it . . ." Her gaze swung back towards Lucy, and she was discomfited to see the depth of bleakness there. "We might as well be divorced."

"Don't say that, Diana—"

"Why not? It's true. Andrew hasn't been back for a weekend since early October." She shook her head, her gaze turning even grimmer. "He's got his own life now, and it doesn't include us. That's what the week down there showed me." She moved off to join her children before Lucy could answer.

"What's wrong with Diana?" Rachel asked as she came over, her hands cradling a cup of soup. "She looks positively thunderous."

"Just the usual," Lucy said, and Rachel nodded knowingly.

"The husband in Manchester? Bad news, if you ask me."

"I think Diana's coming to that realization." She took a sip from her own cup of soup. "What about you? How was the tour of universities?"

"Well, *I* liked them."

"Lily not so much?"

Rachel's face tightened. "She refuses to give anything a chance. She says she doesn't even want to go to university, which is enough to make me tear my hair out."

Lucy had heard this sentiment before, and when she'd met Lily a couple of times, she'd sensed the tension between the two sisters. "Why do you want her to go to college so badly?" she asked cautiously, because she knew this was a touchy topic for Rachel.

"Why wouldn't I? You sound like Juliet. She asked the same thing—"

"Juliet didn't go to university—"

"I know that, and she's done well for herself, but that's not the norm. Education is power, Lucy."

"It wasn't for me. I have a BA in fine art and it's practically useless."

Rachel shrugged impatiently. "Well, Lily isn't going to study art."

"Isn't she interested in graphic design?"

"That's just a phase. She's predicted to get an A star in biology. She could do so much with that. Medicine, research—"

"But if she's not interested—"

Rachel gave her a quelling look. "I think I know my sister better than you do," she said shortly.

"Sorry. I don't mean to push."

Rachel ran a hand through her unruly hair, leaving it messier than before. "I know. I'm sorry to sound so bitchy. It's just that I've practically raised Lily. My mother broke her back when Lily was three years old and I took up the slack. She means more to me than anything, and I want to make sure she has the kind of opportunities I couldn't take advantage of." Rachel pressed her lips together, looking like she regretted admitting so much. "I should go check on her," she said. "And Meghan, my other sister. She's brought her little boy, Nathan, and he's likely to jump into the fire if someone doesn't watch him."

Lucy watched Rachel move off and wondered how long she would be able to carry all of her family's burdens. Her gaze moved around the crowd; she saw Dan Trenton standing by himself, nursing a beer, and Abby on the other side of the bonfire, holding Noah's hand. Oliver Jones had come with his mother, who was still looking shadow-eyed and anxious, but she held Oliver's hand and laughed at something he said.

So many people. *Friends*. She really had made a life for herself here. Then Lucy saw Alex coming towards her with his two daughters in tow. He caught sight of her a second later, and she thought he might veer away and avoid her completely, but Poppy tugged him towards Lucy.

"Why don't we see you anymore?" she demanded.

The awkwardness, Lucy thought, was palpable. "You do see me, Poppy," she said in that cringing too-jolly voice she'd stopped using with children ages ago. "At school every day."

"I don't mean at school," Poppy declared. "At home. You never come round anymore."

As if she'd had a habit of coming round, when

she'd been only twice. But two times to a seven-year-old probably felt like a lot.

"I've been busy," Lucy said feebly, and Alex reached for Poppy's hand.

"Let's get in the queue for hot chocolate," he said, and Poppy turned to him with an eager smile.

"And toffee apples?"

"Fine." He pulled Poppy along, and Bella followed them with one last fleeting glance at Lucy.

Irritation warred with hurt and Lucy decided not to give in to either. This discomfort between her and Alex had to end. Either they could be civil and preferably normal with each other or they couldn't.

"So what do you think of Guy Fawkes Day?" Maggie Bains asked as she came up to Lucy.

"It seems like a nice way to get the village together," Lucy answered. "I don't know about burning effigies, though."

"Oh, we don't do that anymore," Maggie assured her, then added, "Not much, anyway."

"Good to know."

Maggie narrowed her eyes as she cocked her head towards Alex, who had lined up at the food stall with Poppy and Bella. "How are things with Mr. Kincaid, then?"

For a moment Lucy thought Maggie knew about her and Alex. Then she realized Maggie must be asking about work, and relief rushed through her.

"Oh, fine. You were right—his bark is worse than his bite."

"He's a good man really," Maggie said. "But he hasn't had an easy run lately, bless him." She laid a hand on Lucy's arm. "You must give him time, Lucy."

So it seemed Maggie did know about her and Alex. At this rate Lucy wondered who didn't. Soon they'd feature in a question on the pub quiz. *Which staff member was seen entering the head teacher's house?*

"Thanks for the advice," she mumbled, and with a fleeting smile she left Maggie and went in search of some solitude.

She stayed on the edge of the crowd, away from the light cast by the flames of the bonfire, watching as people mingled and talked, laughed and joked. She felt both part and not part of it all; the village had embraced her in so many ways, and she had embraced it. But in a few weeks, if she went back to Boston, this would be nothing more than a quaint and distant memory.

And if she stayed?

Lucy's heart lurched at the thought. She was afraid of so many things: of interaction with Alex being uncomfortable forever, and of not being able to find a decent job. Of failing again, just as she had in Boston. She didn't want the people she'd come to know and like see her fall flat on her face.

And if they did? They might help you back up again.

"Lucy?"

Lucy turned to see Bella standing next to her. Dressed completely in baggy black, the girl was nearly invisible in the darkness. "Hey, Bella," she said cautiously.

Bella dug her hands into the pockets of her hoodie, staring at her feet as she asked in a low voice, "Look, I have to know. Did you and Dad, you know, stop being friends because of me?"

"Oh Bella, no." Lucy started to reach for her to give her a hug, and then thought better of it. She patted her on the shoulder instead. "No, not at all. We're still friends."

Bella glanced at her, scorn combating with uncertainty in her young face. "I'm not stupid. Dad liked you, and now he never talks about you anymore. And like Poppy said, you don't come round."

"I only came round twice, Bella—"

"But you guys liked each other. I'm not a *baby*. I could tell."

Lucy stayed silent, wondering how honest she should be. She felt instinctively that this should be a conversation Alex had with his daughters, not her, but Bella was here with her now and maybe she deserved some straight answers. "You're right, we did like each other, but I'm only here temporarily and your dad has a lot going on in his life. So we decided to take a step back and just stay friends." She blew out a breath, hoping she hadn't opened a Pandora's box of teenage angst. "So it's all okay."

Bella kicked at the ground with her trainer. "It's not okay," she muttered. "Dad's miserable."

Was it wrong for Lucy's heart to lift a little at this admission? Probably.

"He might be," Lucy allowed, "but you know he cares about you, right?" Bella just shrugged and she persisted, "Don't let this stupid grown-up stuff mess up your relationship with your dad, Bella. He loves you. I know he doesn't get it right all the time and it's going to be hard to talk about all the awkward girl stuff with him, but he really does love you. I believe that with my whole heart, and you should too."

Bella was still staring at the ground, but Lucy could tell from the little sniff she gave that she'd gotten to her. Maybe. "I mean it," she added for good measure.

"The thing is," Bella said after a long moment, her voice so low Lucy had to bend down to hear it, "I kind of liked having you around."

"Oh, Bella . . ."

"But I know I didn't act like it, and Dad might have messed things up with you because he thought that would be better for me. But it isn't."

Lucy swallowed past the ache in her throat. "Whatever might have happened between me and your dad, Bella . . . it wasn't just about you and Poppy. It was about us—"

Bella looked up, her expression turned accusing. "You mean because you're leaving? Because you're not happy here?"

"I'm very happy here," Lucy answered. "And the truth is I don't know if I'm leaving or not, but—"

"What?" Bella stiffened. "Does Dad know that? That you might be staying?"

Lucy felt the conversation slipping out of her control. "No, but I'm not sure it really matters—"

"Of *course* it matters," Bella retorted. "Lucy, you have to tell him."

"I . . ." Lucy imagined herself waltzing up to Alex and telling him she was staying in Hartley-by-the-Sea. Somehow she didn't think he was going to snatch her into his arms and kiss her senseless. Her optimism stretched only so far. But she did need to talk to Alex. For all of their sakes. "I will talk to him, Bella," she said. "But don't expect it to change anything."

She found him a little while later, standing apart from everyone else, a cup of soup cradled in his hands. Poppy and Bella were hanging out with some kids from school, and Lucy knew she needed to take the opportunity to speak to Alex when he was on his own.

Sucking in a deep breath, she started towards him. "Hey, Alex."

He turned to her, his expression already guarded. "Lucy."

"I just came over to say that I don't want things to stay weird between us."

"They're not weird," Alex protested automatically, and Lucy raised an eyebrow. "All right, yes, they might be a bit weird," he amended. "But I've never had a—a thing with someone at work before. I'm not even sure what the policy on that is."

"Good thing we ended it before it went anywhere, then." She shifted her weight; her feet were going numb from cold in her Wellies. "How did you meet your wife, anyway?"

"In a coffee shop," Alex answered after a second's pause. "She came and sat down right opposite me and started chatting. She asked me why I looked so serious. She invited me to the cinema that same day." He sighed, his distant gaze on the leaping flames of the bonfire. "I don't think I ever would have worked up the courage to ask her out on my own."

The little snippet of his former life made Lucy feel a rush of sadness—and jealousy. "You must miss her."

"I do, but I miss what we had a long time ago." His mouth tightened. "I shouldn't have moved her up to Hartley-by-the-Sea. She didn't like it here, but I'd always had this crazy dream of living here." He slid an almost embarrassed glance towards her. "I came here as a kid, with a group from the foster home. A day at the seaside, it was, and I remember standing on the beach and looking at all the families with their pails and butterfly nets and ice-cream cones and wanting to be a part of it all."

"Oh, Alex." She knew exactly how he'd felt as a child, because it was the same way she'd felt. On the outside, looking in.

"But Anna didn't have that dream. She was from a wealthy family in Macclesfield, and it was a step down for her to live on my teacher's salary. Her parents kept buying her things—little things, at first, and then a car and a holiday for her with the girls. . . . I tried not to mind, but it always felt like they were showing me up. The last straw was when they bought us a house, this gorgeous Victorian villa in Manchester that cost half a million pounds, at least. And they didn't even ask us first." He shook his head. "I don't know why I'm telling you all this now."

"Maybe you need to tell somebody."

"Maybe," he allowed. "In any case, soon after they bought us the house, I accepted the job as head teacher here. I told Anna it was for the girls, that I wanted them to grow up with the freedom a place like this provides, but I was also doing it to get away from her parents. And if I was chasing that stupid childhood dream, I never found it here. Anna died only six months after we arrived here, and they were a pretty miserable six months."

"I'm sorry," Lucy said. She'd had no idea that asking Alex about his wife would bring up all these bad memories.

"So am I. Sorry I didn't do things differently, and sorry that Anna didn't, either." He turned to her with a weary smile. "And sorry I off-loaded all that onto you."

"I don't mind, Alex."

"I'm sorry things didn't—didn't work out between us," he said in a low voice.

"Me too," Lucy said, and heard the ache in her voice. "But we can still be friends, can't we?" she asked. "I just spoke to Bella and she was worried she'd messed things up between us."

"Bella was?" Alex looked incredulous. "I thought . . ."

"She didn't like me? I did too, although truthfully I don't know if Bella knows how she feels. Teenagers are weird that way, especially teenaged girls."

"And Bella's only twelve."

"You have your work cut out for you, then."

"Lucy . . ." She had the sense that Alex was going to say something important, but it was cut off by the sudden crackle and bang of the fireworks starting. A collective gasp of admiration rose as everyone looked up to see a starburst of greens and reds flare high in the sky.

It was impossible to talk during the fireworks

show, and when it ended ten minutes later, Poppy and Bella rejoined Alex and everyone started trudging back to the village. The moment, Lucy knew, was gone.

Another week passed in a blur of cold, wintry days; Lucy went into Whitehaven and bought herself thermal underwear and several more scarves. She was busy at school, and while the awkwardness had eased a little between her and Alex, she didn't know whether they were actually friends. Besides a bit of chitchat by the photocopier, they hadn't talked much at all.

And she hadn't yet made a decision about whether to stay in Hartley-by-the-Sea.

"You can't have all your ducks in a row before you decide," Juliet said one evening as she chopped carrots for their shepherd's pie and Lucy laid the table. They'd become quite cozily domestic together. "Life doesn't often work that way."

"You must have had a few of them lined up when you decided to stay," Lucy returned. "To buy this house and turn it into a bed-and-breakfast . . . how did you afford that, anyway?"

Juliet hesitated and then bit out a single word. "Fiona."

"*Mum* bought it for you?"

"She sent me a check, after that visit when I was twenty. Blood money, it felt like, and I put it in the bank and didn't touch it as a matter of principle.

And I was tempted, let me tell you. I worked my way up the ladder at the hotel in Manchester the hard way. But then I came here and knew I wanted to stay, and Tarn House was for sale. . . ." Juliet shrugged. "Fiona never gave me a thing my whole life. Why shouldn't she give me this?"

"Do you resent it, though?" Lucy asked curiously. "That you had to use that money?"

Juliet made a half-laughing, half-snorting sound. "Yes, of course I do."

"Well, unfortunately for me, I don't have a big nest egg waiting for me in the bank, so I definitely need a job."

"No, you've had your way paid for since you were a baby," Juliet pointed out. "Not that I'm bitter about it."

"Mum must have paid for you, Juliet, for some things. School—"

Juliet shook her head. "Nothing. Oh, she fed and clothed me, at least until she moved to America."

"But it was your choice not to come with us—"

"Is that what she told you?" Juliet asked, looking almost amused, although there was an edge to her voice.

"I suppose I assumed . . ."

"Fiona didn't want me to come. Oh, she made a song and dance about how I needed to finish my A levels, said I only had one year left, I'd want to go to university in England, and so on. But it was clear she was going off with you and you alone.

And she didn't send a single penny to cover my costs. I was eighteen, so I suppose she felt she'd done her duty by me. I worked nights in a pub to cover my school uniform and to give something to my friend's family, for room and board. They didn't want to accept, but they weren't rolling in it. Not like Fiona was."

Lucy stared at her, appalled. "I had no idea. . . ."

"You just thought I didn't get that wretched pony party?" Juliet surmised with a hard laugh. "Well, that too, I suppose."

"No wonder you're bitter."

Juliet sighed, one hand braced on the counter as she stared out the window at the darkening night sky. "The truth is," she said, "I'm tired of being bitter. Of being angry and hurt and all the rest of it. I just want to let it all go, forget about Fiona, but I can't. I've tried, and I *can't.*"

"Maybe you need to talk to her," Lucy suggested.

Juliet shook her head. "I can't do that, either. I don't have the strength anymore and anyway, the last time I tried, five years ago, she hung up on me."

"*Why?* I mean, why does she . . ."

"Hate me? I have no idea. Maybe she hated my father. Maybe she feels guilty for the way she's treated me."

"I'm sorry, Juliet."

"Not your fault," she answered briskly, and started chopping carrots again.

"I know, but . . ." Lucy shook her head. "I feel like I should have known. I should have reached out more to you, when I was younger."

"Wouldn't have worked." Juliet dumped the chopped carrots into the pot on top of the Aga. "I resented you even when you were a baby. You used to toddle after me and I'd just ignore you. Close my bedroom door in your face. I couldn't stand you, actually, and it had nothing to do with you."

"Oh." Not exactly words to warm the heart.

Juliet cracked a small smile. "But I am glad you're here now, Lucy, and I hope we can make up for lost time."

"I think we are. . . ."

"Then come here and give me a hug," Juliet said, and held out her arms. Lucy stared at her, amazed that her prickly sister could actually be requesting physical affection.

"I'd love to," she said, "but, Juliet? You're still holding a knife."

Juliet glanced at the large butcher's knife she held in one hand and with a laugh she tossed it into the sink. Then she walked towards Lucy with her arms outstretched and gave her a hug.

It was an awkward, clumsy hug, and it was over in about two seconds, but still. They were both grinning as they stepped back.

A week slipped by, a week of Lucy wondering what she was going to do even as she felt herself creeping towards a decision. She stopped by the post office, and to her shock Dan Trenton—who had started chatting to her a little each time she went in—slipped her a bag of chocolate buttons.

"For that lad," he said gruffly, not meeting her eye. Lucy grinned.

"Thank you, Dan," she said, and then because she couldn't resist, "You really are a big old softy."

"Don't tell anyone," Dan answered without cracking a smile. "Can't ruin my reputation."

One Saturday Lucy took Milly and Molly down to the beach and after they'd had a decent run, she tied them up outside the café and went to talk to Abby. The café was nearly empty and Abby made them both coffees as they sat at a table in the corner and Noah played with a couple of battered toys at their feet.

"Juliet gave me the idea," Lucy said, "of maybe exhibiting some of my paintings here, to sell. You could take a percentage of the profits, and it might brighten up the place a bit, to have artwork on the walls. . . ."

Abby's expression, normally so pinched and serious, lightened as she smiled. "I love that idea." She glanced round at the rickety chairs and the peeling Formica. "I've been wanting to spruce this place up, to tell you the truth. It looks like I'm going to be here for a while."

"Is Mary . . . ?"

"She's okay," Abby said, her glance on Noah,

who was now scooting around on all fours and making tractor noises. "But she can't be on her feet all day the way she used to. She needs me here."

"Well, I'm glad you're staying," Lucy said, and Abby gave her a shy smile.

"What about you? Are you staying, then?"

Lucy took a deep breath. "I think so," she said. Admitting that much still made her stomach flip, the way it did when you drove over a hill too fast. "I think so," she said again.

The last week in November Lucy decided to be ambitious and cook everyone Thanksgiving dinner. "Proper American Thanksgiving," she told Juliet. "I'm talking about green bean casserole and stuffing and cranberry sauce and sweet potatoes with marshmallow fluff."

Juliet made a face. "That last one sounds revolting."

"It's delicious," Lucy assured her. "I'll have to find canned pumpkin somewhere for the pie. . . ."

"You could," Juliet suggested, "use a real pumpkin."

Lucy shook her head firmly. "That is so not what Thanksgiving is about."

"Have you had many Thanksgiving dinners?" Juliet asked. "With the turkey and the marshmallow and the rest of it?"

"No," she admitted. "You know Mum. She saw Thanksgiving as another sign of patriarchal oppression." Juliet rolled her eyes and Lucy smiled. "But I've seen enough holiday movies and Norman Rockwell paintings to know what it's supposed to be like."

She spent the next several days searching the Internet for recipes, and waiting for the delivery of canned pumpkin and marshmallow fluff from an online store that sold American products at astronomical prices. She practiced folding napkins into the shape of turkeys—more or less—and bought all the real pumpkins at the supermarket in Whitehaven for a festive centerpiece.

And then there was the matter of the guest list. "I thought I'd invite Rachel and her family," Lucy told Juliet, "and Peter and his father. . . ." Juliet tensed a bit at this, but didn't object. "And the Kincaids."

"You mean Alex?" Juliet said.

"We're meant to be friends," Lucy replied. "And if that's what we're meant to be, then that's how I'm going to act."

"Are you sure this isn't just a way to win him back?" Juliet asked bluntly. "The way to a man's heart and all that?"

"No, it isn't," Lucy replied after a moment, and knew she meant it. "I've learned my lesson there, at least. I'm done trying to insinuate myself into other people's lives, or to convince them they really need me. This is just about being friends and celebrating a holiday. It's as simple as that."

Except it wasn't so simple, Lucy realized as she rushed around the kitchen on the Sunday after the official Thanksgiving Day, trying to make sure everything was ready at the same time. Juliet had offered to help, but Lucy wanted to prove to her—and everyone else—that she could do it on her own. She just hoped she actually could.

At least the napkins looked cute.

By five o'clock everyone had assembled in the dining room and Lucy had most of the dishes on the table, including the promised green bean casserole and marshmallow-topped sweet potatoes. She was saving the turkey for last, wanting to bring it to everyone just like in a movie or a painting, everything golden and gleaming and perfect.

And it was almost like that, except she tipped the platter a little as she set it on the table, and turkey grease dripped onto the once-pristine white tablecloth and splattered onto Peter, so he jumped up and brushed ineffectually at his trousers.

"Sorry!" Lucy exclaimed, and Peter just smiled and sat down again.

A little turkey grease hardly mattered, not when she was sitting at a table with friends and family—Rachel and her family, Peter and his father—Peter had tenderly tucked a napkin into his father's shirt, which had almost made Lucy choke up—Alex and his daughters, and Juliet. People she cared about. People who cared about her.

This was her home, Lucy knew then, without a

doubt. Her home and where her heart was, no matter what did or didn't happen with Alex. Of course she was staying here.

"Lucy?" Juliet's amused voice broke into her thoughts.

"Yes?" She smiled at her sister, and Juliet nodded towards the turkey.

"Aren't you going to carve?"

"Oh. Um." That was something she'd never done before. With a deep breath Lucy picked up the carving knife and fork. She began, tentatively, to saw with the knife and didn't even break through the glossy brown skin.

"You've got to commit," Rachel said with a laugh. "It's dead already. You're not going to hurt it."

"Okay, okay," Lucy said with an answering laugh. "I get it."

Commit. She could do that. She took the first uneven hacked-off slice and put it on Rachel's plate. "Satisfied?"

"I wouldn't recommend you try for a job at a carvery, but yes. It looks delicious."

The evening passed in a blur of good food and conversation; at least, mostly good food. The green bean casserole was burned on the bottom and the gravy was lumpy, but everyone pronounced the meal a success, and Bella and Poppy both gave Lucy a thumbs-up after trying pumpkin pie for the first time.

By nine o'clock everyone was feeling sleepy and satisfied, lolling back in their chairs as Juliet filled glasses with port.

"An English tradition," she told Lucy. "We can't have an entirely American Thanksgiving."

"The English celebrate Thanksgiving?" Lucy teased, and Juliet smiled back.

"We rejoice at being free of you bolshy lot," Rachel chimed in.

Lucy brandished papers and pencils. "And to cap off the evening, a pub quiz! Minus the pub, of course. And all the questions have to do with Thanksgiving."

Rachel took her paper and pencil with alacrity, and then frowned as she read out some of the questions. "Thanksgiving came to be a national holiday thanks to which woman?" She looked up at Lucy. "I have absolutely no idea."

"Take a guess."

"Umm . . . Martha Washington? Betsy Ross?"

"Sarah Hale, editor of *Godey's Lady's Book*," Lucy answered. "That was a hard one. The others are easier."

Everyone grumbled good-naturedly as they tried to answer the questions, and Lucy began to clear the table. The sink was overflowing with greasy pots and pans, and dirty dishes littered nearly every available surface of the kitchen. Cleaning up was going to take all night.

"Would you like help with the washing up?"

Lucy turned around, her heart lurching in spite of her brain's intentions to stay normal and friendly with Alex. He was already rolling up the sleeves of his button-down shirt and just the sight of his strong brown forearms with their light sprinkling of hair made her feel a little weak.

"Umm, sure. You don't want to complete the quiz?"

"I left the girls to it." He moved over to the sink, taking the pots and pans out so he could fill it with hot water. "It looks like a tornado hit in here."

"That's how I cook."

"That's how you live," Alex answered, his smile taking the sting from the words. "You blow into people's lives like a whirlwind."

"Or a tornado."

"Right."

They stared at each other, the moment spinning out until Lucy wondered what it was turning into, if anything. Then the water started frothing up with bubbles and Alex turned off the taps, effectively breaking the moment, if there had ever been one.

Blindly Lucy reached for some dirty plates. She handed them to Alex one by one and he rinsed them off before stacking them in the dishwasher. They worked in companionable silence for a few minutes, but Lucy could feel the tension winding tighter and tighter inside her. She felt as if she might burst with it, with the need to say something.

"I'm staying in Hartley-by-the-Sea," she blurted.

Alex stared at her, a plate nearly slipping from his hand. "Pardon?"

"I'm staying," Lucy repeated. "Not at the school, obviously, since Nancy Crawford will want her job back. But I realized I don't have much in Boston to return for, and I like the life I've made for myself here. Juliet's offered to let me live with her, and so . . ." She shrugged, spreading her hands. "I'm staying. I thought you should know. Not," she amended hurriedly, "that it changes anything, you know, between us."

"No," Alex agreed, and put the plate he was holding into the dishwasher. "No, of course not."

Not exactly the response she'd been hoping for, but the one she'd expected. Sort of. "Well, then." She gave him a cheery smile. "We'll be neighbors. Or rather, fellow villagers, which sounds kind of medieval."

"Fellow villagers," Alex repeated. He slotted another plate into the dishwasher without looking at her. "Yes."

He didn't sound very pleased. Lucy wondered if she should have told him. But he would have found out eventually, and anyway, she thought with sudden savagery, screw Alex Kincaid. He'd have to get used to seeing her about the village, that was all. This was her home too now.

She grabbed the turkey platter and shoved it towards him. She'd meant to hand it to him to rinse, but the platter tipped forward and cold, congealed turkey juices splattered all over Alex's front. The situation was made even worse when Alex reflexively caught the platter and brought it to his chest. He was, Lucy thought with a swallowed bubble of near-hysterical laughter, more covered in grease than when he'd climbed the pole at the Crab Fair.

"I'm sorry," she managed, and realized she didn't even sound all that sorry. She let out a little snort of laughter and then clapped her hands over her mouth as Alex, still holding the greasy platter, narrowed his eyes.

"Are you . . . laughing at me?"

"Maybe," she said between her fingers. "A little."

Carefully he placed the platter down on the counter. His shirt was stuck to his chest with grease. Lucy looked away, only to give a little gasp of surprise as she felt his hand on her shoulder, pulling her towards him.

And then, amazingly, he was kissing her, and she was kissing him back—of course she was—grease and all.

A few wonderful minutes later, Lucy heard the sound of a throat clearing and she broke apart from Alex to see Juliet standing in the doorway, giving them both a narrow look.

"We've finished the quiz."

"Oh—" Lucy could not think what else to say. She pressed her fingers to her lips and felt how she was grinning. She felt as if she were glowing from the inside out.

Juliet turned to Alex, her expression severe. "I hope you're going to be sensible about this."

Alex looked discomfited; he was the one used to giving stern looks, Lucy supposed. "What do you mean?"

"I mean I won't have you hurting my sister. You'd better be serious about her."

Alex looked even more taken aback, but he nodded. "I am serious, Juliet. That's why it took me so long to come around."

"And you too, Lucy," Juliet added, turning that schoolteacherish stare onto her. "Remember that there are two young girls involved—"

"I *know*, Juliet—"

"Does this mean you're staying, then?"

"Yes—"

Alex turned to her. "I thought you'd already decided."

"I had," Lucy said quickly. "I just hadn't told anyone yet."

"Well, then." Juliet nodded, her hands on her hips. "You'd better get in there and mark that ridiculous quiz." The phone rang as she waved them towards the dining room. "I'll get that. You go on."

Lucy walked into the dining room; she felt as if she were floating. Alex reached for her hand and squeezed.

"About the girls—," he began, but Bella was already half-rising from her seat.

"You've got together!" she cried, exultant. "I can see it in your faces!"

Everyone turned to look at them, scanning their expressions. Now Lucy was both blushing and grinning like a loon, and she didn't even care.

"Together? Are you and Daddy going to get married?" Poppy asked, her hands clasped together.

"Don't rush them, Poppy," Bella muttered. "For heaven's sake."

"I think we'll take it one step at a time," Alex said as he sat down at the table. "Now what about this quiz?"

Lucy was just starting to read the answers out when Juliet came back into the dining room. She stood in the doorway, silent, and Lucy hadn't even noticed her entrance until Peter rose from his chair, his forehead furrowed. "Juliet?"

Lucy turned, and saw how strange Juliet looked, all pinched and pale. Before she could ask if she was all right, Juliet spoke.

"The phone's for you, Lucy," she said flatly. "It's Fiona."

28
Juliet

JULIET DIDN'T WAIT FOR Lucy to reply. She certainly didn't want to hear any of her conversation with Fiona. And she didn't think she could stay in this warm, lit room, with everyone smiling and laughing, for another minute. Abruptly she turned on her heel and left the dining room, left the house. She walked blindly down the front path and then stood in the middle of the pavement, the night dark all around her, the still air cold and damp. She breathed in and out and tried to slow her thundering heart.

Fiona. Her mother had called, after five years—no, a lifetime—of silence. And their entire conversation had consisted of three sentences.

"Hello, Tarn House," Juliet had announced cheerfully, still smiling at having caught Alex and Lucy kissing.

"Juliet . . . ?"

Juliet hadn't recognized the husky yet feminine voice. It had never occurred to her that her mother would call her or reach out to her in any way.

"Yes . . . ," she'd said, still in B&B mode.

Fiona had said, haltingly, "It's . . . it's Fiona. Is Lucy there?"

Juliet hadn't answered for a moment; she'd been so stunned to hear her mother's voice. And then to realize that the sum total of their conversation was Fiona asking for Lucy.

"I'll get her for you," she said, and then hated herself for accommodating her mother in any way. For acting like Fiona's behavior was normal, acceptable. Yet she'd already put the phone down and was walking towards the dining room, and in any case she had no idea what she'd say to her mother if ever given the opportunity to speak.

Why?

That, Juliet supposed, was the question that had dominated her life, the question she was both desperate to ask and determined not to. *Why do you hate me? Why didn't you want me? Why?*

And now she was out here in the cold night air with that question pounding through her head and Lucy inside, talking to her *mum*.

"Juliet."

She stiffened as she heard Peter's voice, and then the steady tread of his feet until she knew he was standing right behind her. Felt his hand heavy and warm on her shoulder. He didn't speak, and Juliet closed her eyes, tried to will away the lump in her throat.

"It was my mother on the phone," she finally

404

squeezed out past that lump. She kept her eyes shut. "Fiona. She asked for Lucy. She's *never* asked for me." And because that sounded so ridiculous and childish, she clarified, her voice little more than a whisper, "She's never loved or even liked me. Never even wanted me. She told me that, when I was twenty and I asked who my father was. 'I never wanted you, Juliet.'" She stopped then, with a gasp, as if she'd been running uphill. And maybe she had been running uphill her whole life, wanting her mother to love her. "It shouldn't hurt," she said after a moment, and her voice was thankfully steadier now. "It's been so long, and I've accepted it. It shouldn't hurt anymore."

"But it does," Peter said quietly, and she gave that little gasping sound again, dashing at her eyes.

"I don't want to cry."

"Nothing wrong with a good cry."

"Do you know how much I've cried these last few months? I could create another lake. Julietmere."

She felt rather than saw his smile, and he squeezed her shoulder. "Maybe," he said, "you're making up for lost time."

She laughed shakily. "Maybe. I certainly never cried before Lucy came here."

"I thought you might say that."

"Oh, Peter." It was hard to get words out again.

"I wish I didn't care. I thought if I acted like I didn't care, I wouldn't. But it doesn't work that way."

"No," Peter agreed. "It generally doesn't."

"It should, though, don't you think?"

He put his other hand on her shoulder, and then slowly turned her around. "Yes," he said as he pulled her towards him, "it should."

Juliet remained rigid for a moment, amazed that Peter was actually *hugging* her, and then overwhelmingly grateful because it felt so good. She pressed her cheek against his chest and breathed in the scent of him: sheep and wool and old-fashioned aftershave. She might have messed up her chance at having anything romantic with Peter, but she was glad to be his friend now.

After a long moment she reluctantly pulled away from him. "I should go inside. Clean up . . ." And talk to Lucy. Juliet didn't want to ask her what Fiona had wanted, but she knew she probably should.

"I'll come with you," Peter said, and followed her back into the house.

Rachel and Alex were washing dishes in the kitchen, laughing and joking in a way Juliet certainly hadn't seen Alex do before. Lucy was good for him. Then she heard Lucy's voice from the utility room, a low, urgent murmur, and her stomach cramped.

Why had Fiona called after all this time? Juliet

had the uneasy sense that their mother wanted something from Lucy, that the fragile relationship she and Lucy had built over the last three months was about to be tested.

She finished washing up with Rachel and Alex, and since Lucy was still on the phone, she saw them all off on her own.

"I hope everything's all right," Alex said with a frown, and Juliet smiled tightly in return.

"I'm sure it is." She gave Alex an awkward pat on the shoulder. "You'll see Lucy tomorrow at school, anyway."

"Yes . . ." But he was still frowning, and Juliet could guess why. Alex wasn't the type to dive headfirst into a relationship, even if Lucy was. He'd want things between them sorted before he saw her at school, for his sake as well as his children's, not to mention his staff's. Speculation would be rife.

Eventually everyone headed home; Peter offered to stay, but Juliet could see how William was flagging and she shooed him away. Then she poured herself the last of the wine and sat at the kitchen table and waited.

Finally, an hour after she'd taken the call, Lucy emerged from the utility room, her face pale, the cordless phone clutched to her chest. Juliet nodded towards it.

"It must almost be out of charge."

"Sorry." Lucy put the phone back on the charger.

"Well?" she finally asked when Lucy remained standing in the kitchen doorway. "What did she want?"

"Juliet . . ." Lucy gazed at her, her eyes full of anguish, and Juliet stared back stonily.

"Tell me, then."

"She has cancer."

Juliet blinked. "And?" she said after a brief pause.

"And?" Lucy shook her head slowly, and Juliet suppressed a stab of irritation. Clearly she was disappointing her sister with her lack of response. "And she's having surgery the day after tomorrow. It's breast cancer, and she's having a double mastectomy."

"Fine."

"Juliet . . ."

"What do you expect, Lucy? For me to fall to pieces? I don't have a relationship with her. You know that."

"She's still our mother."

"No," Juliet said coolly. "She's your mother. She forfeited the right for me to call her that. I never did, actually. She wouldn't let me."

Lucy flinched. "Even so . . ."

"No." The single word came out like the crack of a gunshot, and Juliet half rose from her chair, filled with a sudden, surging fury before she took a deep breath, held on to her composure, and sat back down again. "No," she said more calmly.

"There is no 'even so' in this situation." Lucy didn't answer and she took a few steadying breaths before making herself ask, "So why did she call? Just to tell you?" Because Fiona obviously hadn't cared whether she knew.

"No, not just that. She wants me to come home. To be there with her, during the surgery."

Come home. Because Tarn House, and Hartley-by-the-Sea, weren't really home, no matter what Lucy had said. "And you're going?" Juliet asked. "Just like that?"

"I have to—"

"No, you don't. What about your job here? What about Alex?"

Lucy bit her lip. "He'll understand. And Maggie Bains is back. She can fill in for the rest of the term. It's only a few more weeks. I'll be back in January."

"So you just drop everything the second Fiona crooks her finger?"

"She has *cancer.*"

"And when you've been in trouble, has she come running to you?" Juliet demanded.

"That . . . that shouldn't matter."

"No? Why not?"

Lucy lifted her chin. "Because she needs me. For once."

"Other people need you," Juliet pointed out. "What about Bella and Poppy? They danced out of here and now you're going to disappear?"

"I'll explain to Alex tomorrow. And it's only for a few weeks. They'll understand, Juliet. I know they will." Her eyes flashed with temper. "You're the one who has a problem with it."

Yes, she did. Because it felt, reasonably or not, as if Lucy was choosing Fiona over her. "I thought," she said coldly, "that you'd changed."

"I thought you'd changed!"

They stared at each other, the chasm that had been bridged over these last few months opening wider than ever. "I suppose neither of us has changed as much as we thought," Juliet finally said.

"Are you saying you wouldn't go, if she asked you?"

Juliet let out a hard laugh. "She would never ask me."

"But if she did—"

"The point is," Juliet cut across her, "she wouldn't. And she's only asking you because she knows you'll come running. You're like a puppy, Lucy, always eager to please and so easily hurt. *Honestly.* Don't you realize how she's using you? As soon as she's recovered, she'll be grandstanding again. She'll turn your act of service into something to be ridiculed. How My Daughter Tried to Win Back My Love. And you'll just take it, *again*—"

"Why are you being so mean?" Lucy cried. "Or can you not stand the thought that someone needs me? That I'm important to someone?"

"You think you're important to *Fiona?*"

"She needs me," Lucy repeated stubbornly. "When has someone needed you, Juliet? When have you let yourself get close enough to someone for them to need you? You hide in your house, making breakfasts and beds for people you'll never see again. You've never really tried with anyone."

Juliet jerked back. "I tried with you," she said, and Lucy's face crumpled.

"*Juliet.* I don't want us to be like this."

Juliet pressed the heels of her hands to her eyes. "I don't, either."

"Do you . . . do you not want me to come back?"

"No, I don't want you to *go.*" Juliet dropped her hands from her eyes. "Look, I realize I might be overreacting a little."

"It's only a few weeks," Lucy said. "I'll be back by the first of January."

Juliet knew Lucy believed she'd be back; the trouble was, Juliet didn't. Poky Hartley-by-the-Sea with its wind and rain would seem very far away once Lucy was back in Boston, with her old friends, her old life. Maybe that jerk Thomas would get back in touch with her, ask her to babysit his kids. Maybe Fiona would have a change of heart and throw Lucy an art exhibition herself. Or maybe Lucy would just fall back into her old ways. It would be all too easy for her to say she'd changed her mind and stay in Boston instead. And if that was what happened, there wasn't a thing Juliet could do about it.

"Fine," she said lifelessly. "Do what you have to do."

"I don't want to part on bad terms—"

"I'm sorry, but I can't give you my blessing. Not for Fiona. But I understand why you feel you need to go."

Lucy stared at her. "Then I guess I'll have to take that," she said quietly.

29
Lucy

LUCY BARELY SLEPT THAT night; the wind gusted down the street and rattled the window-panes, but it was the thoughts chasing one another in her own head that kept her awake.

The argument with Juliet had stung more than she'd thought possible. She'd craved her sister's support and received her scorn. And she'd hurt Juliet, she knew, with her own unkind words. It felt as if the relationship they'd worked so hard to build had shattered in the first breath of a storm.

And as for Alex . . . and Poppy and Bella . . .

Lucy rolled onto her side and tucked her knees up to her chest. Could she ignore her mother, her mother who had *cancer,* for the sake of little more than a kiss? Alex might have said he was serious about her, but only because Juliet had been lecturing him. They hadn't had the chance to see how a relationship would work out, how she'd fit into his life and he into hers.

And anyway, if Alex was serious, he would wait for her. He'd understand she needed to go to her mother, and he'd wait until she came back. It was only for a couple of weeks.

Although Lucy knew she couldn't promise that it would be such a short time. Fiona might need her for longer than a day or a week or even a month. Surgery, chemo, recovery . . . It usually took months or even years before you were cancer free. Lucy had no idea how much of that process Fiona would need her for. How much she would be willing to stay for.

By six in the morning Lucy was up, showered, and mostly packed. She'd booked a five p.m. flight back to Boston, and arranged to take the train to Manchester Airport. Juliet had already left to walk the dogs; they hadn't said a word to each other that morning.

All Lucy had to do now was talk to Alex. A little before eight she headed up the street to school, a feeling of unreality coming over her at the realization that this was the last time she'd walk into the primary school, turn on the copier and the kettle, and welcome the children who streamed past her window.

Alex came in just as the kettle was coming to a boil; he'd already dropped Poppy off at the Breakfast Club.

"Good morning," he said, and gave Lucy a tentative smile. "I didn't get a chance to talk to you after that phone call. . . ."

"I know. I'm sorry about that."

"How was it? Everything okay?"

"Well, no, not really." Alex frowned and Lucy

continued. "My mother was on the phone last night—"

"I know."

"She told me she has cancer."

"Lucy, I'm sorry—"

She plowed on, knowing she needed to say it all. "She's having a double mastectomy tomorrow. I told her I'd be there."

"Tomorrow? But . . ."

"I need to leave soon for a late-afternoon flight from Manchester. I'm so sorry for the last-minute notice, but I didn't feel I had a choice."

"No, I understand." He rubbed a hand over his face. "The timing's terrible, but that's cancer for you."

"I thought Maggie Bains could cover for me until Christmas. And then Nancy Crawford is coming back."

"Don't worry. We'll manage. We'll be fine." He dropped his hand and stared at her. "But I didn't mean the timing was terrible for school. I meant for us."

He held her gaze and Lucy was the first to look away. "Yes. Well. I hope I'll be back in a few weeks. Sometime in January, maybe."

A second's pause, heavy with meaning. "Maybe?" Alex repeated.

"I don't know how long she'll need me, but I want to come back, Alex. I *will* come back."

She wanted him to believe her, but judging

from the way his expression hadn't altered, she didn't think he did. And she wasn't sure she believed herself. She had no idea what to expect when she reached Boston.

"Well, you have to do what you have to do. Of course." He took a step back, as if distancing himself from her. "Anyway, this might work out for the best. For us, I mean. I haven't even checked the policy about dating staff. It would be better if we didn't announce a relationship until you'd finished at the school."

He sounded as stiff and officious as he had when she'd first met him. Lucy felt as if there was an awful subtext to everything they'd said that she didn't want to be there. This felt like a far more final and formal farewell than she'd meant it to be.

"Okay, well. I can stay the morning, until you can arrange for Maggie to come in. My train for Manchester doesn't leave until two."

Alex waved a hand. "No, I'm sure you have things to do. You might as well go. We'll manage."

"Okay." She wanted to kiss him, or at least hug him, good-bye, but the mood wasn't right and children were starting to come up the hill. "I'll call you," she said, and he nodded.

"Yes. Call me." And he turned away before she'd opened the door to go.

Sixteen hours later Lucy stood in the foyer of her mother's luxury apartment in Boston's Back Bay, exhausted and overwhelmed and emotionally very fragile.

"Lucy." Her mother pressed her cheek against hers, the closest she ever came to hugging. "You're so good to come."

"Of course, Mum," she said woodenly. She'd spent the eight-hour flight from Manchester wondering if she was making a mistake. If she should have made more promises and given an exact date for when she'd return, or even if she should have gone at all.

"How are you feeling?" she asked, and her mother sighed and sat down on one of the ivory leather sofas in the living room. She looked the same, her silver hair cut in a sleek bob, the lineson her face making her look elegant and experienced rather than just old. She wore a loose caftan top in beige silk and a pair of cream leggings, an outfit that would have made Lucy look like a potato but that Fiona wore with glamorous ease.

"Rather annoyingly well. I didn't have any symptoms besides this wretched lump. Thank goodness I had it checked out. I'm going to write a piece for *The New Yorker* about the importance of yearly mammograms. I've already had it accepted, on spec." Her mother smiled, seeming almost contented, and Lucy tried to suppress her irritation and even disappointment. Had she really wanted her mother to fall apart, to make her feel needed?

"Well, I'm glad," she said awkwardly. "I'm terribly jet-lagged myself. I might get some sleep."

"All right." Her mother waved a hand towards the hall leading to the apartment's three bedrooms. "Do you mind using the little bedroom? I haven't made the bed up yet, but I've turned your old bedroom into a home studio."

Even though she had studio space in the city's South End. "No problem," Lucy said, and went in search of sheets.

It was too late to call Alex, but she thought about it. Then she thought about calling Juliet, and realized that was whom she really wanted to speak to. Before she could overthink it, Lucy dialed Tarn House on her cell phone, only to have it ring and ring without anyone picking up. It was the middle of the night there, and she knew Juliet was probably in bed. She shouldn't have called; she might have disturbed the guests. But she'd really, really wanted to talk to her sister.

She lay down on the narrow cot bed in the third bedroom that Fiona used for storage. Boxes were piled all around and canvases lay stacked against a wall. The room smelled both musty and of turpentine, and was hardly the most pleasant accommodation in what was otherwise a luxury apartment. But of course her mother needed her home studio.

The next morning Lucy woke gritty-eyed and

groggy; her mother was in the kitchen, drinking a protein shake.

"I'm packed," she said. "We should leave by eleven."

"Okay."

Lucy sank into a kitchen chair and glanced at her mother; despite the brisk airiness, she looked a little thinner, a little more fragile, her hair more white than Lucy remembered, although she was only fifty-eight. Old age and death would come for Fiona Bagshaw, tour de force though she was, just as they came for everyone.

"How are you feeling about the operation?" she asked, and Fiona gave a twitchy little shrug.

"Well, you know. I'd rather not go through it, but . . ." She trailed off, her expression distant, and for a moment Lucy could see beneath the brisk confidence to a surprising vulnerability and fear. "I do want to thank you for coming back to Boston," she said, still not meeting Lucy's gaze. "I know after everything that happened with that little gallery showing, you probably didn't want to."

Ah, there was the familiar sting. "Little gallery showing, Mum?" Lucy repeated. "It might have seemed little to you, but it was a lot more than that to me."

"Oh, *Lucy*." Her mother drained her protein shake. "You always take everything so seriously."

"And you don't?" Lucy retorted. "You take your

own art pretty seriously." A sudden surge of anger overwhelmed her, surprising her with its fierceness, especially considering the circumstances. Her mother was about to go in for surgery; surely she could let slide a few barbed remarks. "The way you drone on about boobs and penises makes me think you take it very seriously indeed."

Fiona's mouth tightened, just as it always did, just as Juliet's used to. "That's because my art is serious, Lucy, even if you never seemed to think so. Or perhaps you're just jealous."

"Jealous?" Lucy's mouth dropped open. "I've never been jealous of you, Mum, or your success. And although you may find this hard to believe, I wanted you to come to my showing because you're my mother, not because you're famous Fiona Bagshaw, the *artist*." She turned away abruptly, hating that her mother still had the power to hurt her.

Fiona didn't answer for a moment. Lucy could hear the ragged tear of her own breathing and she closed her eyes, wishing that her mother didn't affect her this way. She was too tired and fragile for this now.

"I haven't proved to be much good at that role," Fiona finally said. "I think I'm better as Fiona Bagshaw the Artist than Fiona Bagshaw the Mother."

Lucy stared at her mother with her mouth agape. "I didn't know you even tried," she said, shocked at the spite in her voice and yet knowing she meant it utterly.

"What did you want me to do, Lucy?" Fiona asked, eyebrows raised. "Wear a frilly apron and bake cookies for you and your friends? I was never going to be that sort of woman."

"You don't have to resort to stereotypes," Lucy protested. "But as it happens, yes, baking cookies or even buying them from the store would have been nice. *Thinking* about me once in a while—"

"Do you really believe I never thought about you? Never cared about you?"

Lucy considered the handful of happy memories she had of her mother, of those rare times when she'd felt as if Fiona actually cared. They'd been so *fleeting*. Her mother would give her a moment's attention when she'd been a child and then move on. " 'Never' is a strong word," she said. "But it's pretty close to how I feel."

"I admit I haven't been the best mother," Fiona said after a pause. "But I'm not completely thoughtless. I chose not to go to your gallery showing for your sake, Lucy, not mine."

"So you've said. But I really don't see how writing that awful editorial was doing me a *favor*."

"I know it probably didn't look that way—"

"That," Lucy interjected, "is a *gross* under-statement."

"I wanted you to succeed on your own terms,

Lucy, like I did. Trust me, it means so much more—"

"Fine. I get that. And actually, Mum, I wanted that too. I never traded on your fame. I usually tried to avoid it."

"I know," Fiona said.

"You could have just said you weren't going to go," Lucy said, her voice cracking. *"Privately.* Why did you have to go and write an editorial about it? And trash my paintings in a national newspaper? You were making it as hard to succeed as possible, but I don't even care about that. It was the fact that my *mother* was treating me that way that hurt so much, not that the famous Fiona Bagshaw didn't like my work."

Fiona was silent for a long moment, her face drawn in haggard lines. "I never said," she finally answered, "that I didn't make mistakes."

"Actually, you've always implied that you don't," Lucy replied. She felt tired now, tired and defeated. She and her mother would never see eye to eye on this, or anything. And maybe she needed to accept that. Accept that her relationship with her mother would always be fraught, fractured. Painful.

"What about Juliet?" Lucy asked abruptly, and Fiona stilled, her gaze widening. She said nothing. "I did tell you I've been living with her for the last three months."

"Yes," she answered warily.

"Juliet thinks . . ." Lucy didn't want to betray her sister's confidences, but she didn't want to ignore them, either. "Why don't you ever see her or speak to her?"

Fiona pressed her lips together. "That's not your concern, Lucy."

"She's my sister, and I am living with her. I think I have a right to ask."

"What did Juliet tell you?"

Lucy hesitated and then said, "Not all that much. Only that you never wanted her and the two of you never had a real relationship."

Fiona looked away. "That's true."

"Mum." Lucy stared at her, and reluctantly Fiona turned back to look at her. "Why? Why have you never . . . ?"

"Like I said, that's between me and Juliet."

"But you've never told her, either." Fiona said nothing and Lucy persisted. "Don't you think she deserves to know?"

"Some things," Fiona answered, "are better not known."

"Don't you think you should let Juliet decide that?" Still Fiona said nothing and wearily Lucy shook her head. She was so tired of it all. She half wished she'd never come back to Boston, even though she knew she'd had no choice. Her mother may have let her down a thousand times, but she didn't want to let her down in return.

"I can't let her decide," Fiona said, and to Lucy's shock her voice choked. "I wish I could. I wish . . ." She took a deep breath. "I wish I hadn't made so many mistakes, but I know I did. And maybe the biggest mistake was not admitting that."

Lucy searched her mother's face, saw regret warring with stubbornness. "And now?" she asked.

"I'm about to have major surgery, Lucy. I can't . . . I can't cope with anything else right now."

"But eventually?" Lucy pressed. "Whatever mistakes you've made, Mum, you can still right them. You can still talk to Juliet."

Lucy thought she'd refuse, retreat into hauteur as she often did. Then finally she gave a little nod. "Maybe," she said, and Lucy knew she'd have to be content with that.

A few hours later the surgery was over, and Lucy joined her mother in the hospital room. Her mother was groggy, her chest swathed with bandages, her gaze unfocused.

"Well, I survived."

"Yes, you did. The doctor says it went well."

Fiona glanced down at her bandaged chest. "I suppose I'll need some new artistic inspiration."

Lucy smiled, glad her mother could joke at a time like this. "This might be a whole new start to your career."

"I didn't want a new start," her mother

answered, her face crumpling a little, and then she leaned her head against the pillow and drifted back to sleep.

Lucy gazed at her mother lying so still in the hospital bed and thought how fragile she looked. In sleep, her silvery bobbed hair spread out on the pillow, Fiona appeared diminished, the aggressive vitality Lucy had always associated with her mother now absent.

Her mother, Lucy thought as she sat down next to the bed, was just a woman. Fallible, vulnerable, if not completely lovable. *Human.*

It comforted her, in a strange way, to know her mother was weak. Lucy knew she'd built her mother up in her eyes, ever since she'd been a child. She'd bought into the Fiona Bagshaw the Artist persona just as her mother had, and somehow they'd both forgotten that Fiona was just her mum.

And she was her daughter.

Leaving her mother to sleep, Lucy went out into the hall to check for messages. She switched on her phone, and her heart lightened to see Juliet had called. Twice. Quickly she pressed the button to call her back.

"Hey," she said when Juliet answered with her usual brisk "Tarn House."

"How did it go?"

"Okay. She's out of surgery. The doctor says it went well, but there's still a lot ahead of her.

She's hoping to have breast reconstruction in a few months, when the mastectomy has healed."

"So she can do a whole slew of new sculptures. *My Breasts, Rediscovered.*"

"Probably," Lucy agreed. She couldn't tell from Juliet's tone whether she was still angry with her, but at least she'd called.

"How are you?" Juliet asked. "How's Boston?"

"Fine. I haven't seen much of it. I've just been to Mum's apartment and the hospital."

"Are you going to see your friends?"

She hadn't even texted Chloe to say she was back. "Yes, probably. Since I'll be here for a while."

There was a silence, and then Juliet said flatly, "You mean you're staying through her recovery, until she has the reconstruction?"

Which meant months, not weeks. "I haven't thought that far ahead, Juliet, but I can't just run off."

"I never said that." Another silence, taut with tension. "It's too bad you'll miss Christmas here," Juliet said finally. "The carol service down at the Lifeboat Station with Father Christmas—well, Rob Telford in a shabby old Santa suit. And of course the tractor pull down on the beach on Boxing Day is fun, especially for the children. The Christmas Market in the village hall is small, but sweet."

"I'd love to see all of it," Lucy said. She could feel a lump forming in her throat.

"Maybe next year."

Lucy took what she hoped her sister meant as a peace offering. "Yes, next year," she said. "Definitely."

After she'd hung up from Juliet, she decided she might as well as call Alex. Get all the awkward phone conversations over with.

"Hello?" Alex's voice sounded faintly harassed, and Lucy could hear the girls behind him. It sounded like they were emptying the dishwasher, possibly onto the floor.

"Alex, it's Lucy."

"Lucy—Poppy, a little quieter, please!" There was the muffled sound of his hand on the receiver. "Sorry about that. It's a bit chaotic here."

"I miss that chaos," Lucy said. She heard Charlie bark and her heart gave a sorrowful little pulse.

"How's your mum?"

"Okay," Lucy said, and told him what she'd already said to Juliet.

"So it sounds like you might not be back by January," Alex said neutrally.

Lucy's hand tightened on her phone. "I'm not sure," she said. "It really depends on my mother's recovery and . . ." In that moment she couldn't think what else it depended on. "Well. You know."

"Yes, I know," Alex said, and again she felt that awful subtext running beneath their words.

"Alex, I want to—"

"Look, Lucy," he cut across her. "I understand

that your mother needs you. Trust me, I do. If my mother had stuck around long enough for her to need me, I'm sure I'd have been there like a shot." Which made her feel only worse. "But the truth is, your leaving has made me think." He paused, and she heard him moving through the house, closing a door. "Maybe we should just put things on—on hiatus."

She wasn't surprised, and yet his suggestion still hurt. Unbearably. But she wouldn't beg. Not this time. "If you think that's a good idea," she answered after a pause.

"I do. It's not what I want, but I think it's sensible. I don't want Poppy and Bella to get their hopes up for something that might not happen."

The lump in her throat had grown to golf ball proportions. "You really don't think I'm coming back, do you?" she asked, squeezing the words around it.

"I don't *know* if you're coming back, and I'm not sure you do, either." He hesitated, and then asked heavily, "Do you?"

And Lucy couldn't answer, because she knew he was right.

She ended the call without saying much more beyond a few trivialities, and asking Alex to say hello to Poppy and Bella for her. As she slid her phone back in her pocket, she fought a sense of unreality. Had their relationship ended, just like that? But then, it had never had a chance to begin.

Her mother was starting to stir and Lucy walked back into the room. Fiona's eyes fluttered open; she blinked several times. "My mouth is as dry as a bone. My lips are sticking to my teeth."

Lucy poured water from the jug on the bedside table. "I think that's from the anesthetic. Here." She handed her mother the glass of water, guiding the rim to her lips. Her mother took a few sips, and then sank back against the pillows.

"I'm sorry, Lucy. For everything."

"We don't need to talk about that now," Lucy said. "Although we need to at some point. Especially for Juliet."

"I know."

"Well, then." She replaced the glass of water on the table. "For now let's just think about your recovery."

And what about her recovery? Lucy wondered several hours later as she drove back to her mother's apartment in the Back Bay. She was in Boston with no job, no apartment, no life.

Her life was back in Hartley-by-the-Sea.

At least it had been, although Lucy didn't know where it was now. She'd been back for only twenty-four hours and she already felt as if all the friendships she'd made in England were slipping away from her. Alex had backed off quickly enough. If she returned in a few months, would she feel as if she was starting over yet again? Would everyone wonder why she'd returned?

She didn't have a job; she'd been there for only three months. Now that she was on *hiatus* with Alex, returning seemed less likely than ever.

She pulled into the parking lot by her mother's luxury condo and turned off the engine. The wind off the bay could be unforgivingly cold, colder even than the wind off the Irish Sea back in Cumbria.

Although maybe she'd gotten used to Hartley-by-the-Sea; she'd learned to love the little village and its motley residents, the sweep of wind and even the endless rain. She thought of all the things she'd miss: the Lifeboat Carol Service she and Juliet had been planning to attend; Father Christmas's appearance outside the Hangman's Noose, which she'd wanted to see with Poppy and Bella. Her little chats with Dan Trenton at the post office shop and the children like Eva and Oliver who smiled at her in the school yard; the chance to exhibit her paintings at the beach café; pub quizzes and her friendship with Rachel and Abby; all her art lessons . . .

How could she have just *left?* She'd walked away from everything that was important to her: not just Alex but Poppy and Bella too, Juliet, the friends she'd made at school . . . *everything.*

Juliet had been right to be angry. Lucy had come running the minute her mother had called her, not only because she'd wanted Fiona to need her, but because she'd been afraid to believe in the life she'd been building in Hartley-by-the-Sea.

Because it was easier to run away than to stay and try, and risk failure. Risk hurt.

But she needed to take some risks. She needed to stay for once, to say the things she really felt, even if it meant Alex would tell her no, just as Thomas had done.

Resolutely Lucy dug out her cell phone. Alex wasn't Thomas. And she'd changed. She was stronger now, more confident, more secure in herself. She'd call and she'd beg, damn it.

She called Alex's home phone, but it went to the answering machine. He was probably putting Poppy to bed. Still, she didn't want to let the moment pass. She might not be this brave again, and so she left a message.

"Alex, it's Lucy. Look, I haven't rehearsed what I'm going to say. I just was sitting here in my car realizing how much I don't want to be here. I know I left so suddenly and made it seem like I might not come back, but the truth is my home is there, not here." Her words came faster, too fast. He'd never make out what she was saying, but she'd still try. She'd say it, because that's what she should have done in the first place.

"I don't want to be on a hiatus. I want to be with you, and with Poppy and Bella. I miss all of you. I miss Hartley-by-the-Sea. I even miss the awful weather." She let out a tremulous laugh. "Do you know I thought you'd have sensible shoes and a nasal drip? That was before I met you, of course. Before I saw how gorgeous and sexy you are—okay." She took a deep breath, a realization of all she'd said filtering through her. "Call me," she finished abruptly, and disconnected the call.

Had she really gushed all those feelings into a *voice mail?* He'd have them on record forever. She pictured that voice mail going viral just like her mother's editorial had, and shuddered. Not, she knew, that Alex would ever post the recording online.

Still she winced at some of the things she'd said, and positively cringed at the vulnerability she'd shown. Would she take any of it back?

Maybe the bit about the nasal drip. But no matter what happened now, she knew she was still glad she'd told him the truth. And yet sitting there in her car, the night dark all around her, she also knew there was someone else she both wanted and needed to see again, maybe even more than Alex.

Juliet.

30
Juliet

LUCY HAD BEEN GONE for only three days and Juliet felt the ache of her absence like a sore tooth, a constant, niggling irritation. She'd turn to say something, and Lucy wasn't there. At night she flicked on the horrid reality TV Lucy had made her watch, and could only stomach a few seconds of it. It had been different when Lucy had been there, offering the running commentary on all the contestants, making Juliet laugh. She even missed the tea bags left in the sink, and the shoes in the hall. Her house was too *neat*.

Thankfully she kept busy with a rush of pre-Christmas walkers, and then planning the Lifeboat Carol Service, a village tradition that started with Father Christmas coming down in Cumbria's version of a sleigh—a trailer pulled by a Land Rover—and handing out sweets to all the children outside the pub. Then onto the beach, and an appearance at the Lifeboat Station, where the brass band from Whitehaven led everyone in carols and volunteers from the Women's Institute dressed as elves and handed out mulled wine and mince pies.

It was an event that warmed your heart even as

you froze your tail off at the service held in an unheated shed where the village's two lifeboats were usually stored, and this year Juliet had volunteered to be in charge of the organization. When Rob Telford pulled out of being Father Christmas at the last minute because his father was ill, she flew into a panic she hid by being cross.

"A fine time to tell me this," she snapped. "The day before—"

"Why not get Peter Lanford to do it?" Rob suggested. "He's always willing to pitch in when needed."

Peter. She hadn't seen much of him in the days since Lucy had left; he'd waved to her once from his Land Rover, when he'd been moving sheep, and she'd considered walking the mile up to Bega Farm and—what? Say hello? Ask to come in for a cup of tea or a tot of whiskey? She wasn't sure where their friendship stood, and in any case they were both busy.

But now she had a reason to see him, and so after her call with Rob, Juliet headed up the track to the Lanford farm. She'd gotten only halfway there when she saw Peter out in one of the sheep fields, tossing hay into an enclosure. He stopped when he saw her, then threw his pitchfork into the back of the trailer half-full of hay, and strode towards her.

"Juliet. How are you?"

"All right. Or should I say, areet."

His face creased into a smile. "Good to hear." Juliet thought of the way she'd broken down in front of him after Fiona had called, and she knew then that was the real reason she hadn't headed up to Bega Farm before now. She hated that Peter had seen her at her most vulnerable.

"Rob Telford's backed out of the Lifeboat Service," she said. "And we need another Father Christmas."

"Ah."

"Are you willing? You know we have the suit and beard and the rest of it."

Peter scratched his jaw. "I suppose I could do it. I don't normally go out in an evening, though. Because of Dad."

Juliet knew Peter had arranged for a caregiver to come in during the day to be with William, but evenings were harder. "Can he come along?" she asked.

"I think the crowds might be a bit much. And it's cold out, for him."

She nodded. "I'm sorry, I should have realized. I'll ask someone else—"

"No, I'll do it," Peter said. "Can't be letting the village down." He gave her a crooked smile. "I'll find someone to sit with Dad. Liz Benson might be willing."

Juliet nodded again; she was starting to feel like a marionette. She wanted to say something more, but she wasn't sure what it was, or even if she could. She stared at him instead, noticing a faint peppering of gray in his brown hair, and how reddened his cheeks were from the cold. "Thank you, Peter," she finally managed. She took a step back, and then another, and with a little wave she started back down the track to Tarn House.

The evening of the carol service she stood in her kitchen, tapping one foot in ill-concealed impatience while Peter suited up for the service in the bathroom. He emerged with a self-conscious grin, the slightly moth-eaten beard of cotton wool obscuring half his face, his fingers plucking at the red felt cap in his hand.

Juliet studied him critically, her hands on her hips. "You haven't got enough belly."

He patted his small pouchy stomach. "I put one of the throw pillows in there."

"You need another one. You've got to be a convincing Father Christmas, not one on a diet." She went to the sitting room and grabbed a pillow off the sofa. "Here," she said, and reached for the front of his red suit. She'd already pulled it up before she considered what she was doing; she'd glimpsed Peter's toned stomach before she dropped her hand and stepped back, thrusting the pillow at him. "You do it."

Avoiding her gaze, Peter arranged the other pillow. He looked ridiculous, Juliet thought with sudden affection, in the worn red felt trousers and top, both adorned with fake white fur and silver buckles. Completely ridiculous. He put the cap on his head, pulling it down to hide his brown hair. "Think I'll do?"

"Yes, I'm sure of it," she said with more conviction than she actually felt.

"I don't actually like being out in front of people," he confessed. "But since I'm behind all this rig, I suppose it won't matter."

"You'll be fine," Juliet said bracingly. "Right, we ought to get up to the turning circle at the top of the village. Andrew Lofton is driving you."

Icy rain had been falling for the last three days, and although it had stopped now, the pavement was still slick, and ice-covered black puddles glimmered in the moonlight. Juliet drew in a breath, the air so cold it hurt her lungs. She wondered how many children would even make it out on such a cold, icy night and hoped that at least a few would, for Peter's sake.

They walked in silence up the length of the village; once, Juliet slipped on the ice and Peter reached out and steadied her by the elbow. She nearly leaned into him then, almost put her head on his shoulder in a move that would have been utterly unlike her, and yet she craved his physical touch.

She jerked away from him instead, wishing he didn't affect her this way, every inconsequential interaction making her wonder *what if* . . .

What if she hadn't been so stupid as to bollocks up their friendship with that sperm request? What if she was brave enough now to tell him she wished things were different, that she wanted to be more than his friend?

In any case Peter dropped his hand and they continued in silence up the road.

Andrew Lofton, another sheep farmer, was waiting with his Land Rover at the turning circle at the top of the village. Peter climbed into the trailer in the back; in an attempt to be festive, Andrew had festooned it with Christmas lights and tacked a *Ho Ho Ho* banner to the back of the car. With Peter standing there awkwardly, still a rather thin Santa, Juliet thought it all looked a bit *less than,* but she supposed it wouldn't matter too much in the darkness. In any case, all the children really wanted was sweets.

"Here you go, Peter." She handed him a white cloth sack filled with candy. Peter took it, peering into the depths. "One each, I suppose?"

"That's right, and no arguments. No one saying they don't like Smarties or sour cherries or the rest of it." That had happened last year, and Rob had allowed exchanges of sweets, which had been a disaster of whining children and annoyed parents. "They take what they get," Juliet said sternly, and got into the passenger side of the Rover.

Andrew started driving slowly down the street.

He'd rolled down the windows and had Christmas carols playing on the car stereo, and all in all Juliet supposed it was merry enough, although she still felt a little flat. She remembered how she'd told Lucy about the service, how excited her sister had been to experience it.

She'd called Lucy twice over the past week to check in about Fiona, although she didn't actually care about their mother. She cared about Lucy, and whether she was coming back.

Lucy hadn't made any promises. Fiona had developed an infection and had to stay in the hospital for a few more days, and Lucy had said once again that she hoped to be back in January. Juliet still didn't believe her.

A small crowd of children had gathered by the Christmas tree outside the Hangman's Noose, and they let out a raggedy cheer as the Land Rover approached.

"Ho ho ho," Peter called, and Juliet smiled to hear how his voice boomed. Maybe he could manage this role after all.

Andrew stopped the car and Peter started handing out sweets. Juliet watched from the passenger seat, keeping an eye on some of the older boys who were known to stir up trouble. Oliver Jones could be unruly sometimes, but now she saw him hanging back, holding his mother Lena's hand. A few children asked for different sweets, and Peter refused.

"Maybe I'll give you a different sweet on Christmas Day," he suggested, his voice just a little too hearty, and Juliet heard one of the older boys answer sneeringly, "You're not coming round on Christmas Day. You're not really Father Christmas."

"Shut your mouth, Danny Briggs," Diana Rigby snapped. "You don't know what you're talking about."

Juliet knew that the children of Hartley-by-the-Sea believed in Father Christmas as long as they could, sometimes right up to age ten or eleven. Everyone liked it that way; it was almost a point of pride, how naive the village children could be. How long the magic lasted.

"Who is it this year, anyway?" the boy continued, undaunted. "It's not Mr. Telford from the pub."

"Right, I'd best get a move on," Peter said, his voice still determinedly jolly. "Must see the children down at the beach. And I'm looking forward to a mince pie, myself." Juliet watched as he passed a hand over his face, which unfortunately knocked his beard askew.

A burst of laughter erupted from the children; it wasn't precisely unkind, but it wasn't good, either. Juliet cringed. Even stolid, silent Andrew Lofton winced a bit. *If Lucy were here,* she thought, *she'd manage to make this funny. She'd salvage something from it, but it's just me instead.*

"Get a move on," she told Andrew, and he started driving down the main street again, even more slowly this time due to the crowds around them.

A few of the sneering boys followed the Land Rover; the younger children fell away as they made the turn onto the beach road.

"We know you're not Father Christmas!" one of the boys jeered.

"You're the stupidest Santa I ever saw," another boy called.

"I know who you are!" This from the boy who had started it all, his voice crowing. "You're Peter Lanford, the one with the crazy old father!"

"Right!" Juliet was unbuckling her seat belt before she even realized what she was doing. She flung open the door and jumped out of the still-moving Land Rover, stumbling a bit before righting herself, and pointed a shaking finger at the three boys. "Clear off, you lot, before I box your ears and send you back to your mothers. Look at you, terrorizing everyone and ruining Christmas for a bunch of little children. You ought to be ashamed of yourselves."

Only one of the boys appeared remotely cowed, and even more furious, Juliet took a step forward, her arm raised. "Get away with you!" she shouted, her voice carrying and cracking on the still night. "All of you clear off before I give you a good slap!"

"Juliet." Andrew Lofton had stopped the car and now Peter clambered down from the trailer, and put his hands on her shoulders. "All right, you three," he said to the boys, who were still standing there, looking undecided as to whether they wanted to keep on with their taunting. "Clear off like she said."

The quiet note of authority in Peter's voice convinced the boys in a way that Juliet's shrieking hadn't, and they headed back down the beach road towards the village.

Peter stood with his hands on Juliet's shoulders, and only then did she realize she was shaking. Wordlessly he turned her so she was facing him, and then he put his arms around her and held her in an embrace that Juliet craved with her whole being.

"I'm sorry," she mumbled against his shirt. "I don't know why I was so angry."

"You've had a lot to deal with lately."

"They'll be talking about it for ages," she said with a sniff. "How that old shrew Juliet Bagshaw lost it on the beach road, and spoiled Christmas for everyone."

"Then let's give them something else to talk about," Peter said, and to her amazement he kissed her.

The first thing she thought was how cool and yet warm his lips were; the second was how scratchy his fake beard felt. Laughing a little, Juliet pulled back. Peter frowned.

"Juliet . . ."

"Your beard," she said, and pulling it down, she leaned forward and kissed him again.

After a few minutes Andrew Lofton cleared his throat. "Areet?" he called, and Peter pulled back, grinning.

"Areet," he answered, and still smiling, he climbed back onto the trailer. Juliet got back in the car, not meeting Andrew's unreadable gaze.

"So." She cleared her throat, just as he had. "Are we on time for the carol service?"

"I think we'll make it," Andrew said, and started driving.

A few minutes later he pulled the car up in front of the Royal National Lifeboat Institute, or RNLI, station, now festooned with Christmas lights, the strains of the brass band that was crammed into the narrow shed audible even from inside the car.

"Ho ho ho," Peter called as he waved from the trailer, and Juliet felt herself start to grin again. Peter was a far jollier Santa now than he had been fifteen minutes ago.

He made his appearance, waving and handing out sweets, before the carol service started. Then he changed clothes in the public toilets, bundling up the red Santa suit into a bag, which he left in Andrew's car. Juliet had been waiting for him outside, unsure what to say or even what to think, but knowing she wanted to be with him.

In the end she didn't say anything, and neither

did he. He simply took her hand and walked with her into the carol service. They sat in the back and held hands during the entire service; her hand rested on his thigh, feeling small and fragile clasped in his much larger one.

The service was over by nine thirty, and replete with several mince pies and paper cups of mulled wine, they declined Andrew's offer of a lift back into the village and decided to walk instead.

Juliet almost regretted the decision as they started down the beach road; although the air was still, it was also freezing. But then Peter took her hand again and she knew she was glad they'd decided to walk.

She had no desire for some awkward conversation about the status of their relationship, and Peter didn't seem to, either, for they walked in silence the whole way down the road.

Juliet's steps slowed as they turned off the beach road and crossed the railway; she could see Tarn House in the distance, looking warm and snug and yet also empty. Should she invite Peter in? Ask him to stay? The thought made her hands clammy and her stomach leap with anticipation.

Then she saw the lone figure standing by the door, and her steps halted altogether.

"That looks like . . . ," she began, and Peter finished it for her.

"Lucy," he said.

31
Lucy

LUCY SAW PETER AND Juliet coming down the high street at the same time that they saw her, and for a few seconds everyone just stared at one another. Finally Lucy waved.

"Surprise!" she called, and heard how nervous she sounded. She and Juliet hadn't parted on good terms, and she had no idea if her sister would welcome her back.

"You didn't tell me you were coming."

"Hence the surprise."

She braced herself for one of Juliet's acerbic retorts, but to her relief, her sister dropped Peter's hand and catapulted into Lucy's arms.

"Welcome home," she said.

Lucy hugged her back tightly. This *was* home, and she was glad Juliet knew it. Then she registered that Juliet had been holding Peter's hand, and she jerked back.

"What happ—"

"Later," Juliet muttered, and Lucy wondered how her sister knew what she was talking about. Sibling telepathy, perhaps.

Peter said good night, and Juliet unlocked the

front door to Tarn House. "No guests tonight?" Lucy asked, and Juliet shook her head.

"The ice has kept people away."

"It *is* freezing. It's even colder than it is in Boston, and that's saying something."

They shed their coats and boots and walked into the kitchen; as Juliet flicked on the lights, Lucy's heart swelled with happiness at the sight of the familiar green Aga, the pine table, the poinsettia on the windowsill. She walked towards the range, holding her hands out to its comforting warmth.

"I missed the carol service down at the beach, didn't I?"

"Yes."

"And Father Christmas."

"That was Peter, actually."

"Peter!" Lucy turned around, grinning. "How did he do?"

"Brilliantly," Juliet answered, and Lucy raised her eyebrows, wanting to hear the full story. "Not now," Juliet said, but her lips twitched in an answering smile. "But I think you can probably guess."

"I think I can." They were both silent for a moment, and then Lucy said, "I'm sorry I was gone so long."

"I thought you'd be gone a lot longer." Juliet hesitated, then asked, her tone diffident, "Are you going back?"

"Maybe for a few days here and there. Mum still

has a long road of treatment and recovery ahead of her. But I don't think she needs me every step of the way. And I need to live my own life." She paused, wishing she had more of a sense of Juliet's mood. She'd hugged her and welcomed her home, yes, but she was looking rather stony-faced now. "And I'd like to live my own life here," she continued. "Unless . . . you'd rather . . . ?"

"Don't be daft." Juliet smiled then, a crooked, awkward thing but a smile all the same. "I told you this is your home. I'm glad you're back, Lucy. I'm sorry for the things I said before you went."

"I'm sorry too, for the things I said."

"Well, then, that's put behind us," Juliet said briskly. "Cup of tea?"

"I thought you'd never ask," Lucy answered, and reached for the kettle.

That night she lay in bed listening to the familiar and strangely comforting sound of the wind soughing through the now leafless trees and rattling the windowpanes. Amazing, really, that she'd missed even that. The cold and the rain and everything about Hartley-by-the-Sea.

And Alex.

She hadn't spoken to him since that conversation in the hospital, and he hadn't called her since she'd left that terribly revealing message on his answering machine. His silence was eloquent enough, and yet Lucy knew she needed to see him. Needed to hear face-to-face whether their hiatus was permanent.

At five o'clock the next evening, Lucy headed up to Alex's house. It was already dark, moonless and windy, the pavement icy beneath her feet. No one was outside. The post office was closed and shuttered for the night, and so the walk up the main street felt particularly treacherous and lonely.

A light gleamed from the sitting room window of Alex's house, and taking a deep breath, Lucy knocked on the door. A few seconds later it was flung open by Poppy, who stared at her open-mouthed for a moment before running back towards the kitchen, shrieking, "Daddy! Daddy! It's Lucy! She's come back!"

Lucy's heart felt as if it were beating its way up her throat as Alex walked from the kitchen towards the front door. He had a dish towel thrown over one shoulder and his face was utterly unreadable. She swallowed dryly.

"Hello."

"Hello," he answered back, and she still couldn't tell anything from his tone.

"Let her in, Dad," Bella said from behind him. She stood on the bottom stair, her arms folded, and Lucy couldn't read her expression, either. Why did everyone have to be so damned poker-faced?

Alex stepped back and Lucy came into the house. Charlie trotted in from the kitchen, wagging his tail and offering Lucy one enthusiastic woof. At least he was happy to see her.

"I'm back," she finally said, unnecessarily, her voice cringingly overbright.

"So I see," Alex answered. "For how long?"

"For good. I decided . . . I realized . . ." She licked her lips and swallowed again; her throat felt so very dry and her heart was still beating hard. "I realized I didn't need to be there as much as I thought I did."

"What made you realize that?" Alex asked, his voice toneless. Couldn't he give her just one clue as to how he was feeling?

Lucy glanced at the two girls, who were listening with avid, openmouthed interest. She'd wanted to have this conversation with Alex in private, but it looked like that wasn't going to happen. "Going back to Boston. Realizing it wasn't home anymore—"

"I thought you'd already realized that."

He wasn't making this easy for her. "Didn't you get my message on your machine?" Lucy asked, torn between exasperation and fear. "I sent it nearly a week ago—"

"A message?" Alex frowned. "I never check the answering machine. I really only use my mobile."

"Oh, perfect."

"What was in your message?"

"Well." The things she'd blurted on the answering machine were far harder to say to his face. But maybe she needed to do this, for her sake as well as Alex's. "I'll recap for you. I told you that I was sorry for leaving the way I did, and that I missed you and Poppy and Bella. And that I didn't want to be on a hiatus."

"What's a hiatus?" Poppy asked.

"Something not good," Bella answered.

"Anything else in this message?" Alex asked.

"Well, I said that I cared about you, and that I thought you had a nasal drip—"

Bella let out a choked laugh. "Seriously? A nasal drip? Gross."

"That was before I met you," Lucy said quickly. "Of course."

"Of course." She could see Alex's mouth was quirking up in that lovely little smile she knew so well.

"So I said all those things and then I came back because this is where I want to be." She glanced at the girls, whose gazes darted between her and Alex. "Right here," she clarified, "is where I want to be. If you want me to be here."

Alex didn't say anything and Bella let out a sigh of such utter exasperation that Lucy nearly laughed. "Dad, you're not seriously thinking of turning her down? Because if you are, you're a first-class idiot."

"You really are, Daddy," Poppy chimed in, and then Lucy did laugh.

Alex's small smile disappeared as his mouth

firmed in a line. His arms were still folded. Lucy braced herself. "Well," he said slowly, "I can't be an idiot."

She laughed again as she nearly sagged with relief and Alex reached out one hand and tugged her towards him. She went gladly, pressed her cheek against his chest as he wrapped his arms around her and rested his chin on top of her head.

"Finally," Bella said, and Poppy let out a cheer.

Lucy waved them forward. "Group hug," she said, and Poppy came first, hurtling herself towards Alex's midsection. Bella dragged her feet a little, but she leaned into her dad as he put an arm around her and they stayed there for a minute, the four of them.

Lucy spent the evening with them all, but left before nine, knowing Alex had to get the girls to bed. Knowing too that they would be taking it slow, no matter how serious their intentions.

Still, she and Alex were able to sneak away from Poppy and Bella for a little while, when the girls went upstairs to watch TV; they sat on the sofa and kissed until Lucy's lips felt as if they were buzzing. Eventually, reluctantly, Alex pulled away.

"I need to tell you some things," he said.

Lucy's heart lurched a little at his serious tone. "Okay," she said.

Alex shifted in his seat and her heart lurched again as she wondered just what he had to say. "I

451

reacted badly to your leaving in part because of my history. My history with Anna." Lucy didn't answer; she wasn't sure what to say, and in any case Alex continued. "I told you before that we weren't happy here in the village. Anna didn't want to be here, and I wanted to pretend I couldn't see that. The day she died . . ." He hesitated, and Lucy waited. "That day, before she went riding, she told me she was leaving. For good. I was angry and surprised, even though I suppose I shouldn't have been. Anyway, when you left, even though it was just for a little while . . . it brought back some hard memories, and I reacted badly. I'm sorry."

"Oh, Alex." Lucy swallowed. "I'm sorry. Sorry that I put you in that position." She wanted to ask about a million questions but wasn't sure she wanted to hear all the answers about Alex's marriage. "Do the girls know?" she finally asked. "That she was going to leave?"

Alex shook his head. "No, I never told them, and I never will. It wouldn't do any good."

"No, it wouldn't," she agreed, but she could certainly understand Alex's perspective a lot better now. He smiled then and tugged her by the hand.

"Come back here," he said, and kissed her again.

She left an hour later; the night was still wet, windy, and cold, and the wind had started to howl so Lucy had to clamp both hands down on her hat to keep it from flying away. She came into Tarn House shivering and shaking raindrops from her coat. Milly and Molly nudged their noses against her hip and she stroked their sleek heads fondly. *Home,* she thought again. *This is home.*

She unwound her scarf and hung her hat up on the hook and came into the kitchen, only to skid to a sudden stop. For a moment her brain could not process what she was seeing: two women in the kitchen, the silence so taut with tension it felt as if the air could break in half. Juliet was leaning against the Aga rail, her arms folded, her mouth a hard, compressed line. And standing beside the table, one hand on the back of a chair, was Fiona.

32
Juliet

WHEN JULIET HAD OPENED the door to see her mother standing there, she'd had the same impulse as when Lucy had stood there, all those months ago. She'd wanted to slam the door in her face, and this time she almost did. She started to close it, and Fiona caught it with her hand.

"I know you have every right to shut me out," she'd said quietly. "But please don't."

"Lucy isn't here." Juliet kept her hand on the door, and so did Fiona.

"It's not Lucy I came to speak to."

Shock made Juliet speechless for a moment, and she felt a pressure building in her chest, a pressure she was afraid to release. It might blow up the whole house. It would certainly destroy her. "You could have just called," she finally managed, her hand still on the door.

"I wanted to talk to you in person."

"You never did before."

"I know."

Somehow this honest admission made Juliet relent, if warily. She dropped her hand from the door and stepped aside to let Fiona in.

Her mother was in her house. It was so strange, so surreal, that she could not process how she felt about it. Too many things.

Fiona put down the single bag she'd been carrying and shed her coat, a thing of beige silk that was totally impractical for a Cumbrian, or even a Boston, winter. Juliet waited, arms folded, refusing to help her mother. Her welcome extended only so far.

"Are you all right to travel? With the surgery?" she asked after a moment, then cursed herself for sounding as if she was concerned.

Fiona turned around with a small smile. "No, but I came anyway. I'm not good at obeying orders. Can I sit down, though? It's been a long trip."

Juliet nodded and headed for the kitchen. She retreated to the Aga and leaned against it, her arms still folded. Fiona put one hand on the back of a chair and stood there, looking strangely disoriented, and Juliet wondered if she should offer her a cup of tea. She said nothing.

And then Lucy came in, humming under her breath—a sure sign that things had gone well with Alex—and stopped suddenly as she caught sight of them. Juliet still didn't speak, and Lucy turned to Fiona.

"*Mum.*"

"Hello, Lucy."

"What—what are you doing here?"

"I wanted to talk to Juliet."

Lucy's expression cleared then, and she beamed a smile of such happiness and gratitude at Fiona that Juliet realized at once what had happened. Lucy had asked Fiona to come talk to her. *Of course.* The only reason Fiona was here was because of Lucy. Bile rose in Juliet's throat, the taste of bitterness. She blinked rapidly, hating how disappointed she felt, *again.*

"Maybe you could give us some privacy, Lucy," Fiona suggested, and Juliet unfolded her arms and pushed away from the Aga.

"That won't be necessary. You're only here because of Lucy. You certainly wouldn't be speaking to me for my sake, and I don't think there's anything I want to hear from you anyway."

"Juliet—," Lucy began, and Juliet turned on her almost savagely.

"You asked her here, didn't you? You told her to speak with me. She wouldn't have come otherwise."

"Lucy suggested it, yes," Fiona said calmly. "But I made the trip. I want to be here, Juliet, because I know—I know I've treated you unfairly and I want to explain why."

Juliet froze, her mouth open for a retort she knew she wasn't going to make. Because she needed to hear what Fiona had to say, even if she didn't want to. Even if she was scared, desperately scared, to hear it.

"I'll go," Lucy said, and tiptoed out of the

kitchen. Juliet heard the creak of the steps as she went upstairs.

"I think I'll sit down," Fiona said after a moment, and sank into one of the kitchen chairs. Juliet retreated back to the Aga. "This is a lovely house," Fiona said after a moment, and she actually smiled. It made Juliet feel like slapping her.

"Don't make small talk."

"Very well, I won't." She took a deep breath. "If it helps, I'm sorry for the pain I've caused you."

"If it helps?" Juliet repeated. She felt a fury so fierce and primal, it was like a tsunami about to crash over her. She held it back, but only just. "Actually, it doesn't. Not that I believe you're sorry."

Fiona blinked, clearly shocked by Juliet's response, and she almost laughed. Had Fiona thought it would be that easy? One transatlantic trip, one apology, and boom. They were all good.

"Well, I *am* sorry," Fiona said after a moment. "But I'm not sure I could have acted any differently."

"Which turns your apology into a justification."

Fiona sighed. "Juliet, there are things you don't understand. Things you don't know—"

"Things you never told me, you mean."

"Yes."

"So tell me, then," she said, her voice thankfully even.

Fiona pressed her lips together. "I don't know where to begin."

"You could begin with why you never wanted me. Or why you acted like you couldn't stand the sight of me for my entire childhood. Or who my father is. Take your pick." She spoke almost indifferently, but her nails were digging into her palms.

"They're all related, really."

The fact that her mother didn't deny any of it made Juliet feel like screaming. Or crying. She laughed instead, the sound hard.

"I don't know who your father is," Fiona said flatly. She looked directly at Juliet, and the expression in her gray eyes—the same color as hers and Lucy's—was cold. "I was drunk at a party and I passed out. When I came to, I knew that I'd been raped."

The bile in the back of Juliet's throat rose to fill her mouth. Her stomach heaved, but she swallowed, forced it all back. She didn't trust herself to speak, and after a few seconds she went to the sink and poured herself a glass of water. With her back to her mother she pressed the cool glass against her cheek, took a few deep breaths.

Raped. She should have guessed. She should have realized it was something like this, something so horrible that her mother would feel justified in ignoring and even hating her child. She just hadn't wanted to entertain such an awful

458

possibility. Her father was a rapist. She was the daughter of a monster. She closed her eyes and then took a sip of water. Swallowed again and turned around.

"Tell me what happened."

"I just did."

"You have no idea who it was?"

"Some idea," Fiona allowed. "I was at a party at university. I was in my second year, just nineteen years old." She took a breath and let it out slowly. "Like I said, I got drunk. Really drunk. I was from a conservative family, and I hadn't had much experience with drinking."

"And you passed out."

"Yes, although I don't remember passing out. The last thing I remember is talking to some guy, a third year. And the next thing I knew, I woke up and it was the middle of the night and I was lying on the floor. Everyone had left, and my clothes were torn, my underwear gone. And I could tell . . . well, of course I could tell." She paused, her face contorted before she deliberately smoothed out her expression. "I'd been flirting with a couple of guys. Three of them. I think . . . I think it was one of them. Or maybe all of them." Her voice wavered. "I'll never know."

Juliet could hear her blood thundering in her ears. "Did you report it—them?"

"No. It was the nineteen seventies, Juliet, and I'd been drunk and, many people would think,

459

stupid. In those days no one would have taken me seriously. Even women today often don't report this kind of thing."

"But I thought you would. With all your issues and campaigning—"

"I wasn't always like this. At nineteen I was shy and unsure and quiet. And I became even more so after it happened."

Juliet took a deep breath; her stomach was still churning. "And when you found out you were pregnant? Why didn't you get an abortion?" A question she couldn't believe she was asking. *Why didn't you abort me?* It was horrible, and yet she had to know.

"I didn't know I was pregnant for quite a while," Fiona said after a moment. "I think I must have been in denial, although I didn't have a lot of symptoms. I was nearly five months gone before I finally realized."

"You still could have had an abortion," Juliet protested, hardly able to believe she was arguing the point. "The Abortion Act allows it up to twenty-four weeks."

"Back then it was actually twenty-eight weeks," Fiona answered, "but I couldn't." She shifted in her chair. "Having an abortion at five months is not the same as taking a pill when you've just found out. All of a sudden I realized there was a baby inside of me, kicking and rolling around, having hiccups. Once I accepted the reality of you . . ." She trailed off, shaking her head. "It's a hard choice, and I was scared. I had no one to talk to, no close friends at university, and I was terrified of my family finding out. I couldn't do it."

"You could have had me adopted," Juliet persisted. She knew there was no real point, but she felt determined to show her mother that she'd had options. It hadn't had to be the way it was, terrible for both of them.

"I could have," Fiona agreed. "But that felt like failure. I'd had to endure so much and then I'd get nothing at the end—"

"You'd have got your life back," Juliet cut across her. "Which I imagine is what you wanted."

"Do you really think you can just get your life back?" Fiona asked. "After all that? In any case, I didn't want to pretend it hadn't happened. That felt like cowardice. And it also seemed unfair."

"Unfair?" Juliet repeated, and felt the fury start to surge again. "You want to talk about unfair—"

"I know." Fiona held up a hand to stem the tide. "I know, Juliet. But when I was pregnant, I thought . . . I thought I could love you."

Juliet blinked, tried to arrange the expression on her face into something that wasn't hurt. *Grief.* "But you couldn't." The words fell into the stillness of the room like stones, rippling the heavy silence and then disappearing. Neither of them spoke for several long minutes.

"I was young and alone when I had you," Fiona finally said. "My family had cut me off completely for getting pregnant. My father wouldn't even speak to me after I told him. He never wanted to see you, and my mother only saw you once, when you were a few days old." She pressed her lips together, and for a second Juliet felt a flicker of sympathy for her mother's plight. "They both died when you were little, anyway. And as for when you were born . . . it was a hard delivery, and you weren't an easy baby." She held up a hand even though Juliet hadn't said anything. "I know, I know. These aren't excuses. I know I can't excuse . . ." She paused, and then, taking a deep breath, continued. "I'm just trying to explain how it was. How alone I felt. And I thought I'd be able to keep on at university, but I couldn't. There weren't the child care options available as there are these days, and I didn't have the money. My family was never going to help me. So I ended up living on government benefits and feeling as if my life had ended. And yes, I started to resent you. I'm sorry if that makes me selfish and cruel and what have you, but that's how it was." Fiona broke off and looked away.

Juliet felt no sympathy. If it had been any other woman facing such a dire predicament, poor and pregnant and alone, she would have surely felt compassion and sorrow. But with Fiona she didn't. She couldn't. "I understand how you could feel that way at first," she finally said, keeping her voice level and choosing her words with care. "But you more or less ignored me for my whole childhood. If you couldn't get over your resentment, you should have done something. Sought help, or given me up."

"I wasn't ignoring you on purpose."

Juliet stared at her in disbelief. "Are you joking?" she demanded. "You barely spoke to me. You never came to anything at school—"

"You were so independent," Fiona protested. "You never asked me to come. It seemed you didn't need me."

"I was a child," Juliet shot back. "You were my mother. Of course I needed you."

Fiona closed her eyes. Her face looked gray and drawn. "Look, I know I can't pretend our relationship was normal, but as time went on, it became easier for me to believe it was. To just . . . coexist together."

"And Lucy?" Juliet asked after a moment. "Why did you have her?"

Fiona opened her eyes. "Because I wanted to get it right a second time. I know I failed you, Juliet, and I'm sorry. I failed Lucy too, in a different way. I'm not a maternal person. I suppose I shouldn't have had children at all."

"But you did," Juliet burst out. "And that should have changed how you acted—"

"Yes." Fiona nodded wearily. "I suppose it

should have." She didn't say anything more, and Juliet stared at her, at the sandy hair that was the same as hers and Lucy's, but now streaked with silver. At the gray eyes, even the slightly crooked nose. Both sisters looked like Fiona. Why hadn't her mother been able to see it? Why hadn't she been able to push past the tragedy and heartache, and love the child she'd been given, the child she'd chosen to keep?

Maybe it really had been impossible for Fiona; maybe she just hadn't tried. Either way it didn't really matter.

"So that's it?" Juliet said. "That's all you've got?"

"I don't expect you to understand—"

"No, you do," Juliet cut her off, her voice hardening. "You expect me to understand and absolve you. And Lucy too, although that probably never seemed difficult to you, since she went trotting back to Boston to take care of you." She shook her head slowly. "I think you're the most selfish woman I've ever known. You could have tried just a *little* over the years. You could have reached out to me, even to explain why you couldn't reach out more—"

"Was I supposed to explain to a child that her father was a rapist?" Fiona asked, her voice hardening too.

"I'm thirty-seven. I think you could have found the right time to tell me."

464

"I didn't see the point when you were an adult. We didn't have a relationship."

"At least you're honest about that." She drew a deep breath. "I don't know what you could have done when I was young, but I'll tell you this. Anything, no matter how small, would have been better than what you did, which was bloody nothing."

Fiona rose from the chair; with shock Juliet realized she was actually angry. "I fed you. I clothed you—"

"Am I supposed to applaud?"

"I gave you two hundred and fifty thousand pounds—"

"You can't pretend that was anything but a payoff."

"Maybe it was," Fiona answered evenly. "But it was something. And you never even said thank you."

"Maybe that's because you'd never said sorry," Juliet snapped back. "When I called you on your birthday five years ago, you hung up. How do you think that made me feel?"

Fiona sank back into her chair. "You surprised me—"

"So you should have got yourself together and called back."

"It was easier to pretend you hadn't called at all."

"Right. Easier." Juliet nodded. "I get where

you're coming from, Fiona. Completely." She turned away, everything in her so tight and tense she felt as if she might snap. From behind her she heard Fiona stand up.

"Do you want me to leave?"

Did she? Her mother had come all this way, and for what? To offer up excuses? "You can stay," she said without turning around. "For Lucy's sake. But I suppose we'll just ignore each other as always. The bedroom at the top of the stairs is free."

Fiona was silent for a moment. Then Juliet heard the squeak of her chair and the sound of her mother leaving the kitchen. She let out her breath in a rush and bowed her head, her hands clutching the rail of the Aga. Upstairs a door closed softly.

In one abrupt movement Juliet turned from the Aga and stalked out of the kitchen. She yanked on her boots, grabbed her coat, and headed out into the freezing night. It was dark and moonless; she hadn't brought a flashlight, so she stumbled down the track to the only place she could go, the only place she wanted to be. Peter's house.

Through the window she could see that he was alone in the kitchen, drinking coffee and going over accounts, when Juliet hammered on the door.

"Juliet—" He caught her in his arms as she practically fell through the door. "My God, what's wrong?"

"My mother," she said, and realized her teeth were chattering, and not just from the cold. She felt cold inside, cold with the shock of having her mother come here, and all the awful things she'd said.

"Your mother?" Peter led her to the table, then went for the whiskey. Juliet downed it in one fiery gulp.

"This is becoming a habit," she joked feebly as she placed the glass on the table. Her hand trembled and the glass nearly fell. Peter steadied it.

"What's happened with your mother?"

"She's just come to bloody Cumbria." She let out a wild laugh and then buried her face in her hands. "And she told me why she never wanted or loved me." She looked up at him between her fingers, suddenly terrified that this would change his opinion of her, and yet knowing she had to tell someone, and that she wasn't ready for it to be Lucy. "She was raped, Peter. My father was a rapist."

Peter stared at her for a long moment, a moment that felt endless in its silence, and then wordlessly he covered her hand with his own.

"I'm sorry," he said. "I'm so sorry." Juliet didn't say anything. She didn't think she could.

He squeezed her hand and Juliet sniffed. "I feel like it changes who I am," she said. "I know it shouldn't, but . . ."

"I understand that, Juliet." He hesitated and then said, his voice matter-of-fact, "My father used to hit me." Juliet blinked and Peter continued. "I don't mean the odd slap. Proper beatings, with his belt. I used to hate him. I dreamed about killing him."

She could not imagine Peter dreaming about killing anyone, but neither could she imagine him being beaten as a boy by *William*. "But . . ." she began, although she didn't know what she was going to say.

"It's why my brother, David, left. After my mum died, I was going to leave too, but I was tied to this land and farming's all I've known. So I stayed, and then my father got sick, and I was the only person who could care for him."

"Are you telling me this because . . ." Juliet began uncertainly, and Peter filled it in for her.

"A lot of reasons, I suppose. Because you don't have to be like your parents. I certainly will never hit my child."

"You're the most gentle man I know, Peter."

"And seeing my dad looking so weak and helpless now, it's made me think. He's just a man. He made some mistakes, some bloody great big ones, but in the end he's just a human being, same as me. And there were a few good times, amidst all the bad." He squeezed her shoulders gently. "Were there any good times with your mother?"

Were there? Had the bad memories overwhelmed any good ones? "I don't know," Juliet admitted shakily. "I can't remember. But, Peter, I don't think I can forgive her."

"Of course you can't," he said with a nod. "Not now. Not yet. But one day, for your sake as much as hers, I hope you can."

Juliet searched his face, seeing only acceptance in his eyes. "You're a good man, Peter Lanford."

He smiled at that. "No more than any other, I reckon."

"I don't know if I'm as good as you."

"Then I'm glad this isn't a competition." He pulled her gently to her feet, and then put his arms around her. She pressed her cheek against the rough wool of his jumper, felt the steady thud of his heart. "Give yourself time, Juliet. You're as hard on yourself as you are on your mother."

"So you think I'm hard on her."

He laughed softly, a rasping sound. "I don't care about your mother. I care about you." And then he touched a finger to her chin and tilted her face up so he could kiss her, a whisper across her mouth, and Juliet felt the tightness inside her loosen, just a little.

It was a start, she realized, and kissed Peter back. It was a start.

33
Lucy

LUCY HAD BEEN SITTING on her bed, her hands clasped tightly together, listening to Juliet's and Fiona's voices rise and fall below her in the kitchen. She'd closed her eyes and willed a silent, formless prayer heavenwards. She wanted their relationship to work. She wanted their reconciliation.

At least they were talking for a while. She unclasped her hands because the bones in her fingers had started to ache. She could still hear their voices: low murmurs, and then a sudden rise and fall. And then, after a few more minutes, the sound of her mother coming up the stairs and the distant slamming of the front door.

Not good sounds. Not healing, life-affirming, everyone's-okay-now sounds.

Cautiously she tiptoed from her bedroom and down the upstairs hallway. The house was eerily quiet; Lucy could hear the ticking of the hall clock. She stood at the top of the stairs, not sure what she should do, and her mother opened one of the bedroom doors.

"Mum . . . ?"

Fiona stiffened, her chin rising a notch. "I'm afraid that didn't go very well."

"Where's Juliet?"

"She left." Fiona gestured towards the downstairs. "She stormed off. I don't know where."

Lucy sagged against the wall. "What happened?"

"Oh, Lucy." Fiona's mouth tightened in that old, familiar way. "Did you think we were going to make up just like that? Because I can assure you, too much has happened for that."

"Did you . . . did you tell Juliet why . . . ?" Lucy ventured.

"Yes."

And it obviously wasn't any of her business. "But she's still angry."

Fiona lifted one thin shoulder in a shrug. "Like I said, too much has happened. I think she'll always be angry."

Her mother's tone sounded almost . . . indifferent. "I hope," Lucy said, "for Juliet's sake, she's not."

Fiona considered this for a moment before nodding slowly. "Yes," she said, "I suppose I hope that too."

"You *suppose?*" Lucy stared at her mother, at the weary yet determined lines of her face, and she knew that nothing had actually changed. She was still living in her absurd little bubble of optimism; her mother was still her mother, self-obsessed, determined, arrogant, impossible. She loved her,

Lucy knew; she couldn't help it. But she wasn't actually sure if her mother loved her back. "Why did you come here, Mum?" she asked quietly, and Fiona looked startled.

"Because . . . because I wanted to make amends. Explain things. Facing death does that to a person."

"But what about Juliet?"

Fiona stared. "What about her?"

"I mean . . . don't you care about her?"

"Oh, Lucy." Her mother gave one of her familiar sighs, the sound of weary disappointment with poor, stupid Lucy. "It's not that simple."

Lucy could feel an ache in her throat, and an even deeper ache in her heart. How many times had her mother dismissed what she'd said, believed, or hoped for? But she didn't have to buy into her mother's philosophy anymore. She didn't have to give it a moment's worth of credence. "Actually," she said, "sometimes it is that simple."

She walked past her mother into her bedroom, filled with a sudden, restless anger for Juliet's sake as well as her own. She'd hoped her mother's coming here would change . . . well, everything. Juliet and Fiona would reconcile. They'd finally be a happy family. The End.

She sank onto the bed, annoyed with herself for being so bloody naive, even as she still half wished it could happen. Eventually she heard her mother's footsteps along the hallway, and then the sound of a door down the hall closing. She changed into her pajamas and brushed her teeth, listening for Juliet's now-familiar tread, but she fell asleep before she heard anything other than the lonely rustling of the wind through the trees.

She woke up to rain spattering against the windows, and even though it was nearly nine o'clock in the morning, it was still completely dark out. *Welcome to a Cumbrian winter,* she thought, and almost snuggled back under the duvet before she remembered. Juliet. *Fiona.*

She threw on jeans and a sweater and hurried downstairs. Milly and Molly were in the kitchen by their food bowls, whining and circling them. With a jolt Lucy realized Juliet must not have come home last night.

She took the dogs out into the nasty morning—ice, rain, and wind—and let them do their business while she huddled on the doorstep. Then she fed them their kibble and made herself a cup of tea, wondering where Juliet was and when Fiona would come downstairs.

Then she saw the note.

She eyed it warily, thick cream paper with her mother's elegant script, propped between the salt and pepper shakers, addressed to both of them. Lucy wrestled with indecision for several seconds about whether to wait for Juliet before she plucked the note from the table and opened the folded paper.

I think it's better if I go.
—Fiona

That was it. Seven words and her name. Lucy sank into a chair.

The back door opened and she glanced up to see Juliet coming in, looking decidedly rumpled but also surprisingly composed.

"Where were you?"

"At Peter's." Juliet closed the door and shrugged out of her jacket. "It's horrendous out there."

"All night?" Lucy practically squeaked.

"Yes, but not like that. Well, sort of like that." Juliet reached for the kettle. "Don't ask for details."

She nodded to the kettle. "It's already hot—I just boiled it. And of course I'm going to ask for details—"

"I needed someone to talk to after my conversation with Fiona. Someone who's a little removed from it."

"I can understand that." Lucy waited until Juliet had made herself a cup of tea and sat down. "She's gone," she said, and handed her the note.

Juliet scanned it briefly and then tossed it onto the table. "I'm not actually surprised."

"She came all this way to leave after one night?" Lucy could hear the hurt in her voice. "*I'm* surprised."

"She's probably gone to a spa somewhere in

474

Manchester or London, to recover from her ordeal." Juliet shrugged and took a sip of tea. "Her heart wasn't in it, Lucy."

Even now Lucy couldn't help but say, "She seemed sincere when I talked to her in Boston. . . ."

Juliet grimaced. "I don't know if our mother actually knows how to be sincere. But she gave me some answers, and I'm thankful for that. Mostly."

"Answers . . . ?" Lucy ventured cautiously, and Juliet shook her head.

"I'll tell you sometime, just not right now. It's still . . . raw."

Lucy swallowed and nodded. "Okay."

To her surprise—and gratification—Juliet reached over and covered her hand with her own. "The three of us were never going to be the perfect family, Lucy," she said. "No matter how much you wanted it."

"I know." Lucy gave a sniff and then a half-hearted chuckle. "But I still hoped. I always hope."

"Hope is a good thing. I think. You've got me doing it now too, so it had better be."

"That's a lovely thing to say," Lucy said with another sniff and laugh. "Of anything I could have done for you, Juliet, I think I'd want it to be that."

Juliet smiled and removed her hand. Sentimental moment over, clearly. She nodded towards the dogs, who had crept from their baskets and now lay under the table, their heads on their paws, gazes pleading. "How about we take these two for a walk?"

Lucy gave an incredulous glance towards the window. "It's the worst weather out since I arrived here."

"So? You're a Cumbrian now, aren't you? The weather shouldn't stop you."

"I thought I was going to be an offcomer for another thirty years or so."

Juliet shrugged and drained her mug of tea. "It's all in the attitude." She raised her eyebrows. "So?"

Lucy felt herself starting to grin. "So? That sounds like a challenge."

"You do have sensible gear now, at least."

"That I do."

"So what are you waiting for?"

Lucy glanced once more at the window. It was bucketing down icy rain, and the wind was howling. "Absolutely nothing," she said, and with Juliet grinning back at her, they reached for their coats, called for the dogs, and headed out into the rain.

ACKNOWLEDGMENTS

SOME SAY IT TAKES A VILLAGE to write a book, and in the case of *Rainy Day Sisters*, that was literally true. I am grateful to all the people of my village community who have made me feel welcome, helped me and my family, and of course provided unwitting inspiration for my writing. Thanks also go to my husband, who after seventeen years of marriage has come to recognize the faraway look in my eye that means I am thinking about a story. My five children have been long-suffering but also accepting of my distracted half-listening while I'm typing on my laptop, and I owe them my gratitude. Special thanks go to Eleanor, Anne-Sofie, Aurelie, and Aline—four young women who have each in turn become a part of my family and helped to take care of my children. Finally many thanks to my agent, Helen Breitwieser, for taking a chance on my story, and to my editor, Ellen Edwards, whose help has been invaluable.

KATE HEWITT is the bestselling author of more than forty novels of romance and women's fiction, including the Emigrants Trilogy, set in Scotland and North America; the Hartley-by-the-Sea series, set in the Lake District; and Tales from Goswell, written as Katharine Swartz. Raised in the United States, she lives in England's Lake District with her American-born husband and their five children.

CONNECT ONLINE

kate-hewitt.com
facebook.com/katehewittauthor
twitter.com/katehewitt1
acumbrianlife.blogspot.co.uk

Center Point Large Print
600 Brooks Road / PO Box 1
Thorndike, ME 04986-0001 USA

(207) 568-3717

US & Canada:
1 800 929-9108
www.centerpointlargeprint.com